THE TEMPLE OF
PERSEPHONE

THE TEMPLE OF
PERSEPHONE

ISABELLA KAMAL

**BLACK
STONE**
PUBLISHING

Printed in the United States of America

First edition: 2024
ISBN 979-8-212-53850-3
Fiction / Romance / Historical / Regency

Version 1

Blackstone Publishing
31 Mistletoe Rd.
Ashland, OR 97520

www.BlackstonePublishing.com

To Mama, Baba, Sarah, Reema, Noor, and Connor
for showing me what it is to be loved unconditionally.
To Honora, Radha, Danielle, Esther, and Mia
for showing me the same.

ƟNE

FANCY STRIKING A DEAL WITH THE DEVIL? LONDON'S
VERY OWN LORD OF THE DEAD IS AT YOUR BECK AND
CALL . . .

Persephone Honeyfield had spent the better part of the afternoon
in a frantic search for a very specific book, and getting sidetracked
by a silly headline on one of her younger sister's many scandal sheets
was decidedly *not* on the agenda. She turned her head back to the
shelves that lined the walls of the library, eyes scanning the rows of
books before wandering again to the tempting sheet of paper that
had caught her attention only moments ago. Persephone, bookish
as she was, had never been one for gossip. Still, something about
the bold words on this particular edition of *Treacle & Tea* promised
to be far more intriguing than the everyday scandals that typically
graced the pages. She picked the worn paper up and—

"Persephone."

The sound of her name echoing throughout the silent

library made Persephone jump, and she looked up to see a tall, bony figure standing in the doorway. Solomon Honeyfield regarded her with watery gray eyes, his expression one of complete and utter detachment.

"Papa," she said breathlessly. "You startled me."

He nodded at the scandal sheet she held against her chest. "Taking an interest in London gossip, are we?"

Persephone shook her head. "Not at all. I was only looking for—well, perhaps you've seen it around here somewhere— Mama's copy of *Mythology of the Greeks and Romans*. You know the one. It's green and a little worse for wear."

"I know the one," Solomon said. "You should have seen her other copy."

Persephone stared at her father from across the room. Which other copy? There was only the one from which her mother had read to her every night. She was sure of it.

"Other copy?" she repeated.

"Oh, yes," Solomon replied. "She had two, one of which she'd scribble in all the time."

"Where is it?" Persephone demanded. "Certainly not here, or I'd have found it already."

She was intimately familiar with every book Honeyfield had to offer. They had, after all, been her close companions all these years.

Solomon paused, a frown pulling at his weathered face. "What's the name of that abandoned house? To the east."

Persephone furrowed her brow, wondering if her father's age was finally catching up to him. *Why on earth* would an annotated copy of her mother's book be kept at—

"Ah, Gallowsgate," he said, pleased at having remembered.

"Why would it be at Gallowsgate?" Persephone asked, brow still furrowed.

"If it isn't here, then it must be there. She used to visit the lady of the house." He straightened suddenly, dropping the subject. "Have you seen Venus?"

"Not recently," Persephone said reluctantly, knowing there was little she could do to redirect her father's attention back to the book. She lifted the scandal sheet. "But I've no doubt she'll come looking for this. It looks new."

"Indeed," he agreed. "Well, if you do see her, tell her I need her help sealing the honey jars."

With that, he left, and silence descended on the library once more. Persephone glanced down at the scandal sheet again. The Lord of the Dead sounded like a figure right out of the myths she had been raised on. She was about to prop herself on the edge of the table to read the gossip when a high-pitched call tore through the room. Before she could react, Persephone saw her younger sister burst in.

"I thought you were outside," Venus said. "I've been looking for you for hours!"

That likely wasn't true in the slightest, but Venus had always been prone to exaggeration.

"Well, you've found me," Persephone said with a laugh. "And while you've been looking for me, Papa has been looking for *you*. He needs your help with the honey jars."

"Oh, forget that," Venus said. "I want to show you my dress. I've just finished it!"

Persephone rolled her eyes. "Is that all?"

"I think it's my best work yet!" Venus marched over, ignoring Persephone's decided lack of excitement. She came to a stop as she spotted the paper in Persephone's hands. A cheeky smile bloomed on her lovely face. "You? Reading *Treacle & Tea*? I never thought I'd see the day."

Persephone felt her cheeks burn in embarrassment. "No, I was—"

Venus snatched the paper out of Persephone's hands, eyes scanning the various bits of gossip. "Lord of the Dead, as always," she murmured as if to herself. Tossing the sheet to the side, she took Persephone's hand and began to drag her out of the library. "I wouldn't be surprised if gossip about him overtook the entire sheet one of these days."

"You mean to tell me he's real?" Persephone asked as Venus tugged her up the stairs.

"Of course he's real," Venus said, voice dripping with exasperation. "You'd know that if you kept up with the news from town."

Persephone did not respond, wondering instead what one had to do to be given a moniker as ridiculous as *Lord of the Dead*.

"My dress will be just the thing for when suitors begin to call," Venus said in a burst of excitement.

Venus had reached the marriageable age of twenty-one less than a day ago and was already speaking of suitors. Persephone did not doubt that suitors would come, of course. Venus was a vision—long golden hair with a gentle curl, large blue eyes, and a round face graced with the rosiest of cheeks. Their mother had named her after the Goddess of Love, and Venus had somehow been blessed with her likeness.

Persephone's hand was freed as soon as they crossed the threshold of Venus's cluttered bedroom. Every available surface was covered in scraps of fabric, and none more so than the large piece of unfinished wood balanced precariously atop piles of books to form a makeshift sewing table. From this table Venus lifted what *could* be called a dress but was actually a mess of clashing colors. Venus had recently begun dressmaking and wasn't any good at it yet, but Persephone was glad to see her pour her energy into something, anything to distract her from the loneliness of living at Honeyfield.

"It *is* very good, isn't it?" Venus asked, holding the dress out before her. "Do you think it needs more bows around the neckline?"

Persephone was of the mind that there were already far too *many* bows around the neckline, but instead of saying so, she asked, "What do you think?"

"I think," Venus said slowly, examining the dress with great seriousness, "I can add a *few* more." She looked over at Persephone, eyes twinkling. "You could try it on, you know. Then I'd really be able to tell."

Persephone giggled. "I don't think I'd be able to do it a bit of justice."

"Oh, *please*," Venus begged, batting her eyes and clasping the gown to her chest. "I'll give you some of my pin money in exchange."

Persephone let out an exaggerated sigh, her intuition telling her she'd never see a shilling. "Fine."

Venus squeaked in delight, tossing the dress at Persephone and turning around to drag an old crate out from a corner piled with fabric. She placed it in the center of the room, positioned it to face the mirror, and gestured for Persephone to step atop it.

"I'll make something especially for you next time," Venus promised, dropping to her knees to examine the hemline of the dress Persephone was now wearing. "Then we'll *both* be ready for suitors."

Persephone felt a pang in the vicinity of her heart. It was sweet of Venus to think that one of her creations could pull Persephone Honeyfield off the shelf she'd so firmly sat upon for the past six years. Sweet, but a touch misguided. Dresses were the least of Persephone's problems, even if her hems *were* perpetually muddied.

"It's an idea," Persephone said kindly, if a little begrudgingly.

"Though I really think you ought to be focusing on *your* deluge of suitors, not mine."

Persephone saw Venus's eyes widen considerably in the mirror. "Deluge! How many dresses would a deluge need, do you think?"

"Ten?" Persephone guessed, a smile pulling at her lips. "Fifteen?"

"Oh, dear," Venus murmured, looking a touch stricken.

Persephone hummed in sympathetic agreement, making sure she kept her gaze focused on anything but her reflection. It wouldn't have mattered if her sister had been pinning her into the most beautiful dress in England—Persephone was not one for gazing at herself in mirrors. More often than not, they showed her flaws she could not fix. Flaws her sister did not have.

She desperately hoped that Venus could make it out of Oxbury, that a perfect prince of a man would appear on their doorstep and whisk her away. She was far too lovely a person, full of far too much life, to waste away here.

A comfortable silence fell as Venus worked, and Persephone's mind wandered back to what she'd read in *Treacle & Tea*. "Is the Lord of the Dead *truly* real?"

Venus's eyes twinkled with mischief. "As real as you or I."

"Who is he?"

"Who *isn't* he, more like," Venus said. "He's everything! He's London's very own vampire lord, murderer, organ seller—the list goes on."

"It sounds like he's whatever the scandal sheets need him to be," Persephone said dryly.

"Maybe," Venus said, pushing another pin into the fabric around Persephone's ankles. "I wouldn't be surprised if there were some truth to it, though. I can lend you my old copies of *Treacle & Tea* if you're so interested."

Before she could respond, Persephone's eye caught sight of a

THE TEMPLE OF PERSEPHONE

book wedged underneath Venus's sewing table. The book she'd been looking for *all afternoon.*

"Oh, Venus," she huffed, stepping off the crate.

"Be careful!" Venus scolded. "I could have poked my finger."

Persephone grasped the book and slowly eased it out, taking great pains not to destroy her sister's makeshift table. "Why is this here?"

Venus stood, dusting her skirts off. "I needed something to replace my book of fashion plates. That was the only one I could find that fit."

"It's Mama's book," Persephone said testily, running her hands over the cover, fingertips catching over the title embossed in the center.

"*All* of them belonged to her," Venus said defensively.

"Fine," Persephone conceded. "It was her *favorite* book."

"One you've only read a thousand times," Venus grumbled, kicking at the crate. "You needn't make me feel guilty about using it for the table, you know."

"I'm not trying to make you feel guilty," Persephone said, a touch too sharply. "It's just that—"

"I'll make sure to use a different book next time, all right?" Venus promised. "Now, could you step onto the crate again, please? I was nearly done."

Persephone obeyed, tucking the book underneath her arm and pressing it protectively against her rib cage as irritation pricked at her skin.

"I'm sorry," Venus mumbled softly from her place on the floor. "I know how much you love that book. I wasn't thinking."

"It's all right," Persephone said, the annoyance in her chest disappearing. She paused. "Did you know about the other copy?"

"The what?" Venus asked through a mouthful of pins.

"Papa said that there's another copy of this book at Gallows-gate. One filled with notes written in Mama's hand."

Venus looked up, eyes meeting Persephone's in the mirror. "Gallowsgate? That's the old Barrington estate. Nobody has lived there for years."

Persephone shrugged. "Apparently, Mama used to visit when they did."

"How odd," Venus murmured, placing one last pin in the hem of the dress. "Done!"

"Good," Persephone said. "Now you can go help Papa seal the honey jars."

Venus groaned. "But—"

"Venus!"

Persephone and Venus turned their heads at the sound of their father's voice traveling up the stairwell.

"It looks like you've no choice," Persephone said.

Venus sighed and left the room. Persephone followed, changing out of Venus's colorful monstrosity in her own room and making her way back down to the library. Her eye caught the darkening clouds outside the large window. Her father's lands stretched out before her, a wild and unruly jumble of wild-flowers and shrubs. The estate was one of five on the outskirts of Oxbury, all surrounding the village of Little Oxbury. Stan-cliffe sat south of the village and had been abandoned much in the same way Gallowsgate had been. Hartwell, which was nes-tled next to Honeyfield, was nothing more than a ruin. That left Errwood, which was, thankfully, inhabited by the family bearing its name—a family that included Persephone's closest friend, Christianna. People tended to avoid Oxbury, with its scorching summers and frigid winters. And anybody who *was* willing to put up with the poor weather usually did not want to put up with the fact that Oxbury sat in the middle of the most rural countryside England had to offer, cut off from the rest of the world.

No matter the harshness of the weather, Persephone saw Honeyfield flourish with life every year without fail. Her father's bees dined off what the land provided, resulting in honey so uniquely delicious that word of it had spread beyond Little Oxbury. Sometimes, outsiders would wander in, looking to make a purchase. How frequently visitors came did not matter—in a place like Oxbury, even a single stranger seemed plenty and was enough to cause a ripple of excitement.

Persephone turned toward the shelves just as fat raindrops began to slide down the windowpanes, filling the room with the lovely chorus of a storm. Without looking, she knew that the wildflowers that covered the estate were beginning to dance as the rain came down on their delicate petals.

Many of the thick, dusty books were about Greek culture and mythology, but none were as special to her as the one she held in her hands. Of all the volumes her mother had collected on the subject, she had loved *Mythology of the Greeks and Romans* the most. Stories of ancient gods and goddesses had sparked Emmeline Honeyfield's interest as a young girl—and if Persephone's early memories were anything to go by, that interest must have transformed into something academic long before she and Venus had been born. A crystal clear image of her mother sitting at a desk surrounded by books sprung to mind. Emmeline would read for *hours*. She'd been so invested in her study that she'd even gone so far as to have named her daughters after her two favorite goddesses. Venus had almost been named Aphrodite, but Solomon had swooped in to convince his wife to choose the Roman variant, if only to spare their younger child the embarrassment of having a strange name like *Persephone*.

Venus was lucky, Persephone thought. She was named after

the most beautiful of goddesses, while Persephone was named after the Goddess of Spring—who also happened to be the Queen of the Underworld. Venus did not seem very fussed about understanding their mother's love for mythology. The only reason Persephone found herself revisiting the tome she held in her hands was that she often found herself missing her mother desperately. She could still hear Emmeline's soft voice telling her story after story and answering all her probing questions. Persephone would ask different questions now, of course, but a violent illness had taken Emmeline from them seventeen years ago. It was too late.

Folding herself into a chair, Persephone attempted to read the familiar words before her. Her mind, however, kept wandering to what her father had said about the copy that was tucked away at Gallowsgate. Full of notes, he'd said. Full of her mother's words. Words that would perhaps reveal something of who Emmeline Honeyfield had been—what she'd cared about, which words had moved her—when she hadn't been busy with motherhood.

Gallowsgate was abandoned, so it would be perfectly fine for Persephone to slip in, locate the book, and slip out. Wouldn't it?

She looked back down, eyes catching the passage that described her immortal counterpart pulling a strange flower out of the ground, prompting the Lord of the Dead to erupt from the depths of the Underworld.

Well, Hades. Not London's Lord of the Dead, whoever he was.

TWO

Barrington Funeral Furnishing was established in 1710, long before Aidon Barrington or his brother had come into the world. Anyone who asked a young Aidon about the particulars of what his father did for a living was always given the same vague response. His father furnished funerals. That was all. It was only during his nineteenth year that he learned what that actually entailed—when he'd been given what he later realized had been a sanitized glimpse into the responsibilities that would one day take over his life.

His father had dragged him to the house of a bereaved family, his older brother in tow, as their punishment for appearing in the scandal sheets yet again—Cassius for losing his horse in a wayward game of cards and Aidon for being spotted alone with another unnamed woman in her family's orangery.

"This is your chance to show your father what fine young men you've become," their mother had said.

Aidon, who always bent to his mother's requests, promised they would go, even though he knew Cassius was against it. They both understood there was nothing they could do to earn their father's favor. They were his biggest failure—selfish, unmotivated fools. But at nineteen, Aidon still fully believed that Cassius would take over the business. The future that had stretched out before Aidon all those years ago was one sparkling with social engagements, late nights, and warm, welcoming women.

"It's your fault we're here," Cassius grumbled. They were standing several steps below their father on a staircase leading to Winslow House. "Losing a horse isn't nearly as bad as deflowering Lucy Milton. And you need to learn to say no to Mother."

"*Almost* deflowering," Aidon corrected. He held a wooden box of candles in his arms, which had been foisted upon him as soon as they'd left the carriage. "I was merely doing what she'd requested. And, if I recall correctly, you did the same for her older sister. Where do you think she got the idea?"

Aidon looked up at Winslow House. He doubted that any cost was spared in its construction and maintenance. If the family were truly as rich as their residence implied, then the question of why his father had decided to come here in person was easily answered. Any man of business knew that treating the social elite well was in his best interest. It was what paid for everything Aidon and Cassius took for granted.

Or so Aidon thought, anyway.

"Boys."

They both jumped to attention, backs straight.

Their father regarded them with undisguised suspicion. "You will both remain silent during the appointment. Your only task is to pay attention. Is that understood?"

"Yes, sir," they said in soft unison.

The look on his face made it very clear that he did not believe they were capable of doing what he instructed. Before he could say another word, the door to Winslow House was flung open, and they were allowed inside.

For the first time in his life, Aidon properly understood what his father did for a living. Charles Barrington sat with the recently widowed Mr. Winslow and helped coordinate the late Mrs. Winslow's funeral. He had a contact for everything—he knew all the best coffin makers, knew where to obtain a shroud on short notice, knew exactly which midwives would make the best work of washing the body.

"I've brought candles for you to light while vigil is kept," he said, gesturing to the box in Aidon's arms. "If you have already chosen an appropriate room, I will arrange for it to be draped in the best fabric we have to offer."

Aidon barely noticed the footman that took the candles from him. He was more interested in how his father's entire demeanor had changed. The cold, sharp man he knew was gone, and in his place was a sympathetic, soft-spoken ally. If Aidon didn't know any better, he would have called the man before him sensitive.

What did his family have to do, he wondered, to deserve the same treatment?

Later, Aidon would realize it had been foolish to assume he understood the full breadth of his father's responsibility. He hadn't understood the half of it, and he wouldn't for another four years.

"Sir?"

Aidon looked up, the London of thirteen years ago disappearing from his mind's eye. How long had he been reminiscing? Looking down, he saw that ink had dripped off the tip of his quill onto the funeral contract he had been working on. He'd been so caught up in the past that he had not noticed Michael Chase standing in his cavernous office. Serious, loyal, and trustworthy, Chase had been playing the role of Aidon's assistant for the past ten years. Together, they kept the business running in exactly the way Charles Barrington would have approved of. "What is it? Have you heard back from the coffin maker for the Eythrope funeral?"

Chase glanced around the room nervously before finally settling his gaze on Aidon.

"I'm afraid I'm not here to discuss business."

"Then?"

"You requested I remind you of your appointment with your brother this evening," Chase mumbled.

Aidon's face darkened. Chase wasn't wrong. He was rarely wrong. Aidon *had* asked to be reminded, but the very mention of his brother plucked at his nerves.

Chase examined Aidon before folding his arms across his chest. "I can send word that you are unwell, if you'd prefer."

Aidon sighed, running his fingers through his dark hair. He'd already rescheduled this meeting three times, and a fourth attempt would be enough to bring his brother to his office to harass him. Not to check on him, of course, but to ask for a ridiculous favor or share a salacious story absolutely nobody cared about.

He couldn't have that.

"I should go." Aidon pushed out of his chair and reached for his coat. Hesitation overcame him, and he quickly abandoned the endeavor in favor of tidying the piles of papers scattered over his desk. Not that it did much to improve the condition of the room. With dark wood walls and a dimly lit fireplace, Aidon's office was reminiscent of a mausoleum.

"Perhaps your brother only means to spend time with you," Chase said.

Aidon shot him a look dripping with condescension. "Perhaps. Or perhaps he's already gone through the money I gave him last month."

"You don't know that." Chase walked over and pulled Aidon's

coat and hat off their respective hooks. He cleared his throat and held them out, bringing an abrupt end to Aidon's needless fussing.

"Don't I?" Aidon asked bitterly, pulling the coat over his shoulders.

He didn't know why Chase was dancing around the truth. He had seen this exact scenario play out enough times to understand what Cassius wanted.

"One more thing, sir." Chase held out a scandal sheet. "More gossip about the Lord of the Dead."

"What now?"

"It seems that partaking in your—our—services is akin to making a deal with the devil."

"The *devil*? That's new."

"Would you like me to—" Chase made a halting gesture with his hands.

Both men knew it was pointless, but Aidon appreciated how often Chase attempted to smother the gossip that seemed to haunt him like a specter. The fact that rumors about the Lord of the Dead once again graced the scandal sheets proved that they were fighting a losing battle. He had always had *some* presence in the papers. A decade ago, any interested busybody would have been able to find out what he and his brother had been up to while in town. It was always something to the effect of, *This author has it on good authority that the young Mr. B— spent his time at the Cliveden ball wickedly tucked away in a darkened alcove with an unnamed Miss. What his older brother was up to is not fit to be printed!* As things had changed, Aidon had disappeared from the papers, though his brother had remained a permanent fixture. Recently, however, Aidon found himself the center of the gossip mill's attention once again, his brother thrown to the wayside. After all, there were thousands of rakes in London. There was only one Lord of the Dead.

"The best course of action would be to ignore it."

"Perhaps, but we've been ignoring it for quite some time now."

"And?"

"And—may I speak freely, sir?"

"You may."

"It does not reflect well on you," he said. "The longer you leave it to fester, the more likely it is to impact the business."

Aidon's jaw tensed. "Fine. Try to take care of it, then."

Placing his hat on his head, he left the office and walked out into the rainy night. Droplets immediately began to beat down on him, but he was in no mood to hire a hack to take him to his brother's town house. Why rush over? He knew the night would end poorly. When did interactions with his brother ever end otherwise?

The streets of London were dark and desolate, and as he walked, Aidon began to feel the familiar prick of loneliness creep upon him. It was difficult, doing what he did. He'd lost his position in society, lost the person he had been. Everything was sacrificed for his family's legacy of funeral furnishing.

He wasn't sure who he was now, really.

His older brother was intensely aware of Aidon's complete removal from the world they had once shared but did not seem interested in helping to remedy it. Cassius was fine flitting about, doing as he pleased and frittering his life away. It drove Aidon absolutely mad. Mad, and yet he sometimes felt a strange kind of jealousy blooming in his chest. Cassius lived without a care in the world. No guilt, no shame. Such a life was not possible for Aidon. Not anymore.

He knocked at his brother's door, somehow feeling worse than when he'd left his office. It swung open, revealing the golden devil himself.

"Aidon! To what do I owe the pleasure?"

"You asked me to come here, Cassius."

"Of course, of course! Come in. Mind that you don't drip everywhere. You'd think you'd be able to hire a hack, what with all that money lining your pockets."

Here we go.

Aidon stepped into the town house, wishing he were petty enough to actually drip all over his brother's fine carpets. He stiffened at the sound of chatter coming out of the parlor, which, based on what he could see from his position by the door, was absolutely teeming with people.

"For God's sake, Cassius, I thought we were to speak *alone*," Aidon whispered.

Cassius shrugged. "Must have accidentally forgotten about this little soiree of mine."

A soiree that, Aidon noted, he had not been invited to. Still, he seemed to be presented with the opportunity for escape.

"I'll return another time," he said, reaching for the wet coat his brother had taken from him.

"Nonsense," Cassius replied, shoving the coat at a nearby maid. "Stay here. I'll fetch us some brandy and then we can speak upstairs."

Before Aidon could protest, Cassius disappeared into the parlor. Aidon stepped deeper into the foyer to attempt a curious peek after his brother but was interrupted by the sound of whispers and giggles. Turning his head, he saw a small gaggle of young women who had evidently left the nearby library. They stared at him with round eyes, seemingly rooted in place at the mere sight of him.

Another man might have taken it as a compliment.

"Excuse me," he said politely, stepping out of the way.

The women moved through the doors of the parlor in an audible swish of skirts, their tittering pronounced and accompanied by a hushed declaration of, "The Lord of the Dead, here! I can't wait to tell Annabelle. She'll be utterly scandalized."

Aidon felt a mixture of irritation and embarrassment wash over him, neither of which was assuaged by his brother's reappearance. Leaving now, however, would be putting off the inevitable.

"Off we go," Cassius said cheerfully, shoving a glass of brandy at Aidon before disappearing up the stairs. As he followed his brother to the study, a gasp from another set of newcomers trailed him.

God, he hated being here.

"Well?" Aidon asked as soon as Cassius had shut the door behind them. A burst of laughter from downstairs was blessedly drowned out, replaced with the crackling of the fireplace that sat proudly against a far wall. His brother's guests were, undoubtedly, entertained by the Lord of the Dead's appearance, by *him*, and he would be damned if it gave them yet another thing to gossip about.

"How's business been?" Cassius asked, propping himself against the bare desk. "Any clients from the *ton*?"

"Business has been fine," Aidon replied. "And you know I don't share details about my clients."

"So noble." Cassius grinned, teeth glinting in the light of the fire. "Well, I suppose I'll get right to it then."

"Gracious of you," Aidon said dryly.

"Now, don't lose your temper, Aidon, but—do you remember the money you gave me last month?"

Aidon nodded, already aware of the direction they were going in. It was the direction they *always* went in.

"I know it was a decent sum," Cassius said sheepishly. "Really rather generous of you."

"What did you do this time?" Aidon asked, sinking into

an uncomfortable wooden chair and placing his brandy on a nearby table.

"It was just a little game of cards," Cassius said. "Well, maybe not *little*—"

"You realize you can't keep this up, Cassius," Aidon said. "I can't in good conscience keep funding—" He looked around before settling his gaze back on his brother. "Whatever this is."

"Of course you can," Cassius said. "You have to."

Aidon sighed. He had been expecting this as well. It was where this conversation led them each and every time. The only thing that changed was *how* Cassius had lost his money. Everything else was a reliable constant.

"Father's will *says* so," Cassius reminded him, the sentence spilling out of his mouth like clockwork. "I am to have full access to the family accounts until *you* marry."

Cassius, annoying though he was, was correct. He could continue to siphon from the family fortune until Aidon married. Once that occurred, Cassius would be restricted to a mere five hundred pounds a year.

It would have made perfect sense for the will to favor whichever of them took on the business, but that had seemingly not been enough for their father. The marriage clause had been purposefully put in. Anything for Barrington heirs. Anything to ensure the business was passed down the way it had been for decades. Neatly, to preserve the inner workings of it all, to keep the circle small lest the entirety of London find out just what happened behind the closed doors of the establishment.

Anything to punish the son that did not bend to their father's expectations.

"Yes, well—" Aidon began.

"Which, might I add, is not something that is likely to happen," his brother put in.

Aidon's spine straightened in surprise. This was new.

"I beg your pardon?"

Cassius shrugged. "Come now, Aidon. You and I both know it's unlikely that you'll ever settle down."

Aidon scoffed. "Because I'm busy being an insufferable rake?"

"You *know* why," Cassius said flatly.

He did know why. He also knew their roles might have been reversed if Cassius had only wished it. His brother was not one for responsibility. He was happy enough starting a scandal with any woman silly enough to entertain him and taking money from the business—the business *he* had been offered by their father. Aidon had felt pressured to step in after he'd overheard his brother so nonchalantly turn down the proposal made by their father on his deathbed. It had shocked Aidon at the time—it would have shocked anyone to hear an heir callously turn their family's legacy down—and Cassius's refusal had racked Aidon with guilt. Despite their difficult relationship, Aidon knew how hard his father had worked, how much pride he'd had in what he and his predecessors had built. And though he hated to admit it, Cassius's refusal had also given Aidon one last chance to prove his worth to his father. To prove to him that he *was* responsible, even if he didn't always act it. That he could make selfless choices for the benefit of the family. He was a good son, maybe even one worthy of being loved. So he had stepped in without knowing what exactly he was agreeing to. One short, clipped conversation with his dying father, and Aidon was next in line to run the business.

The business, unfortunately, was funeral furnishing. And as it happened, women weren't very fond of the business of death, which was exactly what Cassius was referring to.

"In any case, you cannot—" Aidon began.

"You aren't one to defy Father," Cassius said thoughtfully, tilting his head.

Aidon opened his mouth to argue, but the words would not come out. Instead, he exhaled, slow and steady. "This is the last time, Cassius. I mean it."

And it would be. Although Aidon had never worked up the nerve to make an offer of marriage, perhaps the time had come to begin considering it. He refused to do it *just* to protect the Barrington coffers from the likes of Cassius, of course. The mere thought of doing *that* filled him with guilt. No, he'd choose wisely. Carefully.

Well, he'd attempt to, at least. He couldn't exactly do away with the whole funeral furnishing situation.

Perhaps settling down would do away with the gossip, too. Well-to-do family men were not given monikers like *Lord of the Dead*. Well-to-do family men were not given monikers at all, really, no matter if they deserved them or not. The amount of gossip in the scandal sheets had slowly but surely increased over the past six months despite Aidon doing very little to incite it. He did his job, that was all.

It had started with a silly story in *Treacle & Tea*, one that implied he could be relied upon by anyone interested in organs that he supposedly harvested from his unconsenting deceased clients. Why waste time relaying gossip about scheming mamas and broken engagements when one could concoct outlandish tales about the Lord of the Dead? And they were, for the most part, just tales. He had read it all at this point—the Lord of the Dead could do away with your enemies, could make your crimes disappear by disposing of your murdered foes. He could do any number of things, but always for a large fee.

Contrary to what the scandal sheets said, Aidon did his work with as much honesty as he could, never shaming families into paying more than they could afford for funeral arrangements, and delivering on his promises to provide coffins made of genuine elm. He ran his business with care, the way his father had—down to the letter. Which was probably where all this damned gossip had come from. Like his father, Aidon *did* offer more than the average funeral furnisher did. And those offerings had somehow found themselves twisted into hearsay that was both ridiculous and untrue.

Perhaps he ought to be grateful they didn't know what he *really* did in the dead of night.

Cassius straightened in a great burst of energy, clapping his hands together in glee. "I'm glad we've sorted this out! Will you join us downstairs?"

"No, I don't think I will," Aidon said, suddenly exhausted. He trailed after his brother until they reached the entryway, desperate to leave and aware of more than one pair of eyes concentrated on his person.

"I'll just be a minute," Cassius assured him. "Need to track your coat down."

Aidon watched him go, curious as to how Cassius had managed to cram so many people into his tiny parlor and wondering how many of them were gossiping away about the Lord of the Dead. At that moment, a familiar face emerged from said parlor.

"I didn't know you would be here," Aidon said.

Ezra Haskett approached, dressed in his usual finery and giving him a crooked grin.

"I didn't know *you* would be here," Ezra said cheerfully. "That is, until I heard—well, never mind. What possessed you to come to Cassius's, of all places?"

Ezra knew of Aidon's general distaste for his brother, but it did not stop him from attending Cassius's social functions. Aidon had met Ezra during a summer in London when they were both relatively young, almost fifteen years ago now. The late Mr. Barrington had spent most of the year in London on business and seemed only to take pity on his wife and sons when he knew the countryside heat of Oxbury would be unbearable. It was during one of these escapes that Aidon met Ezra, then a chubby boy with a crop of curly red hair and a round face sprinkled with freckles. The freckles and curls were all that remained as the Ezra standing before him was almost his height, now more spindly than anything.

"I had an appointment," Aidon said darkly.

"I see. And how is the business?" Ezra asked.

Aidon sighed.

"Still a thorn in your side, hmm?" Ezra said, offering Aidon a sympathetic nod. "And to think you could have had all of this instead!" He gestured dramatically to the parlor.

"Surely there would be other options." Aidon chuckled, shaking his head. "I am not sure this would do, either."

They were interrupted by Cassius, who reappeared with Aidon's coat—now wrinkled beyond recognition.

"I'll send my man around tomorrow," he said, tossing the coat at Aidon before disappearing into the parlor.

"A farewell for the ages," Ezra murmured.

Aidon frowned. "I should be off."

"I'll follow, if you don't mind," Ezra said, his tone irritatingly chipper.

They left the town house in silence. Ezra hunched his shoulders against the cold drizzle, his red hair darkening in the damp. "I remember when I couldn't tear you away from places like this."

Aidon chose not to respond, instead looking out at the empty street glistening with rainwater.

"Look," Ezra said, his tone soft, "why don't you leave London for a bit? I'm off to Oxbury tomorrow. You could come with me."

"Oxbury?" Aidon echoed. Gallowsgate was in Oxbury. His father's estate, now technically his.

"Not to visit your ancestral home," Ezra said, as if reading Aidon's mind. "I'm going to pick up honey."

Aidon cast a weary glance at Ezra. He knew his friend was a little eccentric, but traveling a long distance away for honey was a bit much, even for him.

"You'll regret giving me that look once you've had a taste of it," Ezra said defensively. "I had some of it at my mother's, and she told me that it is quite hard to come by. In fact, it is exclusive to Oxbury."

"Oh, very well. We may as well stay at Gallowsgate, though I doubt Baker will be pleased with our showing up unannounced."

"Excellent!" Ezra chirped, shooting off down the sidewalk. "Tomorrow morning, then!"

"Tomorrow morning," Aidon grumbled. He turned on his heel and began to walk toward his office. It was late, but there would be work to wrap up if he was leaving town. He had not been to Oxbury in an age. Being there had always made him feel cut off from the rest of the world, but perhaps that was what he needed after an irritating evening at his brother's.

Oxbury was far, far away from his brother. And from all the incessant *talk*. What more could he ask for?

THREE

The very next morning, Aidon found himself in a carriage with Ezra, who was too animated for one awake so early.

"Say," Ezra said, attempting conversation for the thousandth time, "I read something curious in the paper the other day."

Aidon, who was desperately trying to sleep, opened an eye. Ezra was staring at him expectantly.

"Well?" he prompted. "What was so curious?"

"Lord of the Dead gossip, of course," Ezra replied coolly. "You drink the blood of your deceased clients, do you?"

"And if I do?" Aidon asked.

Ezra frowned. "Some people take gossip quite seriously, you know."

"I do know," Aidon said, irritation clear in his voice. "There is not much I can do about it."

"I suppose not." Ezra deflated and looked out of the window at the passing countryside. "How long has it been since your last visit to Oxbury?"

Aidon raised his eyebrows. "I've never *visited*. Not since my father died, anyway."

The moment his father died, Aidon had become a permanent resident of London. Not wanting his mother to waste away at Gallowsgate, he'd brought her to live with him. For two years, they'd lived in relative peace, and Aidon mostly focused on adjusting to his new responsibilities. He regretted the way he'd thrown himself fully into learning the ways of the trade. But then, he hadn't imagined his mother would be taken from him so soon. Apoplexy was difficult to see coming, something he'd had to communicate to clients several times in the years since.

It was something he'd had to say to himself, too. He couldn't have seen it coming. She'd been happy, at least. Happier than he'd ever seen her, with her husband dead and buried at last.

"Never?" Ezra sat up a bit straighter. "How do you know it isn't full of beautiful and desperate women?"

"It's all but deserted," Aidon said, trying and failing to suppress a grin. "I thought we were visiting for honey."

"We *are*!"

"Are you in the market for a wife, Ezra?" Aidon asked wryly. "If I recall, you were in my office less than a month ago, insistent that society would be lacking if you did not grace it with your heirs."

"That was said in a moment of weakness, and you know it," Ezra said, his cheeks coloring in embarrassment.

A companionable silence fell, punctuated only by the sound of the carriage wheels rolling over the dirt path.

"I should start considering it," Aidon said quietly.

"Considering what?" Ezra, who had been fiddling with his cravat, left it in a tangled knot and looked curiously at Aidon.

"Marriage."

Ezra's eyes widened. "*You?*"

"Is that so strange?" Aidon asked irritably.

"No, of course not," Ezra said. "It's just that, well—"

Aidon sighed. "I know."

"Not that it shadows all your other qualities," Ezra said, the words tumbling out in a rush. He paused, casting his gaze to the floor as if searching for something, then looked up and snapped his fingers. "You should join me at Honeyfield!"

"Honeyfield?" Aidon's brow knit in confusion. "What the hell is a 'honeyfield'?"

Ezra blinked. "It's where the honey is. Obviously."

"Honey from Honeyfield," Aidon said slowly. "That's—"

"Unbearably romantic, I know."

"I was going to say heavy-handed."

"In *any case*," Ezra said, "I have it on good authority that Mr. Honeyfield named the variant I'm interested in after his lovely daughter—who, by the way, has just reached her majority."

All Aidon had said was that he ought to start *considering* marriage, and already Ezra was trying to play matchmaker. What were the odds that he'd meet his future wife in Oxbury, of all places? Even without the weight of work on his shoulders, he'd never pictured himself lingering there any longer than he'd been forced to. There was nothing there for him, with very little to recommend it. If memory served, the village had regarded itself as a paragon of boring, stuffy tradition, and he certainly hadn't cared for that as a young man.

"Is that so?" Aidon asked.

"It *is* so," Ezra confirmed. "She's said to be a golden-haired goddess tucked away in the countryside."

"In Oxbury," Aidon said flatly. He shook his head. "While I appreciate the invitation, Ezra, I'll most likely be needed at Gallowsgate. God knows it's probably in shambles, with only Baker around to attend to it."

"Suit yourself," Ezra said, leaning back and folding his arms across his chest. He offered Aidon a cheeky grin. "Perhaps I'll bring a jar of honey back for you. That should sweeten you up." Aidon snorted. "Just what I need."

The remainder of the journey was uneventful, and almost three days after they had left London, Ezra's carriage pulled to a stop in front of Aidon's forbidding childhood home. Gallowsgate loomed before them, its stone facade seeming to absorb any and all sunlight in its vicinity. The two men exited the carriage and stood at the foot of the steps that led to the entrance. Standing two stories high, Gallowsgate was as unnecessarily large as Aidon had recalled. The front of the house was punctuated with a series of columns through which the large second-floor balcony could be seen. He remembered that balcony well, mostly because he and Cassius had wreaked all sorts of havoc from it. There was no better way to harass your brother than to empty a bag of flour or a pitcher of water onto his head from above.

But Aidon was an adult now, and there were things about Gallowsgate he could not help but admire. The elegant stonework that connected the columns to the pointed roof, the intricately carved door. And while he could appreciate all that made Gallowsgate attractive, it did not change the fact that his childhood home was a dull, unreflective gray.

"Lovely," Ezra said, clearly lying. "Very impressive."

"Come off it," Aidon returned, giving Ezra a look.

"It isn't that bad," Ezra said, trailing Aidon up the steps. "And look at the grass! Manicured to perfection. You said it would look a mess."

Aidon paused, turning to examine the trimmed greenery.

Whatever Baker, Gallowsgate's steward, was doing, he clearly deserved a raise for it. Aidon had half expected to arrive at a house nestled in a massive bed of weeds and overgrown shrubbery. He lifted his hand to knock at the door, stopping just as his knuckles brushed the polished wood.

Don't worry. I'm sure your father will come to fetch us soon. Why don't you play outdoors with your brother?

His mother's voice, melancholic and distant. They'd been all alone here, cut off from the rest of the world. Violet Barrington, her two boys, and all this *space*.

Too much space.

"Aidon?"

Ezra's voice tore Aidon out of his reverie. He cleared his throat. "Sorry. I was lost in thought for a moment there."

"We could stay at the inn, you know," Ezra said gently.

Aidon shook his head, knocking firmly at the door. "No. No, it's fine. We'll stay here."

Baker appeared almost immediately. If he was surprised to see Aidon, his face did not show it.

"Mr. Barrington," he intoned, shifting his expressionless eyes to Ezra. "I was not expecting you."

"Indeed," Aidon said sheepishly. "I did not have time to send notice."

Baker moved out of the way, allowing the two men into the foyer. "I am afraid the house is not currently ready for guests, sir. I will need a few hours to prepare."

"Not a problem," Ezra chirped, eyes darting around, no doubt in awe at the Gothic interior of Gallowsgate. "I expect to be away until suppertime at least."

"Very good," Baker said, sounding thoroughly unimpressed. "And yourself, sir?"

"I—" Aidon paused, wondering why he felt so damned cold

all of a sudden. It was springtime, for God's sake. "I'll take tea in the gallery."

Baker gave one short, sharp nod in lieu of a response before disappearing into a nearby hallway.

"I should be off," Ezra said.

"I'll be here," Aidon told him. "Enjoy your honey-hunting excursion."

Ezra darted out the door, likely desperate to escape the air of misery that hung over the house. Aidon watched him leave before making the trek to the gallery. He hesitated before pushing the door open, revealing the same cavernous room he remembered from childhood. Save for the paintings that graced the walls, everything was covered in dusty white sheets.

Truth be told, Aidon did not have many memories associated with this wing of the house. There *had* been that one time he and Cassius had accidentally bumped and broken a vase in here, but little more beyond that.

Which was precisely why he had asked for tea to be brought here.

I wonder if I should be rid of this place, he mused, pulling a sheet off a nearby chair before dropping himself into it. After all, what was there to Gallowsgate other than the ghosts of the past?

There was absolutely nothing else that could be found within these walls. That much, he was sure of.

FOUR

"Are you *sure* you won't come with us?" Venus asked, tying the pink ribbon of her bonnet into a pretty bow. "Even Mr. and Mrs. Harding have come to see Papa's demonstration."

Persephone glanced up from her book to raise an eyebrow at her sister. A few days ago, their father had announced that he was expecting a visitor, and the gentleman in question had finally appeared. His appearance had thrown Venus into something of a tizzy because, as she had informed Persephone at least three times in the hour since Mr. Haskett had arrived, they *never* had visitors, and the visitors that *had* come in the past had never been as handsome or charming. Even the Hardings had come from Little Oxbury, having been told of Mr. Haskett's upcoming visit by Solomon. It was doubtful that they had any interest in her father's unique hives. What they had likely traveled for was gossip, which was something of a rare commodity in Oxbury.

And, truly, there was no better subject for gossip than a mysterious gentleman.

"Why are *you* going?" Persephone asked teasingly. "You live here. You've heard Papa talk about his skeps hundreds—possibly thousands—of times."

Venus's face colored. "There's a *gentleman* visiting, Persephone."

"Oh, I'd forgotten," Persephone said. The truth was she needed her father and Venus to leave the house. She had something far more pressing to attend to and was not interested in being questioned about it. Knowing her father, Solomon would keep the group out by the skeps for *hours*. His demonstrations included everything from skep design to honey harvesting. She hoped Mr. Haskett truly was as interested in honey and beekeeping as he claimed.

"Suit yourself," Venus sniffed, straightening her skirts—tailor-made this time, thankfully—and fluffing her beautiful curls in the mirror. She turned and gave Persephone a wink. "If anything exciting happens, I'll be sure to tell you."

Persephone grinned, knowing she could trust Venus for that above all. "I'll try my best to contain myself until your return."

Giggling, Venus waved her fingers at Persephone in a goodbye and slipped out of the library. Persephone allowed a good amount of time to pass before snapping her book shut.

It was time to visit Gallowsgate.

She hadn't been able to stop thinking about her mother's special copy of *Mythology of the Greeks and Romans* since her father had brought it to her attention. It hurt her to think it was sitting in an abandoned house, collecting dust. It deserved to be loved—it *would* be loved. That, and she was absolutely desperate to read what her mother had written inside.

Pulling on her sturdy walking boots, Persephone exited the house through the back to avoid the clearing where the bees were kept. It would take her a good hour to walk to Gallowsgate if she kept to the paths, but only a quarter of an hour if she waded through the thicket, although the shrubbery would likely tear her hem to shreds. *Lucky that Venus will jump at the chance to mend it*, she thought fondly.

While the appearance of her father's visitors had given her the perfect opportunity to sneak off to Gallowsgate, Persephone also knew she was better off steering clear of gentlemen—*eligible* gentlemen specifically. She was terrible at exchanging pleasantries, terrible at flirting, and *terrible* at keeping her opinions to herself. While Persephone and Venus rarely left Honeyfield, Solomon had been known to leave Oxbury every now and again to attend meetings designed to attract beekeeping enthusiasts. He would meet gentlemen on his travels, and two of them had been nosy enough to call, having heard that Solomon had at least one daughter who had reached her majority. They had both appeared six years ago, mere months apart, and had disappeared shortly after, likely chased off by Persephone's decided way of expressing herself. If not that, then perhaps they'd taken one look at her wrinkled clothing and cropped hair and decided that she was no gentlewoman. Or maybe they'd decided to wait for Venus to come of age, which was the most embarrassing scenario of them all. Venus had the world at her fingertips and would likely experience all sorts of things before Persephone did—*if* she ever did. Things like love and companionship.

Passion.

"It's too late, now," she grumbled, almost tripping over a large root. The fact that she hadn't had a single proposal at twenty-seven meant it was time for her to start settling into spinsterhood.

A very small part of her hoped, though. But in Oxbury, hope was a waste of time. Its emptiness aside, Persephone doubted very much that Oxbury could attract her perfect match, whoever that was. She knew she did not need a man to take care of her or compliment her appearance. She knew she wanted to be seen. Yet every time she tried to imagine a fully formed man, she came up short. The truth was she wasn't even sure she could be loved at all.

It was, she noted, a little easier to be hopeful when one was away from Honeyfield. As much as she loved her home, it was the site of all her failures. It was too small, too cramped, a catalyst for her endless restlessness. If only she had another place to go.

Once or twice, she had considered asking to stay with relatives for a season to see what it would be like. Her father's distant cousin lived with his family in Bath, which made them a viable option, but she had never been able to gather the courage to actually do it. No doubt it would have ended in failure, with her returning to Honeyfield before the season was through. The thought of all those people *looking* at her, silently judging her way of being, was a bit too much to bear. She wouldn't know how to handle the pressure of living under the eye of society—she could barely do it here.

"So, you're saying, if I intend to leave Honeyfield," Persephone had said to her only, and therefore closest, friend, Christianna, "I should accept the next man who comes around?"

"It's the only way," Christianna had replied. "But if you do get married first, promise you'll help me escape next."

Christianna would tell anyone who listened about the romantic dreams she was *sure* would come true, no matter the man she married. Persephone fancied she'd be rather good at playing matchmaker for her friend, having read more than her fair share of romantic literature. She'd sooner help than face her own secret desires. It hurt less when one had other things to dwell upon.

And besides, Persephone thought, wincing at the sound of

ripping fabric as she clambered over a particularly large shrub, it wasn't as if marriage didn't have its own set of risks. She'd had her faults pointed out to her more than once. By her father, even by Venus, who sometimes spoke without thinking. Certainly by the few inhabitants of Little Oxbury. She remembered the day she had gone with Venus to fetch fabric scraps from the Grants' store. Mrs. Grant, as usual, had plied Venus with praise. To Persephone, she had recommended a good softening up.

"Don't worry, child," she'd said eventually, her ruddy face graced with a knowing grin. "Marriage will be the thing to change you."

But Persephone didn't *want* to change. The faults she'd been made aware of weren't *truly* faults. There was nothing wrong with being serious. Or opinionated. Or sharp. Men were allowed the luxury of all those characteristics. On Persephone, they were simply *unseemly*.

Perhaps marriage would be an acceptable compromise, helping her escape all the talk so she might finally find her peace. Maybe she *would* be wise to marry the next man who came along.

"Although," she said under her breath, "you are quite literally avoiding a gentleman at this very moment."

Finally emerging from the thicket—and likely looking a fright—Persephone laid her eyes on what had to be Gallowsgate. Large, foreboding, and built out of fine gray stone, it was Honeyfield's perfect opposite. Even the land, which was overgrown and colorful at Honeyfield, was a flat, perfect green at Gallowsgate.

She frowned. Who was caring for the gardens? All of her digging on the subject had confirmed one very crucial detail: nobody lived here. Nobody had for at least a decade.

Perhaps whoever *had* owned it had made arrangements to

have the land cared for. Yes, that made sense. Perhaps they were looking to sell it.

She snorted. As if anybody would willingly move to Oxbury.

Persephone made a slow, cautious circle around the house until she spotted an open window. It must have been left unlatched, allowing the wind to manipulate it with ease. Peering through it, she saw all the furniture inside covered with sheets. Abandoned. Just as she'd been told.

Hiking her skirts up, Persephone climbed through the window, her boots leaving footprints in the dust that coated the marble floors. She concluded that she was in a drawing room of sorts. The walls had been stripped bare except for a faded painting that hung over the fireplace. Persephone squinted at it, barely able to make out the stern, unyielding face of a man, his hand placed possessively on the shoulder of the woman standing beside him.

Venus had called Gallowsgate the Barrington estate, a name Persephone hadn't heard in years. The door let out a loud creak as she pushed it open, causing her to grimace. She walked slowly down the hallway, covered in dark wood paneling. In fact, she noticed, almost *everything* about Gallowsgate was dark. She found it a bit difficult to picture her mother visiting this place. For her part, Persephone could not recall ever interacting with the family that had resided here, nor could she particularly recall the guests her mother had received at Honeyfield. Clearly, whatever had connected Gallowsgate and Honeyfield had died with her mother.

Persephone looked into an open door, excitement flooding her as she realized she'd stumbled across the library. The shelves were uncovered and, to her astonishment, stretched all the way to the ceiling. She quickly scanned the room, worry beginning to build in her veins. Compared to the drawing room she had crawled into, the library looked almost lived in. Perhaps the open window hadn't been a random stroke of luck. Maybe someone *did* live here. The desire to turn around came hard and fast, but Persephone stamped it down. She'd come all this way, and she trusted that she could be quiet and quick. Luckily, there were far fewer books here than there were at Honeyfield. She began to scan the spines, taking advantage of a wheeled ladder propped against the shelves. Excitement flooded through her as she spotted a particularly promising book. Reaching over, she pulled it off the shelf. Just then, a deep voice cut through the heavy silence of the room.

"Who are you?"

Persephone gasped, the book slipping through her fingers. She screwed her eyes shut in terror, waiting to hear the thud of the book hitting the floor. But she didn't hear a thud at all. She heard a *thwap* and a grunt of pain.

Her eyes shot open.

FIVE

Aidon had been sulking in the gallery when a noisy creak resounded through the house, followed by the sound of footsteps echoing down the hallway and to the library. He had assumed it was Baker, accidentally bringing the tea tray to the wrong room.

That was what he had expected to find, at least. What he *hadn't* expected was to see a woman at the top of the ladder that leaned against the shelves, reaching for a book.

He also hadn't expected said book to be dropped right onto his head, but that was his fault for quietly approaching before announcing himself.

Bending down, he picked the large volume up off the floor. The words *Mythology of Ancient Greece* were pressed into the dark green leather in intricate silver lettering. He turned to the woman, finally able to get a good look at her. The words that had been ready to leave his mouth were quickly lost as he took in the sight of her, hanging on to the rungs of the ladder and staring at him with brown eyes the size of saucers. She looked like a little forest nymph, clad in a white dress that appeared a little worse for wear. The hem was muddied, and parts of it were torn to pieces.

His eyes slid up to her hair, so short that it may as well have been fashioned after a man's. It stuck out haphazardly in every direction, revealing a high forehead. The light that filtered through the window illuminated her, making her hair shine in shades of golden honey and her skin glow with freckles that appeared to be composed entirely of sunlight. She stared down at him, eyes curious. The silence stretched on, an unreadable expression on her face. She remained high above him, knuckles white from her grip on the ladder.

"I am very sorry," she squeaked, making no move to descend.

"Whatever for?" he replied, despite knowing that she was technically trespassing on his property and therefore did owe him an apology.

She raised an eyebrow. "For dropping the book on your head."

He looked down at the book and then back at her. "Of course."

She was no conventional beauty, yet he was sure he'd never come across a more bewitching creature.

"What does the cover say?" she demanded, squinting at the book he held in his hands.

"*Mythology of Ancient Greece*," he replied.

She sighed. "That's not right."

"It isn't?"

She scaled down a few rungs and wedged herself against the ladder, making a seat out of it. Up close, he saw that everything about her was small, down to her delicate, slender fingers. She reached for the book with one hand, the back of which was dusted with freckles.

Aidon wasn't quite sure how to put a name to the emotion coursing through him. Curiosity? Confusion? Or—and thinking this almost had him wincing outwardly in embarrassment—was it attraction? How long had it been since he'd been alone with a woman?

"My name is Persephone," she said.

Of course it was. He was hallucinating the physical embodiment of a goddess, staring down at him with large, questioning eyes.

He continued to study her small face, her slender neck, the unbearably luscious swell of her bosom, the—

"And yours?"

He lifted his eyes back to her face. "I beg your pardon?"

"Your name?"

"My apologies," he said quickly. He gave an awkward bow. "Aidon Barrington."

"But—you aren't supposed to be here," she said slowly, a frown marring her delicate features.

"Aren't I? Gallowsgate belongs to my family," he said, feeling equal parts dazed and confused.

Her dark eyebrows shot up. "Yes, but you don't *live* here, do you?"

"No," he corrected quickly. "I live in London. I'm just—visiting."

"Oh," she exhaled, her shoulders relaxing. "I wouldn't have climbed into the window had I known anyone was here. Everyone in the village said this place was abandoned."

"It is," he told her. "Well, partially, but—what are *you* doing here?"

This *was* his house, after all. The idea that any number of people might have climbed through the window over the last decade and gone through what was left of his family's possessions brought a twinge of discomfort and the urge to guard Gallowsgate from prying eyes. With Baker as its only guardian, Gallowsgate may very well have become an easy target for anyone curious to know what remained within its walls. Granted, the woman before him did not exactly give the impression of a thief. And if she was, she was not a very good one.

Persephone gave him a blank stare. "I'm looking for a book."

"I gathered," he said wryly. "*Why* here? It's not often people go looking for books in abandoned houses."

"I have reason to believe what I'm looking for is here. I did not choose a random house to search through, I'll have you know."

"No, of course not," he murmured, struck by the oddness of the exchange. "What book are you after, exactly? Perhaps I can help."

It was a ridiculous thing to say, given that he hadn't been to Gallowsgate in years and had absolutely no clue what books the library even held.

"It's called *Mythology of the Greeks and Romans*," she said.

"And *Mythology of Ancient Greece* won't suffice?"

"No, it won't." She paused. "It'll have the same stories, I'm sure, but it isn't what I'm looking for."

He looked up at her. "Do the mortals tell your tale correctly in books, Persephone?"

She hesitated, and he wondered if he'd overstepped. God, he was rusty.

"No," she replied. "I'm afraid they do not."

"Is that so?"

"For one, I was not dragged into the Underworld kicking and screaming," she said mildly.

He gave her a curious look.

Persephone lifted her chin. "I went of my own volition. And I was not tricked into eating those pomegranate seeds. I asked to have them."

He chuckled. "You wished to remain in the Underworld?"

She nodded. "The Underworld needed a queen, and I needed a change from the monotony of spring."

"How fortunate for Hades that he was able to capture your heart."

Color crept across her cheeks, and Aidon felt a thrill at having caused her to blush. That she had broken into Gallowsgate was already forgotten.

"I'm not quite sure he has. Though I am certain I have captured his," she replied, eyes glittering mischievously before shifting back to the shelves that lined the wall. "Would you help me? Find the book, I mean."

"Of course," he said, a touch too quickly.

"It belongs to my family," she blurted out, pushing *Mythology of Ancient Greece* back into its proper place. "I'm not looking to steal anything from you."

"You'd be welcome to it either way," he said, hoping he sounded polite instead of desperately foolish. "I'm not really one for books."

"That's a shame," she said, looking down at him. "Perhaps you ought to try something new."

It was not what she was referring to, but he had the distinct feeling that his something new was staring right at him.

"What would you recommend?"

"It depends on what you've already read," she said, eyes scanning the room. "And it depends on what you've enjoyed. You'll have to think on it."

He was enjoying *this*. He hadn't enjoyed something so much in the ten years since he'd taken on his father's business. Who knew that running into a strange wisp of a woman in his library would be just the thing to bring him back to life?

Suddenly intent on pleasing her, Aidon began to look through the shelves, hunting for the book she was so desperate to find. They searched in perfect silence, occasionally checking in with one another until Persephone let out a long, exasperated sigh from the ladder, which now sat two bookshelves down from where it had originally been propped.

"Where *is* it?" she grumbled. "I doubt I'll get back before Venus and Papa now."

"Back?"

"To Honeyfield," she explained. "I live there with my sister and father."

Honeyfield. When Ezra first mentioned it, it was as if Aidon had never heard the name at all. It had been so long since he'd thought of Oxbury at large—the only part that had lived on in his mind was Gallowsgate, isolated and oppressive. Nothing else had existed in his memories, mostly because nothing else had really mattered. His father had not allowed them to mix with the other families beyond going to the village, though a part of him vaguely recalled his mother receiving visitors while Charles had been away—perhaps someone from Honeyfield. How else would the book have found its way here? The only thing he was certain of was that he and Persephone had never met.

He would have remembered her.

"The honey," he murmured. "My friend Ezra's at Honeyfield."

"Oh!" she gasped. "You know Mr. Haskett."

"We came here together."

"Why aren't you at Honeyfield, then?" she asked. "Surely you've come for the same reason as Mr. Haskett."

"Not quite," he said. "Only Ezra is here for honey. I'm here for a change of scenery."

She nodded, as if all had been clarified. "I see. Well, I really should return. If you don't mind, I'll come back another time to look for the book. Or you could let me know if you come across it. I doubt you'd want me back here tracking mud on your floors."

He frowned. What could he do to keep her from leaving so soon?

"Stay for tea," he blurted out.

"I shouldn't," she said quietly, making her way down the ladder.

He quickly approached her and offered his hand. She hesitated for a moment before slipping her delicate hand in his. Pure electricity shot through him at the contact, the force of it dizzyingly delicious.

She had to have felt it, too. What were the odds of their meeting? What were the odds of it being so perfect? Free from the wandering eyes of society, free from propriety, free from the presence of nosy gossips. *Perfect* didn't even begin to do it justice.

At that moment, Persephone's boot caught the torn hem of her muddied white dress. A loud tearing sound cut through the room, and in less than a second, she had toppled off the ladder and straight into his arms, a large chunk of white muslin hanging pathetically onto the rest of her dress by a thread. He could feel the warmth of her, one hand against her back, the other having found purchase underneath her now bare knees. She blinked at him, cheeks crimson, the force of her heartbeat apparent even to him.

"I am so—" she began, voice hoarse.

"Are you—" he said at precisely the same time.

Neither of them could complete their thoughts because, without any warning, Ezra burst into the room. He was accompanied by a tall, elderly gentleman, a young woman with blond curls, and a middle-aged couple who looked absolutely stricken.

"Oh, no," Persephone whispered, barely audible. She wiggled in his arms. "Put me *down*."

Aidon snapped out of his daze and slowly lowered her to the ground, clearing his throat. "Ezra. I wasn't expecting you back so soon."

"I can see that," Ezra said cheerfully.

Aidon shot him a look that made the smile disappear off Ezra's face.

"Everyone was curious to see Gallowsgate," Ezra explained. "I thought we could have tea here before returning to Honeyfield for the rest of the demonstration."

"And it seems we arrived at the perfect moment," the middle-aged woman said, her horror seemingly forgotten as she began to practically vibrate with glee.

"There was no perfect moment, Mrs. Harding," Persephone corrected sharply.

"A lovers' rendezvous," Mrs. Harding said in a loud stage whisper to the man next to her.

"Persephone!" the blond woman cried out, hands flying to her mouth.

"I was just—" Persephone sighed in exasperation. "I came here to look for the book, Venus."

Venus's attention turned to Aidon, eyes widening as she examined him. "Did you—did you find it?"

"No," Persephone said. "In fact, I was about to return home."

"Such scandal," Mrs. Harding crowed. "And in Oxbury, too! And to have Miss Honeyfield in the center of it is simply—"

"There is no scandal," Persephone protested. She looked up at Aidon pleadingly. "Tell them there is no scandal."

"Miss Honeyfield is correct," he said, stepping forward. "I was only assisting in her search for a book."

"Alone, Mr. Barrington?" Mrs. Harding asked.

It seemed he could not be free of gossips, not even in Oxbury. So much for the perfection of their encounter.

"Mr. Barrington," Venus said slowly, as if testing his name out. "Aidon Barrington? Aren't you the Lord of the Dead?"

"Excuse me?" Persephone said, putting her hands on her hips.

Aidon let out a long exhale, dread barreling through him.

"So he is!" Mrs. Harding exclaimed. "We heard all about it from Mrs. Murphy when she returned from London."

"Right," Persephone interrupted. "I think we have taken far too much of Mr. Barrington's time already."

"We have not, however, been given sufficient explanation as to your activities here," Mrs. Harding insisted. "Look at her *dress*! The poor thing's almost had it torn right off her."

This time, Aidon saw that even Venus was casting a look of utter astonishment at the older woman. Mrs. Harding was hell-bent on conjuring a scandal out of this particular misunderstanding, and there was nothing anybody could do to stop her.

"Such an unfortunate situation your daughter has found herself in, Mr. Honeyfield. And with the Lord of the Dead, no less!" Mrs. Harding continued with clearly feigned sympathy. "Thank goodness your dear wife is not here to see this. Her eldest daughter ruined! She simply would not have been able to cope."

"Mrs. Harding!" Venus chastised.

"Do not think you are unaffected by this, my dear," Mrs. Harding said, beady eyes darting to Venus. "What gentleman would willingly marry into a family stained by such impropriety? Oh, what a waste of your beauty. The entire village was quite convinced you'd be the one to marry well. Surely you did not foresee being forced to remain at Honeyfield for the rest of your days with your ruined sister in tow. I shudder to think what will become of the two of you now."

Venus's cheeks flushed crimson. "*I* think we'll—"

"Papa," Persephone interjected desperately, turning toward the thin man who had, thus far, been silent.

"There is no scandal to speak of, Mrs. Harding," Mr. Honeyfield said, his words measured and slow. "This was not the way we wished to announce the news, but my daughter and Mr. Barrington are"—he paused here, as the entire room awaited his final word—"engaged."

Aidon's mouth dropped open just as Persephone let an entirely unladylike curse slip from her lips.

Ezra, meanwhile, gave Aidon a smug smile. "And you said there was nothing to be found in Oxbury."

Six

That night, Persephone was lost in thought. What had she been *thinking*? She ought to have excused herself as soon as Mr. Barrington had appeared. But her mind had been clouded over by the immediate, overwhelming sense of comfort that had overtaken her as soon as he'd spoken. It was a feeling that had only increased as they'd exchanged words, and one she wasn't sure she had ever experienced with another person before. Something about the whole encounter had been . . . different.

It hadn't hurt, of course, that Mr. Barrington was painfully handsome. He'd been dressed very finely in a crisp white muslin shirt, a pressed black waistcoat, tight black trousers, and shiny black boots. His cravat had been perfectly starched and folded in the most complicated knot she had ever seen. With his angled jaw dusted with black stubble, his sharp, straight nose, and his dark hair, Persephone had had a very difficult time tearing her gaze away from him.

But that wasn't what had made her feel so blissfully comfortable. It was those grass-green eyes of his and the way he'd *looked* at her. Eagerly, with interest. Almost desperately at times, as if he'd wanted her to stay. Wanted to hear the next words out of her mouth.

You're being silly. And if you had left, you wouldn't be in this mess, would you?

Her father had ushered her and Venus back to Honeyfield shortly after announcing Persephone's engagement—*engagement!*—to Mr. Barrington, claiming a sudden headache and rescheduling the remainder of his beekeeping demonstration. He asked Mr. Barrington to visit Honeyfield the following morning. To Mr. Barrington's credit, he had not denied the engagement. He'd agreed to visit and simply watched them go, more than likely completely and utterly bewildered by what had occurred.

Denials, Persephone was sure, would come later.

Solomon entered the shadowy parlor, a cup of tea clinking in his shaky hands. He sat in an armchair by the window, peering at her in silence.

Just get on with it, she thought impatiently. When he didn't, she realized he expected her to break the dreadful silence.

"I know, Papa," she said flatly. "I shouldn't have gone to Gallowsgate."

Her father took a sip of tea and did not say a word.

"And I should not have been alone with Mr. Barrington. I was only looking for Mama's book. I didn't expect—"

"No, of course not," her father said gently. "That is not the issue here, Persephone. I need you to understand why I did what I did."

"I do understand," Persephone said, sitting up straighter.

"Mrs. Harding is a notorious gossip," Solomon said.

"You were trying to protect—"

"If you'd been ruined, think of what that might have meant for Venus."

Persephone flinched, her father's calm words a dagger

through her chest. Mrs. Harding had said something to that effect as well. Was that the only thing that had spurred Solomon to act? Would Persephone's ruination have been acceptable to him had she been an only child?

"Surely you do not expect Mr. Barrington to agree to this," Persephone said, voice steady so as not to betray her heartbreak.

"That is for me to sort out," Solomon said.

"And what if *I* don't agree to it?" Persephone demanded. "Surely you do not expect *me* to—"

"Have you other options?" Solomon asked directly, though not unkindly. He sighed. "What else are we to do with you, Persephone?"

Accept me as I am. Love me as I am.

Instead, she said, "You don't have to do *anything* with me. Nobody does."

"Are you to stay in Honeyfield for the rest of your life?" Solomon questioned. "I won't be here forever, my girl."

Persephone blinked slowly, processing her father's words. But—was this her only chance?

Why, in God's name, would Mr. Barrington agree to this? He had no reason to protect her reputation, had no reason to want to marry *her* of all people.

She thought of Venus, hopeful about suitors and deserving of her own great escape. Persephone could not—would not—be the thing that shut the door on the excitement that undoubtedly lay in wait for her sister. Her father's haphazard announcement had softened the situation at Gallowsgate considerably, leaving Mrs. Harding with a story devoid of the sort of scandal that would properly ruin a lady. At best, the state in which Persephone had been found would result in a few interested whispers, which would be easily eclipsed by news of her engagement.

As if summoned by Persephone's thoughts alone, Venus appeared, dressed in her nightgown, with a plate of biscuits in her hands. She seated herself by Persephone as if to shield her from their father's interrogation.

Solomon stared at them both, seemingly unmoved, before standing up and bidding them good night. Venus watched him go before turning to Persephone.

"What's to happen?" she demanded, dropping the plate of biscuits on a nearby table with a noisy thud.

"Father seems to think he'll be able to convince Mr. Barrington to agree to this nonsense," Persephone grumbled, burying her face in her nightgown. She peeked at her sister. "I was only looking for the book."

"I believe you," Venus said soothingly. "All that gossip floating around London is about Mr. Barrington, you know."

"It's all that Lord of the Dead business, isn't it?"

Venus launched into a description of all she had heard about Mr. Barrington, providing far more details than the first time they'd discussed the Lord of the Dead. Some things seemed plausible, such as his position as head of a highly successful funeral furnishing establishment in London. Other things, like claims of vampiric habits and connections to the devil, were clearly the product of silly people with wild imaginations and far too much time on their hands.

"I've heard that his family has always run in circles far loftier than their own," Venus said. "It seems that their clientele leans rich and aristocratic. Is that not strange?"

Persephone shrugged. "Rich people do die, Venus."

"Yes, but there are any number of respectable businesses for them to go to," Venus countered. "It's almost as if Barrington Funeral Furnishing offers services they cannot obtain elsewhere."

"Like deals with the devil?" Persephone teased.

"Gossip isn't always entirely made up," Venus said. "It's not all devils and vampirism. It's about who people rely on when they want to make their secrets disappear."

Persephone considered this begrudgingly. It made sense, and she was *sure* deals of a scandalous nature happened behind closed doors, but—he'd seemed so *nice* and gentlemanly.

You know better than to be fooled by such behavior.

Yes, Persephone was smart enough to know that men were skilled at using gentility to gain people's trust. A false compliment here, a carefully placed smile there, and some women could be fooled into believing all sorts of things.

"There were even a few columns about the cemetery at Gallowsgate mysteriously growing," Venus added in a hushed tone. "I think everyone in the village likes that bit of gossip the best because it includes Oxbury in all the excitement."

"What nonsense," Persephone said in an attempt to calm her unsettled nerves.

Venus shrugged. "Nonsense to you, but I doubt he is entirely unaffected by it. In fact, I'm sure he longs for the gossip the scandal sheets *used* to print about him."

"There's *more*?"

"I've heard that a 'Mr. B' used to feature in *Treacle & Tea* years ago before he disappeared from the papers."

"And what did they have to say about him?" Persephone asked, not entirely sure she wanted to know.

A cheeky glint appeared in Venus's eyes. "That he was a consummate rake."

"Don't tease, Venus," Persephone said.

"I'm not!" Venus insisted. "Mrs. Murphy goes to London often, and she says it's true!"

"So you mean to tell me that the consummate rake turned into the Lord of the Dead?"

"Why not?"

Rakes were skilled at deception. How else did they manage to coax women into shadowed corners? Into their beds, even?

Stop.

Venus interrupted Persephone's train of thought. "Do you think you'll go to bed soon? You should rest."

Persephone shook her head, running her fingers through her wild hair. "The sooner I sleep, the sooner I'll have to deal with what is to come."

"Is what happened bad, really?"

Persephone's mouth dropped open. "Venus! Of *course* it's bad!"

"If Papa is successful, you'll find yourself married to a handsome, rich gentleman," Venus said pointedly. "Gossip not-withstanding, of course."

"How on earth would Papa succeed?" Persephone asked, heart twisting in her chest. "No sane person would agree to such a thing."

"Would *you* agree to it? If it came down to your decision?"

Persephone turned toward the dying fire, as if the answer would make itself visible in the ashes. She'd have reason to leave Honeyfield. Nobody would be able to say another unkind word about her. She wouldn't spend every waking moment feeling as if she'd failed, as if she'd missed some arbitrary date by which she was supposed to have achieved all that was demanded of women. She'd have her own space, and—

"I suppose," she said slowly, unable to meet Venus's eyes.

"And the funeral furnishing bit wouldn't bother you?"

She did not have the luxury of being so picky as to reject a man based on the nature of his work. Still, to be so closely connected to death, to have that be such an integral part of life, was not exactly enticing.

"I'd learn to live with it," she said. "Though the very idea of my agreeing to all this is so . . . pathetic."

"It's not pathetic!" Venus burst out, taking Persephone's hands in her own. "It's your chance to chart your own course, Persephone! You'd want the same for me, wouldn't you?"

"Of course," Persephone said emphatically, looking at her sister's lovely, rosy face.

"And, just to remind you," Venus said, "there is such a thing as fate. Papa doesn't have all the power."

Persephone laughed. "Thank you, Venus. I'll remember that."

Aidon couldn't sleep. The Honeyfield family had left Gallowsgate quickly after the debacle, leaving Aidon to handle the Hardings, who had been overly congratulatory for two people who had just wreaked havoc on both his and Persephone's lives. Ezra had failed to lure them away, only finding success when he'd offered to give them a tour of the grounds. He'd shot Aidon a comically panicked look—one that was entirely appropriate given that Ezra had never been to Gallowsgate before and was, therefore, utterly unequipped to give a tour of any kind—but Aidon was grateful for their departure. After all, it wasn't as if the Hardings would know the grounds any better than Ezra.

Aidon, meanwhile, had made himself scarce, his mind running through the events that had led to the announcement of his engagement—*engagement!*—to Persephone Honeyfield.

Staring up at the dark ceiling, he sighed. His current bout of insomnia made sense, then, as his mind still had not settled. As stunned as he was, part of him couldn't help but linger on the image of Persephone, with her high cheekbones, dark, inquisitive eyes, and the freckles that dusted the back of her right hand—the very picture of asymmetry. He thought about her hair, wild and untamed and completely out of the ordinary for a young woman of any standing.

But perfectly suited to her.

Despite his better judgment, he closed his eyes and thought about other things, like the way her dress had clung tightly to her slender form, pushing her lovely breasts into view. How her hands would look laced in his, or even splayed across his chest, grasping desperately at his shoulders—among other places.

His eyes shot open. This was ridiculous. He didn't know her, and she'd undoubtedly talked her father out of his ridiculous scheme as soon as she'd returned to Honeyfield. She had no reason to—well, no, that wasn't entirely true. If she agreed to it, it would be to protect herself and her family from ruination.

And as for him, he'd just been thinking of marriage, hadn't he? This could be the answer to his problems with Cassius. It could very well distract the scandal sheets from spinning tales about the Lord of the Dead. If he gave the impression of respectability, the ton would be less interested in whispering about him. It was easy to believe that an unattached man, one who lived alone, could get up to all sorts of antics under the cover of night. A married man, less so. Barrington Funeral Furnishing had always been a family business—perhaps the *family* part of it was what had been lacking all this time. But there was something else, something about Persephone that was just *right* in a way he couldn't describe. It sounded foolishly starry-eyed, and maybe a touch desperate.

You are desperate, Lord of the Dead, he reminded himself wryly.

Still, there was an attraction. He'd felt it in his bones, seen it in the crimson of her cheeks. No doubt it would help things along.

Things. What things? He didn't even know if Persephone would agree to this. Didn't even know if her pretty blushes were the product of embarrassment rather than attraction. He was weaving a sickeningly romantic tapestry out of nothing.

Overcome with restlessness, Aidon dragged himself out of bed. Perhaps something warm would help him settle. He walked down the hall only to see that Ezra's door was slightly ajar, light spilling out of the room. Aidon knocked gently, almost jumping when the door swung open instantly, revealing a bright-eyed Ezra.

"You're still awake," Aidon said.

"I was just about to say the same to you," Ezra said, moving aside to let Aidon in. "Mr. Honeyfield lent me a book on bee-keeping, and it's been very difficult to put down."

Trust Ezra to latch on to a zany new hobby less than a day into their visit to Oxbury. Aidon dropped himself into an armchair before the fire. Ezra looked at him expectantly.

"What?"

"What?" Ezra repeated, flopping onto the bed. "You're the one who's come to my room in the dead of night."

"I couldn't sleep," Aidon said.

"And no wonder." Ezra grinned. "What happened, exactly? You'd all but disappeared when I finally got rid of the Hardings."

"Exactly what we'd explained. She was looking for a book," Aidon said helplessly. "And I was helping her. That was all."

"Not quite sure how that would end with her in your arms, but I'll take your word for it."

"You are welcome to fall off a ladder in my presence, Ezra," Aidon replied. "Perhaps you'll be able to put the pieces together if I am inclined to catch you."

"I realize that her father was merely trying to smooth over a—uh, complicated situation," Ezra said slowly. "But what are *you* going to do?"

"I—I don't know."

Which was only partially true. He knew what he *wanted* to do, just not what he would actually do.

"I only ask because I saw the way you looked at her."

Aidon's eyes met Ezra's. "I beg your pardon?"

"If I didn't know any better, I'd say you looked a little love-sick," Ezra said teasingly.

Aidon felt his face begin to warm. There was no point in denying it. "The whole situation was—odd."

Ezra tut-tutted in disapproval. "Is that all?"

Aidon stood and began to pace around the room. "Not odd in a bad way, just *strange* and *right*, and I . . . can't quite describe it, really."

Ezra was silent for an unusually long time before letting out a low whistle. "I don't think I've ever seen you this worked up."

"I'm not worked up," Aidon snapped.

"Irritable as well," Ezra murmured, sounding quite like a doctor listing off a patient's symptoms. Which was appropriate because Aidon certainly did feel as if he'd come down with something.

"I think . . ." he said softly, his tone hesitant. "I think it wouldn't be such a terrible thing. Marrying her."

It had been so much easier to think on it when he'd been tucked away in his bed, alone. But there was something pleasant about having it out in the open nonetheless.

Ezra nodded. "It would save her from ruination, that much is certain."

"Yes, but—" Aidon shook his head. "I don't think it's ever felt so natural."

"Indeed," Ezra acknowledged. He smiled. "You know, I think this could be good for you, Aidon. You haven't had an easy go of it lately."

"That's an understatement," Aidon said, collapsing back into the chair. "All of this feels *mad*, though."

"I hate to say this," Ezra said gingerly, "but I don't think Miss

Honeyfield has much of a choice. I have no doubt that Mrs. Harding has let the entirety of Little Oxbury in on the news."

Damned gossips. He hated that, the implication that Persephone didn't have a *choice*. She deserved to have choices. She likely deserved someone far better than him, deserved to have her pick of all the men in England.

"I'll have to go to Honeyfield tomorrow," Aidon said.

"Yes, you will. You also owe me an apology."

Looking up, Aidon frowned. "What for?"

"You didn't believe me when I suggested that you might meet your match at Honeyfield," Ezra said in mock seriousness. "As it happens, I predicted all of this. I ought to start charging for my fortune-telling services."

"Shut up, Ezra," Aidon grumbled, exhaustion suddenly weighing heavily on his shoulders. He stood and made his way to the door. "I'll see you in the morning."

"Good night, Romeo," Ezra crooned.

"That play ends terribly," Aidon reminded him.

"Does it?" Ezra asked. "I wouldn't know. Never got around to reading it."

SEVEN

The next morning, Persephone found herself up in her favorite tree. It was a great gnarled thing, older than Honeyfield, more ancient than Oxbury. She loved the feeling of the rough bark underneath her hands and the quiet swaying of the sharp-edged leaves. The leaves reminded her of herself: soft, patterned with a delicate map of veins, but surrounded by serrated, jagged edges. The aroma of damp earth and flowers swirled around her—a scent she usually found comforting.

She climbed down the tree until her feet were once again firmly planted on the ground. She had left two bowls of water and a small packet of sugar by the roots. Sitting on one of the roots, she began to combine the ingredients. Her father, having seemingly forgotten that her life was in complete chaos, had tasked her with discovering if the bees preferred to be supplemented with sugar water or syrup. Once she had prepared the concoctions, she approached the hives, which hummed and pulsed with a restless energy that matched Persephone's thoughts.

"What should I tell him?" she asked aloud, mixing the thick syrup. She began to pour it into a shallow tray.

In the early hours of the morning, Persephone had made a decision. She would accost Mr. Barrington before he made it to the house and convince him to agree to marry her. She would protect Venus's reputation as well as her own, despite hers being considered largely unimportant by her own father—and she would finally have reason to leave Honeyfield.

The issue, one of many, was that men usually weren't very interested in her. There were simply things about her they did not like, and Persephone did not feel that those things could be corrected. It wasn't so much that she needed to brush her hair or press her dresses. It felt more like she had a cloud hanging over her, one that told potential suitors she was too difficult, too spirited, too *unlike* Venus, who she was always compared against. Venus was heartbreakingly beautiful and so sincerely sweet. Persephone loved her for it and often wished she were the same. Instead, she was always sharp and guarded.

"Why should Mr. Barrington want me, then?" she demanded bitterly, directing her question at a bee that had landed on the tray. It ignored her and continued to observe the syrup with great interest.

Useless.

Nothing was stopping Mr. Barrington from returning to London and choosing a lovely, gentle girl. After all, there were scores of them in England. There was no reason for him to feel the need to protect her reputation.

She took a deep breath and moved to another hive, hoping to calm the wild beating of her heart. Something else had been plaguing her since dawn, something that had plagued her since Mr. Barrington had encountered her in his library.

Persephone huffed, waving off a passing bee as she set up a tray of sugar water. As much as it embarrassed her, she couldn't stop thinking about the lovely warmth that had spread through her at the feel of his skin against hers when he'd caught her after she'd fallen off the ladder. She'd spent half the night thinking about his strong jaw, dusted with a dark shadow that she was sure he meticulously shaved off every morning. His thick black hair that curled ever so slightly, untamed and very handsomely tousled. And his eyes—so clear, and the loveliest shade of grass green she had ever seen. When he held her against him, she had felt the straining of his muscles, had been enveloped by his sheer sturdiness. For the first time in her life, she was hyperaware of the fact that she was a living, breathing woman.

A living, breathing woman who was capable of actual, palpable desire.

It was difficult to feel like much of anything when one rarely strayed from Honeyfield. Oxbury was boundless, but there was nowhere for her to go. She'd even started to avoid Little Oxbury once she'd grown tired of all the misplaced advice given so freely by its inhabitants. There was no use in advice that always boiled down to "be completely different."

But Gallowsgate *was* a place she could go. It was a place her mother had been, a place Persephone hadn't even thought to seek her spirit out. Emmeline had been the only person to truly understand her—the only person who had been proud of all that made Persephone different. When she died, Persephone had felt that understanding fade like smoke. While the library at Honeyfield continued to hold much of her mother, the years had made it more difficult for Persephone to connect with her. She read Emmeline's books on a constant loop, searching the pages for the understanding that had been torn from her. With every year that passed, it had been harder to find, leaving her with the distinct feeling that there was nothing left of her mother to cling to anymore. But Gallowsgate offered her a new thread to follow. She felt inexplicably drawn to it, the same way her namesake had been attracted to the narcissus.

And yet, despite all that was calling her to Gallowsgate, she heard Venus's voice in her head. How much was Persephone willing to risk for a chance at freedom? For the off chance that she might find pieces of her mother to hold close to her heart? For all she knew, Mr. Barrington lived his life as unassumingly as she did. Although . . . Venus had mentioned he'd disappeared from the papers, only to reappear as the Lord of the Dead. Which, Persephone had to admit, was strange. What had he been doing while the busybodies weren't looking? What had triggered his return to the scandal sheets, this time in the leading role of London's very own Lord of the Dead?

Persephone shivered, willing her mind to quiet. She had already made her decision. And there was nothing she would not risk for her sister—and for the only chance at freedom she might ever have.

Now, if she could only convince him to—

As if on cue, Persephone heard the sound of hooves hitting the ground. She dropped the tray she'd been holding on top of a nearby hive and scrambled toward the trees. Peeking around a trunk, she saw that Mr. Barrington had arrived and was guiding his horse through the confusing maze that was Honeyfield. Taking a deep breath, she cleared her throat delicately. Mr. Barrington turned to face her, a warm smile blooming on his handsome face as their eyes met.

"Miss Honeyfield," he said politely, sounding entirely too pleasant for someone who had likely come to embarrass her.

"Mr. Barrington," she said, voice sharp and businesslike, "might I have a word with you?"

To her surprise, he instantly dropped his horse's reins and followed her without question as she led him to the honeybee clearing. The trees on the outskirts filtered the sunlight and offered plenty of shade, making it the perfect place for them to speak. As with the rest of Honeyfield, wildflowers threatened to take over, and a breeze brought the scent of lavender along with it, familiar enough to steel her nerves.

Crossing her arms against her chest, she looked up at him. Had he always been so tall?

"I should apologize for my father," she started hesitantly. "I am sure you know this already, but he was only trying to save me from further embarrassment."

"Of course," was the gracious response.

"I know you are in no way obligated to agree to this," she continued, feeling as if her heart was stuck in her throat, "but I was hoping—no, not hoping." Pausing, she searched for the right word. Unable to conjure it, she said, "You are here to speak to my father, are you not?"

He blinked at her. "I am here to speak to you."

Persephone's eyebrows shot up. "Me?"

"Yes, you," he repeated softly. Offering a teasing grin, he said, "The woman I am allegedly engaged to."

Persephone felt her skin prickle with awareness. "Yes, well, that is precisely what I wanted to discuss."

"We are of the same mind, then," he said.

"Yes!" she blurted out. "Maybe—it is really rather unlikely that we are of the same mind, which is why I thought to accost you."

The corner of his mouth lifted in a devastatingly charming smile. "Is that what this is?"

"I should think it was obvious," she retorted. Smoothing her hands down her dusty pink skirts, Persephone took a deep breath. "What happened yesterday—well, what's done is done. I've no doubt the entirety of Little Oxbury knows of it already."

"I'm sorry," he murmured. "I should have done a better job of—"

She shook her head vehemently. "No. They should have listened to *me*."

"Yes," he agreed. "They should have."

Persephone let out a long exhale. The conversation was already going nowhere, and it was entirely her fault. "In any case, that is not what I wanted to discuss. I wanted to talk about the—the engagement."

"Ah, yes," he said mildly. "Our engagement."

Just say it.

"Would you consider it?" she said, almost choking on the question. "Consider me, I mean."

She cringed once the words had left her mouth, realizing how foolish they must sound to him. Mr. Barrington's eyes widened, his dark eyebrows knitting together as he stared at her, seemingly speechless.

"I appreciate your silence," she said dryly, attempting to protect her wounded pride. "I understand that this is all rather strange, but—"

"But?" he echoed, sounding a little bewildered.

"But my sister's reputation is at risk," she said briskly. "And it is important to me to try to protect her."

He gave her an unreadable look before asking, "And what of your reputation?"

Persephone sighed. "*My* reputation is of no importance."

"I don't think that's true."

Unsure of how to respond, Persephone walked over to a buzzing hive, running her fingers along the wooden edge of it. "Do you know that most skeps require the keeper to kill all of their bees just to harvest a little bit of honey?"

She was sure the change in subject confused him, but she

needed a moment to gather her thoughts. He hadn't responded to her suit, and that in and of itself was rather telling.

He nodded, and she continued. "Papa has always been terribly against it. Against hurting any living thing, really."

Bees began to hover around them, as if attracted by their presence.

"I feel very much like one of them," she said, gesturing to the hive. She lifted her eyes to meet his. "Restricted to a very small place. No matter how far they go, they always return to Honeyfield."

"Miss Honeyfield, I—"

"You can call me Persephone," she interrupted. She bit her lip. "You came here to end this entire farce, didn't you?"

She had to know.

"That's just it," he said, taking a step toward her. "I came here to ask you the very same thing you just asked me."

Something unidentifiable exploded in Persephone, something that was composed of equal parts fear and relief. Mostly fear, if she were being honest. Who would believe she had come by this match properly?

"I appreciate your silence," he said wryly, using her own words against her.

"I didn't think—"

"You want to protect your sister's reputation," he said simply, "and I would protect yours. We are of the same mind after all."

Persephone felt her lips part in surprise. This was what she'd been hoping for. And yet—and yet, she'd never been more terrified in her life.

"Is your father in? I should like to speak with him."

Venus's words about fate echoed in her head.

Honeyfield was quite literally like nothing Aidon had ever seen. Everything around him was an unruly expanse of multicolored flowers and large swaying trees. It was absolute chaos and looked as if it had been purposely left to fall into disarray.

Despite that, all he could focus on was Persephone. He'd come here to talk to her, to see if she might consider a proposal, even if it had come on the heels of her own almost-ruination. But she had found him first and asked him the very same thing.

Again, what were the odds?

His pride was wounded a little, knowing she was mainly doing it for her sister's sake. But even he had held back from telling her his own reasons. His need to be rid of the constant thorn in his side that was his brother, his desire to stymie the gossip that only served to complicate his life, even the longing for companionship that was brought on by ten long years of lonely solitude—there was nothing he could share that would not make him look like a fool or, worse, a self-serving reprobate.

"I've never seen anything like this place," he told her as they walked toward the house. Standing by her side, he noticed that she was really no more than five feet tall. She walked barefoot, her hem muddied beyond repair.

Lifting her thin, sloped nose, she regarded her home with an air of detachment. "No, I suppose you wouldn't have."

"It suits you," he offered, meaning it. Persephone looked as if she belonged to Honeyfield as much as the trees and overgrown lavender.

She tensed her jaw at this and did not respond. Instead, she showed him where he could tie his horse before leading him into the house, which was outfitted exclusively in pastels and positively bursting at the seams with books. He was half surprised to see that the flora of the outside hadn't managed to worm its way in. She led him to what he assumed was her father's study, gesturing at the door.

"Go on. He won't mind being interrupted. Not for this."

Aidon knocked, entering when called. He found himself buckling under the weight of Solomon Honeyfield's gaze.

"Mr. Barrington," he said, remaining seated. "Thank you for coming. I expect I owe you an explanation for yesterday."

"Not at all," Aidon said quickly. "I've come here to ask for your daughter's hand."

Solomon leaned back in his chair, looking mildly impressed. "Then you have saved me time."

"I am in no hurry," Aidon added nervously. "Perhaps Miss Honeyfield would rather we—"

"We should post the banns as soon as possible," Solomon interrupted.

Three weeks.

"If that is what Miss Honeyfield wishes," Aidon said slowly, wanting to make it clear he was not comfortable making decisions without her input.

Solomon gave him a long, steady look before barking, "Persephone!"

The door opened instantly, making it painfully obvious that Persephone had been listening at the door. Her face, Aidon noted, looked a bit pale.

"Yes, Papa?"

"Mr. Barrington has asked for your hand," Solomon said, words emerging from his mouth at a snaillike pace. "Which means we have given Mrs. Harding one less thing to gossip about. I suggested we post the banns immediately, but Mr. Barrington was hoping to hear your thoughts on the matter."

Persephone turned her head in his direction then, a slight

frown pulling at her face. It deepened as she examined him, and Aidon suddenly felt this was going terribly.

"I should not like for the banns to be posted."

At all?

"Now, Persephone," Solomon chastised.

"You could obtain a common license, couldn't you?" she asked, directing the question at Aidon.

Of course he could obtain a common license. He had the money for it, but why not do things the way they were normally done? She looked white as a sheet, her peachy skin drained of all life.

"As you wish," Aidon agreed, wanting to make this easy and hoping to one day understand the reason behind her request.

"And I don't want a large gathering." This, Persephone directed toward her father.

Ignoring his daughter, Solomon slid his gray eyes from Persephone to Aidon. "I must ask, though you mustn't think it changes anything—what is this Lord of the Dead business about?"

"Papa!" Persephone gasped.

Aidon glanced at her to see she looked quite offended on his behalf. It was sweet, and he did not deserve it in the slightest.

"A perk of working in funeral furnishing," he lied.

It came as natural as breathing now.

"It seems that not a one of us is free from gossip," Solomon said serenely.

"I will ensure that Miss Honeyfield remains untouched by it," Aidon promised, wondering if that, too, would end up a lie.

After a moment's silence, Solomon stood up and grinned. "Well, I suppose this is settled. Our family thanks you, Mr. Barrington. I expected to have to use my powers of persuasion to convince you to protect our good name."

Aidon heard Persephone scoff softly. She kept her gaze firmly away from his, face still milky white. Something had changed since the library, since the honeybee clearing, even—but he couldn't put his finger on it. Whatever it was, he was sure it would come out in time. She was, after all, to be his wife.

"Please," he said to Solomon, "the pleasure is all mine."

EIGHT

Persephone asked to walk her new fiancé out of the house. Her father agreed, a pleased glint in his eye. She turned to look at Aidon as soon as the front door was shut.

"I did not expect today to end like this," she admitted.

In truth, she wasn't sure what she *had* expected. Was it possible to want and *not* want something in equal measure? This was the change she had been seeking, and yet fear had won out over excitement with very little effort.

"Neither did I," he said before fixing her with a curious look. "Is there a reason you refused to have the banns posted? It would have given us a little time."

Persephone knew that. She knew it quite well. But she had been possessed with the same age-old fear that had plagued her for her entire life. She did not want to be looked at, did not want people to wonder what Mr. Barrington was doing with the difficult, plain daughter of Solomon Honeyfield. With the posting of the banns, everyone in Oxbury would have three full weeks to wonder about her dowry, gossip about her appearance, and whisper about ulterior motives. She simply would not suffer through *weeks* of it before she even made it to the parish. She refused to.

"Will you return to London?" she asked suddenly, desperate to change the subject. "I should hate for your business to suffer because of all—this."

Aidon shrugged. "Most likely."

"I see."

A strained quiet settled. All Persephone had done yesterday was go to Gallowsgate in search of her mother's book. Now, she was officially engaged.

"Perhaps this was fate," Aidon said abruptly.

"Fate?" she repeated in disbelief. What was it with everyone and *fate*?

"A romantic way of looking at things, is it not?" he asked.

Persephone gaped at him. Here they stood on the steps of her family home, pushed into an engagement because she'd fallen off a *ladder*, and he was speaking of romance?

"I am not very fond of romance," she lied.

He gazed at her in silence for a moment before glancing at the carpet of greenery that stretched out before them. "I would think that living here would leave you particularly fond of romance."

Persephone turned to look at Honeyfield, trying very hard to see what he was seeing. It was beautiful, and there was nothing she loved more than the chaos of springtime, but it was also lonely. It had made her who she was, and that person was by no means ideal.

Something he would find out in due course. Another thing to be scared of.

Then, she thought, *I am sure to disappoint him.*

"I suppose you will be reviving Gallowsgate in the meantime," she said, swiftly changing the subject again.

"Gallowsgate?" he choked. "Surely you do not intend to remain in Oxbury."

"I'll need some time to adjust to—married life," she said, panic coursing through her veins as the possibility of leaving all she had ever known began to settle in. "Please. We needn't stay here forever—just for now."

Aidon looked at her for a long time, and Persephone could not help but fidget under his gaze. He was probably regretting his decision already. Venus would have jumped at the chance to be married and go to London. True to form, Persephone had managed to turn the whole thing into a muddled and difficult affair. Even if she was drawn to him, even if fate was playing a role in all of this, even if she knew this was the quickest way for her to expand her world—

"Very well," he said.

He took the reins of his horse, preparing to depart, but then dropped them, turning toward her.

"Persephone," he began, giving her a helpless look.

"Later," she said, desperate to be alone with her thoughts. "We will have all the time in the world."

"So we shall."

He held out his gloved hand, and she glanced down at it, slightly bewildered.

"May I?" he asked, jolting her into action. She gingerly placed her hand into his and watched in utter amazement as he lifted it, pressing a kiss to her bare skin. The featherlight touch set off an explosion of butterflies inside of her so raucous that her knees almost buckled. Gently releasing her hand, he gave her a polite bow and left her on the steps.

Persephone watched him mount his horse and ride off, and only when he was out of sight did she sink down on the steps and shiver. The door behind her opened, and Venus's voice floated out.

"Papa told me what happened," she said, sitting next to her. She tucked her hand into Persephone's before continuing.

"Thank you. I know this was for me, but I hope it was only *partially* for me."

I did this for me, Persephone thought.

"Everything will be fine," she said aloud, squeezing her sister's hand.

"Persephone!" a voice called. "Venus!"

Both women looked up to see Christianna walking down the path, her thick chestnut hair tousled from the walk from Errwood. She came to a stop in front of them, her grin disappearing as she examined their faces.

"Whatever is the matter?"

"Persephone is engaged," Venus said somberly.

"Engaged!" Christianna shrieked. "I did not think I would return from London to *this*!"

Persephone gave Christianna a helpless look. They had known each other their whole lives. Christianna lived in a neighboring estate, and her father's sprawling farms generated masses of wool that were traded in Little Oxbury and beyond. They'd spent their childhoods playing and running through the unruly wilderness of Honeyfield, with Persephone always luring Christianna into some kind of mischief. Now, her friend was crouched in front of them, bubbling with curiosity.

"What happened?" she demanded.

Persephone sighed and launched into the whole sordid tale. Christianna hung on to her every word, gasping and shaking her head when appropriate.

"That Mrs. Harding," Christianna said. "She is absolutely ridiculous." She gave Persephone a knowing look. "But you wouldn't have agreed to this if a part of you didn't want it, Persephone."

"Their meeting was fate," Venus said. "Or that's what I told her, at least."

"I mean, think of all you'll experience!" Christianna

continued, her gray eyes starry with excitement. "Didn't I tell you that this was the only way to make life in Oxbury bearable?"

Persephone nodded. "And you still think so, do you?"

"Of course I do," Christianna said confidently. "I think you'll find that you'll see the world in a whole new light. Oxbury after marriage will certainly be different from the Oxbury we are living in now. You'll have far more freedom than Venus and I do, I assure you."

Persephone cautiously believed that Christianna was right. Something new *would* make Oxbury bearable, and the fact that this something new was a strange, magnetic pull she had never felt before seemed to sweeten the pot considerably. The possibility was dizzying.

"When will the banns be posted?"

Out of the corner of her eye, Persephone saw Venus shaking her head at Christianna.

"No banns?" Christianna asked aloud, as incapable of subtlety as always. She looked at Persephone, sinking her teeth into her bottom lip. "Oh, Persephone."

She knew why Persephone would have refused the posting of the banns. Even Venus knew. Both of them knew Persephone's whole heart. There was no need to discuss it any further.

"It doesn't matter," Venus said, jumping to Persephone's defense. "Mr. Barrington is to obtain a common license."

"How lovely," Christianna said, though her words sounded a little forced.

"I can't wait to fall in love," Venus blurted out.

"Love?" Persephone echoed, turning to face her. "I am not in love."

"Yet," Christianna said, twirling the ends of her chestnut hair.

What had felt so impossible was now a reality, and Persephone was finally free of all the pressure and hopelessness that had haunted her entire adult life. For once, she did not have the suffocating feeling she usually felt when her sister and friend spoke of love and courtship.

If she had grown up in a grand place like London, she would have found another way to chart her path. She was sure of it. But that had not been her lot in life.

You would want this regardless, a voice sang in her head. *Want him.*

"I still don't know where Mama's book is," Persephone grumbled. "That's the worst part of all of this."

"You'll find it," Christianna said soothingly. She gave Persephone a strange look. "It's a little funny, you know."

"What is?" Persephone asked.

"All of this—it's almost your myth come to life."

"It's nothing like her myth," Venus disagreed.

It occurred to Persephone that her myth was one of restlessness. And while Venus was correct in that the past few days hadn't been a perfect reflection of the story in their mother's books, there was something oddly familiar about it all. Traveling from the cradle of spring that was Honeyfield to dark, forbidding Gallowsgate was apt for someone named Persephone.

"Well, either way," Christianna said, dropping the subject, "it looks like we have a wedding to plan."

NINE

The carriage ride after the ceremony from the parish to Gallows-gate was bumpy but arguably less trouble than trekking through the thicket. Persephone and Aidon sat across from one another, an awkward silence permeating the air and making Persephone wish she were elsewhere. Her stomach had twisted into knots the minute she stepped foot in the carriage. The ceremony had been short and to the point, attended by Venus, Solomon, Christianna, and her parents. Persephone wanted so badly to be brave, to simply trust she'd made the right decision, but it was proving difficult. Only a week and three days had passed since their slapdash engagement, which had left Persephone plenty of time to agonize over all the ways this scheme of hers could go awry. She and Aidon had not communicated since his visit to Honey-field. That is to say, he had written her, and although his letters had mostly consisted of pleasantries, she had been too much in her head to respond. Persephone convinced herself that she ought to say as little as possible to him, lest he really come to know her and regret his choice.

She stared out the window, taking in the flat, uninhabited

landscape of Oxbury. It was so *empty*. There weren't many suitors for young women, and yet young women were still expected to make a match before spinsterhood came knocking at their doors.

Very suddenly, a man *had* appeared. Or rather, Persephone had appeared at his house uninvited. Either way, she was now sitting across from him. Married to him. She absently wondered if the Goddess of Spring had found her journey to the Underworld as awkward as Persephone was currently finding this ride.

He may come to regret this match, a wicked voice in her head sneered. *You haven't forgotten what people have said about you already, have you?*

Persephone sighed, exhausted by her traitorous mind, and felt Aidon's eyes flicker to her for a moment. So much had happened, and all so quickly. One minute she was climbing trees and reading books, and the next, she was falling into a handsome, wealthy man's arms.

She imagined very few people were enthused by his line of work. Frankly, Persephone wasn't too fond of the idea herself, but she supposed she could stand it. After all, it was his business, not hers. She could acknowledge that funerals were important, even if women were not allowed to attend them. After Emmeline's funeral, Solomon had seemed lighter, as if a minuscule but weighty part of his devastation had been buried with his wife. Persephone had toyed with the idea of sneaking to the parish to watch the funeral proceedings, but she'd been tasked with caring for Venus, still an infant. She often wondered if being at the funeral would have helped any. By the time she'd gone to the gravesite, it was as if all traces of her mother were gone. There was nothing to visit. So she'd looked for her elsewhere, finding her far more easily in the pages of her favorite books. And while the myths Emmeline had favored often dealt with death, Persephone tried not to dwell on it overmuch. Gods and goddesses did not die, after all. Mortals, however, did. All her mother had done was catch a chill, and that was that. Death had snatched away the person she loved most, and it was difficult not to resent it even if she knew it was simply the way of things. But death was now linked to her livelihood, whether she liked it or not.

And from what she had heard, it was *incredibly* lucrative. Not only was she being offered security, but she was also going to be mistress of her own house.

And a wife. What did husbands and wives discuss, anyway? What did they *do*?

Persephone felt her cheeks warm. More than a few of her mother's books had been inappropriate, to say the least. It was safe to say that Persephone knew more about what happened in the marriage bed than any of the other young ladies in Oxbury. She used to shock Christianna with the details, laughing the entire time.

She wasn't laughing now.

A part of her couldn't imagine, not for one second, that her husband would want to lie with her. Another, larger part of her was thinking of her body pressed against his in the library and the sensation of his lips brushing gently against the back of her hand. How that tiny, delicate touch had sent a burst of electricity dancing through her veins. And how she wanted more.

Some women, Persephone thought, had a certain charm to them, a certain air that made men weak. She was quite sure she didn't have that charm. Generally speaking, she did not find any part of her particularly inviting. She was a bit bony, not at all lush like Venus and Christianna. And yet, he'd—

Perhaps it would be for the best if he didn't want her in his bed. That way, she wouldn't have to waste time feeling so self-conscious. She felt her skin begin to prickle in discomfort.

"Persephone."

The sound of her name startled her, and she felt her face warm again as she realized that she had been staring. At her *husband*.

The word seemed so foreign in her head.

"I . . . I did not mean to stare," she stammered apologetically.

He shook his head. "It's not that." He nodded at the window. "We've arrived."

Stepping out of the carriage, Persephone realized she likely looked an odd contrast against the stone facade of the house. She was a spot of pale yellow sunshine against the gloom, having changed into a pastel day dress as soon as possible.

As they ascended the shallow steps that led to the door, they were met by a man who looked less like a person and more like a fragile skeleton.

"Baker," Aidon told her. "Gallowsgate's steward. Baker, my—my wife."

"Persephone Hon—" Persephone cut herself off, realizing she no longer had Honeyfield attached to her name. Clearing her throat, she covered the gaffe up with a polite smile. "Barrington."

"A pleasure, Mrs. Barrington," Baker intoned, either polite enough to have looked over her hiccup or so detached that he simply did not care.

Stepping inside, Persephone took a moment to absorb the interior of her new home properly. The entrance was far bigger than the one at Honeyfield, decorated with the same wood paneling she had noticed during her last visit to Gallowsgate. Dark furniture melted into the walls despite the light that spilled in from the large windows that framed the front door. To the right sat a wide staircase, and she noticed a series of paintings had been hung alongside it, disappearing into the second floor. From where she stood, she saw they were portraits—the past masters of Gallowsgate, no doubt. In the center of the room sat a small table with a vase of carefully arranged flowers. The sight of them unwound something in her chest, their familiarity comforting.

"It's a little sparse," Aidon said from beside her.

"It is," she agreed, a sense of awe washing over her as she tilted her head up to examine the high ceilings. "There's so much to *do*."

So much change to oversee, so much to distract herself with.

"And that is a good thing?" he questioned, lifting an eyebrow in her direction.

"Of course it is," she said, wandering through the grand entrance and running her fingers along the wood paneling. "It must be odd for you, being here."

The statement seemed to confound him. "Odd?"

"You've been away for so long," she explained. "To the point where everyone thought the house had been abandoned."

He paused, looking around the entryway before settling his gaze onto her. Something she could not identify flickered in his eyes. "Not odd, but different. As I am sure it is for you."

At this, Persephone began to walk through the corridors, all of her worries temporarily banished. Aidon trailed behind her, waiting patiently and answering all her questions as she nosily poked her head into every room they came across. Persephone, ever curious, wanted to know when things were built and where all the art had come from. She did not comment on the fact that most of the rooms were in desperate need of care, many of them still in partial disarray after years of disuse.

"It's so much bigger than Honeyfield," she said.

Less restricting.

"We can change anything you like," he said, and she almost thought he sounded eager.

The tour of the ground floor brought them back where all of this had begun: the library. It had changed since she'd last been to Gallowsgate. The furniture glistened with polish, and the books had been rearranged into tidy rows on the shelves. Persephone wandered over and picked out the first book she saw, turning it over to see that it was a small collection of Shakespeare's plays.

"I love these," she said softly, flipping it open to the middle of *The Winter's Tale*. "But only the happy ones."

"No tragedies?" he asked.

Persephone shook her head. "There's nothing harder than writing a happy ending. Cynicism is much easier." She offered him a sheepish grin. "I would know."

He looked at her then, an intensity in his green eyes that made her slightly uncomfortable.

She snapped the book shut. "Could I be shown to my room, please?"

Silently, he handed her off to a newly employed maid, who led her up the stairs. The woman opened a large, heavy door, revealing Persephone's room. Persephone dismissed her quickly and politely and took a minute to examine her new surroundings.

It was as dark as the remainder of the house. The large four-poster bed was constructed of mahogany with a headboard patterned with intricate carvings of leaves. Deep crimson sheets were topped with black furs meant to protect her from the coming winter. She wryly thought that whoever had chosen the bedding did not know one would melt under furs this time of year in Oxbury but forgave them when she felt their softness underneath her fingertips. A fireplace crackled happily across from the bed. Walking over to the window, Persephone pulled the heavy drapes open a fraction. The late afternoon light illuminated the gardens below, revealing perfectly trimmed shrubbery.

And tombstones.

Many, many tombstones in a cemetery that sat close to the house, surrounded by an iron gate. The sight of it transfixed her, her eyes scanning the neat rows as she mindlessly counted. One hundred and six markers exactly. A shiver ran up her spine, and she quickly turned away. She remembered what Venus had told her about this very cemetery. It couldn't be true, of course.

Could it?

"Don't be silly," she scolded herself. She would not ruin her newfound freedom by thinking on idle gossip. Turning her attention back to the room, she was pleased to see a bookshelf, bare for her use, and a plump chair upholstered with maroon velvet. A small desk sat nearby, perfect for her letter writing. Overall, the room was well furnished, despite being outfitted in such somber colors. Just as she moved to open one of her trunks, her eyes caught sight of another door, only steps from her bed. Straightening, she walked toward it and opened it a crack.

Persephone's eyes widened. She'd never seen anything like it—a room with a fireplace, in front of which sat a large copper, linen-lined tub. An intricate screen stood a few steps away, concealing a corner behind it. A wide porcelain dish sat on a stand across from the tub, and a small shelf above it held a selection of what appeared to be oils.

Such rooms were typically reserved for the aristocracy or the incredibly wealthy. It surprised her, this revelation that there was *this* much money in death.

Persephone saw yet another door across from where she stood. She ventured into the bathing room and hesitantly placed her hand on the doorknob. Perhaps it led back to the hallway or into yet another finely furnished room. She opened the door very slightly, grateful that it wasn't creaky. She poked her head inside for a moment before sharply pulling away.

Another bedroom. *His* bedroom. She felt her heart hammer in her chest as she closed the door softly. It made sense that he would be nearby. She just hadn't given it much thought. It would take him very little effort to walk directly into her room if he wished it.

If he wished it. And, just like that, Persephone's anxiety returned with a vengeance.

Trunk. Go unpack your trunk.

Knowing that distraction was the only thing that would quiet her thoughts, she slowly put her things away, happy that the sight of her books on the shelf brought some much-needed color into her dark cavern of a room. At the very bottom of the trunk was her white cotton nightgown, soft and worn from years of use. She placed it gingerly on the bed and continued to unpack.

Hours later, after the sun had made way for the moon, she carefully wiggled out of her dress and stepped into the soft, familiar cotton. Dinner had been brought to her room on a tray, the maid explaining that the dining room was not quite ready for use.

So much for a wedding night.

Sitting on the edge of the bed, Persephone sighed. She'd wanted out of Honeyfield, and that was what she'd gotten. She could now do whatever she pleased without being constantly reminded of all the ways she was *wrong*.

This was freedom.

But it wasn't a love match.

Surprise bloomed inside her as she gripped the edge of the bed, feeling the heavy furs tickle her palms. It was a silly thing to want, yet here she was, wishing desperately that she'd managed to find it somehow.

Persephone lay back, staring at the canopy of her new bed. There was little point in dwelling on all of this. She'd planted her seeds. Now, she had to see what would come of them.

TEN

A long time ago, Aidon thought, being in the presence of a woman would have been simple. His interactions with Persephone would have been filled with easy smiles and sweet nothings.

But things had changed, and he was unsure of himself.

He'd been surprised at her reaction to Gallowsgate. Her expression hadn't been one of wide-eyed disappointment, but rather wide-eyed wonder. Of course she saw Gallowsgate for the dazzling house it was. He wished he could look at the house through her eyes, but far too many unpleasant memories had been absorbed by these walls.

He remembered his mother, always sighing and melancholic; his father, stern and forceful. He and his brother would make themselves scarce when their father was home, typically choosing to play outside on the perfectly manicured grounds, mussing up the groundskeeper's hard work. He and Cassius had left as soon as they'd been able, storming London with all the passion of young men who'd had a lifetime of pent-up energy to spend.

He suddenly realized that Persephone hadn't had that luxury—the ability to just up and go. He'd taken it for granted.

And now he'd returned. The only thing that made being at Gallowsgate bearable was Persephone, with her bright dress and curious eyes.

A shame that he no longer possessed the charm or skills to inform her of the fact.

Aidon looked down at the sheet of paper on his desk, knowing he would have to seek her out before it got too late. It was what was expected. But he was struggling to finish reading the letter before him, covered in splotches of ink and crossed-out words. He despised receiving these letters. But he was duty-bound to honor the requests within, just as his father had.

You wouldn't have to if you'd only just—

No. He had to. And he would.

But his response would have to be left for another time. He knew he also had to write to Cassius to inform him of his new annual income of five hundred pounds. Granted, he could have spoken to him in person while he'd been in London, but he'd known better than to let his brother get a whiff of his impending lifestyle change. He'd be furious, of course, but perhaps it would inspire him to find a vocation of his own. After all, the Barringtons had always been a working family.

Aidon snorted. Wishful thinking.

He folded the letter in half, taking great pains to hide it in a locked box at the very back of a drawer. Heaven forbid anyone should find it. Heaven forbid *Persephone* should discover—

Though she'd have to know at some point, know that the next Barrington heir would have to—

She is going to come to regret this.

He slammed the drawer shut. That was a problem for another day. Now, he had to find Persephone. The very idea flooded him with heat, making him aware of every bone, every sinew in his body. God, it had been a long time.

At that moment he heard the sound of a door closing and footsteps echoing down the hall. He froze. It had to be Persephone. He was suddenly overcome with a desperate hope that she'd taken it upon herself to come to him.

But the sound of her footsteps softened as she continued down the hall, passing his door entirely. It seemed that it was a night for wishful thinking.

Where was she going? It was late—very late. Aidon slowly opened the door and stepped out into the hallway, his body somehow knowing where to take him. He walked down the staircase, remembering how terrifying this house had seemed at nighttime when he'd been a boy. It was less dark than he remembered, though that was likely because he had spent time in far darker corners of the world since then.

The soft glow of candlelight spilled out of the library, and he saw Persephone once again perusing the shelves, likely searching for the book she'd initially come to Gallowsgate for. She was dressed in a white nightgown, made translucent by the candlelight.

Christ.

"Persephone," he said, his voice low and soft. She started, snapping shut the book she held in her hands. "My apologies. I did not mean to interrupt."

Persephone blinked at him with her dark, inquisitive eyes. "There was no interruption," she said. "There—there's nothing to interrupt, really. Did I wake you?"

He shook his head.

"Oh, good," she murmured, fidgeting a little. "I couldn't sleep, so I thought I'd come down here and—"

"Look for your book?" he guessed, hoping he could slip back into his old charm if he tried. "We keep meeting here, don't we?"

She swallowed. "Yes, I suppose we do."

"You mentioned that it belonged to your family—that you

had reason to believe it would be here," he said. "Do you know who might have brought it from Honeyfield?"

"It must have been my mother," she replied, her tone reverent. "Do you recall receiving a Mrs. Emmeline Honeyfield at Gallowsgate? It would have been a long time ago."

He shook his head. "She must have come to see my mother."

Persephone brightened at this. "Perhaps I might ask her more about it, then. Does she live in London?"

"She passed away eight years ago."

"Oh. I'm sorry."

"I would suggest searching her rooms, but she cleared them out herself before leaving Gallowsgate."

She seemed to wilt at that. "I see."

He got the distinct feeling that a change in subject was warranted.

"I didn't see much of you this afternoon."

"I was unpacking," she said, turning away from him to push the book back onto the shelf. He could see the outline of her bare body underneath her nightgown.

Patience.

"Is the room to your liking?" he asked, walking toward her. Her wide eyes tracked his every move, the air in the room thick with tension.

"It matches the rest of the house," she said, and he wasn't sure if that was a compliment or a complaint. "The cemetery was a surprise."

"Cemetery?" he repeated, suddenly rooted to the floor.

"I hadn't expected it to be within such close proximity to the house." She continued, voice light, "Was it intended to be? I wondered if it might have outgrown its original size."

Aidon's jaw tensed. "It has always been nearby."

Damn that gossip. It had even reached Oxbury, for God's

sake. He would not let it get in the way. Not when she looked so delectable, only a few untied ribbons away from being completely undressed.

"Well, I should—" she began.

"I was going to come looking for you," he said abruptly.

"You were?" she asked, crestfallen. "Whatever—oh."

He approached her slowly, carefully. She remained still, studying him with her perpetually curious air. She bunched her hands in the cotton of her nightgown, and he thought he saw understanding flicker in her eyes. When he came to a stop, it was close enough to hear her soft intake of breath. He could have reached out and touched her but instead offered her his hand, showing her that the decision to proceed was ultimately hers. "May I?"

She nodded, color creeping across her high cheekbones. Taking her hand, he gently tugged her toward him. He leaned in slowly, taking great care not to startle her, his lips a whisper away from hers. He could smell the lavender and honey rising off her skin, remnants of Honeyfield. Something deep inside him, something he had buried years ago, wanted to claw its way to the surface. It was the part of him that would have never hesitated to press her against the shelves, fists full of her flimsy nightgown.

The part of him that would have happily taken her on the floor of this room.

In another life, they would have been a rake and a wallflower in the library of a conveniently empty house late at night. There would have been no hesitation from either of them—he would have been too charming, and she would have been itching for his touch.

He felt her breath catch, her mouth parting slightly. Just a little closer, and he would have her fully in his arms. Or he would have if guilt hadn't suddenly overtaken him.

She had no idea who she'd married. She deserved better,

and he was every bit as selfish as his father had believed him to be. He'd selfishly wasted his youth engaging in all manner of unspeakable behavior. Now, he had selfishly drawn Persephone into his web, risking a reenactment of the strained relationship his mother had shared with his father.

He pulled back as her eyes fluttered open.

"Is—is something the matter?" she whispered.

"No, nothing."

He looked down at her hand, so small and delicate, and yet roughened with calluses that she'd likely earned from all her outdoor activities. He noticed again the freckles that dusted the top of her right hand.

"They're a little strange, I know," she said, following his eyes. "It's an odd place for freckles."

He needed to push his doubts out of his mind and into the closet with the rest of his skeletons—and he would. He simply did not believe he had it in him to rise above them *tonight*, even as his blood boiled with desire.

She watched as he ran his fingers across her knuckles. Turning her hand over, he pressed a kiss to her palm before gently releasing her hand. She pulled it away, holding it to her chest.

"Are you quite sure you're all right?" she asked. "I was under the impression that—well, I suppose it doesn't matter."

"I've disappointed you," he said, desperately wishing he could be less of a coward.

"No!" she exhaled. "In fact—I'm very grateful that we've come to—to this."

This? What was this?

Before he could ask, she'd turned to the shelves again. "Reading until sleep comes knocking sounds like a good idea."

He almost laughed at that, at the sweetness of it. "Then, if you'll excu—"

She turned around. "Where are you going?"

"Upstairs?" He was suddenly unsure what she expected of him now that he'd turned their wedding night into an incredibly awkward affair.

"I know you're not one for books," she said, pausing before removing one from the shelf, "but I've been told that I am quite skilled at reading aloud."

She wanted him to stay. She wanted him to stay so she could *read* to him. Knowing how much a part of her life books were, the suggestion felt far more intimate than what he had planned.

"That is to say, I've only been told that by Venus—"

"I am sure she and I will be in agreement. What are we reading?"

"*Measure for Measure*," she said, settling down on a chaise and tucking her knees underneath her chin. Her nightgown hung over the edge of the sofa, covering her like a shroud. "It's very good, though not nearly as popular as Shakespeare's other plays."

He took a seat on the same chaise, leaving space between them. He didn't want her under the impression that he thought to distract her.

Not that he'd be able to tonight, anyway, given the way his mind was still racing.

"It's quite scandalous," she announced, raising her eyebrows pointedly in his direction. "Which is something you and I are becoming rather well acquainted with, don't you think?"

"Unfortunately, I do," he agreed wryly.

"*Fortunately*, we've managed to worm our way out of it." She cracked the book open, eyes scanning the page.

"That is fortunate, indeed."

If only she knew, he thought bitterly.

She gave him a sweet smile, though her cheeks and neck were still tinged with a rosy flush. "Shall we begin?"

"Yes, let's," he said, her intoxicating, overwhelming presence already putting his doubts to rest.

Perhaps there was hope for him yet.

ELEVEN

A few days later, Persephone once again found herself in a tree, this time on the perfectly manicured grounds of Gallowsgate. While her heart did feel lighter here, her restlessness had been replaced with a fear she really ought to have anticipated. Even though every interaction with her husband had been pleasant, Persephone felt herself struggle not to put up invisible walls. Without them, she feared that he, too, would realize the ways in which she was not enough.

She had heard it all, from the nosy inhabitants of Little Oxbury to her own well-meaning father. If the misplaced guidance had come only from the village, Persephone might have been able to put up with it. But after her second caller had excused himself and never reappeared, her father had taken her into his study. His counsel had boiled down to one thing: be more like Venus.

Persephone wondered if it was even *possible* for one to change so much.

Perhaps more than freedom from criticism, Persephone had been yearning for understanding. And the silly, naive part of her had seen a glimmer of it in Aidon Barrington—the man who had been all gentle understanding even as she'd accidentally trespassed onto his property.

He was also the man who had not tried to touch her since their wedding night. And what a strange wedding night it had been. After her voice had finally tired of reading aloud, they politely bid each other good night. She could have sworn she'd seen hesitation cross his features before they'd parted, as if he'd had more to say—or do. But it had lasted only a moment, and she still wondered if she'd imagined it. The evenings since had seen nothing but courtesy and awkwardness between them. She felt out of place, as if she'd forced herself into a position she had no idea how to fill. She had no idea how to be a wife. Mothers typically sat with their daughters before trips to the parish were made, dispensing advice and allowing them to ask questions. Persephone hadn't had the opportunity to have such conversations with Emmeline. This was, for better or for worse, something she had to navigate in her own clumsy way.

Truth be told, she was almost certain that what he was grappling with was regret. He was still endlessly kind, but he continued to keep his distance from her, as if he hadn't almost kissed her that night in the library. He was distant in other ways, too. When they were together, it was almost as if he was holding himself back.

Glancing down at the unannotated copy of *Mythology of the Greeks and Romans* she held, she ran her fingers over the frayed edges of the book and sighed. To top everything off, she was yet to find her mother's special copy and was beginning to doubt it had ever existed. After all, her father was known to be a little detached from the real world. Perhaps he'd conjured it up, a creation born from the painful memories of his late wife.

Persephone looked out onto the grounds, letting her leg

slip off the branch. She swung it back and forth lazily. Gallowsgate was nothing if not tidy. The grounds that stretched out underneath her were uniformly green, each bush, shrub, and plant pruned to perfection. It was unlike Honeyfield and, therefore, very much unlike her. She wondered if living here might change her, transform her from a woman with perpetually muddied hems and improperly styled hair into one who fit into the confines of fine society. Perhaps she would no longer recognize herself in a few years.

It needn't be as dire as all that, she thought.

She leaned back against the tree trunk, letting the silence envelop her. Slowly, she closed her eyes. What could she do, she wondered, to feel less afraid? To make this easier? She knew that the pull she felt to Aidon was not one of friendship. It had dug up desires that frightened her. Desires that a small, insistent part of her was longing to indulge.

"Persephone?"

Startled, Persephone jerked in surprise, her book dropping from her hands—and straight onto her new husband.

Again.

Aidon was scared.

He hated admitting it to himself, but he was. Scared that he would overstep—hadn't he always, in the past?—scared that he'd somehow offend Persephone, and *terrified* that she would begin to ask about his work. And if she *did* ask about it, how would he even begin to respond? It was easy to lie to everyone else around him, but he knew he would be tempted to spill every last secret into her open arms.

It wasn't that what he did was wrong, but even he knew it

was not quite right, either. Although it seemed more right than wrong to him, there was no telling how she would react. How quickly she would wish she had accosted another gentleman.

Yet there was nothing he could do about the business, about his work. He'd been doing it for ten long years, and he would do it for every year that came after. He knew the purpose, knew to what end he did what he did, and Persephone's presence did not change that. But he would not sabotage his own marriage in the process.

Despite concluding that he was not *nearly* deserving of her, his attraction had not waned in the slightest. It became a struggle, even, to be around her, to listen to the passionate, sure words that rolled off her tongue every time she had something to say. And any time silence fell, his traitorous mind was given the opportunity to think on all the things he'd do to Persephone if allowed. An inkling of interest from her would most likely dash away every single one of his fears.

Earlier, he had glimpsed Persephone through the window of his study, wandering through the gardens. Despite her willingness to share her mind with him, there was something of an aloofness to her—surely he was to blame. After all, the absurdity of their wedding night had been his fault. He pushed himself out of his chair, determined to begin behaving like the husband he'd promised to be. He would find her, they would talk, he would make her smile and laugh. He would at least attempt to bridge the distance between them instead of constantly retreating to the familiar comfort of his own company. Whatever happened after that was entirely in her hands. He would not be the one to deny her, not anymore.

Moments later, Aidon found himself overcome with déjà vu as he rubbed briskly at the shoulder that had been attacked by his wife's heavy book. Persephone dropped out of the tree, her expression one of utter mortification.

"I am so, so sorry," she said, rushing toward him, cheeks red with embarrassment. She reached up to lay a hand on his shoulder, and the way his skin tingled at the contact did nothing but prove just how ridiculously touch-starved he'd become. "Did I hurt you?"

"Not at all," he lied, picking her book up off the ground. "I startled you."

He glanced at the cover. Wasn't this the book she'd been searching for? He raised his head, giving her a questioning look.

"It's a different copy," she offered. "The other one is full of notes."

"Yours?"

She shook her head. "My mother's."

He saw that the cover was a little worn and the spine creased from use. "You must read this often."

She blushed. "I do. Although"—she looked up at him, tone spirited—"I might have been tempted with a different book had your collection been a little less boring."

He laughed, handing her the heavy volume.

"Tell me what you'd like to read, and I'll make sure the library is brought up to your standards," he said fondly. He allowed himself a moment to study her. She was wearing a green dress today, earthy and warm. Her hem, however, wasn't muddied—the grounds were too well-maintained for that. Her cheeks were rosy at his words, and her head tilted upward toward his, a soft smile on her pretty face. He felt his heart squeeze. This would be the perfect time to give in and—

"My mother loved mythology," Persephone said, pressing the cover to her chest.

"Hence your name."

She nodded. "And Venus's. But the myth of Hades and Persephone was her favorite. She would read it to me all the time. As a child, I was half convinced that I was doomed to be kidnapped and taken to the Underworld."

He thought about how to respond, suddenly feeling the immense pressure of being in a delicate situation. After days of mere pleasantries, this was the first genuine conversation they'd exchanged, and he was anxious about ruining it. Before he had a chance to open his mouth, Persephone sat on the ground, her back against the tree. She looked up at him expectantly.

"You can sit if you'd like," she said.

Aidon sank down next to her. There was nothing charming about sitting on the cold, damp ground with your new bride, was there?

"She always knew just what to share—always knew what would pique my interest. She understood me."

"You must miss her terribly."

"I do. Even after seventeen years," she said. "The doctor said something about her lungs being too weak to cope with the chill she caught, but I think that was just because he felt that something needed to be said."

"Yes," he said softly. "That is often the case."

"Honeyfield was never the same after that," she said. "She took everything that was kind and understanding with her, and I've—I've been searching for it ever since, which likely sounds nonsensical."

"Not at all," he said, realizing that his life had felt the same when his own mother had passed. The difference between him and Persephone was that where she had continued searching, he had never begun. Once his mother died, he'd convinced himself that whatever light she had brought to the world was gone for good.

"That's why finding the other copy of this book is so important to me," she said. "I want to know what she thought to write in it. I want to know everything I can about her." She opened the book to an image of the Goddess of Spring in Hades's chariot and pointed to a block of text. "Look at this. Persephone is described as incandescent. Beloved, even. That doesn't sound like me at all."

But it does, he thought.

She looked at him briefly, her expression guarded. "I don't know that I'd describe myself as beloved." Her voice dropped to a near whisper. "*She* would have had more than two suitors, and they would not have run back to London a day into meeting her."

Aidon's eyebrows shot up in surprise. Two suitors had come to call? And *both* of them had left without attempting to make her theirs? Impossible. The hymn she read from seemed unbearably accurate to him. She was full of life, leaving the heartbreaking smell of lavender and honey in her wake, bringing fresh air to this dead estate.

"It suits you," he said, feeling foolish as soon as the words left his mouth. "The hymn, not the—"

A puff of air left her pink lips, and she rolled her eyes. Their gazes met, and she broke into nervous laughter, the sound melodious and airy. He would pray at her temple every day if it meant he could hear her laugh. Overcome by a lovestruck daze, Aidon reached over to her gently, brushing a lock of hair out of her face. Her laughter died down, but her blush remained, so he ran a thumb across her cheek, grazing her sharp cheekbone. Warmth coursed through his body, and he gave her a helpless, lovesick smile. Her eyes were wide and dark and questioning, and he could have sworn she was the first to lean forward.

In response, he angled his body toward hers, cupping her face so that he might pull her to him.

"Aidon," she said, her voice soft and hesitant.

"Yes?"

She reached up, placing her small hand on his wrist, barely circling it. He felt her lips brush against his as she said, "It's nothing."

One kiss, and he'd leave her be. He would indulge whatever rakish part of him had survived these ten years, the part of him that had reared its head that night in the library, and finally put it to rest.

He committed to closing the gap between them once and for all. And he'd have done it, too, if not for the sound of someone bellowing his name.

Who—

Biting back a curse, Aidon pulled away. Persephone looked at him, bewildered. They were both greeted by the sight of a shiny pair of black boots, worn by none other than Cassius.

Aidon stood up abruptly, offering his hand to Persephone. She did not take it, electing instead to pick herself up and dust off her skirts.

"There you are," Cassius said cheerfully, clearly pleased at having interrupted them. "I had it on good authority that you'd found yourself a wife." He looked at Persephone, very obviously allowing his gaze to travel up her lithe form. "How rude of you to keep your ravishing bride away from me."

"I beg your pardon," Persephone said quietly. "I don't believe we've met."

"Cassius Barrington." He took Persephone's hand and pressed a kiss to her knuckles, the affectionate gesture inspiring a burst of violence in Aidon. "He hasn't spoken of me, has he? Typical."

"My older brother," Aidon mumbled, furious and dangerously close to punching Cassius.

"I wasn't interrupting anything, was I?" Cassius asked innocently.

"Not at all," Persephone replied politely, her gaze shifting between Aidon and his brother. "We were about to return to the house. Won't you join us?"

"I'd *love* to."

Aidon watched Cassius offer his arm to Persephone. No doubt his brother had come to investigate, and to discover a way to squeeze more than five hundred pounds out of the family accounts. Much to Aidon's surprise, Cassius seemed as relaxed as ever despite having heard the news—and his new financial situation—from town gossip. Or, rather, from Ezra, who had more than likely been the one to let it slip. Aidon could admit he should have prioritized writing Cassius to inform him of the changes to the family, but he'd been far too distracted.

Persephone gingerly took Cassius's arm—why hadn't she taken Aidon's hand first?—and they began to stroll toward the house.

Damn it all to hell.

TWELVE

Opening up to someone new felt foreign, but there was something about Aidon Barrington, something that made Persephone feel like she was bubbling over with things to say. He had listened so intently that she'd felt her stomach twist with a mixture of embarrassment and delight when he'd expressed his opinion that, yes, the poems that described her namesake as incandescent and beloved *also* described Persephone Honeyfield, a mortal who had never felt like either.

And, oh, that almost-kiss. The eager, dazed look on Aidon's face had all but banished Persephone's self-doubt. It had felt different from the other night in the library. Then, their lips almost touching had been laced with a sense of urgency. This time, however, there was a sense of intoxicating tenderness.

Her belief that he couldn't possibly desire her had begun to crumble that night in the library and was hanging on for dear life now. If he did want to touch her, she hoped it was not because of some foolish husbandly obligation.

You want him to touch you.

She did. For as little as they truly knew about each other, she wanted him to touch her. And she wanted to touch him, too. She'd spent the past few nights in her dark, empty room thinking about his broad shoulders, the muscles she was convinced were under those crisp shirts of his, if what she'd felt the day he'd caught her was any indication—and about those unbearably desperate green eyes. Was he desperate for her? Was it possible for a man to look at her with desperation?

Persephone would have had ample time to consider the questions floating around in her head if she wasn't currently walking between the two Barrington brothers, the friction in the air almost suffocating in its intensity. Part of her hated the newly arrived Cassius for interrupting the moment she'd almost had with Aidon. Another part of her—the part that recognized the novelty of yet another newcomer to Oxbury— was inflamed with curiosity. Cassius was sandy-haired and lively, chatting her ear off as they walked toward the house. Aidon walked beside them silently, dark-haired and brooding, his mouth a hard, straight line. It was clear to Persephone that he was not at all fond of his brother. Not only did they look nothing alike, but their personalities appeared to be on opposite ends of the spectrum.

Once they reached the house, Cassius disappeared to the stables to check on his horse. She and Aidon stood on the steps, waiting for Cassius to return so they might see him inside. The moment they had shared under the trees was gone, leaving something unrecognizable in its place.

"I didn't know you had a brother," Persephone said, breaking the silence. *I don't know very much about you at all*, she thought, and the truth of it filled her with a muted sort of nervousness. "Is it just the two of you?"

Aidon replied with a clipped, "Yes."

She looked at him out of the corner of her eye in an effort
to better identify how he was feeling. Gone was the soft, eager
man she'd been with. In his place stood a grim, straight-backed,
no-nonsense gentleman. His tense expression brought out the
hard angles of his face and the sharpness of his jaw. She winced
inwardly, reminding herself that this was *not* the time to admire
her husband. In an attempt to disrupt her train of thought,
Persephone did what she did best—she impulsively blurted out
the first thing that came to mind.

"You don't seem to like your brother very much."

She cringed, wishing she could kick herself.

Aidon turned toward her and raised a single eyebrow. "Is
it obvious?"

Persephone let out a little exhale, pleased she hadn't upset
him with her words. They stood in silence for a moment, and
Persephone wasn't sure if asking why was appropriate. She folded
her arms across her chest and took a deep breath.

"He's irresponsible. Unimaginably so," he said. He shrugged,
a smile tugging at the corner of his mouth. "I could tell you
wanted to ask."

She stared at him in bewilderment. How could he have
possibly—

"You can be very expressive."

Persephone felt heat rise to her cheeks. She'd always thought
herself to be stony-faced. Impenetrable. If he could tell that she'd
been curious about Cassius, then it followed that he might have
sensed just how badly she'd wanted him to kiss her. The very
thought made her want to bury herself on the perfectly manicured grounds.

"Irresponsible in what way?" she asked, bringing the subject back to Cassius.

Aidon's face darkened once more. "Cassius's singular focus

in life is to enjoy himself. Gambling. Skirt chasing. He traipses all over London making a fool of himself."

"As is his right, I suppose," Persephone murmured. She could understand not being particularly enthused about it, but it was clear that Aidon's feelings on the subject ran deeper.

"Indeed," he said flatly. "And yet it was meant to be much different. The business was intended to be his."

Persephone dropped her arms to her sides, eyes widening. "Oh."

"He is the eldest, after all." Aidon shrugged. "But he pushed the responsibility aside because he was unwilling to compromise."

"Why did you take it, then?" Persephone asked. If it had been such an undesirable proposition, she would have understood if both brothers had decided against taking on the job.

"I had to," he replied, emotionless. Then again, more softly, "I had to."

Persephone studied him, catching the sadness that flickered in his eyes. "Maybe it's for the best," she said, forcing brightness into her voice. "Perhaps the job would not have suited him."

"The way it suits me, you mean?"

Persephone bit her lip, wanting once again to kick herself. Earlier, he'd been kind enough to tell her that the lovely poetry in her book had suited her. Now, she was telling him that the dour and depressing job of funeral furnishing was perfect for him.

"No, I—"

For the second time that day, they were interrupted by Cassius.

"Sorry to have kept you waiting," he said cheerfully. "I got caught up with the stable boy. Talkative fellow." He turned toward the house and regarded it with a strange, unreadable expression. "Shall we?"

Without waiting for either of his hosts to respond, Cassius bounded up the marble steps to the great house. Persephone and Aidon trailed behind him, the tension between them palpable.

"You are very good at your job, I'm sure," she whispered, a pathetic peace offering.

"I have to be," he said. Once in the entryway, he gave his brother a curt nod. "If you'll excuse me."

Persephone watched him stalk off, likely making a beeline for his study.

"Aidon's in one of his moods, is he?" Cassius asked from beside her.

"Not at all," Persephone said, somewhat defensively. "He's just busy with work."

"*Work*," Cassius repeated, shuddering dramatically before giving her a devilish smile. "In any case, it looks like *you* have been left to fend for yourself."

It did look like that, Persephone thought bitterly. She would have appreciated *not* being abandoned but was quite used to fending for herself.

"Indeed," she said, leading him to a nearby drawing room and ringing for refreshments. "It will give us time to become better acquainted."

Cassius fell into a chair, that same devilish smile on his lips. "Uncovered my motive for visiting, have you?"

Persephone sat down in a nearby armchair, aware of a strained smile on her own face. She was not used to a person being so *much*. Cassius appeared full of energy, his curious eyes glittering with mischief as he studied her.

"Tell me," he said conspiratorially, leaning toward her, "is the story true?"

"What story?" she asked.

"The one that says you and my brother were caught in a most *compromising* situation," he said.

Persephone laughed nervously, shaking her head. "Oh, no. That was all a misunderstanding."

"A wedding still followed," Cassius said, raising an incriminating eyebrow in her direction.

Persephone smiled gratefully when Baker arrived with the tea tray as it gave her a moment to think of how to explain. Cassius was a stranger to her, which meant that her father's ridiculous cover story would have to suffice. "That was going to happen either way. We were already engaged."

"Were you, now?" Cassius asked, taking an indelicate bite out of a biscuit. He leaned back again, giving her a leisurely once-over. "How did that come about?"

"We happened to meet while he was visiting with Mr. Haskett," she said, not wanting to go into too much detail. "It was clear to us both that we were well suited."

"And Aidon just *jumped* at the opportunity to make things official, did he?"

Persephone blinked, confused. "I . . . I suppose you could say that."

Something flickered in Cassius's eyes, so fleeting that Persephone did not have the chance to identify it. He quickly replaced it with a cheeky expression, plucking another biscuit from the tray. "I see."

Letting another nervous laugh escape her, Persephone said, "Surely you did not come all the way to Oxbury to have gossip confirmed for you."

Cassius laughed. "Nonsense. I came to indulge my curiosity. Aidon didn't write me about the wedding."

"Oh," Persephone said, keeping her tone measured. "That is—odd."

Why wouldn't Aidon have informed his family of their marriage? He had, after all, returned to London before their wedding, and she'd just assumed—

"I'm not surprised," Cassius said matter-of-factly. "Aidon tends to keep things from me, even when they're *important*."

He put special emphasis on the last word.

"I can assure you that nothing else of importance has occurred," she said politely. "And it *did* all happen rather quickly, so perhaps it simply slipped his mind."

Cassius gave her a toothy grin. "Perhaps."

They sat in awkward silence, and Persephone was reminded that she was a poor excuse for a hostess.

"I brought this along," Cassius said suddenly, rummaging through his pockets and producing a crumpled sheet of paper. "A little memento from London."

Persephone took the paper from him, eyes quickly scanning it. The words *Treacle & Tea* were printed at the top.

"You brought a scandal sheet?" she asked.

"Don't play coy, my dear," he drawled, folding his arms over his stomach. "Surely you know that you are married to the most notorious man in London."

Persephone glanced at the paper, seeing the words LORD OF THE DEAD—CONNECTED TO MISSING LIVESTOCK? in bold letters halfway down the page.

"An exaggeration, surely," she said, folding the sheet in half and handing it back to him. "I am not really one for gossip."

For a fleeting moment, she wondered if there was any truth to all the whispers about her husband. She wondered if she should be afraid of him, if a more sensible woman would have been nervous, if she was a fool for being so trusting.

"Of course you aren't," Cassius smirked. "It all comes together very neatly, I must say."

"What does?" Persephone questioned.

"Never you mind." Cassius looked around the drawing room before settling his gaze back on her. "What does one do in this damned place? I haven't been here since I was a child."

Persephone shrugged. "Anything one wants, I suppose."

"Anything, eh?" Cassius jumped out of the chair and held his hand out to her. "Well, then, let's get cracking."

Persephone almost choked on her tea. "Cracking? On what?"

"I do believe you are meant to keep me entertained," Cassius said, hauling her out of her chair. "We can start with a tour."

"A tour?" Persephone sputtered. "But you've *lived* here."

"Then pretend I haven't," Cassius said impatiently. "Call it a test of your skills as a hostess."

"I *have* no hostessing skills," she grumbled as he led her into the entryway.

"Oh, very well," Cassius said, impatience melting away to reveal a wicked smile. "*I'll* entertain *you*."

"You will?"

"Yes," he purred. "I most certainly will."

THIRTEEN

Aidon watched his brother at the dinner table grumpily, unwilling to join the lively conversation Cassius was having with Persephone. His older brother had apparently intended to stay for a day, but one day had turned into two, and two days had turned into an entire insufferable week. Cassius monopolized Persephone's attention, and Aidon was in no position to compete. He hadn't been for a long time now. Cassius was the superior conversationalist, better at coaxing laughter out of women, more skilled at telling animated stories that captured the attention of anybody in his radius. And Persephone, it seemed, was just as susceptible to Cassius's charm as the next person. He heard her laugh at something his brother said and felt jealousy bloom in his chest.

He had no right to feel jealous.

"How long do you mean to stay?" Cassius was asking, gesturing to the room at large. "In this barren hellscape, I mean."

Barren hellscape? The house was a little dark and sparsely furnished, but it was no hellscape. Aidon glanced at Persephone, who had her lovely dark eyes concentrated on him over the rim of her wineglass, and realized he would have been inclined to agree with his brother had she not become a permanent resident of this once miserable house. Her mere presence had changed the very fabric of Gallowsgate, something Cassius would never see or understand.

"I'm surprised you even came here," Cassius continued. He turned to Persephone. "You should have whisked your lovely bride off to London as soon as the papers were signed."

Aidon remained silent. He hadn't intended to stay in Oxbury. He was only waiting until Persephone felt comfortable enough to leave. But he hadn't thought about the *when* in days now. In fact, London rarely crossed his mind. Returning to town had seemed like the natural thing to do. But now he couldn't help but care about what Persephone might think of him—what she might notice—if she saw him through the harsh lens of London.

Here, Persephone was unable to see just how unwelcome he was in his brother's social circles. She didn't have to suffer the weight of being married to a man who worked with grieving families, taking their money in exchange for the false comfort of respectable funeral services. Maybe he was trying to protect her—maybe he was trying to protect himself. Selfishly delaying the inevitable.

"I'm not sure I would even like London," Persephone said. "I've spent my whole life in Oxbury."

Aidon felt a momentary burst of relief. She would not hold him to London because she was most at home in Oxbury.

She was at home in Gallowsgate. *With him.*

"I am able to work from here," Aidon added.

Cassius perked upon hearing Aidon suggest work, likely sensing an opportunity to embarrass him. He immediately turned toward Persephone with a cheeky glint in his eye. "Has it frightened you to bits yet?"

"She has no involvement in it," Aidon said sharply, not giving Persephone a chance to respond and attempting to cut the conversation short.

"No, of course not," Persephone agreed. To his surprise, she sounded slightly chagrined. Her cheeks turned a dusty shade of pink, and she focused her gaze on her plate, pushing at her food with a fork.

"Probably for the best," Cassius said. "It's a sad thing, Sephie. Too sad for a sweet little thing such as yourself."

Sephie?

"Suits Aidon, however," Cassius continued, lowering his voice to a stage whisper as if Aidon wasn't currently sitting to the left of him.

Persephone shifted her gaze to Aidon, her eyes wide and melancholic. Gently, she pressed her teeth into her small pink lips.

He was instantly gripped with the desperate need to kiss her. He wanted to kiss the melancholy out of her, wanted to return to that blissful moment under the trees with her reading hymns that had Aidon convinced the ancient poets had been writing about her, only her.

Instead, they were stuck in this cold dining room, Aidon at the head of the table, Persephone on one side of him, and Cassius on the other. He had to be patient. Once his brother left, he could coax that bright, airy laughter out of her again, bring that same rosy color to her cheeks.

But that would not happen until Aidon engaged in the conversation Cassius was clearly here to have—a conversation Aidon was tempted to initiate tonight just to be rid of him. Aidon needed a few hours to himself first as he could only take his brother in small doses. Even this meal was enough to leave him with worn nerves.

After dinner, Aidon once again excused himself to his study. Relief coursed through him as he settled behind his desk, even as he knew he'd be faced with Cassius again in no time. The subject of work, too, sat heavily on his shoulders, a reminder that he'd be taking part in his least favorite part of the job tomorrow, the part that had made his father a favorite among the aristocracy and the rich. He was fortunate to be able to perform most of his duties by post—funeral furnishing was mostly about coordination, anyway—but tomorrow's client had insisted on traveling all the way to Oxbury. Aidon knew his presence comforted them, if only because it reassured them that nothing about the business had changed since his father died. That their secrets would be kept as promised. As he moved to dip the tip of his quill in an inkpot, a knock came at his door. Cassius appeared, having apparently refused to wait for Aidon to call him in.

"I'm working," Aidon said.

Cassius shut the door behind him, dragging a chair away from the fireplace and placing it squarely in front of Aidon's desk. Suppressing a sigh, Aidon put his quill down and eyed Cassius expectantly.

"That wife of yours is a curiosity," Cassius began, propping his ankle up on his knee and giving Aidon a toothy smile.

"What do you want, Cassius? We needn't suffer through pleasantries every time you need something from me."

The smile disappeared from his brother's face, replaced with a grim expression. "You know damn well the old man put that clause in his will to drive a wedge between us."

"I do not think that at all," Aidon said calmly. *Cassius* had destroyed the bond they'd had when he chose to abandon Aidon in the cloud of misery left behind after their father's passing. When he chose to turn a blind eye to the splintering of Aidon's life, far too consumed by his own freedom.

"It was Ezra who told me, you know," Cassius said. "About your marriage."

"I gathered as much."

"It's lucky," Cassius grumbled.

"What is?"

"How you managed to track down the only woman in England who doesn't care for gossip," Cassius said bitterly. "Clever of you to keep her tucked away here."

"I am not keeping her prisoner," Aidon snapped. "She asked to stay here."

Cassius raised an incredulous eyebrow. "She simply doesn't know any better. How could she? She grew up in complete isolation."

Aidon frowned, overcome with the urge to jump to Persephone's defense. "You underestimate her intelligence. She is fully capable of making her own decisions."

Based on the little she knows of me, he added silently.

"Maybe so," Cassius allowed, leaning back with a sigh. "It is no matter. The fact is I cannot survive on five hundred pounds a year, Aidon. I know you know that."

Aidon hesitated before responding. He knew what the will stated. He also knew his father would be deeply disappointed at the spark of guilt Aidon suddenly felt in his chest. No matter his feelings toward Cassius, he was still the only family he had in the world. And for once, his brother seemed to be speaking sincerely, his gaze unguarded and anxious.

It was one thing to triumph over his brother in theory and an entirely different thing to do so in practice.

"I will pay for the household expenses," he offered. "That gives you the full five hundred to use as you will."

"Still a marked reduction from last year's income," Cassius muttered under his breath.

"Indeed," Aidon agreed. "You'll have to manage, as we are held to Father's word."

Cassius rolled his eyes. "Oh, fine. Your generosity is appreciated, as always."

An awkward, mistrustful silence fell as the two brothers regarded one another.

"You have me considering marriage, you know," Cassius announced.

"*You?*" Aidon asked. "Don't be ridiculous."

"Why not? I'm sure I'd have a far easier time of securing a wife than you did."

Aidon sighed, entirely unsurprised that Cassius would turn this into some kind of nonsensical competition. "Thank you, Cassius. Now, if you don't mind, I have a few things I'd like to do before tomorrow, so—"

"Fine, fine," Cassius said, hopping out of the chair. "I know when I'm not welcome."

Aidon watched him go, then looked down at the work on his desk. He had no doubt he would see his brother again. Cassius had never known how to leave well enough alone. If he returned, it would be with some ridiculous plan for revenge in tow or with the intention to annoy Aidon into folding.

Even if he had already folded, at least a little.

He shouldn't have given in, shouldn't have felt even a sliver of guilt. While he'd cut out a large portion of Cassius's income, he hadn't stuck to his original plan, which had been to punish his brother for his irresponsible ways, to—

To punish him for refusing to take on the business.

Aidon's shoulders sagged. It took a decidedly petty person to still feel this way after ten long years. Perhaps it was time for him to make his peace.

After all, Cassius couldn't have known all that their father's work had entailed. How could he have? Aidon himself had been completely in the dark until after he'd taken on the mantle of owner.

And besides, all of it had brought him to Oxbury, had put him in the exact place he'd needed to cross paths with Persephone. There was little point in hanging on to all that had preceded their meeting.

It was, of course, easier said than done. Guilt, shame, resentment—they had been his constant companions all these years. He had no idea if he even knew any other way to be, any other way to feel about the misfortune—the plain *unluckiness*—of it all.

He thought about Persephone, tucked away in Oxbury all these years, all forms of excitement held just outside her reach. He'd resented growing up here, resented the silence and dullness. He wondered, if he'd been in her place, whether he'd have been able to come to peace with his lot in life as she appeared to have done. Maybe he would have remained resentful and angry if he'd stayed in Oxbury a minute longer. Maybe that was the sort of person he was, doomed to marinate in all that was negative and pessimistic.

Maybe, but—things had felt different recently. For the first time in a long time, emotions like curiosity, eagerness, excitement—desire—were intermingling with the familiar sentiments of the past. And all could be credited to Persephone.

Lifting his quill again, Aidon dipped it in the inkpot and began to write. Finding peace was far easier said than done, yes, but it was not impossible. Not with Persephone by his side, reminding him of all his life could be if he only made space for it.

And he would make that space. He would, at the very least, begin to try.

FOURTEEN

After the initial shock of his presence wore off, Persephone found that she did not mind Cassius's company in the slightest. To her, he seemed nothing more than overly energetic and perhaps a bit tactless, never seeming to think before he spoke. It was hard to imagine him as any worse than that. He was charming, yes, and perhaps a bit pushy, but certainly not ill intentioned. She knew he purposely struck at Aidon's nerves, but his large, noisy presence left her no time to dwell on her anxiety. Aidon spent time with them in carefully controlled bursts, rarely speaking and always watching Cassius with suspicious eyes. He would, without fail, eventually excuse himself, as if he could not stand to be around his brother for longer than a half hour at a time.

Persephone had not forgotten what Aidon had told her about Cassius and his proclivity for leisure. She remembered it well but was quite swept up in her new role as hostess despite being rather poor at it. Besides, there was no gambling to be had here, no skirts to chase. If anything, it gave her a glimpse of who her brother-in-law truly was, once distanced from all his vices.

On Cassius's eighth and final day at the house, they lounged in the library, drinking tea and discussing whatever crossed their minds. Persephone had never been one for mindless chatter, but Cassius had an easy way about him that had her rambling.

"I know you aren't one for gossip," he said cheekily from behind his teacup, "but surely you must have *some* opinion on all of this Lord of the Dead nonsense."

Persephone shrugged. She knew Aidon well enough to believe he wasn't some bloodthirsty murderer, vampire killer of livestock, or whatever else *Treacle & Tea* saw fit to label him as. "You've just said it yourself. It's nonsense."

"I'm only surprised it doesn't bother you," he said. "It is one thing to be disinterested in gossip, and another when the gossip is about you or, rather, your husband."

"Should it bother me?" Persephone placed her teacup down and tucked her legs underneath her skirt. "People have said all manner of things about me. It doesn't mean they're true."

Cassius raised his eyebrows in surprise. "Now, what could people possibly have to say about *you*?"

"I won't bore you with the specifics."

"I *demand* you bore me with the specifics," he said theatrically.

Persephone smiled and shook her head. "Nothing interesting. Just that I'm a bit too sharp, a bit too opinionated. What people normally say about women who don't quite fit in. It's never a good idea to let on how different you are in a place like this."

"It's been a long time since I've lived here, so you'll have to indulge me with an explanation," he said.

She hesitated, unsure if she should open up to him. He was family, though, wasn't he? Families were not meant to hold each other at arm's length.

"It was not so much the things I said, but rather the things I didn't," she said. "It seemed a bit shocking to people, I suppose, that I never mentioned the desire to be a wife and mother. In fact, I avoided the subject altogether."

"You *are* a wife now," he pointed out.

"Yes, but surely women can be more than one thing," she replied, feeling all the defensiveness of her youth return to her. "Men are not restricted to only being husbands or fathers. Women deserve that luxury extended to them, too."

"Fair enough," he said, surprising her.

"In fact, I think every single luxury extended to men should be extended to women."

"A scandalous declaration," he said cheekily.

"The people in Oxbury would agree," she said. "They have always thought me the oddest thing in England, and not in a charming way."

"*That* is nonsense," he said vehemently. He lowered his voice. "Especially when I know you to be the exact opposite."

"Thank you," she said hesitantly. Leaning forward, she asked, "What do people say about *you?*"

He laughed. "Quite brazen of you to assume that I am gossiped about at all."

"Aren't you?" she asked.

He gave her a wicked smile. "Of course I am. Do I look boring to you? Only boring people find themselves free of gossip."

"Well?"

"Let's see," he murmured. "They say I am an incredibly charming rogue of a man, who is very good at throwing parties and very *bad* at being like his responsible, dour younger brother."

"I see."

"*Women* say that my skills as a bedmate are unmatched," he added, winking. "But don't go spreading that one around. I'm already up to my knees in eager ladies."

Persephone snorted, even as she felt heat rise to her cheeks. She had no doubt that what he said was true. He was tall and well built, with a blinding smile and perfectly tousled golden hair. Still, true or not, she certainly did not want to discuss anyone's skills as a bedmate with Cassius. Not when she herself hadn't—

"How do you do this all day?" Cassius groaned, stretching his legs out before him. "Sit around in this great big house with nothing to do?"

Persephone looked around the library. The room was slowly coming together, more furnished than the other sitting rooms, with mahogany shelves that she planned on absolutely packing with novels. She and Cassius sat by one another in chairs upholstered with forest-green silken fabric, chosen to give the room a warmer feel. The large windows, now washed and nearly transparent, let in far more sunlight than they had the day she'd come to Gallowsgate in search of her book.

"There's plenty to do," she said eventually, if not a touch defensively. "There is a lot of space that still needs attention, and I enjoy talking to your brother."

She said the last bit rather pointedly, even if it had been frustratingly difficult to indulge in conversation with Aidon when he could not stand his brother's company. When Cassius did not respond, she stood up and retrieved a book from a nearby writing desk.

"Books are helpful," she continued.

"Oh?" Cassius asked. "What's that one about?"

Persephone sat down and ran her hands over the cover. "It's *The History of a Young Lady*. The heroine leaves her husband for a terrible rake. Is that exciting enough for you?"

His eyes sparkled with interest. "And how does it end?"

Persephone grinned. "She dies alone."

"That's no fun," he said with a pout. "Well, books aside, I do wish you had more to occupy yourself with."

"I've just told you that there is plenty to do here," she reminded him.

"But you'd be happier if there were *more*," he shot back emphatically.

Persephone could not help but silently agree. It was likely not what Cassius was referring to, but she *had* been hoping for a bit more excitement following her departure from Honeyfield. As much as she valued and appreciated the slow, tentative way in which Aidon was getting to know her, she also desperately wanted to—

I am at fault, as well, she thought begrudgingly. If she had wanted things to move quickly, then she really ought to have tried harder. Cassius's presence in the house was another obvious obstacle, but at least it wasn't one of her own making. Any lady would have taken advantage of her first few days as a new wife to explore all the ways marriage was different from regular companionship. Any lady, but not Persephone.

Cassius's voice pulled her out of her thoughts. "It's a terrible shame that Aidon has become such a bore."

"Don't say that," Persephone said quickly and a little forcefully.

He shrugged. "It is true, though. He wasn't always like this."

Persephone thought about the Aidon she knew. Kind, patient, ever gentle—save the intensity she'd noticed behind his eyes that night in the library or during that moment under the trees.

"What happened?" she asked, guilt following the question. It was one she should have asked Aidon himself.

"Oh, who knows," Cassius huffed, sinking deeper into his chair. "I suppose he thinks this is what responsible gentlemen behave like."

"Like bores?" Persephone said, echoing his words and giggling despite herself.

"Precisely." He gave her a wolfish grin, leaning across the armrest toward her. "I think you could do better than a *bore*, Persephone."

"Clearly not," she replied, chuckling nervously.

"Shall we put that to the test?" he murmured, grin widening.

"I'm not sure how we would," she said, confused. "And besides—"

At that moment, Baker entered, a fresh pot of tea in his hands. Cassius cursed quietly under his breath.

"The man is like a damned ghost," he grumbled once Baker had left.

"You become accustomed to it," Persephone responded, their conversation forgotten.

Cassius paused and examined her. "I wonder if you might do me a favor."

Persephone placed her teacup down, eyebrows lifted. "What sort of favor?"

"I think," he said slowly, "it is high time I work on repairing my relationship with my brother."

"After you've just called him a bore?"

"Ignore that," he said impatiently. "I'm due to leave for home this evening, which means I don't have time to appeal to Aidon."

"What could I possibly do?" Persephone asked, suddenly feeling very put-upon.

"Perhaps you might convince him to visit London," Cassius suggested. "Far easier for me to impress him in my own domain. There are too many memories in Gallowsgate, and I imagine each one of them reminds him of why he dislikes me so much."

"I'm not sure," Persephone said, biting her lip. "I don't think I should involve myself in—"

"Christ, but the two of you behave as if you aren't married

at all," Cassius said. "Of *course* you should involve yourself. Trust me."

Persephone thought about how odd and distant from one another she and Aidon must seem to an outsider. Cassius's observation stung, but she could see a kernel of truth in it. Perhaps going to London made sense. It would certainly force them together, removing the sheer size of Gallowsgate from the equation. She didn't love the idea of leaving Oxbury, of putting herself in society's line of sight, but she reasoned that there was very little reason for anyone to notice her anyway.

She nodded. "I will speak to him."

"Excellent," Cassius crowed. "Now, what shall we do for the rest of the afternoon?"

Before long, Persephone was waving Cassius off, his absence leaving a vacuum of silence in its place. Knowing she would lose her nerve if she did not act immediately, she went to seek Aidon out. She hadn't seen him at all today, which was a bit unusual. He'd made an effort to share meals with her and Cassius over the past week, but he'd skipped today's entirely.

Approaching his study, she saw that the door was ajar. Poking her head gingerly into the room, she spotted him at his desk. There was something strange about his appearance, something exhausted and disheveled. With his rumpled shirtsleeves and wrinkled cravat, he looked as if he'd spent the day overexerting himself somehow. He looked up, having felt her eyes on him, and quickly stood, running his hands through his hair in what seemed to be an effort to tidy himself. Persephone eyed him guardedly, an unwanted thread of anxiety worming its way into her chest.

"Where's Cassius?" he asked.

She entered the room and propped herself on the arm of a chair. "He's just left. He wanted to say goodbye, but we hadn't seen you today and I couldn't convince him to look for you."

"I left the house early this morning," he said vaguely, his tone betraying the fact that he did not care that he'd not seen Cassius off. He seemed to catch his own gruffness and offered her an encouraging smile. "Did you enjoy his visit?"

"I did," she said, and she swore she saw a flicker of annoyance cross his face. "You two are very different from one another."

"Yes," he said slowly. "We are."

She bit her lip and decided to take the plunge. "I would have appreciated your company while he was here, especially during the first few days."

His dark eyebrows shot up, his green eyes stricken. "Persephone, I—"

"I know you don't enjoy being around him," she said softly.

"I didn't realize," he muttered, gaze breaking from hers. "I didn't *think*. That was—that was selfish of me. I apologize."

"It's quite all right," she said, forgiving him instantly. She had not come here to bicker or to demand that he do better next time. His reaction alone told her he would, and so she pushed on. "Have you ever considered making peace with him?"

"Sometimes," he grumbled, folding his arms protectively against his broad chest. "Not often, admittedly, but sometimes."

"Perhaps he will surprise you," she murmured.

"I highly doubt that."

"Would you give him a chance?" she coaxed. "He's tasked me with bringing you to London."

Aidon's brow knit in confusion. "London? Whatever for?"

"He would like to spend more time with you," she said. Pausing, she added, "Away from Gallowsgate."

He pressed his mouth into a firm line, the underlying

meaning clear. It made sense to her that Aidon's tumultuous relationship with his brother could not be repaired within the walls of their family home. There was too much history here, too many reminders of a childhood long past.

If she knew more about it, she might have had an even deeper understanding, but—

"Would you like to go?" he asked hesitantly.

Her eyes snapped to his, recognizing the uncertainty in his tone and seeing it plain on his handsome face. Affection bloomed in her chest at the idea that he'd ask her such a thing, at the implication that his decision hinged solely on doing whatever made her most happy.

It was what husbands did for wives. Cassius was wrong, then, in saying they did not act like a married couple.

"I would," she replied. "It could also give us some time together."

"Together?" he echoed.

Be brave, Persephone Honeyfield. Well, Barrington—oh, who cares.

"Yes, together," she said, a bit more evenly this time. "I have barely seen you this past week."

"I apologize," he said again. "I should not have let my—my issues with Cassius overshadow my responsibility to you."

Responsibility.

Who was Aidon when he was not being perfectly responsible? It was impossible for a person to be wholly one thing or another, wasn't it?

"You needn't apologize again," she said gently. "I simply said that I have not seen very much of you this week."

She examined him once more, this time with an air of scientific curiosity. He looked as if he hadn't gotten very much sleep at all. If he'd left early, it must have been *very* early.

"Where did you go this morning?" she asked, feeling as though she ought to stretch her bravery as far as it would go since it rarely showed its face as it was.

"I had work to attend to," he said, the response stilted and automatic.

She could not tell if he was lying.

"You don't typically leave the house for work," she observed.

"No, I don't," he said. "Not often, anyway. Only—only sometimes."

Persephone sighed. It was clear to her that Aidon did not enjoy discussing his work with her, and since she did not enjoy torturing him, she decided to drop it. Even if she *did* find his responses a little strange.

The unease in her chest spiked for a brief, uncomfortable moment before settling once more.

"I see," she said, effectively ending the conversation.

"Persephone—" he began.

She cut him off. "We should go to London. Together."

"Yes," he said. "Yes. Anything you want."

"Good," she said, jumping to her feet to conceal just how sharply her heart had twinged at his words. "I will write to your brother. Will you be at dinner?"

"Yes," he said quickly. "I will."

Nodding, Persephone excused herself from the room. London would be good for them, she thought.

She scoffed as she made her way down the hall. There was another reason behind her agreeing to Cassius's plan, one that she had refused to acknowledge in the moment. She was doing what she always did instead of facing her fears head-on. She was indulging herself in distraction, creating a buffer between herself and what she needed. It was all well and good to list out all the things she *wanted* in her head, easy to say them aloud, even, but actually pursuing them, actually being *open* to them was another story.

She sighed. Aidon and Cassius's relationship wasn't the only broken thing that needed mending.

If only she did not feel so beyond repair.

FIFTEEN

London was like nothing Persephone had ever seen. She had read and heard about it, of course, but nothing could have prepared her for the real thing. She had felt uncharacteristically sure of herself during the journey, pleased at her decision. Cassius was not nearly as bad as Aidon believed him to be. She was sure she could help bring them together, if she only tried.

Cassius had, in his roundabout way, implied that Aidon had lost his spark. To be more precise, he'd said that Aidon hadn't always been such a "bore." While Persephone did not think the word suited her husband, she did wonder if helping him reconnect with his brother would bring him back to himself—and to *her*.

Whoever that man was.

She had spent the past few nights lying awake in inns, always in her own room, becoming deeply invested in this new scheme of hers. She crafted scenario after scenario in her head, ultimately convincing herself that this trip was destined to be an utter triumph. It was a welcome distraction from the tedium of travel, as well as from the tension that invaded the carriage every time the door was shut behind her and Aidon.

All of her scheming, however, came to a grinding halt as soon as they arrived in London proper, the sheer size of it occupying her senses. It was thoroughly crammed with people, the roads a crush of horses and carriages. She saw women dressed in finery that would have put Venus in an absolute tizzy.

Even the air was different. Heavier, somehow, which left her feeling deeply grateful when the door to her husband's town house was shut behind them.

The decor in the house reminded her very much of Gallowsgate. It lacked a feminine touch, making her miss the cool colors of Honeyfield. She wandered deeper into the entryway as her husband exchanged words with a footman at the door, feeling inexplicably drawn to a portrait of a woman painted in muted tones. Her eyes were a dazzling green, peering out at Persephone, her face framed by a halo of glossy black curls. Her expression was melancholy. Distant.

"Are you all right?"

Persephone turned to see Aidon, who was holding a crumpled note in his hand.

"Yes," she fibbed.

He looked over her shoulder at the portrait.

"My mother," he said, voice emotionless.

Persephone whirled around to look at the sad painted woman once more. "I should have known. You take after her. It's—it's a lovely painting."

She then offered him a friendly smile, hoping to coax one out of him as well. He had been tense the entire journey over, and Persephone had discovered he was a man of very few words when preoccupied.

"I would have gotten rid of it long ago if it didn't help me to remember her face," he said bitterly.

Persephone's eyebrows shot up in surprise. Why anybody in

their right mind would get rid of a portrait of a beloved parent, she did not know. She only had a miniature to remember her mother by, and she treasured it with every bone in her body.

"I've shocked you," he said, watching her face closely.

"No!" Persephone said, a little too quickly. She felt heat begin to rise up her neck. "I just—it's yours to do with as you please."

"She looks miserable, doesn't she?" he asked, his eyes leaving Persephone.

She felt herself relax, no longer under his searching gaze. "Did she have reason to be?"

Not your place.

Except it was, wasn't it? She remembered Cassius's words, remembered how she was meant to involve herself in more than what lay on the surface of Aidon's life.

He let out a long exhale and began to tug nervously at his cravat. "My father was a difficult man. He was—controlling, in the way only a shrewd businessman can be. He preferred the lot of us tucked away in Oxbury, only bringing us into town when my mother was reduced to begging."

Persephone could not quite place the emotion in his voice. It *should* have been laced with bitterness or hate. Instead, it just sounded exhausted.

"But my brother and I were not easy. On either of them."

The words left unsaid hung between them, heavy and dark—placing the blame on Aidon and Cassius for their mother's misery and father's controlling nature.

"You weren't easy on either of them," Persephone said, stepping into the heaviness. "How is that?"

"I—we—we were terrible children," Aidon stammered. "Rough. Noisy. It took quite a lot of effort to bring us to heel."

Persephone's mouth almost dropped open in disbelief. An

empty feeling settled in her stomach. She glanced at the portrait of his mother, wondering—

Ask, the painted green eyes seemed to say.

"Who told you that?" she blurted out, looking up into his face.

"That we were terrible?" he asked, voice tinged with discomfort. "It was quite obv—"

"No," she interrupted. "That you had to be brought to heel."

A long, pregnant silence settled over them. He studied her, and she wondered if she'd finally crossed a line.

"My father," he said, right as the silence was at risk of becoming insufferably long. "Those were his words exactly."

Taking a small, shy step toward him, Persephone placed her hand on his forearm, feeling his solid warmth beneath her fingers.

"You were children," she said quietly. "Both of you. You do realize that, don't you?"

"I . . ." he trailed off. He laughed, the sound breathy and nervous.

She pulled her hand back, placing it awkwardly at her side. "I hope I haven't overstepped."

"No," he said quickly. "No, I'm just not used to it. Forgive me. I've never spoken about any of this. To anyone."

"There's nothing to forgive," she said. "And you should never have heard those words from your father."

He looked at her then, gaze searching and sad. Persephone felt herself begin to crumble, her eyes darting around, searching for something else to speak of.

"Is that a note?" she asked, spotting the creased paper in his hands.

"Ah. Yes. I hope you're prepared for some excitement," he said flatly. "My brother has invited us to dinner."

"How kind of him," she said encouragingly. Frowning, she looked at a nearby clock. "Isn't it a bit late for dinner?"

Aidon gave her a cynical smile. "Cassius is not one for propriety. We should leave at once, if we want to make it back before midnight."

Before long, Persephone was in a parlor filled to the brim with far too many people. Cassius had been a welcome sight, but he had disappeared into the fray shortly after showing them in.

She had not counted on an audience.

"I did not realize so many people would be here," she said, allowing herself to be led into the emptiest corner of the room. "Is it always like this?"

"It is," Aidon said, and she thought she heard a hint of smugness in his voice.

He thought he was making a point—about Cassius, who Persephone spotted engaged in flirtatious conversation with a tall, shapely woman. She looked away, still determined to fulfill the promise she had made to her brother-in-law.

"Fancy seeing you here!"

Ezra Haskett was a breath of fresh air in the otherwise stuffy room. He gave her a quick bow and flashed a smile at a stony-faced Aidon.

"I did not think I would see *you* here again," he said to Aidon. "I heard Cassius visited Gallowsgate."

"He did," Aidon replied stiffly.

"And he managed to convince you to return to London!" Ezra crowed. He gave Persephone a cheeky grin. "No small feat, my lady."

Persephone laughed, shaking her head. "I am no lady, sir."

Not in title, and certainly not in appearance.

Persephone had seen one or two people whisper to their companions as she'd passed them by, shocked by her plain dress and short hair. She did not care, she thought to herself.

She tried not to care.

The fact was she had not anticipated being faced with this many people. She had changed into an evening gown because it was what one did before sitting for dinner, but her burnt-orange muslin could not compare to the finery around her. Though it was trimmed with a simple pattern of beads around the collar, it paled in comparison to the silk and gauze ensembles that sparkled in the candlelight. Nothing about her gleamed. Even the sparse beading she had once admired on her own dress seemed dull in the grandeur that filled the parlor. She missed Venus, wished desperately that her sister was with her, a buffer against all the discomfort Persephone was suffering.

To her surprise, she longed for Honeyfield. For the safety of home.

Ezra's presence was a welcome addition to this so-called dinner, which so far seemed like an excuse to gather people in one room and ply them with drink. He brought with him entertaining tales, told in his happy-go-lucky, easy way of talking. He even managed to coax a laugh out of Aidon once or twice.

"Hello, Mr. Haskett!"

They all turned to see a young lady approach them, a grin on her face. Her dark hair was perfectly coiffed, contrasting beautifully with the teal of her evening gown.

"Mrs. Reeves," Ezra said. He nodded in Persephone's direction. "You've yet to meet Mrs. Barrington, I gather."

"I haven't had the pleasure," Mrs. Reeves said, twinkling in Persephone's direction. She turned to Aidon, still smiling. "I must say, you're an unexpected sight."

"Ezra already said as much," Aidon responded. He did not seem very enthused at the interruption.

"Mr. Barrington was a friend of my husband's," Mrs. Reeves told Persephone, who did not miss her use of the past tense. "They were rakes of the worst kind, running amok all over London."

"Indeed?" Persephone said politely.

"Oh, yes," Mrs. Reeves said, ignoring Ezra and Aidon entirely. "Do you know, Mrs. Barrington, that you are married to the man who once occupied the leading role in many a young lady's wicked daydreams? Why, you could not go to a ball a decade ago without hearing tales of a scandalous rendezvous or stumbling across something rather risqué—"

"Mrs. Reeves," Aidon said, tone clipped.

"My apologies," she giggled, turning toward him. "Mr. Reeves has been reminiscing lately. He thinks back on his time in your circle quite fondly."

"I believe, Mrs. Reeves, that your husband made the decision to remove himself from my *circle* very soon after my father's death. Does he reminisce about that as well?"

Persephone suppressed the expression of surprise that threatened to take over her face. She had not thought Aidon capable of such brusqueness. Next to her, Ezra sighed.

Mrs. Reeves responded with a tight smile. "Indeed, he does not. I think I hear my cousin calling. I will bid you good evening."

They watched her disappear into the crowd in silence.

"Aidon," Ezra said.

Aidon let out an exhale. "I know. I shouldn't have."

"She's going to recount your exchange to every person she sees," Ezra said, a frown marring his usually smiling face. "It's like you *want* people to—"

Once again, their conversation was interrupted—this time

by the arrival of a harried-looking man whose red face very clearly showed his agitation.

"Mr. Barrington," he said, mopping his brow with his handkerchief. "A word?"

"Lord Follett. Of course." Aidon managed a quick bow before being pulled away. Persephone watched in confusion.

"Who was that?" she asked.

Ezra shrugged. "I've no idea."

Persephone wondered if he was telling the truth but did not push any further. Instead, she asked, "Do you really think Mrs. Reeves took great offense to what Aidon told her?"

"Absolutely," Ezra said. "He knows better than to speak to people like that, even if it *is* warranted. Before—well, you've likely heard enough about his past for one night."

"Not at all," Persephone said, sure nothing could shock her further.

"He would have dealt better with it before, that's all," Ezra said. "Charm used to come so easily to him. It can defuse any awkward conversation far better than politeness can."

"What charming response would you have given?"

Ezra chuckled. "If I possessed any amount of charm, I wouldn't have envied Aidon so much for his. I suppose he simply does not have the energy for it anymore."

Persephone sighed, suddenly overwhelmed by the sheer number of people around her. "Perhaps coming here was a mistake."

"Well, now!" Ezra laughed. "You sound just like your dour old husband."

She grimaced and looked up at his freckled face. "I rather thought bringing him here might help him reconnect with his brother."

Ezra's eyes widened. "A noble quest."

"But an impossible one?"

"I have tried everything," Ezra admitted, running a hand through his red curls. "Aidon will not budge."

"No," she said, pouting.

"Neither will Cassius," he added. "Not when I've tried to reason with him, at least."

This surprised her. Cassius had been so eager to ask her help, making Aidon seem like the main obstacle toward familial bliss. She wondered what could possibly have changed his mind and why he had trusted her with the task when Ezra had known both brothers far longer than she had.

"What would it take, do you think?" she asked casually.

"All Cassius needs to do is admit that he should have taken responsibility for the business," Ezra said, lowering his voice. "Or so I should think."

"That doesn't seem very likely," Persephone said, thinking back on the time she had spent with Cassius.

"Precisely." Ezra gave her an odd look. "Why the interest in their relationship?"

"Oh!" Persephone felt herself blush. "I—I thought it might help Aidon to be happier."

"I'm sure you are doing a fine job of that yourself," Ezra said. "Some things are not meant to be repaired."

He left her with that, having caught sight of yet another acquaintance.

Suddenly feeling as if she were suffocating, Persephone began to walk, intent on leaving the parlor for a bit of air. She saw Aidon across the room, still deep in serious conversation with the red-faced man. She followed the wall, running her hand along the wood paneling until she found her way to a hall. She saw one open door a few paces down and was relieved to see it led to a small study.

Entering, she leaned against the cool wall and let out a long exhale.

This was silly. *She* was silly. A sensible woman would have simply stayed at home, her relationship with her husband her singular focus.

A swish of skirts caught Persephone's ears as a gaggle of women stopped in the hallway, speaking in low whispers.

"I am surprised at him," a girlish voice said. "Of all women! You really have to wonder what he sees in her. She looks as if she's never spent a day among fine society in her life. Did you see her dress? And that *hair*?"

"You can't be *that* surprised," another voice said. "It isn't as if any of *us* would have had him. Can you imagine! Married to the Lord of the Dead."

Persephone winced at their words, barbs directed at both Aidon and herself. This was exactly what she'd been trying to escape when she'd left Honeyfield. To think it could follow her everywhere she went was hopelessly terrifying. The women moved along, their whispers and giggles following them down the hallway. She wished she had refused this trip when Cassius had suggested it. If this was what he called his domain, then she wanted no part of it.

She would give anything to be at Gallowsgate, alone. Alone with Aidon, who did not deserve to be gossiped about. Who had never once implied that she wasn't enough. Who did not deserve her trying to change him by meddling in his personal affairs. She wondered where he was, if he was even looking for her.

I should return to the parlor.

Maybe she could convince him to leave, pretend she was feeling unwell. There were too many people here. She could not stand it.

She pushed herself off the wall, only to see the doorway crowded by Cassius's tall figure.

"There you are!" he said, stepping into the study. "I've been searching for you."

Persephone felt her stomach sink, though she wasn't sure why. After all, she had brought them all this way to see Cassius. And now here he was.

"I was in need of some air," she said.

"It's a bit much, isn't it?" Cassius smiled. "You'll come to enjoy it."

She very highly doubted that.

"I think I shall find Aidon," she said quickly, taking a step forward, expecting him to make way.

Instead of stepping aside, he moved into the room.

"I've done some reading," he said.

Unease threaded through her. "Oh? Did you pick up *The History of a Young Lady*?"

He shook his head. "Nothing quite so grave. I was reading about *you*, Goddess of Spring. You and your dour husband."

"Me?"

"It starts with brothers," he said, taking slow, measured steps toward the window. He peered out of it, Persephone unable to see his face. "They draw lots and Hades gets the Underworld, of all things. Terrible luck. It must have made a resentful bastard of him."

Persephone remained silent. He turned to look at her, an indulgent smirk on his face.

"It's no wonder he risks everything to make Persephone his," he said. "Poor, innocent goddess. She was just miserable down there, wasn't she?"

"I—I don't know."

Cassius gave off an overbearing air, very different from the man she had spent over a week with. "How could she not long for someone else, someone *better*, trapped in the Underworld for six months at a time?"

"I am sure she had much to busy herself with," Persephone said, glancing at the open door.

"But did she busy herself with her husband, I wonder?"

"I think, perhaps, you've been reading too much between the lines," she said sharply, fixing her gaze upon him. "You are overcomplicating a very simple story."

"I might be," he agreed. He stepped away from the window, drawing closer to where she stood. "But I can't help but wonder if *you* are busying yourself with your husband, little Persephone."

A short, nervous laugh bubbled out of her as he approached, forcing her to retreat until she felt the desk press against the backs of her thighs.

"I am not very fond of teasing," she said, gripping the tabletop, trying desperately to convince herself that she was misreading his tone.

"Teasing?" he repeated. She looked up into his glinting copper eyes, the edge of the table pushing painfully into her skin. "You have mistaken me."

He's drunk, she thought. Or rather, hoped.

"Has my brother been taking proper care of you?" he asked, tilting her face toward his own. She pressed herself back, but there was nowhere for her to go.

"I'm sure he wouldn't appreciate my discussing it with you," she said, annoyed that her voice emerged a shaky whisper.

He ran his thumb along her jaw, leaving a frigid trail in its wake. She pressed her lips together.

"No, then," he murmured. "Aidon can be so foolish. So focused on his work that he's unable to see that he has a flower before him, ready to be plucked."

"I am no flower," Persephone said hotly. Impulsively.

"Oh, don't be like that," he said, running a hand lightly up the side of her bodice, stopping right under her breast. She felt frozen in place, unable to find the strength to at least *try* to move out of his reach. "There is no need to play coy. No woman alive would choose him over me."

Persephone stared at him, bewildered. What in God's name was he *talking* about? Did he think she was a pawn in some ridiculous, competitive game between brothers? What was he trying to prove? She looked up at him, taking in the ridiculous grin he probably thought incredibly suave, and felt anger melt her frozen body. She took a sudden step forward, forcing him to stumble back. And hard as she could, she slapped him across the face.

It felt good.

Much to her disappointment, it must not have hurt him as much as she'd intended because all he did was give her a look of complete astonishment. He opened his mouth to speak, but she interrupted him.

"Your brother was right about you."

To her displeasure, Cassius laughed. "Oh, he warned you, did he? It's a pity, you know. Having you for a night would have been the easiest way for me to get back at him."

For what?

She let out a firm, "Leave."

He shrugged, making his way lazily toward the door.

"It makes sense, my brother choosing you." Over his shoulder, he gave Persephone a toothy grin. "No gentlewoman would have ever had him, so he was forced to go to godforsaken Oxbury to find someone who would."

Persephone refused to respond, despite how sharply his words had struck. She stood there until he left, letting out a long breath as soon as he disappeared from view.

Briskly, she walked toward the door, desperate to leave, only to see yet another man crowd the doorway.

Aidon.

SIXTEEN

She looked unsettled.

Aidon stood in the doorway of his brother's study, taking in Persephone's flushed face and large, glimmering eyes. He could have sworn she was relieved to see him, her shoulders slumping as her gaze met his. She looked as if she had folded into herself for protection, the very air around her agitated and restless.

"I was coming to look for you," she said breathlessly, and he felt his heart skip a beat. Lord Follett had kept him too long, the fool. "Did—did your brother—is he in the parlor?"

An odd question. Aidon took a step into the room. Persephone stepped backward, giving the impression of a nervous little bird trapped in a cage.

"Was he here?" he asked slowly.

"Yes," she stammered. "No." Walking up to him, she placed her hand on his sleeve. He felt the slight pressure of her grip as her fingers pressed into the fabric of his coat. "Would you mind terribly if we left?"

The dying glow of the fireplace cast shadows across

Persephone's sharp jaw. She radiated tension, her mouth pressed in a straight line and her brow distorted.

"Persephone." He carefully placed his hand over hers, feeling her flinch beneath his touch. Something had happened, he was sure of it. "Was Cassius here?"

"It does not matter," she said, looking up at him beseechingly.

So he had been. Cassius, when he had a mind for it, was incredibly adept at saying or doing whatever he could to leave a person feeling distinctly unsettled. But that side of him was typically reserved for those he disliked, not for someone like Persephone, whom he'd seemed intent on getting along with. What could have possibly changed in the time between Cassius's visit to Gallowsgate and now? What could have possibly happened?

"It does matter if he has done something to upset you," Aidon insisted.

"I would like to return to Gallowsgate," she said desperately, and the plea would have reduced him to a puddle had it not been for the context.

Guilt coursed through his veins as he recalled his conversation with Lord Follett. "I . . . I have business I must attend to."

Her face fell.

"But we can return to the town house," he offered quickly.

She nodded, her grip on his sleeve tightening. "Should— should we say goodbye to Mr. Haskett?"

Aidon looked down at her, so small and devoid of the spark that usually lit her up from within. He would, he realized, do anything to reignite it.

"We can send him our regards from the house," he said, his words causing her to relax visibly.

They left quickly and quietly. In the carriage, Aidon watched the shadows of the city travel across Persephone's face. As he

studied her guarded expression, his mind replayed the conversation they'd had in front of his mother's portrait. He had felt
equal parts defensive and awkward in response to her questions, simply because no one had ever asked them before. But
here was lovely Persephone, so deeply invested in knowing and
understanding and fixing things that nobody had ever even noticed were broken. She shifted in her seat uncomfortably, and
he wished desperately that he could do something, say something, that would make her feel as understood and safe as she
had made him feel then. As they alighted from the carriage, she
darted into the town house.

"It was not my place to bring us here," she said, pausing
inside the entryway. She looked at him with wide, glossy eyes,
folding her arms against herself. "I'm sorry."

Aidon reached for her without thinking, her apology tearing right through his soul. She did not turn from him, instead
nestling herself within his arms. Warmth spread throughout his
entire body as she positioned herself against him, taking a deep
breath as she did so.

"You've nothing to apologize for," he murmured.

She sighed. "I think I do. I heard women whispering
about—about the Lord of the Dead. I should have said something to them."

Aidon brushed a wayward lock of hair from her forehead.
"That is not your battle to fight."

And it was a battle. She just didn't know it. But every passing minute brought with it the temptation of telling the truth,
of finally being truly open with her. He continued to resist it,
continued to remind himself that it was quite likely she would
respond poorly.

Or leave. And he couldn't have that.

"It's unfair," she said, stepping out of their embrace. He had to force himself not to reach for her again. "But if it makes you feel any better, they talked about me, too."

"You?" he asked in disbelief. "What could they possibly have had to say about you?"

Persephone responded with a perplexed expression of her own. "The same things people have said about me my entire life."

He had no idea what that meant or how anyone could look at Persephone and not instantly recognize her brilliance.

"If you think they're wrong about me, then they are wrong about you," he said finally.

A rosy flush bloomed across her cheeks. She paused, and he got the impression that she wanted to argue but could not find the words. "I suppose I cannot argue with such logic."

"There," he said gently. "Nothing to worry about, after all."

"No, but—" She let out a small huff of frustration, gesturing around the entryway. "I'm sure you've realized that I'm not good at any of this. Society, crowds, I—none of it has ever been for me. And I'm sure that's disappointing."

"What is for you, then?"

Persephone frowned. "That is not the point."

"I think it very much is the point," he responded. "Because whatever is for you is also for me."

"I—I'm sorry?"

He shook his head. "There is nothing disappointing about you, Persephone. If something isn't for you, then it isn't for us. It's as simple as that."

She blinked rapidly, as if trying to process his words. "You can't mean that. There is so much that isn't for me. It's bound to inconvenience you."

"It won't," he assured her.

A breathy laugh escaped her. "I had no idea you were so stubborn."

A corner of Aidon's mouth hiked up. "And are stubborn men for you, Persephone?"

"Maybe," she said, laughing again, cheeks still rosy. "I shall have to think on it."

He gave her what he was sure was a dazed smile, and in return, she quickly pushed herself up on her toes to press a kiss to his jaw. Lightning shot up his spine at the contact, and balling his hands into fists at his side was all he could do not to pull her against him for a proper kiss. But there was something about her that was still on edge, something that told him now was not entirely the right time.

"It's late," she said, turning to go upstairs. "I will see you tomorrow."

"Wait," he said, impressed that he was still able to form words.

She paused on the first step, looking at him out of the corner of her eye. "I will be just fine."

"And you won't tell me what it was that occurred," he said slowly. He desperately hoped it had nothing to do with all that damned gossip about the Lord of the Dead.

Persephone shook her head in a silent *no* before disappearing up the stairs, her grip on the banister tight, as if she were trying to anchor herself.

Aidon had been convinced that in London he could try to coax out a shadow of his past self, try to show Persephone that he, like his brother, was capable of charming conversation and flirtatious banter. What had felt impossible in Oxbury had seemed a touch closer to reality in London. Now, as he let himself into his bedchamber, he felt foolish for ever having thought that at all. He'd been imagining the London of his past, as if he did not intimately understand how things had changed. Worse still, he did not know what had happened or what Cassius had said to Persephone. What he knew was that his bond with his brother was almost damaged beyond repair.

Blowing out the candle by his bedside, he lay back and stared at the dark canopy above. He was suddenly struck by the shouldn't-couldn't-wouldn't clauses he'd built into his life over the past ten years. He shouldn't pull his focus from his work, couldn't indulge in distractions of any kind, wouldn't prove his father right by being anything other than rigid and responsible. And that was only a sampling of the rules he'd unthinkingly imposed upon himself. After all this time, had any of it been truly worth it?

A small, tentative knock broke through the silence of his room. Aidon sat up, confused, as the door creaked open. A low-burning candle came first, its owner following. She was clad in the same white nightgown he'd seen before—soft fabric and pretty ribbons.

"Persephone," he murmured, a delicious, anticipatory sort of anxiety spiking through his veins.

She stared at him in silence for a moment, her dark, owlish eyes large in her pale face. "I woke you. I'm sorry."

"Not at all," he choked out, desperate to know what she was here for.

Desperate to give her whatever she asked for.

"Good," she breathed. After another moment's silence, she said, "I was hoping I could sleep by you tonight."

"Oh?"

"Just—just sleep," she clarified, her blush so furious that he could make it out in the weak candlelight. "And only for tonight."

It was clear to him that whatever Cassius had done had well and truly rattled her. Pushing aside the urge to strangle his brother, Aidon nodded. She took small, hesitant steps toward the bed before placing the candle down and blowing it out. He felt her climb onto the mattress, her movements nearly undetectable.

She curled up beside him, just barely close enough to touch, and did not say another word.

"Persephone," he whispered.

She turned toward him, eyes wide in the darkness.

"How can I fix things if you don't tell me what happened?" he asked.

"There is nothing to be fixed," she said quietly. "Actually, this makes me feel better than discussing it would."

"This?" he echoed, trying to make her out in the light of the moon.

"Being beside someone," she explained. "Being beside you."

The simplicity of her words tore into his heart. Reaching over, he brushed her hair back before tracing the outline of her jaw. She shivered beneath his gentle touch, the air in the room charged with something he could easily identify.

"I am at your disposal," he told her.

"I . . . I'm starting to understand that," she said. She pulled her hand out from beneath the pillow, her fingertip brushing down the bridge of his nose. "This will do for now."

He was too taken by her presence next to him, curled up in the most intimate of places, to feel even a hint of disappointment. He wanted her; that much was certain. If he hadn't known it before, he certainly would have discovered it now with the way his blood had heated at her touch. He had wanted her the minute he'd seen her teetering on the library ladder at Gallowsgate. Nothing would change that, and certainly not however long it took her to decide that she wanted him, too.

Perhaps it would take longer than he hoped. Insecurity gnawed at him, a wicked voice in his head telling him she would never deign to warm the bed of the Lord of the Dead.

She's here, he reminded himself, forcing his thoughts to the present. *She wants to be here with you.*

"Are you comfortable?" he murmured.

"Yes," she whispered. Then added, "I feel safe."

Safe.

He'd wanted so badly to make her feel as safe as she did him. Somehow, he was doing so just by lying next to her. It was an overwhelming realization for someone whose presence had never been considered worth much of anything.

"If I ever make you feel otherwise—"

"You won't," she interrupted. "Not you."

"I feel safe with you as well," he told her, unsure if she would find the sentiment laughable coming from a man.

"That's something," she said sleepily. "Isn't it?"

"It is," he agreed, still wide awake, eyes focused solely on her.

"A good something, of course," she yawned.

He chuckled softly. "Naturally."

Persephone's eyes fluttered closed, sleep finally overtaking her. Aidon watched her for a long while, his mind overrun with thoughts. In the early morning hours, just as exhaustion was about to drag him into slumber, only one thought remained at the forefront of his mind.

It told him, with complete certainty, that he was, for the very first time in his life, at risk of falling in love.

Seventeen

Persephone appeared to recover rather quickly after the innocent night spent in Aidon's bed, but she continued to dismiss his efforts to discover just how Cassius had offended her. Two days after his brother's debacle of a dinner, they returned to Oxbury, Aidon focused on one thing alone—making Persephone happy. He still didn't know, might not ever know, what Cassius had done, but he still wanted to at least attempt to make it right.

The way any well-to-do gentleman would, he began to buy her gifts. He offered to take her to the best dressmaker—in actuality, the only dressmaker—in Little Oxbury so that she might have more dresses for her wardrobe. She agreed shyly and, predictably, was now due to own dresses in every pastel shade and floral pattern known to man. He made plans to fill the library with books of her choosing and asked her to provide him with an exhaustive list of everything she'd ever wanted to read.

When the latest gift finally arrived from London, Aidon sought Persephone out, finding her in the parlor with a letter in her hands. The room, which had been austere in its appearance, now looked lived in. Persephone's wrap was hanging over the edge of the chaise she sat on, and a vase of flowers rested on the table next to an open atlas.

"There you are," he said, hearing how desperately pleased he sounded. He cleared his throat in an effort to regain some of his composure. It was ridiculous how he missed her now as soon as they parted after breakfast. He seemed to miss her more often since their return from London, particularly at night. But, true to her word, she had not come to him again. Still, he felt as if something had shifted between them. Her smiles came more quickly now—a promising sign of affection.

He nodded toward the letter in her hands. "Good news?"

"No news, which I rather think is the same," she said. She placed the letter on the chaise before standing up and smoothing her bodice. His eyes tracked the movement, spellbound. "Venus and Papa send their regards. They keep meaning to visit, but they are easily distracted with the hives as it's collecting season."

He studied her, noting a hint of melancholy in her expressive eyes. "You must miss them."

"I do," she said eventually, her intense gaze meeting his. "I know it's only been a little over a month, but I don't think I've ever gone so long without seeing them."

He nodded. "And Honeyfield?"

A small frown pulled at her pink lips. Aidon thought he had discovered why she *hadn't* rushed back to visit her family, choosing to remain at Gallowsgate instead. He remembered when she'd compared herself to the bees, restricted to Honeyfield. It was difficult for him to see how Honeyfield could ever suffocate anybody. Persephone had seemed to belong there, as much a part of the land as the flowers and trees.

"I do miss some things about it," she added lightly. "But it's not important. I live here now."

I live here now.

She did, and he desperately hoped that Gallowsgate would never become suffocating or lonely. So much of the house seemed different to him. Even the simple act of conversing with his wife seemed to air the place of bad memories.

"What do you miss most?" he asked.

She turned her head to look out at the perfectly manicured grounds. "The chaos of it all, I suppose. The flowers." Her eyes met his again, and she laughed. "I would have much preferred to *not* love flowers as I do. Persephone Honeyfield loves flowers. It's a little ridiculous. It sounds as if I'm trying to play the part."

"It suits you," he said eagerly. "And—and I'd like for Gallowsgate to suit you as well."

She cocked her head to the side. "You may regret saying that. What if you awake one day to grounds overrun with weeds?"

As long as Persephone was among them, happy and rosy-cheeked, he wouldn't care. He reached for his coat pocket, remembering the gift that had arrived from London. Fishing it out, he handed her the tiny paper parcel.

"Here. For you."

Persephone took it gingerly, the paper crinkling in her small hands. "Another gift?"

She unwrapped it to reveal a pair of earrings. Little golden pomegranates with shining ruby seeds.

"Pomegranates?" she laughed, the sound piercing his heart. She looked up at him, her expression mischievous. "If I take these, I'll be forced to spend eternity here, which could be quite awful for you."

"I'm not sure I would use the word *awful*." Aidon grinned. "Bearable, maybe."

"Bearable is far better than awful. I will accept bearable." She smiled, putting the earrings on. "Thank you, but—"

"But?"

"I cannot keep accepting these gifts. It's too much, and I—have nothing to give you in return."

Aidon could think of plenty of things Persephone could give him. He would never ask, never imply that he expected *her* in exchange for gifts, but the thought lingered in his mind nonetheless.

"You needn't give me anything," he said quickly. "I enjoy it. In fact, you might tell me what it is you'd like me to give you. It would make it easier."

She blushed, and he felt a buzz spread throughout his body. He wanted to kiss her. Wanted to do so much more than that. He didn't even know why the imaginary boundary between them was even *there*.

"Well, there is one thing," she said shyly. "Besides my mother's book, of course."

"Which we will find," he promised. He knew that every time Baker declared a section of the house fit for use, Persephone would look through it. So far, she had come up empty-handed each time.

"You've just given me the idea, actually," she said, looking up at him with those intelligent eyes of hers. "Seeds."

"Seeds?" he said, confused.

"The gardens *are* a little dreary. I think I might plant some flowers." She paused, considering. "We could plant them together."

Aidon thought back once more to the unearthly shock of color that decorated Honeyfield. Unruly and untamed, just like Persephone. He had told her he wanted Gallowsgate to suit her, and she was two steps ahead. She was already thinking about how to emulate what she'd loved about her home—already trying to make Gallowsgate *more* of a home. She had not hesitated for a moment, and the realization filled him with a deep, aching hopefulness.

If she wanted seeds, then seeds she would have. Anything to make her feel at home. Here, with him.

Not two days later, Persephone entered her room to find packets of seeds, and alongside them, a bunch of flowers wrapped in a pale blue ribbon. Aidon, of course, had done what she'd asked as soon as he'd been able to. The distant fondness she had held for him was quickly evolving into something entirely different with every word exchanged. It had taken quite a lot of courage for her to ask to sleep beside him that night in London, but her desire to feel safe had won out over her anxieties. She had never felt so safe in her entire life.

Since returning to Gallowsgate, a few specific anxieties were crumbling into a very fine dust. It was becoming more and more difficult for her to convince herself that Aidon would dislike the imperfect person she was. Now, they were dancing around each other, the steps becoming closer by the minute. She had no doubt it would end in a collision, one that she could possibly inspire, but—

A different woman might have seduced him by now.

Persephone felt terrible, felt like Aidon deserved better. She thought about Cassius's words, about how Aidon hadn't been able to find a gentlewoman to take him. She could not fathom how the entirety of London could be so wrong.

He had not enjoyed being in London very much, if their horrible trip was any indication. She wondered if that was why they were still in Oxbury.

As dreadful as London had been, there was still the question of his work. She knew he was able to attend to his duties via post, and that he had a colleague in London, but there was nothing to like about Oxbury, either—unless he was doing this for her.

Whatever is for you is also for me.

Persephone gathered up the seed packets. She wanted to do this with him, and it occurred to her that his easy, accepting ways were making it very difficult for her to keep her walls up. She wandered down the hallway to knock softly at his study door, poking her head around it before she was called in.

Aidon sat at his desk, illuminated from behind by the large windows that opened out over the gardens. He was surrounded by piles of papers, his cravat loosened.

He was the very picture of temptation.

Feeling slightly embarrassed, she shook the packets of seeds in her hands. "How did you manage to track these down so quickly?"

He gave her a crooked grin. "I have my ways."

"Well!" She exhaled, willing herself to be brave. "Shall we?"

The words seemed to light a fire underneath him because he stood up with such urgency that a few pieces of paper were knocked to the ground. He bent to pick them up, the muffled sounds of "Yes, of course" coming from underneath his desk.

Persephone felt a sharp pain in her chest. Sharp, but somehow still pleasant and promising and terrifying all at once.

The ground in the garden was still damp from the rain. Without thinking, she led them to the cemetery. It was peaceful there, if not a little unnerving. The tombstones were a little weathered, but not much grew around them. The earth looked healthy, however, and the area desperately needed some brightening up.

"Why don't we start here?" she said, handing him a packet of seeds. She went to the very first marker, leaving Aidon a few steps away. Eager to begin, she started to push the seeds into the damp earth with her bare hands and was finding a rhythm when she heard Aidon awkwardly clear his throat. She looked up, startled to see he hadn't moved.

"Is everything all right?" she asked, dusting her hands on her skirts.

"I don't know how to do this," he admitted softly, clearly embarrassed. "I've never—planted anything."

Persephone bit her tongue to stop herself from laughing. Only Aidon could make complete and utter hopelessness seem charming. She walked over to him and placed a hand on his wrist, immediately aware of the warmth emanating from his skin.

"Here," she said gently, the way she wished she'd been spoken to when she hadn't known how to do things, "let me show you."

They knelt in the dirt together, and she watched patiently as he mirrored her movements.

"Deeper," she said, placing her hand over his and directing him to push the seeds into the damp soil.

He cleared his throat again, a blush blooming across his cheekbones.

"My mother always wanted to do this," he said, planting the seeds perfectly on his next attempt. "But Father wanted to keep things tidy."

"He'd have hated Honeyfield," she said wryly.

He probably would have hated her, too.

"My mother would have loved it," Aidon said, and Persephone felt her cheeks warm.

When a comfortable silence finally settled, she went from marker to marker, counting under her breath and pushing seeds into the earth. Some of the tombstones were unmarked, which she found a little strange. Maybe the engravings had faded, victims of time.

She reached the one hundred and sixth marker, only to see one more right next to it.

That can't be right.

Unless she'd miscounted that first day at Gallowsgate. She didn't think so, but she *must* have. Tombstones did not materialize out of thin air. The one hundred and seventh tombstone was unmarked, just as some of the others had been. She glanced at Aidon, who was working diligently a few rows behind her. The rumors about the Lord of the Dead—about her husband—began to flutter into her head.

She'd have known if somebody from the family had died.

I must have miscounted, she told herself firmly. *Those rumors are nothing but silly gossip. He deserves better than that.*

Persephone hesitated to plant seeds over this new-to-her plot. But she had to because she'd done it for the others. She bent down, pressing the seeds into the ground, telling herself that gossip was for nosy busybodies, and—

"Persephone," a deep, delicious voice said from behind her. She dropped the seeds in her hands, and they scattered around her feet. She looked up, eyes meeting Aidon's.

He offered her a hand, and she took it, allowing herself to be pulled up. He held tight, his grip firm and warm.

"Thank you," he said, running a thumb across her knuckles. She felt her breath catch in her throat.

"Whatever for?" she choked out.

"I've never done anything like this before," he said. "I've never had the privilege, I suppose."

"Just the privilege of being a wildly rich man of business?" Persephone grinned.

He laughed, the sound rumbling through her bones.

"And nobody has ever done anything like this with *me*," she added. "Something so menial in such comfortable silence. I wouldn't even know how to begin to thank you for *that* privilege."

"I suppose we have a lifetime of menial tasks ahead of us," he said.

Because it had come from Aidon, because he made her feel so safe, his response injected her with a healthy dose of courage.

She looked up at him through her eyelashes, feeling warmth creep up her neck. "I don't know how to thank you," she murmured, tossing aside her inhibitions. She reached up to grip his lapel, and he allowed himself to be pulled down to her height. "Perhaps this will do."

Persephone pressed her lips against his gently, and she felt Aidon stiffen even as every nerve in her body stood to attention. The kiss was chaste, her mouth kept closed and soft against his. Releasing him, she took a small step back, running her hands over her skirts. Her entire body felt as if it had been set aflame.

"That won't do at all," Aidon said.

Persephone's eyebrows shot up in surprise. "I beg your pardon?"

Embarrassment flooded her, and she began to fidget. Truly, this was the worst possible outcome.

"I'm not sure I understand your meaning," she stammered.

"Then allow me to demonstrate."

Taking her slender wrist, Aidon pulled Persephone's lithe form against his, claiming her mouth in a heated kiss. He cupped her head in one hand, allowing the other to circle her waist. Persephone was stunned, but as he probed deeper, she returned to earth with a jolt, threading her arms around his neck and pushing herself up on her tiptoes. She could hear the blood rushing through her veins, keenly aware of the warmth erupting through her body. Aidon's hands wandered gently, moving from her waist and up toward the swell of her breasts. They broke apart, breathless.

Before she could speak, a voice rang through the air. Persephone jumped away from Aidon, turning to see none other than Ezra Haskett bounding toward them.

"What in the *hell*?" Aidon muttered.

At least his sentiments mirrored her own. Small blessing, that.

EIGHTEEN

Aidon had never felt the urge to strangle Ezra until this very moment.

His friend leaned over the black iron gate of the cemetery and flashed them a shameless grin. "Aidon! I don't think I've seen you work outside the entire time I've known you."

"Ezra," Aidon said, his tone measured, "we weren't expecting you."

Persephone stood off to the side, shuffling nervously in place as she looked between the two men.

God, he wanted to touch every inch of her. She had unknowingly opened the floodgates of mindless desire, and the only thing that had stopped him was the fact that they were out in the open. That, and Ezra.

"I told you," Ezra said impatiently. "I'm in Oxbury to study skep design with Mr. Honeyfield."

"When did you tell me this?"

Ezra paused for a moment. "In London?" He took in Aidon's expression. "No? Then I *meant* to tell you when you were in London."

Typical.

"I must have," Ezra insisted. He gave Aidon a look reminiscent of a puppy left out in the rain. "I can leave and come back when it's more convenient for you."

"No, no," Persephone said, joining them at the gate. "Not after you've come all this way."

She was a far better person than Aidon; that much was clear. He could still smell the lavender coming off her sun-warmed skin as he'd kissed her.

Ezra brightened immediately. "You have my thanks. It'll only be a week. Less, even," he promised. "I'm surprised your father didn't mention it to you."

"My father is forgetful," Persephone said. "The both of you have that in common."

Ezra laughed and did not have the decency to look even slightly embarrassed. He seemed ready to continue his incessant chatter but was halted by the arrival of yet another person—Christianna, whom Aidon had not seen since his and Persephone's wedding day.

For the love of all that was holy, was *every* person in Oxbury going to invade Gallowsgate today?

Persephone perked at the sight of her friend, wiggling the gate to the cemetery open and rushing over to meet her. Aidon watched them embrace, then turned to Ezra, who was taking in Christianna's rosy-cheeked face and the deep chestnut hair that sat on her shoulders in dark contrast to her pale blue dress.

"A friend of Persephone's?" Ezra asked, failing miserably at nonchalance.

"Ezra," Aidon said tiredly.

"What?" Ezra said, still unable to take his eyes off Christianna. "You'll introduce me, won't you?"

"Ezra," Aidon repeated.

"It's the polite thing to do, Aidon," Ezra said, finally turning to look at him.

Aidon sighed. Ezra had never had very much luck with women. Not because he was plagued by gossip, but simply because he always seemed to make a fool of himself eventually. He meant well, but there was only so much women could put up with.

There was also only so much Aidon could put up with. He and Persephone needed their privacy now more than ever. They were on the precipice of something wonderful and decidedly *not* guest friendly.

"Well?" Ezra pressed.

"Aren't you here to study bees?"

"Skep design, thank you," Ezra sniffed. "*Some* of us weren't distracted by women the last time we were here and learned quite a lot."

"Some of us are distracted right now," Aidon grumbled.

Persephone rejoined them with Christianna by her side. "Christianna heard we'd returned from London," she said. She looked between her friend and Ezra. "Oh! Christianna, this is Mr. Ezra Haskett. Mr. Haskett, this is Christianna Errwood. She lives on a neighboring estate."

Ezra shot Aidon a smug look despite knowing that Persephone was not the right person to have made the introduction. He gave Christianna a polite bow.

Christianna giggled, and Ezra's freckled face lit up. Aidon could sense a weeklong headache coming on.

"Shall we go to the house?" Persephone asked, herding the group out of the cemetery. Ezra and Christianna walked ahead, making polite small talk. Aidon trailed behind with Persephone.

"I should apologize for him," he said. "Ezra can be a little overeager."

"So can Christianna," Persephone observed. "But she's lovely and gentle and—she has the biggest heart of anybody I've ever known."

He couldn't resist. "Quite like yourself."

"Better," she said. A smile pulled at her lips. "Far better. You know, I've always thought she deserves someone kind and intelligent and handsome. Someone who can provide for her so that she may spend her days doing whatever she pleases without worry."

Aidon wondered, truly wondered, if Persephone knew just how perfectly exquisite she was. There was, of course, her fae-like form and her sharp, expressive face. But there was more to her, too. He could clearly see how deeply she cared for her friend, how deeply she cared about most things that crossed her path. He hoped she knew that care—that *love*—she gave was nothing short of a blessing to whatever she thought to bestow it upon.

"Someone like Mr. Haskett," she finished, triumphant in her suggestion.

"Not you as well," Aidon groaned as they walked into the entryway. Baker led their guests to the parlor as Persephone turned to give Aidon a quizzical look.

"Not me as well?"

"Ezra asked to be introduced," Aidon said.

Persephone brightened. "That's good, isn't it?" She looked around before pulling Aidon into the library and shutting the door behind them. "I'm sure Christianna would be flattered."

"Of all times for Ezra to descend upon this house," Aidon grumbled.

Persephone raised an incredulous eyebrow. "Is there something else you would rather we do?"

"I thought you'd never ask."

Persephone was in trouble.

Here she was, standing in the library, her husband pressing hot kisses to her neck, whispering sweet nothings into her ears. She was completely at his mercy, and she loved it.

She had been on the verge of distracting herself with yet another project. As soon as she'd seen Ezra and Christianna together, something in her mind had clicked. Christianna had spent their entire adolescence and adulthood waxing poetic about love and marriage, but there had been nothing of the sort for her in Oxbury. Now an opportunity had presented itself, and as distracted as Persephone had been by Aidon, even she could tell that they made a handsome pair.

"I've wanted this for so long," Aidon murmured, his voice low and heavy. "Since the day I found you on that ladder."

All thoughts of matchmaking dissolved from Persephone's mind, and she felt a thrill shoot up her spine at his admission. He'd wanted this, wanted her, the day they'd met at Gallowsgate. Her! Undesirable, unlovable Persephone, who had paled in comparison to the lovely Venus her entire life. That she felt any surprise at all made her realize how often her mind refused to accept the simple truth.

Persephone Honeyfield had never been one to attract affection. What a terrible belief to hold on to—and what a difficult belief to shake.

Her mind suddenly went blank, her thoughts interrupted by a series of warm kisses down her neck.

How could something feel so utterly electrifying? Worried that her knees might buckle, Persephone held onto Aidon's upper arms, marveling at the hard feel of them under his layers of clothing. She felt warmth bloom in her stomach, traveling down, down, down—until she realized that she had to put a stop to this before it truly became torturous and impossible to do so.

She broke away, easing herself gently out of Aidon's arms and taking a small step away from him for good measure. His dark hair was wonderfully tousled, his overall appearance one of delicious dishevelment.

"We should go to the parlor," Persephone said, desperately hoping that her voice didn't let on how overcome she was. "We have guests."

"Of course," he said breathlessly, sounding disappointed.

They left the library and entered the cavernous parlor in silence, only to see Ezra and Christianna lost in animated conversation by the window. Persephone shot Aidon a triumphant glance, gesturing for him to stand outside the room with her. She was intensely aware of his body next to hers as she willed her boiling blood to cool. Aidon glanced at her with his irresistible green eyes. She looked up at him, the lazy smile on his face making her heart squeeze in her chest.

"What is it?" she asked.

"You're lovely, do you know that?"

Persephone felt her face warm, sure she had just turned an embarrassing shade of red. Nobody outside of her family had ever called her lovely before.

"I've been told once or twice," she said, feigning confidence. She looked away, unable to maintain eye contact. "But never by a stranger."

She felt her husband's featherlight touch as he tilted her face toward his own. "Am I a stranger to you?"

"No, no," Persephone said quickly, burning with embarrassment. She should have interrupted the conversation in the parlor. "I just—Venus *is* my sister, you know."

She mentally kicked herself. This was *not* the time and place to bear her soul to him.

He tilted his head in confusion. "And?"

"It's nothing." Persephone looked down at her balled-up hands. "Thank you for the compliment. Should we go inside?"

"Come now," he said softly. "Tell me."

Persephone realized she did not want to fight him—did not want to fight *this*.

"It's a little silly," she admitted. "I grew up hearing people rave about Venus's beauty, and I convinced myself that I didn't possess any because nobody ever spoke of it."

He opened his mouth to respond. Persephone shook her head, silencing him.

"I did this as a result," she continued, running her hands through her short hair. "An old friend of my mother's was going on and on about Venus's lovely hair, and I saw how much she struggled when she turned to address me. She could not think of anything to say. So, I marched upstairs and took a pair of scissors to my head." She laughed. "Papa was horrified. I rather like it, though."

"I wondered," he said, reaching out to touch the crown of her head.

Persephone took his wrist gently, lowering his arm. She kept hold of it as she spoke. "If I had a shilling for every time someone commented on my hair, I would be richer than you are." She released him and sighed. "Since you don't seem inclined to go into the parlor, you should tell me something about yourself. It's only fair."

He chuckled. "What is it you wish to know?"

A hundred questions flooded Persephone's thoughts, very many of them having to do with the extra tombstone she'd counted. But she couldn't ask that.

"Why do people dislike you?" He raised his eyebrows, and she quickly corrected herself. "That is, why do they gossip about you so?"

Aidon shrugged. "They've no better use for their time."

"Yes, but why *you*?" Persephone pressed. "Surely there are other funeral furnishers in London to gossip about."

"My father's business—*my* business—is the most well-known in London. And—well, the gossip is partially my fault."

Persephone looked at him in surprise. "It is?"

"I changed quite a lot after my father died. You've already heard as much."

"Yes, but I'd like to hear it from you," she said.

"It is as Mrs. Reeves said in London. I was very much like my brother. But my father's death . . . it hurt, and I had to take on the business shortly after. Responsibility changes a man, and that change was noticeable enough for people to begin to whisper."

If Persephone hadn't heard it multiple times now, she'd have never believed Aidon capable of being a skirt-chasing, pleasure-seeking fool like Cassius. The man standing before her was sturdy and dependable, not flighty and unprincipled. She felt her heart soften a little at his words. She couldn't imagine dealing with the death of her father while taking on a responsibility as massive as an entire funeral furnishing establishment.

"Aidon," she said softly. He looked at her with desperate green eyes. "This might not matter, but I am glad you changed."

He gave her a hopeful smile. "You may be the only one."

Persephone felt a strange affection blooming in her chest,

unfurling like a newly sprouted flower. She knew she was in trouble. Of course, she'd known that from the start.

"I'm glad we planted those seeds," he said.

Persephone blushed despite herself. "As am I."

He stood up a little straighter. "Would it be too forward of me to ask why you kissed me? Instead of simply thanking me, that is."

Now *that*, Persephone was not expecting. She thought about how to respond, finding herself vaguely distracted by the incessant chatter that spilled out of the parlor and into the hallway.

What a ridiculous place to be having this conversation.

"I just wanted to."

"As did I," he said, his words causing heat to flower in Persephone's stomach again. "I only regret that I was not the one to do it first." He gave her a warm, searching look. "I wanted to."

"Yes, you—you said," Persephone stammered.

"I meant it. There's something about you that drives me mad, Persephone. I'm afraid I do not have the eloquence to describe it."

She had never in her life been spoken to in this way, had never heard words tinged with need and passion. It had only happened in her daydreams, and those had always seemed out of reach. These words were meant for someone far prettier, far gentler, far kinder. And yet they were being said to her. She felt a tightness in her throat, swallowing hard to be rid of it.

She grinned. "Will you tell me when you find the words? I am rather curious."

Aidon chuckled. "You'll be the first to hear them." He turned to glance at the parlor door. "Should we interrupt them?"

"I think we should," Persephone said, nodding. "I should ask Christianna to dine with us, as well."

"Then I suppose we'll be seeing them both at dinner," he

said, resigned. He bent down and pressed an innocent kiss to her cheek, murmuring softly in her ear, "And perhaps I will see you *after* dinner, if you'll allow it."

Persephone followed him into the parlor in a daze, feeling like an entire colony of cocoons had burst open in her chest, leaving her more butterfly than woman.

Nineteen

Persephone had often thought she'd make a very good match-maker. She was just the right sort of person for it, perceptive and capable of hatching a good scheme. That aside, she was the *perfect* person to help Christianna make a match. She knew her friend as well as she knew her own heart. Better, even.

All of this, of course, was happening at a most inconvenient time. If the opportunity to meddle in Christianna's affairs had appeared earlier, she might have snatched it up. The part of her that would have rushed headfirst into a matchmaking plot was understandably hesitant after her doomed trip to London—and her failed reunion between brothers. Then there were her feelings for Aidon to contend with. For one, she was out of her mind with want for him. For another, there was the nagging thought of the tombstone in the cemetery. As it turned out, suspicion and desire did not mix well.

Even when desire was winning.

The sound of her name brought her back to the present.

"I have known Persephone my entire life," Christianna was saying cheerfully. She had been seated strategically before Mr. Haskett, who was drinking in her every word with great interest.

Persephone was glad everyone was absorbed in Christianna, because she was very much on edge. Every so often, she would catch Aidon looking at her. There was a glint of something new in his eyes, something she could only identify as hunger.

Something she could only identify because she felt it, as well.

This was part of her newfound freedom. She'd secretly always wanted to experience passion, and now the promise of it was prostrating itself before her. She knew now that it was inevitable—she was desirable and *wanted*. But kisses and sweet nothings did not— could not—fully undo years of grappling with self-loathing. She'd been so sure leaving Honeyfield would have freed her from it.

She promised herself a little grace. Something she had never extended to herself.

"She is the best of us," Christianna gushed. "Nobody has stood up for me quite like she has."

Surely they cannot still be speaking of me.

Aidon glanced at her, a grin pulling at his lips. "You are very lucky to have found each other."

Persephone felt heat spread across her cheeks. "It's not as if Christianna had very many options," she mumbled. Desperate to no longer be the center of attention, she shifted the conversation in what she believed could be a more productive direction. "I am the one who is lucky. Christianna is like no other."

"A few minutes in her company assured me of that," Ezra said after a moment spent processing Persephone's pointed look.

"The feeling is quite mutual," Christianna said shyly.

The remainder of the dinner went smoothly, ending with the gentlemen and ladies breaking apart for evening conversation. As soon as Persephone shut the door to the library behind her, Christianna broke into nervous giggles.

"What are you laughing about?" Persephone asked, despite being fully able to hazard a guess.

Christianna flopped down onto a maroon chaise, her face high with color. "What do you think?"

"Hmm, I'm not sure," Persephone said, feigning innocence. "Could it have to do with a certain Mr. Haskett?"

"You didn't tell me your husband had such charming friends!"

Persephone took a seat by her friend and smiled. "I should have reported this very vital fact to you immediately."

"Don't tease," Christianna said with a pout. "Do you think he liked me?"

He'd adored her in the way everybody who met Christianna did. She had always been easy to love.

"If he didn't, he's a fool," Persephone said plainly.

Christianna let out a contented sigh, turning her head to look out the window. "I've dreamed about this for so long." Her gaze met Persephone's, a guilty smile appearing on her face. "Do you know I was ready to settle for one of the boys in the village?"

Persephone's mouth dropped open. "What?"

"It's true!" Christianna laughed, shaking her head and sitting back. "But now I can barely remember his name."

"Your father would have gone mad," Persephone said. "Why didn't you tell me?"

As innocent and silly as it was, Christianna's admission had stung. They had always shared secrets with one another, so it seemed inconceivable that she hadn't opened up to Persephone about something as significant as her future.

"I thought you might judge me," Christianna said after a long moment, her gray eyes serious. "I was wrong, of course. You've always been a safe place for me to go, Persephone."

"Don't forget that."

"I won't." Christianna giggled again. "Besides, it is of no matter now. Will you help?"

"With what?"

"Mr. Haskett, silly," Christianna whispered, as if she were telling a secret. "I should spend as much time with him as I possibly can."

"You *want* me to meddle?" Persephone asked, raising an eyebrow.

"Yes!" Christianna breathed. "Please meddle."

Persephone smiled. It was one thing to meddle unprompted, and an entirely different thing to meddle when asked. Besides, she could never refuse her closest friend. And, at the very least, she would be meddling in a familiar place, on behalf of a person she knew well, without any of the unknowns that had awaited her in London.

"Have you been getting along with Mr. Barrington?" Christianna asked suddenly, fixing Persephone with a curious look.

They were meant to be discussing matchmaking, not her marriage.

"We get along well enough," Persephone said eventually.

A pause.

"That's *it*?" Christianna demanded. "You get along well enough?"

Persephone huffed in frustration. "Well, what would you have me say?"

That he wants to bed me?

"Oh, I don't know." Christianna gave Persephone a probing look. "Do you love him?"

"*Love?*" Persephone repeated, almost choking on the word. "It's a bit too soon for that, isn't it?"

"Is it?" Christianna asked in disbelief. "I think I fell in love over the course of a single meal."

"Did you?" Persephone laughed. "I wish it were half as easy for me to love people as you do."

"It can be," Christianna said firmly. "You only need to *allow* yourself to love people. The very thought of marriage *and* love, all tied together with a tidy bow is—is—well, I'd do anything for it."

"You've always said so."

"Tell me what I should expect!" Christianna said impatiently.

Persephone sighed, unsure how to answer. "What do you want to know?"

"Everything!" Christianna chirped. "How does it feel?"

Confusing.

"Fine," Persephone said evenly.

"If it were *fine*, you wouldn't be blushing," Christianna said triumphantly, leaning back against the chaise.

"I'm not blushing," Persephone muttered.

"You are," Christianna shot back. "I can only imagine how lovely it must be. The company, being gazed at like you're the most perfect being in creation. I can't wait."

"Yes," she said, wanting to appease her friend. "It's just like that."

"I knew it!" Christianna crowed happily. "Oh, Persephone. I am so happy for you. Really, the ladies of Oxbury deserve nothing less after the hand we've been dealt." A cheeky grin graced her pretty face. "And I should hope to be happy for myself *very* soon, if you understand my meaning."

Persephone laughed and rolled her eyes, pleased that the conversation was back to Christianna's new infatuation with Mr. Haskett. "I think I understand you *very* well."

"Excellent," Christianna said conspiratorially, lowering her voice. "Tell me, how should we proceed?"

"I think I'm in love," Ezra declared dramatically, throwing himself across the chair in Aidon's study.

Aidon tried very hard not to react. This wasn't the first time Ezra had put on such theatrics, and it likely wouldn't be the last. Unless, of course, everything came together just the way Persephone and Ezra hoped it would.

He knew he was being overly pessimistic about all of it, but he'd been desperate for a night alone with Persephone. No Ezra, no Christianna, and certainly no budding matchmaking scheme.

"Do you think she liked me?" Ezra asked pathetically, staring up at the ceiling.

Surprisingly, Aidon did think she'd liked him. She'd responded so well to Ezra's clumsy charms that it had bordered on unusual.

Deciding to take pity on his friend, he said, "I think so."

Ezra shot up and turned toward Aidon. "Oxbury is *magical*. I can't believe you ever thought to leave it."

Yes, magical. As magical a place could be with a forever melancholic mother and a stiff, controlling father. Certainly, his life would have been very different if he'd wandered over to Honeyfield. Persephone had been within arm's length for a sizable portion of his life, tucked away in a floral haven. But he would have been the wrong man for her then, and so fate had led him to London.

"You'll help me, won't you?" Ezra asked, pulling Aidon out of his reverie. "With Miss Errwood, I mean."

"What could I possibly do to help?"

"Oh, come now," Ezra said, cocking his head to the side. "Teach me your ways, Aidon Barrington. You were once one of London's most notorious rakes, after all."

Aidon cringed in embarrassment. "Former rake, thank you."

"Still, you *must* have some advice to give."

"Actually, I do," Aidon said. "Are you ready?"

Ezra nodded, eyes wide with interest.

"Never take advice from a rake."

Ezra deflated. "Why not?"

"Because you aren't one," Aidon said patiently. "And you could never hope to turn whatever nonsensical advice a rake would give you into real action." Pausing, he added, "That was meant to be a compliment."

"Oh, fine," Ezra grumbled. He gave Aidon a pleading look. "You'll still try to help, won't you?"

"I'll see what I can do," Aidon conceded. "Ezra?"

"Yes?"

"Are you serious about this?"

"Of course I am!" Ezra declared. "I knew the minute I saw her. You understand, don't you? You must have known the minute you laid eyes on your wife."

So he had. The minute he had stumbled across her in the library, some part of him had known she was necessary to his very existence.

Aidon examined Ezra for a long moment, taking in his reddened face and nervous demeanor. He was dramatic and ridiculous and quite possibly as serious as Aidon had ever seen him.

"I understand," he said softly, finally. "Though, again, I'm not sure what I could possibly—"

He was interrupted by a knock. Persephone stuck her head around the doorframe as if summoned by their conversation.

"Christianna is about to leave," she said, nodding at the both of them. "We should see her off."

"I'll see her off!" Ezra said, launching himself off the couch. He hesitated at the door. "If that is agreeable to my hosts, of course."

"She hadn't been expecting to stay for so long, so she'll be needing someone to escort her," Persephone said, raising an eye-brow at Aidon and looking pointedly at Ezra.

"I'll take you to the stables," Aidon said, nodding at Ezra, who was all but vibrating with excitement. He darted out of the study and down the stairs before Aidon could blink.

"Well?" Persephone said.

Aidon went to join her at the door. "I never once pictured myself playing matchmaker," he admitted. "I don't think I can talk Ezra out of this."

They walked out into the hallway, their voices kept low.

"You won't have to," Persephone said, suppressed laughter tickling her voice. "Christianna is smitten."

"With Ezra?"

"You don't think he has his charms?"

"He's eager to please, I suppose."

Persephone looked up at him through the corner of her eye. "As Christianna is easily pleased, I'd say it's a perfect match." A smile bloomed on her lovely face after a moment of contem-plation. "I never thought I'd be able to help Christianna like this. It's rather exciting."

Her smile and eager manner of speaking quickly convinced Aidon that he would do anything to help, given how much it clearly mattered to her. As much as he resented Ezra for gracing them with his boisterous presence, playing matchmaker *could* give him a chance to show Persephone just how far he would go to ensure her happiness.

Granted, he could think of at least one other thing he wanted to pour his focus into, but he'd always been able to multitask.

As they descended the stairs, Aidon saw Ezra and Christi-anna once again occupied in enthusiastic conversation by the entrance. Baker stood nearby, holding the door open with an unaffected look on his face. A cool breeze came in from the out-doors, which was now fully plunged into darkness.

"Mr. Haskett said he'd be in Oxbury a week," Persephone whispered conspiratorially. "It isn't a lot of time, but we can work with it."

"Plotting already, are you?" Aidon asked, amused.

"I doubt we'll have to do very much," she said, nodding at the couple by the doorway. "They're already halfway there."

Aidon took her hand and pressed a kiss to her knuckles. "Then I suppose we'll have to help them the rest of the way."

"Yes," Persephone said eagerly. "Christianna's happiness is more important to me than my own."

And yours is important to me.

"I'll be back soon," he promised, running his thumb across her freckled hand. "Very soon."

TWENTY

Persephone paced around her room, feeling like a bubble on the verge of bursting. Aidon wanted her, she wanted him, and yet an unforgiving combination of excitement and dread had her unable to sit still.

And with Mr. Haskett escorting Christianna home, she and Aidon would be alone.

The kisses they'd shared had been deliciously perfect, so it followed that there was absolutely nothing for her to be worried about. But Persephone, for better or for worse, was a worrier. Put her alone in a room, and she could emerge having thought through no less than a hundred scenarios born entirely out of anxiety.

Whenever she was alone with Aidon, she felt like she was on the precipice of something. She had agreed to this marriage to protect her family, yes, but also because she'd known, deep inside her, that it had the potential to bring her closer to something like happiness—freedom.

And if she hesitated to explore every facet of what this marriage had to offer, it was because a small part of her still insisted that she did not deserve affection, and especially not from such a frustratingly handsome, kindhearted man. How would he react upon seeing her naked body, free of the soft curves men were known to favor? And would he notice the not-so-smooth skin on the backs of her thighs? The freckles that dusted the gap between her breasts? She'd told Aidon that she had never heard anybody wax poetic about her beauty, and that was true. She had good days despite it all, but she also knew that some wounds might simply never go away. They would heal, but a scab would always remain. Some insecurities were hard to shake.

"Maybe I should take a bath," she mumbled to herself. The warm water would relax her. She called for a maid and asked for a bath to be prepared, hoping desperately her nerves didn't show. If they did, the elderly woman who appeared to help did not seem to mind. Persephone exchanged awkward small talk with the maid, hoping to distract herself. She was still not used to relying on servants and had a hard time making casual conversation with them.

As was their custom, the maid asked if Persephone required assistance with bathing and was politely declined. She was left alone in the bathing room, steam wafting up from the hot water that filled the deep copper tub. Walking over to the neatly stocked shelves that lined the wall, she selected a glass bottle of lavender oil for her bath. She watched as the oil drops hit the water. Carefully, she removed her clothing and eased herself into the tub, letting a puff of air escape as she adjusted to the temperature of the water. The wet linen felt pleasant against her back, and she reclined, sinking down.

The warm, fragrant bath was meant to distract her, but it was doing a poor job, as Persephone was already thinking about Aidon. She had felt embarrassed before he'd pulled her into that second kiss, thinking she'd mucked up the first one. A rush of affection flooded her as she recounted every last detail of that kiss—and the ones that had followed. While she was still quite sure she knew nothing of love, she was certain of her overwhelming fondness for Aidon. That he was a wonderful kisser helped, too.

Their kisses had been deep and passionate, and she had distinctly felt his hand travel up her slender waist and stop right before he'd reached her breasts. She wondered what it would have felt like if he'd ventured further and, without thinking, ran her palms along her breasts, shivering at the idea of his strong hands grazing her nipples.

Maybe she *did* deserve his affection. Or she would pretend she did, at least in this moment. The bathing room felt safe and separate from the rest of the house, so she could do as she pleased. Long ago, Aidon had been a different man, and she reasoned that his past had likely left him an experienced bedmate. She closed her eyes and ran her hand down, feeling the muscles of her taut stomach spasm in anticipation. If Aidon was experienced, then he would know just how to touch her. She paused at the mound of curls between her legs, easily picturing his handsome face, with its well-defined jaw, proud nose, and those *eyes*. She could see them in her mind, grass green and clouded over with desire. He'd wanted her from the very beginning. There was something about her that drove him *mad*. His words danced about in her head as she gave her core a featherlight touch. It felt different than it usually did because it had never been accompanied by such vivid images. She'd never had urgent kisses to recount or passionate words to remember.

Now, she had Aidon. And, at least in this moment, she was going to enjoy him.

Aidon shivered as he came in from the cold. Ezra, of course, had decided to launch into an entertaining story right as they'd reached the stables, which had kept the whole lot of them out for longer than anticipated. Christianna had listened in fascinated silence, and Aidon had seen just how ridiculously, blessedly easy all of this was going to be.

The polite thing to do would have been to find an appropriate chaperone for Christianna's sake, but Aidon was disinterested in politeness tonight. He and Persephone would have at least an hour of uninterrupted peace, and he meant to take advantage of every minute. Knowing Ezra, he would find a way to linger at Errwood. For once, Aidon was grateful for his friend's penchant for chatter.

He stopped by his room, overcome with the silly desire to check his reflection in a mirror before he sought Persephone out. He assumed he would find her in the library, curled up in the chaise with a large, heavy book. He saw a flicker of his youth in the image reflected back to him, a shadow of a time when women and sex were all he knew. But it was only a flicker that remained, the rest of it having been buried piece by piece over ten long years. Taking one last look in the mirror, he made his way back to the door. It was then he heard the whispered sound of his name.

He paused, confused. Perhaps his mind was playing tricks on him. His eyes traveled around the room, large and outfitted with dark furniture—indeed, no one was there, hiding in the corners. His gaze rested on the door to the bathing room that connected his bedchamber to Persephone's. He swore that he could hear the gentle sloshing of water.

It couldn't be.

Aidon walked toward the door, placing his hand gently on the knob. Perhaps it had been accidentally left open by a maid doing her daily pass through the rooms. He stood there, debating with himself. If Persephone were bathing—and it seemed she was—then he should respect her privacy and leave her to it. What were the chances that she had left the door open on purpose? The very idea that this might be an invitation sent a rush straight to his groin, causing a tightening of his grip on the doorknob.

He would leave her to it. As badly as he wanted Persephone, he was a gentleman. Gentlemen left their wives to bathe in peace. He must have misheard—there was no reason for her to be calling his name.

Well, not yet, anyway.

Just as Aidon released his hold on the knob, he heard his name again, clear as day. It was Persephone, and the sound came out in a heated whisper, just loud enough for him to hear. His entire body stood to attention. She was murmuring his name, and he was suddenly desperate to see what was coaxing such sweet sounds out of her.

He pushed the door open ever so slightly, reveling in the sight before him. She lay in the bath with her eyes shut, steam swirling around her slight, naked body. The heady smell of lavender invaded his senses as he watched her run a hand along her breasts, stopping momentarily to tease a pebbled nipple. Her other hand was out of sight, but it didn't take a scholar to know what she was doing with it.

Aidon watched her in fascinated disbelief. Not only was she touching herself, but she was doing so while thinking of *him*. And if it was him she wanted, then, well, he would be at her beck and call.

Stepping into the room properly, he cleared his throat. Persephone's large eyes shot open, and she sat up in shock, water spilling out of the tub and onto the floor.

"You called?"

Persephone was sure that this was the worst thing that had ever happened to her in her twenty-seven years of living. Embarrassment invaded her veins as she stared at Aidon, who was watching her with a lazy smirk on his face. His eyes traveled downward, and she realized that sitting up had brought her breasts into full view. She blushed violently and sank down, the water lapping at her chin.

"No," she eventually said, her voice coming out in a frustratingly small squeak.

"Are you quite sure?" he asked, taking a few slow steps toward the tub.

Persephone froze, unsure of what to say or do. This *would* happen to her.

"Yes," she squeaked. She cleared her throat and tried again. "Yes, I am quite sure."

But the smirk hadn't left his face, and she was, unfortunately, trapped naked in a tub of hot water.

"Well," he said, the timbre of his voice deliciously low, "as I am already here, perhaps I ought to offer my assistance. After all," he added with a wolfish grin, "it *would* be the gentlemanly thing to do."

Persephone was at a loss. Aidon had always been kind and gentle with her, but even she'd sensed that his kisses hinted at something more. And here that something more was. Standing before her, still slowly approaching the tub, was the confident, experienced man she had been fantasizing about.

The adventurous streak in her decided to rear its wild head, urging her to play along. Persephone, still embarrassed, made a feeble attempt to shoo it away.

She followed Aidon with her eyes, but he soon stepped out of sight, coming to a stop behind her. She remained still, hyperaware that any movement might reveal more skin than was appropriate.

Has propriety ever mattered to you?

It hadn't, yet somehow it was suddenly of utmost importance.

Persephone willed herself to speak in a firm, commanding tone. "While I do appreciate your offer, I am almost done with—"

She was silenced by the delectable sensation of Aidon's lips pressed against the back of her neck. He must have crouched down to her level.

"Done with what?" he asked innocently. Persephone cursed her choice of words as he continued. "What *were* you doing, Persephone?"

The way he said her name sent a fresh jolt of electricity throughout her body. It rolled off his tongue, reverent and sinful all at once: *Per-seph-on-e.* And as for his question, she had been having a grand old time before she'd been interrupted. Perhaps this was punishment for trying to enjoy her body in such an unladylike manner. He pressed another warm kiss to her damp neck, coaxing an answer out of her.

"Nothing at all," she breathed. "I was simply daydreaming. I'm not sure it was very polite of you to interrupt."

"Perhaps not," he murmured, his breath hot against her ear. "What were you daydreaming about?"

Persephone cringed inwardly. She'd started out by recounting their kisses, but her mind had eventually drifted. She'd fallen back into an old and embarrassing favorite, a daydream in which she was the Goddess of Spring. It had been a*lmost* the same, but this time she had been in the Underworld at the mercy of Aidon and his wicked ways, and, dear *God*, it was too embarrassing to even think about.

Lie, damn you.

"Mythology," she blurted out.

What part of "lie" did you misunderstand?

"*Your* myth, perhaps?" he purred.

Persephone suddenly felt like the bath was far too warm. There was no way out of this, and truth be told, a part of her was rather enjoying it. But the weight of her inexperience was telling her to cut this particular encounter short before she made a fool out of herself. Unless, of course, making a fool out of herself was exactly what this situation called for. Perhaps she could embarrass them both out of this room.

"Yes," she said, her voice soft and confident. "I had just found myself in the Underworld."

Another kiss, this time at the junction between her shoulder and neck. Her skin tingled at the contact. He remained silent, apparently waiting for her to continue.

"The wicked Lord of the Dead was just about to have his way with me." She let out a disdainful sniff, hoping he didn't sense how out of her mind with mortification and desire she was. "It is a shame that I was interrupted."

He leaned over, his lips finding her jaw. "A shame indeed. You have my apologies." He ran his fingers along the length of her neck. She shivered. "Please, allow me to make it up to you."

His hand on her damp skin set her entire body aflame. He hadn't seemed to mind her silly little fantasy. In fact, she could have sworn she'd heard a satisfied hum come from behind her. Her embarrassment faded slightly, replaced by curiosity.

"Persephone," he murmured, his hand ghosting along her shoulder, "what would you have me do?"

Persephone swallowed, hard. Was he going to make her *ask* for it?

"I'm not sure," she said shyly, shivering. Every scandalous thing she had ever read flew out of her head and was replaced with a thick fog.

"Let me help you," he offered. "Would you like me to touch you? Help you finish?"

She sighed at the suggestion. This was absolute madness. How had she found herself in this situation? All she'd done was drop a book on a man's head, and now she was in his house on the verge of begging him to touch her.

"Yes, please," she whispered.

She watched in wonder as his fully clothed arm broke the surface of the water. She was trembling in anticipation, and she had to bite down on her tongue when his hand found her breast. As he explored, she wondered how it might feel if he were to use his mouth instead. Oddly, she did not think about how small her breasts were, or whether he might come across a fold of skin.

"You are *lovely*," he growled. He peppered kisses along the back of her neck, and despite how hard she tried to suppress it, a little moan escaped her lips. She had already been close to her peak before he'd entered, her entire body still sensitive.

"Aidon," she forced out, "please."

"Please?" he repeated between hot, tantalizing kisses placed wherever he could reach.

"Just—just touch me. Please."

Persephone's words were music to Aidon's ears. He'd just needed her permission, her shy consent giving him all the courage he needed. Her little Underworld fantasy was utterly beguiling, and it was very clear who she had been picturing as the counterpart to her Goddess of Spring persona.

Persephone's body was soft and taut all at once. Aidon's hand wandered deeper into the water, feeling the warm contours of her figure. He thought about lifting her out of the tub and taking her to his room but decided to let this tantalizing situation play out to completion instead.

"Christ, Persephone," he murmured. "You've no idea how badly I want you."

Fragments of his past self began to creep out, but it was different in a way he couldn't quite describe. He was different, and she was different from any woman he had ever been with.

He finally complied with her request, pushing into her folds to find she was enticingly wet. She gasped as he found her sensitive bud, and he grinned against her neck as she involuntarily pushed against him.

"Is this all for me?" he asked, delving down and dragging her sweet, silky wetness up toward her clitoris. He was rock-hard, and he resisted the urge to attend to himself with his free hand. This was going to be about Persephone, and Persephone only.

"Yes, yes," she said breathily. He felt a thrill shoot through him as she placed her small hand over his much larger one, directing him on how she wanted to be touched. It was clear that she had done this before, the realization causing the tightness in his trousers to become almost painful. He allowed her free rein, following her lead until she came, her hand entwined in his.

She held him against her until she regained her composure. Eventually, she loosened her grip on his hand, and he drew it out from the water, tilting her head toward his for a kiss. Persephone turned to face him fully, the lavender-scented water splashing around her. Sitting on her knees, she placed her hands on either side of his face and kissed him. Aidon wrapped his arms around her naked body, cursing the layers of clothing between them. He felt her damp breasts push against his chest as she pressed against him, breaking away to kiss his face and neck.

The idea that she might want more almost had him reeling. He pulled her to her feet, tugging her out of the bath. She stepped onto the chilly floor and shivered.

"Are you cold?" he asked.

"No, I—"

Persephone suddenly seemed to realize where she was. She crossed her arms over her breasts in a poor attempt to hide them. Her eyes darted around the room, but there was nowhere to go. Aidon gently pried her arms away from her body, bringing a blush to her cheeks.

"There's no need to be shy," he said, giving her what he hoped was an encouraging smile.

"I'm not shy," she protested. He noticed that she kept her eyes on his face, never once straying.

He did not argue. Instead, he wrapped her in a towel that had been sitting on a nearby stool. She looked up at him with her wide, dark eyes as he draped the fabric around her.

"I did not expect you to be so *rakish*," Persephone said quietly.

Aidon froze, his hands resting gently on her hips. If he had overstepped, there would be no going back. If he had disappointed her—well, she would be joining a long, long line of people who felt the same.

"If you'd prefer me otherwise—" he began, but she cut him off with a shake of her head.

"No. It was surprising is all I meant."

Surprising was not disappointing. It was not offense, either. He looked at her, half-drowning in the massive towel, droplets still clinging to her dark eyelashes. The look in her eyes was hopeful. She bit her lower lip delicately, and the gesture almost killed him.

"Well, then." Surprising was not disappointing, he thought again. "Why don't you let me show you just how rakish I can be?"

After Aidon had pushed her over the edge, Persephone had felt bold and uninhibited. *She* had pulled him into that delicious kiss, and *she* had enjoyed the feeling of her bare body pressing against his tragically clothed one. But as soon as she had stepped out of the bath, mortification had seeped back into her bones.

She had only ever done such things in private. Alone, she did not have to worry about how she looked or sounded. Now, it was all she could think about. And *why* had she told him about her silly fantasies?

While Aidon pulled her arms away from her chest, Persephone stole a surreptitious glance downward. The sight of his very obvious erection dashed all insecurities from her mind and replaced them with a new set of worries. What if he wanted her to return the favor? She wanted to, of course, but she didn't know *how*. She had no practical experience to speak of, and she was beginning to realize just how much detail the books at Honeyfield had left out.

"Well, then. Why don't you let me show you just how rakish I can be?"

Persephone felt his bold words travel up her spine.

"What do you have in mind?" she asked, pretending to be brave.

"A kiss," he said innocently, pulling her toward him.

"Is that so rakish?" she asked against his lips.

"Ah, but I didn't say where, did I?" he murmured. He allowed her one quick kiss but swiftly moved on to her jawline, then her neck. She trembled as he pushed the towel off her, the softness of it pooling by her feet. She ran her hands through his dark hair as he came to her breasts, taking her already stiff nipples in his mouth. She let out a soft moan, a noise she had never heard herself make before today. But it just felt so *good*.

How else was she supposed to react? He began to travel downward, settling onto his knees before her. He placed a kiss on her stomach, and she shivered.

"What are you doing?" she gasped, the words strangled.

He planted kisses on her hip bones. "Patience."

Persephone watched as he kissed the tops of her thighs. Her body was unbearably warm, and each kiss sent thousands of sparks down her spine and straight between her legs. She was only vaguely sure of where he meant to go with this, though it seemed innocuous enough. That is, until he placed a lingering kiss on the inside of her thigh. Suddenly, she knew what he meant to do. She felt heat flood her but quickly pushed her desire aside. She was not brave enough to do this here, fully naked, while he remained safely tucked into his disheveled clothing.

"Aidon," she said abruptly and firmly.

He looked up at her, his usually clear eyes clouded with hunger. "Persephone," he responded roughly. He was positioned right at the junction of her thighs, mere inches away from her.

"Mr. Haskett will return soon," she said.

He raised an eyebrow. "Knowing Ezra, he's struck up conversation at Errwood."

"I just—" Persephone pressed her thighs together. "If he were to come back—"

Aidon looked up at her, his expression shifting from one of passion to thoughtfulness. To her relief, he stood up. "You are right. I was not thinking."

Neither was I.

How could she have been? Thinking around Aidon was impossible, and not having her senses about her felt dangerous.

"I will meet you downstairs to wait for Mr. Haskett," she

promised, picking the towel up and wrapping it protectively around herself.

"Perhaps we can continue this another night," he said.

Persephone found herself agreeing before she could even think.

TWENTY-ONE

Matchmaking was blissfully easy when both people were half in love already. After a day of painfully observing both parties tiptoe around each other, Persephone and Aidon had cobbled together a childishly simple plan to grant Ezra and Christianna some privacy with the hopes that it would move things along. Persephone had directed Christianna to meet her in a specific hall on the ground floor so that they might take a turn around the house. It was the same hallway that Mr. Haskett tended to pace in the early evening, muttering facts about beekeeping and skep design under his breath in preparation for her father's grueling tests. Persephone would not be present, naturally. Neither would Aidon, which meant that Ezra, too, would have nobody to converse with *but* his newly discovered object of affection. Persephone did not fault them for their shyness, of course. They were two eager, hopeful romantics with little idea of how to proceed.

In the meantime, the upstairs drawing room in the west wing had finally been deemed acceptable for use, which meant Persephone had a new room to search, this time with Aidon in tow. Combing Gallowsgate for her mother's book had been somewhat disappointing thus far. With about twenty-five rooms to explore, Persephone knew she would soon run out of options. Even with the meager staff he'd requested, Baker was making quick work of the house.

"Was this room used often?" Persephone asked. The drawing room was small and decorated with striped paper-hangings that had not been used anywhere else in the house. A small desk sat in the middle of a row of large windows. On either side of the fireplace sat a pair of low, freshly dusted shelves, the tops of which were decorated with white porcelain figures. Persephone walked over to examine them, picking up a shepherdess with a finely painted pink skirt.

"We mostly used the downstairs parlor," Aidon said, coming to stand behind her. "My mother loved those figurines. She regretted leaving them here, she always said. I should have brought her back to fetch them."

The regret in his voice was palpable. Persephone gently returned the figurine to the shelf. "I'm sure she wouldn't have wanted you to distress yourself over it."

"No, she wouldn't have," he said. "She could never bring herself to inconvenience others. Only herself."

Persephone nodded. That was simply the way women were raised to behave.

Trinkets aside, the shelves were empty. Persephone wandered to the center of the room, examining the upholstery on the chairs that had been arranged in a circle, with small tables scattered among them to hold tea or biscuits. The fabric was a slightly frayed deep purple, something that could be easily addressed with Baker's help.

Against the right-hand wall stood a chest of drawers, begging to be searched. The first drawer was empty save for a single book. It was too small to be the one she was looking for, but Persephone picked it up all the same. Flowers had been pressed between its blank pages, and as she flipped through them, she realized that they were all flowers she'd seen at Honeyfield. She imagined Emmeline bringing them here to stark Gallowsgate, where Aidon's mother had endeavored to preserve them.

"Do you think Christianna and Mr. Haskett are sorting themselves out?" she asked, gingerly turning the page of the book to see what appeared to be the remnants of a small primrose. She glanced over her shoulder to see Aidon pulling open the drawer of the writing desk.

"I should hope so," he said, shuffling through a few pieces of paper. "Though Ezra might have lost his ability to form coherent sentences in Miss Errwood's—"

He stopped speaking so abruptly that Persephone stopped what she was doing to cast a worried look in his direction. "Aidon? What is it?"

"A letter," he said, holding it out for her to take. She placed the book of pressed flowers back in its drawer and went to his side, eyes scanning the page she now held.

7 August 1793

Dear Tabitha,

Thank you for your letter. I do so appreciate your invitation to spend autumn in Kent with your family, but I doubt my husband will hear of it. He prefers for the boys and I to remain at Gallowsgate this time of year, though I could not tell you the specific reason why. It has been terribly lonely and gray here as of late. I've been instructed not to mix with the other families, and it has been a long, long time since I have been allowed to see the only friend I've made here. I suppose I could do it in secret, but I fear Charles's reaction should he find me out. Oh, Tabitha. I wish I could leave! I so badly want to run away, even if that is not an option for myself or any other woman in my position. What would become of the boys? Unless I were to prevail myself on family, I could never scrape together the means to care for them. And I would never leave them with their father—never. We have never discussed it directly, but I know they are aware that Charles holds no affection for them. He simply does not understand that they are children, and if he showed them love and patience, they would grow up to be perfect gentlemen.

I cannot, naturally, send this letter now. What would you think of me? You'd shake your head and think, 'Oh, dear, Violet has gone mad, imagining—

The letter cut off suddenly, as if its writer had been interrupted.

"Your mother wrote this?" she asked, looking up to see a distant look in Aidon's eyes. She glanced back down at the letter, rereading the line about the only friend Violet had made in Oxbury.

Emmeline, no doubt.

He nodded grimly, taking the letter from Persephone. "Responding to her second cousin."

"She loved you."

"Yes," he said. "But it would be another ten years before my father died. If it hadn't been for us, perhaps she'd have found a way to escape him."

Persephone shook her head. "Do not torture yourself with things you know to be untrue. Women rarely have the means to escape."

He dropped the letter back in the drawer, sliding it shut. "A hopeless situation, then."

She took his hand in hers, giving it a reassuring squeeze. "Not hopeless. She had you and your brother."

"And look at us now," he said bitterly.

Persephone gave him a gentle smile. "Look at *you*. She would be proud of the life you've built for yourself—for us."

Something softened in his eyes. "She'd have adored you."

They stood in silence, focused intently on one another. Memories of the bathing room came flooding into Persephone's mind, and she felt heat creep up her neck.

Of all the inappropriate times!

"I think we've given them enough time to leave for that walk, don't you?" she asked, referring to Ezra and Christianna. "I don't think we run the risk of interrupting them. Though let me just—" She returned to the chest of drawers and pulled the remainder of the compartments out. Empty.

"I'm sure it'll turn up," he said.

Persephone swallowed her disappointment and turned to him with a smile. "Yes, I'm sure. Shall we?"

They made their way downstairs, where, to Persephone's surprise, they heard voices. And footsteps. Before Persephone could think, she shoved her husband into a convenient alcove, making sure to pull the curtain shut behind them. She then heard Ezra and Christianna walk by, snippets of their conversation reaching her ears. They were talking about—*wool*?

"They must have decided to take a turn around the house," she whispered, realizing the alcove was far too small for two.

"If you wanted me alone, you could have asked," Aidon said, amused. "We needn't have come downstairs at all."

Persephone was at a loss for words, still trying to figure out where her calculations had gone astray and trying very hard not to think about how perfectly her body fit against his.

"Were they discussing *wool*?" Aidon asked.

Persephone sighed. "They keep quite a lot of sheep at Errwood."

"Perhaps we might encourage them to take a more direct approach." Aidon shifted against her, and it felt *good*. A liquid heat began to pool in her stomach as he brushed against her again, the alcove unforgivingly tight.

"That won't work with Christianna," she forced out, heart close to bursting right out of her chest. "And besides, what does that even—"

"May I show you?"

"I asked, so—"

She was interrupted by Aidon capturing her mouth in a searing, desperate kiss. Her knees buckled almost immediately, and she balled her fists up in his crisp white shirt for balance.

"What was that for?" she whispered when they parted, his warm breath fanning across her cheek.

"You asked what taking a more direct approach meant. That was your answer."

"Christianna would never do that," Persephone said, still holding onto Aidon for dear life. "It'd be improper."

"And what of us?" Aidon murmured.

Persephone strained to read his expression in the low light. "What of us?"

"The sooner this is over, the sooner the two of us can be alone."

"Is that what you want?"

"Of course it is," he said breathlessly. He paused, his next words hesitant. "Is—is that what *you* want?"

Persephone had no idea why the prospect of letting him in completely was so terrifying to think about. Her body wanted it with an intense fervor, yet her mind couldn't stop listing all the things that could go wrong, and her heart—well, she didn't know what her heart wanted. Aidon had gone along with every little thing she'd suggested, never once making her feel silly or power-less. He made her feel wanted in a way she had never felt before.

"Persephone?"

"Yes," she said, the word leaving her mouth before she could even think. "Of course it's what I want." She let out a breath. "I should find Christianna."

"What happened to not wanting to interrupt them?"

"They're discussing wool," she said flatly, wiggling out of the alcove. She saw that the hall was blessedly empty, until—

"I thought I heard you!"

Persephone jumped, turning to see Christianna and Ezra rounding a corner to approach them.

"Oh!" Persephone said, casting a surreptitious glance at Aidon. "I was supposed to meet you. I'm so sorry."

"It's all right," Christianna said, her cheeks rosy with ex-citement. "Mr. Haskett kept me quite amused. I just wanted to make sure I found you before I left."

"So soon?" Persephone asked.

"I am off to Honeyfield," Ezra said, his face also flushed. "I offered Chr—Miss Errwood an escort home if she desired it."

"Honeyfield?" Persephone echoed.

"Your father and I are off to buy supplies at dawn tomor-row," Ezra said, sounding rather put-upon. "He's invited me to spend the night so as to avoid any delay."

"Allow us to walk you to the entrance," Aidon said gra-ciously, though he trailed behind with Persephone. "It seems that we'll be getting exactly the time we need."

Persephone's heart hammered in her chest. "It seems so."

Aidon watched Persephone as she sipped her wine at the dinner table. He focused on the curve of her pink lips, the gentle slope of her nose, the fire behind her large, deep-set eyes. Dinner had barely started, and already he felt it was dragging.

The clearing out of Gallowsgate had been nothing short of a miracle, but he still wondered if Persephone would join him after dinner. She had vocalized as much, but he'd been able to see the uncertainty in her eyes in the bathing room even through the fog of his desire. He'd relented, giving her space, even though it had taken Ezra hours to return. Worry coursed through him as he considered that their guest may not have been the only issue—what remained of the scoundrel in him had come so easily to the surface, desperate to please her. She had taken it in stride, seemed to enjoy it, even, but perhaps he should have tried harder to suffocate his impulsiveness. It should not have been a challenge—it was what he had done for the past ten years, after all.

Persephone caught him studying her, and he was pleased to see a pretty blush creep along her skin.

"Is there something wrong?" she asked, self-consciously running a hand through her short hair.

"Not at all," he said, offering her a charming smile. "I was simply thinking."

"Will I regret asking you to elaborate?"

Ah, there was the mischievous streak he adored. He debated whether to let her know just what had been on his mind but remembered the worry that had clouded her eyes and the pregnant silence that had descended upon them in the alcove—and decided against it.

"How long until an engagement, do you think?"

Persephone's face brightened. "Not long. They would make a wonderful couple. Mr. Haskett is easygoing and kind—just the sort of person Christianna deserves."

"What of yourself?" he asked, derailing the conversation.

"I beg your pardon?"

"What did you think you deserved?"

"I'm not sure I understand your question."

He knew she did. The shy, unsure expression on her face betrayed her.

"Who did you picture for yourself?" he questioned. Smiling, he added, "Back when you had the luxury, I mean."

"Nobody," she said swiftly.

He raised his eyebrows in surprise. "Nobody at all?"

"Women do think of other things, you know," she said dryly over the rim of her glass. "It seemed a little pointless, being in Oxbury."

"You had suitors, though," he reminded her.

She grimaced. "I was embarrassed by the speed at which they excused themselves, but it was likely for the best. It always felt wrong, somehow."

"Tell me about them," he said, unable to help himself.

Persephone propped her head in her hand. "The first one was *very* interested in the business of honey—so much so that I suspect he'd mostly come to assess Honeyfield's suitability over mine. Though I suppose both of us failed that test. The second man was looking for a wife to prepare his wards for their debut. I do not need to explain how I did not fit his needs. So it is just as I said—I pictured nobody." She glanced at him over the rim of her glass. "Who did you think you would marry?"

He'd never had a list of requirements or hidden desires. For ten years, he hadn't thought about it at all until he'd felt the need to cut Cassius off from the family accounts.

"Nobody," he said, grinning.

"I suppose I am something of a step up from nobody," she said primly.

"As am I," he countered.

She laughed at this, the sound melodic and lovely. "Christianna always had a *somebody* in mind. Maybe it wasn't Oxbury. Maybe it was me. I couldn't have matched her knight in shining armor if I'd tried."

"You could still try," he said.

He might have fit the part had he not been labeled the Lord of the Dead. But Persephone wasn't the knight in shining armor type—she struck him as the sort of person who had always fought her own battles, as well as the battles of those she loved. She'd sooner need a squire, being something of a knight herself.

"Perhaps," she said shyly, slowly, breaking eye contact. "If I had to *try*, I suppose I'd picture someone just like you."

Twenty-Two

The truth was Persephone did not know what she deserved. She'd always had a vague idea of the sort of man she'd hoped to marry but had never allowed herself to construct an imaginary partner, knowing it would lead to disappointment. But when Aidon had asked her to try, an image had appeared in her head with very little trouble.

If she'd let herself try over the years, she would have easily pictured someone like Aidon.

Her response had ignited a flame in him, and his hot kisses passed that hunger along to her. She was now inside her husband's bedchamber, pushed against the door by his strong body. They were both partially undressed already, his thigh finding its way between her legs. She wiggled against the fabric of his trousers, reveling in the shocks of pleasure that coursed through her. She didn't have time to think or feel insecure or even worry— what was it she had been so concerned about earlier in the week? She could no longer remember.

Persephone freed Aidon's crisp shirt from his black trousers, letting a curious hand travel along the planes of his abdomen.

He was hard beneath her touch, just as she'd imagined he'd be. Aidon hummed in pleasure at her exploration as he ran his lips down her neck. He broke away, pulling his shirt over his head. Persephone pressed a hand to his chest before he could continue his ministrations.

She began to remove the rest of her clothing, distracting herself by taking a long, appreciative look at her husband. His chest was dusted in dark hair, and she took note of a slightly visible trail that led to his barely concealed erection. A spurt of worry bubbled up, disappearing when she met Aidon's eyes. He was looking at her as if she were the most exquisite creature he had ever seen. She smiled shyly at him as her clothing fell around her feet, revealing her naked body to him for the second time. He sighed, seemingly in approval, and pulled her against him. She pressed a kiss against the corner of his mouth, relishing the sensation of her breasts against his well-defined chest.

Persephone gasped as Aidon lifted her off the floor, tossing her easily over his shoulder. He set her down gently on the foot of the bed, falling to his knees before her and taking her face in his hands.

"Tell me what you need," he said.

Persephone blinked rapidly, her hand finding its way to his wrist. She felt incredibly small, sitting here before him without a shred of clothing on. What *did* she want?

Ask him to continue what he started, a voice in her head suggested. She balked at the thought. She'd been flooded with uncertainty the last time he'd kneeled before her. Why would she want to revisit that?

Persephone looked down at her own body, catching sight of the way her pale skin glowed in the firelight. She absentmindedly thought it a pretty picture, made prettier by Aidon waiting patiently, caressing her face and allowing his thumb to trace the outline of her lips.

"What you tried to do in the bathing room," she said meekly.

He smiled, but only briefly. "You are sure?"

So he had seen the doubt in her eyes before.

"Yes," she said. Then softly, sweetly, "Please, Aidon."

Persephone was momentarily shocked at herself. She hadn't been aware of her ability to speak with such sugary lightness, and she had never been one to beg. What was he *doing* to her?

He pressed a soft kiss to her stomach, and she felt her muscles tighten.

"Lie back," he said, placing a reassuring hand on her hip. "And if you need me to stop, I will. You have my word."

Strangely, it was those words that caused her to become aware of the slick ache between her legs. She lay back, staring up at the dark canopy of his bed. Persephone closed her eyes, shuddering at the sensation of Aidon's lips ghosting along her inner thigh. The light scrape of his jaw against her skin would have made her giggle if it hadn't also sent a shot of desire straight to her center. Just as she wondered what she was meant to do with her hands, Aidon ran a finger up her slit, causing her to grasp the crimson sheets with a sudden ironlike strength.

She was very, *very* wet, she knew. Aidon wrapped his strong hands around her thighs and pulled her slightly toward him, propping the backs of her knees on his broad shoulders. Now she was fully open to him, with no way for her to hide. Persephone tilted her head up to look at him, catching sight of his satisfied, wolfish smirk.

"Must you look so proud?" she demanded.

He did not respond. Instead, he lowered his head and ran his tongue between her folds, pulling a moan from her throat. The sensation was like nothing she had ever felt before. A delicious, frantic buzz overtook her body as he continued to explore her, savoring the sensitive bundle of nerves that so desperately called for his attention. Persephone felt her entire body grow hot. She gripped furiously at the sheets, trying and failing to keep her composure. Gasps and moans escaped her, and she soon gave up trying to keep them to herself. A delightful, intense pressure began to build, and she knew she was only moments away from becoming completely undone.

"Aidon—I—" she forced out, cut off by her own gasps.

"Come for me, Persephone," he coaxed, and it was those shockingly inappropriate words, words that she had never heard said aloud before, that sent her over the edge.

Persephone felt herself burst, a thousand sparks traveling in waves throughout her body. She lay back, allowing her climax to run its course. She shivered in delight, finally able to loosen her grip on the sheets. Aidon pressed a kiss to her hip bone, pulling himself up to align his body with hers, the push of his thigh between her legs sending another shower of sparks shooting through her. He kissed her, and she could feel his smile against her jaw.

She was unsure of what to say, so she simply said, "Thank you."

"Do not thank me just yet," he murmured, nuzzling her neck. "I am not done with you."

He shifted, and the push of his erection against her leg filled her with anticipation and anxiety.

"How are you feeling?" he asked, his clear green eyes searching. Every look he had ever given her had been so open, so transparent. She was nothing like that, and the realization made a tiny seed of guilt sprout in the pit of her stomach.

She turned away. "Must you always ask me questions?"

Aidon took her chin in his hand, forcing her to look at him. His expression was playful, and there was a glimmer of something else in his eyes. Something like awe, something that told Persephone he took pleasure in having her with him. "You are welcome to ask me a question instead, if you prefer."

Ever the gentleman, except when I am at his mercy, she thought wryly.

"Very well," she said. She ran her fingers through his soft, disheveled hair. "What do *you* need, Aidon?"

He chuckled, the sound dark and low. "I need to—"

Persephone did not find out, as they were interrupted by a sharp, loud knock before he could form the words.

Aidon cursed, fully prepared to brutally murder whoever had knocked on the door. Persephone shot up in surprise, scrambling to pull a sheet over her naked body.

"I should go," she said nervously, casting her gaze to the door that led to her bedchamber.

Aidon retrieved his shirt from the floor, pulling it haphazardly over his bare chest. "No. Stay, Persephone."

She remained on his bed, wrapped up and looking very small and unsure. He was desperate to return to her, to hold her against him. Whatever the disturbance, he would take care of it quickly.

He cracked the door open and was surprised to see Baker on the other side.

"I apologize for the interruption, sir."

"What is it?" Aidon demanded, fully aware of how harsh his tone was.

"Urgent post from London," Baker said simply, handing Aidon a letter. The lettering on the front indicated that the message was from Chase. Aidon took the note, thanked Baker, and retreated into the room.

Persephone had not budged. She was biting at her lower lip in worry.

"Urgent?" she echoed.

It had better be, he thought.

With an apologetic glance, Aidon tore the wax seal on the letter and quickly began to scan its contents. A string of curses popped into his head. Did this have to happen *now*? He sighed, suddenly angry at his father. He crumpled the paper up in his hands, concealing what Charles Barrington had worked to hide for years. Persephone watched him nervously. She had loosened her hold on the sheet, giving him an enticing look at her soft, luminous skin.

"Persephone, I—"

She shook her head. "I understand."

She did not, and he was glad for it.

Persephone slid off the bed, leaving her covering behind. She seemed completely unaware of what the sight of her naked body did to him as she gingerly picked her clothing up, holding the small pile against her chest.

"Persephone," he said, strangled.

She walked up to him, placing a butterfly-light kiss on his cheek. "I will see you in the morning."

He watched her leave, gently closing the door behind her. He sighed and turned back to the letter. It seemed that the Lord of the Dead had some work to do.

Twenty-Three

Persephone awoke before the sun, her room still awash in moonlight. She turned over in her bed, hoping in vain that a new position would help her sleep. But it was no use—she was wide awake. Wide awake, and with a head full of unruly thoughts.

Allowing herself to be known was nothing short of mortifying—and freeing. She felt closer to Aidon with every passing interaction and every fleeting touch. And it had happened no matter how hard she'd tried to prevent it, no matter how terrified she'd been. A deeper part of her had wanted to reach out, to be seen, and that was the part she had ultimately listened to after having ignored it her entire life.

And the more time she spent with him, the more she saw that her husband was as softhearted as they came. She could hurt him very easily if she were not careful.

Persephone snorted into her pillow. Aidon was not the only softhearted being in this house. She herself had gone soft. She heard it in her voice, and she felt it in her chest. She'd thought herself capable of detached indifference, which was almost amusing considering the intense pull she'd felt when they'd met in the library that first day. She felt her body grow warm under the sheets as she remembered what had transpired between them mere hours ago. She hadn't imagined it possible, but he'd made her forget all her insecurities with a single tender touch. It made her question how well she truly knew herself. Perhaps Aidon saw what she had not allowed herself to see all these years.

She also wondered at the urgent post he'd received, allowing it to fuel the fire of her imagination. Was it from his brother, perhaps? She hoped not, as the very thought of Cassius sent a shiver of discomfort through her. It most likely had to do with his work. But if it was about work—what were the odds of it being related to the gossip that relentlessly hung around him like a haunting specter?

You are being foolish, she scolded herself. Perhaps she was desperately looking for a scandal, searching for a fault to protect herself from the inevitable. And, truth be told, she did not want to think too deeply on what the inevitable was. It was a feeling too deep for her even to imagine, and she was at risk of falling right into it.

Persephone thought back to what Aidon had told her about his past. If he had been like Cassius, he must have been loved like him, too. Now he was little more than an outcast, seemingly pushed away by a social circle that had preferred merriment over responsibility. She understood him in a way because she had been an outcast on the rare occasions she had been given the opportunity to socialize with strangers. It was not easy, and she could not imagine putting up with it after having had a taste of popularity. Aidon did not deserve the gossip, nor did he deserve his loneliness.

And for all the hearsay, Persephone had remained untouched by his allegedly unlucky profession. Perhaps living in London would have made it more difficult to forget, but Aidon seemed content to stay in Oxbury. She imagined it made very little difference to him. Being isolated in Oxbury had to be easier than being isolated in town, where unwanted seclusion was indicative of a poor reputation.

Finally, she drifted to sleep, waking up from a fitful, shallow slumber the next morning. Almost immediately, she was presented with a letter from Venus. She read it in bed, wishing she had more time to rest. Apparently, Mr. Haskett's tutelage was ending soon, and Venus and Solomon were making for the seaside for two weeks after he returned to London. Persephone was being asked to watch over Honeyfield during their absence. An inconvenient request, but she knew her father likely saw shutting down the entire household as a waste of time. The irony of being asked to return to care for her realm of springtime and flowers after a stint at dark, sterile Gallowsgate did not escape her. To her surprise, the thought of returning to Honeyfield did not fill her with dread. It seemed that time away from it had transformed it in her mind. In the past, she'd thought of it as a cage. Now, she simply thought of it as her old home. And she did not have to remain there for longer than necessary. Having the option to leave made everything that much more bearable.

A gentle knock pulled her out of her reverie. Persephone had no time to leave the bed before Aidon slipped into the room, closing the door behind him. She felt strangely shy seeing him in the light of day, especially after the intimacy they had shared the night before. He, too, appeared exhausted and disheveled, and Persephone wondered if he had stayed up all night, drowning in work.

"Good morning," she said, hoping to ease the awkwardness in her chest. Her pulse spiked as he came to sit beside her, reaching out to caress her face. She felt herself grow warm at the contact, suddenly desperate to kick the coverlet off her body.

"I thought I might check on you," he said, exhaustion apparent in his voice. "You usually leave your room well before noon."

"Is it truly so late?" Persephone asked, shaking her head in disbelief. "I had trouble sleeping."

"I must apologize for last night," he murmured. "That is not the way I had intended for it to end."

"Do not apologize," Persephone said, feigning confident nonchalance and hoping he could not hear the wild beating of her heart. "It was not your fault."

"No." He fixed her with a searing look. "But you deserved far more than that."

Persephone stared at him helplessly, wishing she had the courage to say the same to him. After all, he deserved his share of pleasure as well. The words would not leave her mouth.

"I've been asked to go to Honeyfield," she said abruptly, offering him the letter. He took it from her gently, quickly scanning its contents. His face fell in dismay.

"Two weeks," he said softly, looking up from the letter.

"It will give you time to attend to your work," she said, taking the letter from him and folding it up into a neat square. "There will be no distractions."

He grinned, leaning toward her for a kiss. "Ah, but you are a most welcome distraction, Persephone."

She indulged herself by closing the gap between them and slanting her lips over his. She was tempted to deepen it, to drag him toward her, but he pulled away.

"I suppose it will give me time to return to London," he said, lips still grazing hers. He pulled back to give her a devastatingly charming smile. "Speaking of London . . . Ezra is heading back soon."

"Perhaps you can travel together, then. Will you encourage him to return to Oxbury?"

"He likely already has plans to," he said with a laugh. "For all we know, he'll be ready to propose before you've returned from Honeyfield."

Persephone tugged at his shirt, drawing him toward her. She pressed a kiss to his jaw. As time-consuming as matchmaking could be, there was something pleasant about working to bring people together.

Aidon cupped Persephone's face in his hands, regarding her with such tenderness that she was unable to hold his gaze. "When will you go?" he asked gently.

"Tomorrow," she replied. "I am far too tired to even think of moving today."

"As am I." He cast a suggestive glance at the empty space in her bed. "Might I join you?"

Persephone felt a smile tug at her lips. "And what are your intentions, Mr. Barrington?"

He gave her a look of complete and utter innocence. "They are entirely honorable, Mrs. Barrington."

Persephone felt herself blush at his use of her married name. It was not as if she hadn't heard it before—it simply sounded different to her now, somehow *meant* something different.

"Very well," she agreed, forcing seriousness into her voice. "But do behave."

"You have my word," he said.

The phrase brought back vivid memories from the night before, and she found herself wishing that they had not been interrupted.

They curled into one another, and Persephone welcomed the warmth that radiated off his body. He held true to his word, drifting off to sleep with Persephone following not far behind.

Aidon shifted, reveling in the sensation of waking up with Persephone by his side. They had taken an odd, winding path toward intimacy, but he was glad of it, glad that they had given it the space and time it had needed to blossom properly. He had spent so long struggling to find his place in the world following his father's death, never fully able to extricate himself from the work he'd taken on. Every time he'd thought about returning to *living*, returning to the social engagements and company, he'd heard his father's scolding voice in his head. And when he'd finally allowed himself to look up, it was too late. It had felt as if whatever place he might have occupied no longer existed. But it seemed that struggle had led him straight to Persephone.

Based on the shadows that stretched across the room, they had slept the entirety of the day away. His exhaustion did not surprise him, given how he had ended the previous night. Chase had enclosed a lengthy list of questions from a new client, with a note that indicated a swift response was necessary. He often received such letters, ones that demanded reassurance written by men who were particularly protective of their secrets. With no other choice, Aidon had spent the night penning a response with the sole purpose of quelling his client's nerves.

He felt Persephone move against him, her thin cotton nightgown soft beneath his palms. She spoke, her voice thick with sleep.

"Is it nighttime already?"

"It is," he replied quietly.

She turned toward him, large eyes glowing in the bright moonlight. "It seems your intentions were honorable after all."

He smiled, deciding that decency would be wasted at this hour. "At the moment, my intentions are anything but."

"You would think otherwise if you saw me properly. I'm sure I look a fright."

He regarded her carefully, drinking her in. Her short hair was sticking up in every direction, and she was still blinking the sleep from her eyes.

"You are beautiful, Persephone," he whispered. Her tone had been teasing, but he wanted—needed—her to know.

She did not reply, instead placing a tender kiss on his neck. He gathered her close, inhaling the now familiar smell of lavender.

"Your intentions," she reminded him, speaking into his shirt.

He delighted in her transparent effort to tempt him. If it was what she was after, then he would not deny her.

"I want you," he said. He felt her tighten her grip on his shirt. "I wanted you the day I saw you. Is that what you want to hear? You were unlike anything I had ever seen before. I was sure that you were a forest nymph or some other figment of my imagination."

"Imagine your disappointment at discovering that I am very much human," she said dryly.

He laughed, running a hand through her soft hair. "I would not call what I felt disappointment."

Persephone hummed in acknowledgment, the sound happy and satisfied.

"Do you want me now?" she asked innocently.

"Desperately," he replied, his voice strangled. "And yourself?"

"Your questions are maddening," she said, exasperated. She gripped the collar of his shirt and gave him a hungry kiss. He held her against him for a moment before lifting himself over her. Trailing kisses down her neck, he snaked a hand underneath her nightgown to brush at her center. The anticipation had made her wet, just as it had made him hard. She sighed at the touch, lifting her hips to push against him. He needed her like nothing else he had ever needed in his life. He sat back on his knees, and her protests were silenced as he slowly, deliberately peeled her nightgown off her. The moonlight illuminated her skin, giving her an otherworldly glow.

That was his Persephone. Not of this world. So unique were her features, sharp and soft all at once, and so intelligent and fiery was her nature that she had to be visiting from beyond the veil that separated humans from the fae-folk, or from Mount Olympus itself.

He pulled his shirt off and stepped out of the bed to remove his trousers, desperate to be rid of his clothing. Persephone sat up to watch him, instantly taking note of his freed erection.

"Will you fit?" she asked, uncertainty and nervousness lacing her voice. He knew she did not mean it as a compliment but rather as an acknowledgment of the glaring size difference between their bodies.

He kneeled on the floor, pulling her toward the edge of the bed, hands pushing into her soft, pliable skin.

"Don't worry, my love," he rumbled, the endearment slipping out without thought. "I will make sure you are good and ready."

Persephone opened her mouth to question him further, but his tongue between her thighs pulled a pleasant gasp out of her instead. He took his time, enjoying the mewling sounds of pleasure that escaped her. The noises she made were soft, but her tight grip on the sheets told him that she was in ecstasy. He focused on her sensitive nub, and she placed a small hand on the back of his head in an attempt to keep him in position. He very carefully pushed a finger into her, and she shivered. He moved slowly, only adding a second finger when he felt she was ready. When she was gasping his name, unable to take it any longer, he stopped.

She sat up, indignant. He gently pushed her onto her back, silencing her. Positioning himself over her, he wedged his hips between her slender thighs. He kissed her face gently.

"I need you, Persephone," he murmured. "But if you ask me to stop, I will."

She nodded, her trustful gaze making him aware of his wildly beating heart. He fit himself against her and pushed his way into her slick heat as slowly as he possibly could. She held onto his shoulders with an ironlike grip until he had buried himself to the hilt inside of her. He remained motionless, giving her time to adjust.

"You feel so good, Persephone," he panted, pushing his self-control to its limit. "So good."

Persephone looked up at her husband, blood hot in her veins as he showered her in whispered encouragements. Her entire body was aflame, having almost been brought to climax by his deft tongue and nimble fingers. But this was better than that, more intimate, and she had only felt the slightest shock of pain before adjusting. He had promised that she would be ready, and she was.

She had instigated this for no other reason than the fact that she'd wanted to. She'd worried about being rejected, about her forwardness, but she hadn't felt any shame. She wanted this, wanted him, and had felt the same lustful spark he had admitted to when he had first stumbled upon her in his—now their—library.

He began to move, each thrust stronger and less controlled than the last. Persephone ran her fingers though his hair, down his arms and shoulders and back, gasping out his name before he captured her lips in a bruising kiss. She loved the way his large, muscular body felt over her slight one, the way his stubble scraped over her skin, the way he chanted her name as if he were praying to the actual Goddess of Spring. He ran his hands down her sides, cupping her breasts to tease her nipples. She felt that now familiar pressure begin to build in her belly, sending shocks of delicious pleasure throughout her entire body.

"I am going to—" she forced out, cut off by an intense orgasm that shot through her veins with abandon. She clenched around his length, and he carried her through her climax with smooth, deep thrusts. He came soon after, growling her name into her ear.

Persephone panted, trying to catch her breath. Aidon pushed himself off her, laying on his side and gazing at her reverently, a flicker of worry ghosting across his handsome face.

"I didn't hurt you, did I?" he asked, cupping her cheek in his hand.

"No," Persephone laughed. "I think you did the exact opposite."

He gave her a rakish grin—goodness, how she adored that grin—and leaned over to kiss her gently. He pulled her toward him, tangling his limbs with hers. They lay together in silence, and he eventually drifted off to sleep. Persephone lay in his arms, sleepy, but also alert, and focused on one particular thing.

He had, after all, called her *my love*.

TWENTY-FOUR

Sunlight filtered through the curtains of Persephone's room. She stretched her naked body languidly and sighed.

She had not slept very well. The echo of Aidon's endearment had plagued her. He probably had not meant it to be taken seriously, but the words had been startlingly new to her ears. Sleep had only come when she had convinced herself that he'd said them in the passion of the moment.

Aidon still slept, and she shifted to look at him. He looked peaceful, his brow smooth. Light shadows lingered on the delicate skin beneath his eyes, and Persephone wondered if he had gotten very much sleep himself.

"Have you had your fill?"

The words, spoken in what sounded like a purr, made Persephone start in surprise. Aidon was smiling, his green eyes focused on her.

"I didn't mean to stare," she said, embarrassed.

He stretched, and this time she *did* mean to stare. She was mesmerized by the hard planes of his body and the muscles of his arms. They had felt so delicious against her own pliable softness, her sharp hip bones be damned. She was so distracted that she barely felt him pull her naked form against his. He pressed a kiss to her forehead.

"Can I convince you to spend another day in bed?" he asked, grinning wolfishly.

Persephone blushed, her skin tingling where his hands stroked her body. "I'm afraid I'm needed at Honeyfield."

He sighed. "And I am needed in London."

She studied him, noting the tension he now held in his jaw.

"I'm sorry," she blurted out.

"Whatever for?" he asked.

"London distresses you."

His expression softened. "You've no need to apologize for that."

"You won't see your brother, will you?" she asked softly. Anxiously.

"No," he answered immediately. "He and I—some things are too far gone to be repaired, and I think we crossed that line a long time ago."

Persephone remembered Ezra's words. He had said something very similar.

"Was it always like this between you?" she asked, curious.

He turned, his gaze focused on the canopy above them. "Actually, no. We understood each other quite well. A consequence of being so alike, I suppose."

"But then he refused to take on the business," she murmured, studying his serious face.

He frowned. "I heard my father offer it to him. It was a few days before he passed. When Cassius refused, Father begged him to reconsider."

"Why would he do such a thing?"

Aidon glanced at her from the corner of his eye. She caught a glimmer of pain flicker across his face.

"*Aidon will drive it into the ground,*" he said slowly. "I didn't know—he had always been disappointed in the both of us, but I didn't know that he'd seen me as the greater of the two evils."

"You aren't," Persephone said. She sat up, crossing her legs beneath her and giving him a hard look before repeating, "You aren't."

He looked up at her. "Perhaps I was. When I heard Cassius refuse, I was fully prepared for everything to be handed off to the next cousin. Anyone but me. But when I heard what Father said, I—I felt this intense desire to prove him wrong."

"You took responsibility," Persephone said gently, brushing a lock of hair away from his face. "I understand."

"I became *obsessed* with making sure I did not disappoint my father any longer. And that meant running the place exactly the way he had, with plans to eventually pass it down to my child. Continuing what he started." He turned to look at her, his tone apologetic. "And, like a fool, I bring up the subject of children without even asking you if it is something you even want. It has been ten years, and *still* the selfish parts of me slip through with little trouble."

Persephone was bewildered and completely caught off guard. She placed her hand over his and bent so that she could look him right in the eye. "A different man would not have given a second thought to what it is I want."

A long silence passed before he responded. "But is that something you want?"

"Children?" Persephone said, tilting her head. The thought terrified her, but then most things did. She'd always assumed she would one day be a mother, and now she was being given the chance to *choose* when that time would come. "Someday, though not today."

He let out a relieved exhale. "I am in no rush. It is your decision to make—do what you will to keep it from taking."

The intensity with which he put her desires before his rocked her to her core. Another man might have demanded she begin carrying children immediately. A more patient man might have been open to waiting but would never have suggested taking measures to prevent a pregnancy. He was unlike any man she had ever spoken to, or even read about.

"Aidon," she said. He looked at her desperately. "What your father thought about you was wrong. He was wrong. Family is not always right about us."

"Your family adores you."

"Maybe. But I was still a disappointment to my father, especially when compared to Venus."

She said the words without thinking, lulled by the security and comfort of the soft bed covers and the warm, handsome man by her side.

You're going soft.

"What could possibly have disappointed him about you?" he murmured in disbelief.

Persephone laughed bitterly. "My father orchestrated our engagement to stem the flow of gossip, yes, but he also did it because he believed I would never have other prospects. He felt fully justified in his actions because, well, look at me."

Skinny, sharp-tongued, unable to keep her mouth shut.

"I am looking at you," he said, his words heavy and soft all at once. Persephone's train of thought was interrupted, and her heart squeezed painfully. "I have been unable to look at anything else since the day we met."

Persephone felt the color rise to her cheeks. "I do not understand that," she admitted. It felt good saying it aloud. "Anyone can see we make an odd picture. If the banns had been posted—"

He sat up, alert. "*That* is why you refused to have the banns posted?"

The color that had risen to her cheeks spread to her entire face and neck. She looked down and began to pick at the coverlet. "I just—people would have thought it odd, seeing you choose someone like me. I thought I was avoiding embarrassment for us both."

He took her face in his hand, tilting her chin up. She looked at him, at those frustratingly desperate eyes. "Whoever made you believe that you are anything less than utterly bewitching was either lying or just *wrong*."

Persephone felt as if he were staring right into her soul, right at the shabbily healed wounds in her chest. The feeling was overwhelming. She did not understand how he was able to see someone completely different. But a part of her fully believed him, even as the rest of her continued to struggle against accepting his words as truth.

Unable to stand another second under his searching, sympathetic gaze, Persephone pushed him back onto the bed and straddled him.

"It seems that family is not always right," she said, half-believing her own words as well. "You do not see what my father saw—and I do not see what yours did."

"I've changed," he said softly.

She bent forward, her lips grazing his. His muscles tensed between her legs, and she felt a now familiar ache bloom inside her.

"Aidon," she murmured against his lips. She felt his rising erection press against her backside. She was almost driven to distraction but managed to force out the words. "Whoever you were then has made you who you are now, and for that I am grateful."

"Persephone—" His voice was strangled. Ragged.

She reached behind her, meaning to guide him into her aching center. Pausing, she cast him a questioning look. "May I?"

The intensity disappeared from his face, replaced instead by a smile. He laughed, the sound pulling at her heartstrings. "Must you ask?"

"Something I learned from you," she said pointedly.

"Yes, well, you *may*," he chuckled, his hands running along her thighs. "But first—" He sat up slightly, his grip keeping Persephone in place, shifting her so she almost sat in his lap. He began to guide her upward. She hesitated.

"Where am I meant to be going?" she asked sheepishly.

He pressed a warm kiss to her stomach, and she shivered. "Let me show you," he murmured. "Hold onto the headboard."

Persephone allowed him to position her just so, her sensitive entrance level with his face as her hands held onto the headboard. She felt him trace her slick folds with a single digit, her grip tightening on the headboard in response.

"Aidon," she gasped, unsure.

"Trust me."

Anticipation crept over Persephone as she realized she had no way of knowing what he was going to do next. She jerked in surprise and pleasure when she felt the flat of his tongue drag over the sensitive skin of her thighs. He focused his attention on her warmed skin, leaving her aching bud unattended.

"Would you hurry?" she asked, frustrated.

He chuckled against her. "Hasn't anybody ever told you that patience is a virtue?"

"No," she said, eyes focused on the wall. "Hasn't anybody ever told *you* that it is impolite to keep a lady waiting?"

"No," he said, echoing her tone. "I was not aware you were waiting for something. Would you care to enlighten me?"

Trapped again. She would probably never learn to avoid his little games, but she quickly thought of a way she might wiggle out of this one.

"I was expecting you to make me come," she said bluntly, glad he could not see that she was blushing furiously.

With no warning, Aidon ran his tongue firmly through her folds and up to the pulsing bundle of nerves at her apex. She let out a squeaky little moan, the sensation unbearably intense.

"Now, didn't that feel good?" he said, his mouth still against her. She felt the timbre of his voice rumble through her. "All the better for having waited like a good girl."

She had never heard the phrase *good girl* sound so sinfully filthy. But this was who he was at his core, wasn't it? He was a reformed scoundrel who could twist even the most innocuous phrase into temptation.

Tightening his grip on her thighs, he supported her weight as he slowly ran his tongue up her slit, the bridge of his nose grazing her most sensitive parts. Her knees buckled, and she allowed him to hold her as he continued his slow and deliberate ministrations. He sucked gently at her bud, pulling a mewling cry out of her as his hands began to roam, dragging firmly against her thighs and backside.

Unable to stand the slow pace any longer, Persephone began to rock against him, chasing her own release. She held on tightly to the headboard with one hand, using the other to run her fingers through his tousled hair.

She cried out as she came, pushing herself unabashedly against him, shivering as she released the headboard and fell into his lap. She was damp with sweat, her chest heaving with exertion.

When she finally felt brave enough, she glanced up at Aidon. He was looking down at her with wonder, his expression tinged with a hint of smugness.

"All right, my love?" he asked gently. Her entire body stood to attention at the endearment.

"Yes," she breathed, an unfamiliar feeling blooming in her chest, painful and ecstatic all at once. "Are you quite sure you've changed?"

His face fell. "What do you mean?"

"A gentleman would have *never*—what you just did—"

"What would a gentleman have done?" he asked.

His face told her that he thought she was scolding him. She stifled a giggle before bringing herself to her original position.

"Nothing I would have cared for."

I must be dreaming, Aidon thought. Never in his wildest fantasies had he imagined himself back in Oxbury, back at Gallowsgate, in bed with a woman.

And not just any woman. *Persephone.*

"Look at me," she had said, her voice tinged with years of hurt and bitterness. And he did. He saw the glint of her rare smile, the flash of intelligence in her dark eyes. He heard her tinkling laugh, though he would have gladly taken a breathless moan in its place.

And she had redeemed him somehow.

Perhaps she would take it back in time. How could he consider himself reformed, no longer a scoundrel, when he continued to keep things from her?

There is no redemption for the Lord of the Dead.

He thought about his father and wondered how much his secrets had led to the crumbling of his own marriage. Charles Barrington had been a cruel man, and for the first time in his life, Aidon questioned whether his father's responsibilities had made him crueler. Was that what lay ahead for him, too? For Persephone?

But he could not dwell on these thoughts, not as Persephone was guiding him into her, sinking down with a deep, fluttering sigh. Awe ignited in his chest as he watched her move. It felt like *heaven*.

No, like Elysium. It felt like he had been welcomed into Persephone's realm. He remembered thinking how he would pray at her temple every day if it meant he could hear her laugh, but now he knew he would pray *every waking moment* if it meant he could see her like this.

She reached down, gently taking his hands and placing them on her hips.

"Persephone," he choked out.

"I want it to feel good for you, too," she said, her breath short. "Show me."

And he did. Religiously.

TWENTY-FIVE

Persephone waved a hand at a nearby bee. She could not help but smile at the stretch of wild land before her. Honeyfield. Home. It felt different, less suffocating and more like the Honeyfield she had known in her childhood.

She let herself in the front door, immediately spotting Venus sitting on the first step of the staircase with a massive straw hat perched atop her golden curls.

"You're late," she huffed. But she could only hold her grim expression for a moment before wrapping Persephone in a perfumed hug. "I suppose I forgive you. What kept you so long?"

Persephone put every ounce of her energy into making sure she did not blush. The answer was simple: Aidon. But Venus did not need to know the specifics.

"I woke up later than planned," she lied, hoping it was convincing.

Venus giggled. "Is your husband keeping you up at night?"

So much for hiding it.

"Venus!" Persephone shook her head at her grinning sister. "No. *No.*"

"Oh, fine." Venus pouted. "Keep the details to yourself then. But don't expect to hear anything from me when it's *my* turn."

"I would want nothing less than to hear your—your *details*," Persephone said, crinkling her nose.

"You say that now," Venus grinned. "I *have* missed you, Persephone. Papa said I should give you space to allow you to settle into your new life, but since he isn't here, I have to ask—can I come visit?"

Persephone felt affection for her sister swell in her chest. "Of course you can visit. Why didn't you ask me instead of taking Papa's word?"

"He was rather insistent about it all," Venus said with a shrug.

"Where *is* Papa?"

"Here."

Persephone turned to see her father, the companion to Venus's straw hat sitting on his graying head. She rushed to give him a hug, all of her longing for what had been comfortable about Honeyfield bubbling beneath her skin.

"Has Venus finally convinced you to take her to the seaside?" she asked teasingly, arms still wrapped around his middle.

"I will have you know that Papa convinced *me*," Venus said. She fluffed her pink skirts primly. "I'm simply going to keep him company."

"I am going to a meeting," Solomon said. "About skeps."

"Of course," Persephone laughed. "Of course you are."

Solomon held her at arm's length, staring directly into her eyes. She shifted uncomfortably under the sudden intensity of his gaze.

"Are you well?" he asked.

"Quite well," Persephone answered quickly. Honestly.

She had never felt better in her life. "Did my letters imply otherwise?"

"I suppose they did not," her father replied. "Will you be all right here by yourself? Where is Mr. Barrington?"

Persephone felt color creep across her face. "In London. On business. I will be fine. Why didn't you invite Mr. Haskett to go with you?"

Solomon sighed. "That boy is in love, and bees are the last thing that would lure him away for two weeks. I would not be surprised if he returns here before I do."

"I'm surprised you noticed."

"Am I not perceptive?" her father asked, his tone devoid of emotion.

Venus dissolved into giggles. "You are the least perceptive person I have *ever* met, Papa."

"I disagree with that," Solomon said seriously.

Venus giggled again as Persephone herded them out the door.

Right before she shut them out, she could have sworn that her sister winked at her over her shoulder. Persephone rolled her eyes and walked to the parlor. Immediately, her ears perked at the sounds of buzzing and chirping.

Honeyfield was noisier than she remembered. Even the windows did very little to dampen the lively sounds of the outside. Had she gotten so used to the eerie silence of Gallowsgate so quickly?

Gallowsgate.

Persephone shivered, her mind betraying her with thoughts of Aidon. Frankly, she couldn't remember the last time she had thought of anything else. How easy it was to lose yourself in another person, particularly when that person did not want to change a single thing about you. She tried to think of something else but could not. All she could see in her mind's eye was Aidon. Polite, but with a rakish smile. Gentle, yet in control. And skilled—so very skilled.

She sighed and took herself to the library. She would bore herself into focusing on other things. She could read, care for the bees, even climb the trees she'd loved so well while living here. How hard could it be?

Days later, having failed at redirecting her mind to other things, Persephone reminded herself that it didn't suit her to be thinking on romance so much. She picked a book out at random from the overflowing desk in the library, willing to give reading another go. Walking out the front door, she sat in a patch of wildflowers near the path that led up to the house.

Taking a deep breath, she crossed her legs and looked down at the book she had chosen.

Mating Rituals of Bees.

"Oh, for God's sake," she grumbled. She cracked the cover open, unable to find the energy to return to the library. Just as she was about to read the first few words, she heard the crunching of footsteps.

Aidon?

Persephone squashed the hopeful thought instantly, feeling distinctly embarrassed. It couldn't be him—he would be in London by now.

She watched as the person in question approached, her eyes narrowing as she tried to focus in the bright sunlight.

Cassius.

Persephone stood up abruptly, pleased to see that she had startled him. "What are you doing here?" she asked sharply.

He held an exaggerated hand to his chest and gave her a toothy grin. "Ah, my darling Persephone! Fancy seeing you here."

"You didn't answer my question." She folded her arms across her chest, shielding herself.

"I was in the area," he said, his voice irritatingly cheerful, "and I thought I would come take a look at the famous Venus."

Persephone bristled. "This is not a museum. You cannot walk in to *take a look*."

His face fell. "Are you angry with me?"

"Angry?" She took a step forward, still keeping her distance. Fury and adrenaline coursed through her veins. "Angry! You propositioned me in London."

He laughed. "Will you hold the actions of a drunken fool against him? Be reasonable."

There was nothing Persephone hated more than being told to be reasonable, and she had heard it more times than she could stand.

"I will not be any such thing. Leave."

He sighed dramatically. "Well, I suppose I can do without seeing Venus. You're here, after all."

"Your teasing is not helping things. Leave."

The smile disappeared from his face. "God, you're just as boring as my brother." He turned his back to her and took a few leisurely steps before facing her once more. "Do you know who you are married to?"

"Of course I do," Persephone said, wrapping her arms tighter around herself. "Now—"

He cut her off. "Do you know why they call him the Lord of the Dead?"

"It's silly gossip," she said, wishing desperately that he would just leave. She felt the hairs on the back of her neck stand up.

"Is it? They called my father that as well. And his father before him. Never in the scandal sheets, of course—both of them were far better at their jobs than Aidon could ever hope to be. Much more discreet." He paused before adding, "They might have called *me* that if I hadn't had the sense to turn the bloody business down."

Persephone felt her blood run cold.

His father, too?

"Leave," she forced out, hating how weak her voice had turned.

He began to pick his way back up the trail before stopping again. "Do you know why he married you?"

"We have already had this discussion," Persephone said shortly. "We—"

"Your being *well suited* had nothing to do with it," he interrupted. "My brother—your noble *husband*—was looking to cut me off. You just happened to be the first woman he ran into."

Persephone drew her eyebrows together. "That—that can't be true."

"It's in Father's will," Cassius said, voice deceptively pleasant. "The fool who runs the business gets full control of the Barrington accounts once married. The clever spare is stuck with a pathetic five hundred pounds a year once the papers are signed."

"I don't think—"

"You were a means to an end," he said sweetly before turning his back to make his way off the estate. "Aidon Barrington is not a man of honor, *Persephone*. He never was. You would do well to remember that."

Persephone did not respond. She remained rooted in place until she could no longer see his retreating form. He had to be lying. She hadn't heard a thing about Aidon wanting to cut Cassius off from—

Why would he tell you?

Nausea slammed into her mercilessly, forcing her to sink

down into the wildflowers again. Aidon was kind; he had wanted to protect her reputation, *Venus's* reputation, even—

Nobody is that kind.

Persephone's hands began to twitch, itching for something to mangle. She had to do something, needed to do something, before her mind abandoned all reason and spiraled out of control. Her hands went to a wildflower first, pulling it out of the ground by its stem. Slowly, she tore the petals off one by one, dropping them to the ground. She pulled another one up, then another, until she had a whole fistful. Wrapping a hand around the heads, she ripped them off in one swift motion. Only when she saw the stems in one hand and the crushed petals in the other did she feel a jolt of guilt. She *loved* these flowers. They did not deserve to be on the receiving end of this. Standing up, she made her way to the house, stopping by the kitchen to grab a pair of scissors. Marching up to her old room, she positioned herself in front of the mirror and washbasin.

Better her than the flowers.

Snip, snip, snip.

The blades wreaked havoc on her already short hair. She snipped haphazardly, not particularly caring if the cuts were even. She preferred her hair shaggy and untamed, though she usually dedicated a lot more focus to the task.

Scissors held in midair, Persephone peered at herself in the glass. Dark, deep-set, owlish eyes that were too big for her face stared back at her. She frowned.

Aidon couldn't have wanted her from the moment they'd met. The confidence that she had been nurturing, the confidence that had been coaxed out of hiding by Aidon's shows of affection—by his want for her—fell to pieces inside of her chest, leaving her as shattered as she had been before she had signed her name onto the parish register on her wedding day.

How fragile it all had been.

Her mind turned to Cassius's other declaration. The late Mr. Barrington had been called the Lord of the Dead, too? She had convinced herself that it was just gossip meant to punish Aidon for leaving his life of frivolity behind him. Words from peers meant to penalize him for taking away a source of entertainment and scandal. If what Cassius had said was accurate—

She wouldn't believe him. She had done so before, charmed by his easy smiles and silver tongue.

But—what of the grave, the one she'd thought newly appeared? The late-night business matter delivered urgently via post?

Work that she was meant to stay out of. Work that she didn't know a thing about. Other people were not impressed with his job, but maybe it was because they actually understood what it *was*. He had never seemed to want to tell her about the family business, and that was yet another bitter truth to swallow.

Persephone laid the scissors down, sitting on her bed with a heavy thud. Did she know Aidon at all?

Yes, you do.

For once, the voice in her head was not bitter or judgmental. It was hopeful, urging her to reconsider, pulling her mind away from dark places. She did know him. He was kind and gentle, and every time she was with him, she forgot about all her faults.

Aidon was not the sort of person who would marry simply to cut his brother off. If he had done so, then there would have been no reason to treat her as perfectly as he had.

When he looked at her with those devastating green eyes, it felt as if he was actually *seeing* her. Everything she had struggled with he admired. Every look he gave her was appreciative, and every touch overwhelmingly reverent. She had almost forgotten what it was to doubt herself.

Perhaps all she had needed was for someone to listen and understand. She had been stuck in Honeyfield alone, with a beautiful sister who could not have possibly understood and a father who had been distracted and distant since her mother had died.

Mother.

Persephone felt an old sadness descend upon her, and she sighed, running her fingers through her freshly cut hair. She wished she could speak to her, wished she could ask her what to do or how to confront this.

"This is silly, isn't it?" she asked aloud, her voice wobbly. "My imagination is making this seem worse than it is."

Nobody answered. Cassius had managed to worm his way under her skin, that was all.

"He is so good to me," she continued, undeterred. "Maybe I don't know all of him, but I know enough. Don't I?"

She didn't know.

She wanted so badly to resist suspicion.

She had managed to ignore the gossip, hadn't she? And she had probably miscounted the headstones in the first place. As for the late-night work, people died at all hours, didn't they? And the accounts—perhaps that was a clause of the will, but it didn't mean it had informed his decision to—

He had gone along so easily with everything she'd wanted. He'd stayed in Oxbury, buried his hands in the damp earth with her, helped her bring Christianna one step closer to freedom. And she had felt loved.

Her body started at the thought. Love?

Did he make her feel *loved*?

I wouldn't know, she thought. *What does it even feel like?*

She wondered what he felt when he was with her because it couldn't have been love. It couldn't have been because she didn't—

Persephone knit her brow and shook her head. How could she confront Aidon about all of this?

Her insides refused to settle.

Venus could be trusted to know more about the Lord of the Dead than anyone else, but she was at the seaside. The only other option was to go to the source: her sister's precious gossip rags. Persephone pushed herself off the bed and made her way across the hall.

Venus's room was as Persephone remembered it, packed with trinkets and shiny things. Pretty glass bottles sat on the wooden surface of her makeshift worktable, scattering pinpricks of light all over the room. Every other available bit of space was covered with scraps of fabric, finished sewing projects, and formless mounds on their way to becoming dresses.

Persephone, for the first time in her life, regretted that she had not paid more attention to Venus's love for gossip. She had always only half listened to her sister's reports on what was going on in Little Oxbury, London, and beyond. She did know, however, that Venus kept all of her precious papers as they were rather hard to come by when one did not live anywhere near town.

Feeling guilty, Persephone rummaged through her sister's big trunk and closet, finding nothing but piles and piles of odd-looking dresses.

Venus originals, of course.

Then, suddenly, it came to her. She kept her precious, secret things underneath her bed. Falling to her knees, Persephone peered under Venus's rickety bed, and lo and behold, she found a tin box. It scraped along the floor as Persephone pulled it out, and the lid easily popped open. Inside were a few scraps of ribbon, a small journal, and a stack of neatly folded papers. Although curiosity instantly gnawed at her insides, Persephone

put the journal aside. She would not add to her list of wrong-
doings by nosily going through Venus's secrets.

She pulled the stack of papers out of the box, spreading them
around her. She went in order, unfolding one thing at a time
and searching for any mention of the Lord of the Dead. She
found mostly what she expected—that he drank the blood of
his deceased clients, that he prowled the streets of London with
his vampire's teeth bared unabashedly for all to see, and so on.

A waste of time.

She began to fold the papers up again, frustrated with herself for indulging her ridiculous suspicion. Then, a smudged
sentence caught her eye.

> *This author has ample evidence to inform our readers
> that a certain Lord K— has privately exchanged funds
> with London's own Lord of the Dead. What dastardly
> deed would he have the Lord of the Dead do, you ask?
> Well, dear readers, that is for our source to know, and for
> all of London to discover . . .*

She had never heard of the Lord of the Dead working for
anybody, let alone for the aristocracy—this was the first mention
of anything of the sort. Why would a lord privately exchange
money with Aidon? It seemed odd, if not a little alarming. Cassius's words echoed nastily in her head.

Tucking her knees underneath her chin, Persephone closed
her eyes. A thread of terror began to tie itself around her insides.
She was nothing if not resilient. She had been able to overcome
every unhappiness, every disappointment, every unwelcome surprise her life had thrown at her. But resiliency could not protect
her from the heartbreak that threatened, nor could it promise a
full recovery. If there was any truth to Cassius's words, even to

her own panicked thoughts, then she would be shattered. And there was no telling if she'd ever be able to put the pieces of herself back again in the aftermath. Not this time.

Her mind suddenly and very calmly focused singularly on one thing: his study. If there was anything to hide, anything that would prove the silly gossip that had been plaguing him for the past ten years, then he would hide it there. Persephone replaced Venus's tin box underneath the bed and pushed herself up off the floor.

She would return to Gallowsgate, but only to prove Cassius wrong.

TWENTY-SIX

Gallowsgate felt large and empty, the way Oxbury always had to Persephone. She had never noticed how her footsteps echoed as she walked through the entrance, the clicking sounds bouncing off the fine marble floors and disappearing into thin air.

Baker had let her in, seeming to believe her when she told him she had forgotten to take some crucial items with her to Honeyfield. He had simply shrugged and did not pry, and for once she was grateful for the awkwardness she shared with the staff.

That awkwardness allowed her to move through the house like a ghost. She heard her heart hammering in her chest, amplified by Gallowsgate's eerie and uncomfortable silence. The hallway leading to Aidon's study was mercifully empty. Persephone stood by the heavy wooden doors and hesitated.

You won't find anything, she told herself. *Gossip is simply—gossip. Although, it would be wonderful to prove Cassius wrong.*

Yes, it would. And that was what she was here to do. She wiggled the doorknob and found that the room was unlocked. This should not have surprised her, given that her husband was nothing if not trusting. He was in London and thought her to be at Honeyfield. There was no point in locking any of the doors here. She remembered all the times she had walked in freely, pulling him out of his den of funeral furnishing. He had never refused her, and he had never appeared startled. She had never once seen him shove papers aside or away. He'd never behaved suspiciously in the slightest. So why was she here?

She sighed, stepping into the study. There was no use in stewing in her guilt. She shut the door softly behind her and walked purposefully over to his desk. Papers were neatly stacked on one side of the tabletop, but secrets, she thought, would be tucked away.

That is, if he had any. Which he did not.

She pulled gingerly at a drawer, opening it with a piercing scrape that made the hairs on the back of her neck stand up. The contents were neat, and she vaguely remembered admiring his starched cravat the day she had met him and thinking how meticulously he must shave every morning. He was meticulous and thorough in *all* things, a thought that sent heat creeping up her chest.

There is nothing here, she thought, running her fingers across the tidy stack of envelopes and cards inside. The pile shifted slightly, and a crumpled corner caught her eye as she moved to pat them back into place.

It was a little odd, especially considering how fine and flat everything else was. She pulled at it, the paper crinkling between her fingers. The writing on the front was an almost unintelligible scribble. It was a quarto sheet, the linen rough beneath her fingers. She unfolded it carefully, barely making out the words *E. Follett* at the bottom of the letter.

She had heard that name before.

London.

Lord Follett was the nervous red-faced man that had pulled Aidon aside in the crush of Cassius's parlor. What had he been so nervous about? Persephone began to lower herself into a chair, barely sitting when the doors to the study flew open. She jumped in surprise, crumpling the letter in her hands.

"Baker," she said, heart hammering in her chest. "May I help you?"

"Apologies, madam," Baker said from the doorway. He did not look suspicious, but then, Persephone could not remember ever seeing anything other than an expression of neutral distaste on his weathered face. "I thought I would open the windows to let in some air."

"Yes, of course," Persephone said a little too quickly. "I came here for—a book."

Her saving grace sat on the table, a large leather-bound volume engraved with the title *A Treatise on Preventing Bodily Decay.*

"Just what I was looking for," she said breathlessly, wishing she could stop talking.

"Taking an interest in the business, madam?" Baker asked, moving silently past her to the windows.

"Quite," Persephone said, hearing how terribly false her tone sounded.

"Most impressive," he said. "As I have you here, I would like to inform you that only one more room requires restoration before we may call the task of bringing the house to working order fully completed. I apologize for the time it has taken, but I have always preferred overseeing a tight staff. Fewer people to keep an eye on, you understand."

"Yes, of course," Persephone said, distracted. "That's wonderful news, Baker."

"There is an issue, however."

That drew her attention. "Oh?"

"The door is locked. I was aware of its inaccessibility when I was overseeing the maintenance of the house myself but did not have the time to undertake a thorough search for the key. I have instructed the staff to prioritize locating it, however, so that you may have full use of Gallowsgate."

"Do you know what the room was used for?"

"I believe it was designated for the late Mr. Barrington's use," Baker stated. "It is the smallest room of the house, and we were not to disturb him there."

"I see," Persephone said. Perhaps Mr. Barrington had sought to conceal secrets behind the locked door, secrets Cassius had alluded to. She had to know. "Please tell me when you find the key. I should like to see what was left behind."

"Yes, madam," Baker said. "Though I doubt there will be much to see. Many of the late master's personal effects were kept in London."

"Thank you, Baker," she said, the sharp edges of the crumpled paper in her hands reminding her why she was here. "I should be going now."

He bowed, and Persephone slowly and calmly walked the excruciating distance between the desk and the door before darting to the entryway and crossing the thicket back to Honeyfield.

Two days later, Persephone was once again lounging in the wildflowers, keeping a lazy look on the house. The letter she had whisked away from Aidon's desk still remained unread, crumpled alongside the books that sat beneath her bed.

The guilt of taking it was eating her alive, and she refused to read it. Cassius had just been lashing out, she reasoned, angry that someone would choose his brother over him.

Despite herself, despite what she had been told, she missed Aidon and was uncharacteristically determined to hold on to that feeling, reveling in it like the heroines of the dramatic novels she liked to read. She had never missed anyone with such intensity before. It was almost enough to quell the suspicion and worry wedged in the back of her mind, collecting dust with the letter from Lord Follett. She could not betray Aidon, could not believe that he had married her for his own purposes, could not believe in the gossip that haunted him. Not after everything he had said to her, all the ways in which he had helped her heal. She had taken the letter to avoid being caught, not because she thought it held information of interest.

Or so she had told herself.

Persephone lay flat on her back, her gaze following the movement of the wispy clouds in the late afternoon sky. She very badly needed to talk to someone, to release this anxiety from her chest and be told there was nothing to fear.

Christianna, she told herself. *You need to talk to Christianna.*

She stood and, after dusting herself off, began the familiar trek to Errwood. Over the years, she and Christianna had discovered all manner of shortcuts between their homes, primarily using them when needing to divulge matters of great importance. Persephone took the fastest route, hopping over a creek and trudging through a rough, prickly stretch of bramble before seeing Errwood in her line of sight. It was a beautifully constructed manor, the white marble of its facade winking in the waning sunlight.

Persephone was let in by the cheerful housekeeper and taken straight to the appropriate drawing room before she could say a word. Christianna sat on a powder-pink chaise, surrounded by flawlessly matched wall-hangings. Like a proper lady, she was attempting to perfect her needlework. Which she might have continued doing if she hadn't dropped it carelessly to the side the minute she saw Persephone.

"I wasn't expecting you!" she said, rushing over to pull Persephone into a hug.

"What are you working on?" Persephone asked, her heart suddenly wedged in her throat.

Christianna released her and returned to the chaise. She picked up her needlework with a sigh. "I rather thought I would try to re-create Errwood and have it surrounded by sheep, but it's looking a bit lopsided."

Persephone sat next to her and leaned over. The outline of the house had been mapped out in neat stitches, with shapeless blobs making up the sheep. "It's quite good."

"I appreciate the fib," Christianna said with a giggle, tossing her work between them. "I'm glad you've come, actually. I wanted to tell you something."

For the first time since she'd entered, Persephone noticed that Christianna was all happiness and confidence, the nervous energy of last week nowhere to be found. "Go on."

"I think your matchmaking has worked!"

"I knew it would," Persephone said, trying very hard to mask her lack of surprise.

"Papa has told me that Ezra—Mr. Haskett, I mean—has written ahead to request a private meeting with him. And one with me, too! We both know what that means."

"He intends to propose?" Persephone asked with a grin.

"Yes! How can I ever begin to repay you?"

"There is nothing to repay," Persephone said firmly. "He was half in love with you the moment he saw you." Her heart was on the verge of bursting, her worries momentarily forgotten. "Aidon helped, too."

"Oh, Mr. Barrington!" Christianna gasped. "What have you

done to him, Persephone? I've never seen a man look so lovesick at the mere sight of a lady."

He would change his tune if he knew I went rummaging through his study.

"When did you find the time to notice that? Were you not distracted by your soon-to-be husband?"

"If you think that Ezra and I have not discussed your effect on Mr. Barrington, then you are quite mistaken," Christianna said smugly. "In fact, it was one of the first conversations we had with one another."

"Oh, don't tell me that." Persephone blushed. "That's ridiculous."

"And the more we spoke of it, the more we realized," Christianna continued, undeterred by Persephone's embarrassment, "that there is no other explanation. He must be desperately in love with you." Her final sentence was said with pride, a cheeky glint in her eye.

Persephone felt her heart sink. He shouldn't be in love with her. Not when she had believed that he would marry to protect his coffers, and not when she had gone through his desk under the ruse of trying to prove Cassius wrong.

It had all been a ruse, she thought sadly.

What a complete and utter disaster.

"Christianna, I—" Persephone cut herself off, unsure of what to say. How could she even begin to explain the situation she was in?

"Are you all right?" Christianna asked. "You've gone a bit pale. Surely the news that your husband is in love with you isn't *that* much of a shock."

Persephone picked up Christianna's needlework, running her fingers over the stitches. She could picture the newly wedded Mr. and Mrs. Haskett living in a perfect house just like Errwood.

No secrets between them, only implicit trust and happiness. The image brought forth a twinge of envy.

There was nothing she could say to Christianna about what she was feeling. It was as if the words were stuck in her throat, made all the more impossible to let out in the wake of her friend's happiness.

"I see that you and Mr. Haskett are well matched in imagination," she said finally.

Christianna shrugged, unbothered. "Believe what you will. But don't expect me to keep my composure when you come to tell me that you're in love as well."

"Me?" Persephone scoffed, still scrambling to hide the tempest raging inside of her. "Why would you wish such a thing on the poor man?"

Christianna laughed, leaning over to press a kiss to Persephone's forehead. "I would wish your love on any decent person, Persephone. It has changed my life in the most wonderful way. Now, why don't you help me pick a dress for when I am proposed to? I intend to look my absolute best."

Persephone took a steadying breath. "I'd love to."

TWENTY-SEVEN

In London, Ezra was buzzing with more nervous energy than usual. He seemed almost irritable, his expression lovesick as he informed Aidon of the great lengths he'd gone to obtain the perfect ring to present to Christianna.

God, I hope I don't make those faces.

"So you know," Ezra said, "I do not mean to stay at Gallowsgate when we return to Oxbury. I couldn't steal away your privacy like that."

"You didn't seem to have an issue with doing so before."

Ezra laughed. "Maybe I've matured some over the past few weeks."

"Doubtful," Aidon said. "Have you made travel arrangements? Perhaps we should return together."

"I couldn't," Ezra said. "I am soon to be a married man, Aidon. I must secure my own lodgings and organize my own travel."

"I . . . have no idea what either of those things has to do with marriage."

"Isn't it romantic?" Ezra said, ignoring Aidon's comment. "Aidon Barrington and Ezra Haskett, two of London's most

eligible and, dare I say, underappreciated bachelors, both finding love in Oxbury. It's the stuff of poetry."

"I will admit to your being underappreciated," Aidon said
fondly.

"Thank you," Ezra said. "Putting romance aside for a
moment, have you heard from your brother?"

"No," Aidon said. "Why do you ask?"

Ezra shrugged. "I haven't heard from him since I returned.
He used to send me at least one invitation a week. I heard that
he's been looking rather run-down as of late."

"Run-down?" Aidon repeated. "Run-down how?"

"He's been in his cups more than usual, or that is what
Reeves told me, at least. And he did not join the others at the
club this week. Is that not strange?"

It *was* strange, but Aidon decided not to comment on it
any further. His brother had no part in his life any longer. But
his face must have betrayed *some* slight concern as Ezra added,
"Oh, for all we know, he is luxuriating at the estate of some lord
or earl we have never heard of. As one does."

Convincing Ezra to join him on his trip back to Oxbury
was embarrassingly easy. That was who Ezra had always been,
easygoing and easily convinced. As it happened, Christianna was
the same, and the realization that Aidon attracted the same sort
of people as Persephone did amused him to no end.

Persephone.

Being in London without her had been agony. He was
almost grateful to Ezra for being so hell-bent on finding a ring
without delay because it meant they could return to Oxbury—
something Aidon had never imagined himself wanting to do. He
had spent the majority of his time there trying to leave, waiting
patiently for his father to take pity on them and summon them
away from the countryside.

How things had changed.

Aidon spent the better part of the carriage ride to Oxbury making sure Ezra knew how to word his proposal like a perfect gentleman. After all, they were no longer in London, and Oxbury was quite different from Cassius's parlor. He was filled with a strange, enjoyable sort of nervousness now that he was returning home and was so close to Honeyfield—and Persephone. He accompanied Ezra to Errwood, the sprawling estate that belonged to Christianna's family. Unlike Honeyfield, and quite like Gallowsgate, the lands were carefully maintained. The one glaring difference was that Errwood was dotted with an inordinate number of sheep. Ezra had been to the estate before and was already acquainted with Christianna's parents, so Aidon found it very easy to make a quick exit.

He went to Honeyfield, impressed that he was able to navigate the overgrown chaos of it. The sounds of Honeyfield were a welcome change from the bustle of London, the air filled with the rustling of leaves and distant birdsong. It was a day perfectly suited for an engagement—and a reunion. He walked up the pathway to the house, his body abuzz with anticipation.

Had she missed him? Would she be happy to see him? Had she, like him, spent every stray moment thinking on the passion they'd shared?

It had been more than passion. There had been tenderness. Understanding. *Acceptance.* Everything he had been craving.

He spotted a figure lying among the grass and wildflowers. It was Persephone, clad in a plain brown dress. Her eyes were closed, and her chest rose and fell slowly. Her hair was shorter now, he noticed. The sun illuminated her high forehead, and her dark eyelashes rested sweetly on the delicate skin beneath her wide eyes. A novel still rested in her right hand, the page she had been reading lost as she had nodded off. She looked so peaceful that he almost hated to wake her, but he was desperate to do so.

Softly kneeling beside her, Aidon cupped her face, running a thumb across her cheek. She stirred, opening her brilliant eyes, and graced him with a dreamy, sleepy smile.

"Hello," she said, her voice still thick with slumber.

"Hello," he replied.

She sat up suddenly, as if having registered whom she was speaking to. He thought he saw uncertainty flicker across her face, but it was quickly replaced with a little smile.

"Are you all right?" he asked, still kneeling before her.

She looked around at Honeyfield, her dark eyes resting on him after a prolonged silence. Or rather, a silence filled with the busy chattering of birds and the dull buzz from the skeps nearby. "Yes," she said, her voice clear. "I heard about Christianna and Mr. Haskett."

"Ah, of course," he smiled. "Though I had hoped to be the one to tell you."

She beamed at him, her smile widening. "Christianna told me about Mr. Haskett writing ahead to her father. Are they pleased?" she asked, her face hopeful. He wanted very badly to kiss her but held himself back.

"Deeply." Aidon grinned. "You were right, of course, about them being a good match for one another. I daresay it was love at first sight on Ezra's part. I can't say we had a very difficult job to do."

She did not respond, so they simply sat there, gazing at one another. He could not help but think about the way he'd felt when he'd seen her for the very first time. The way he felt every time he looked at her.

"It's quite nice," Persephone said suddenly, her soft voice bringing him back to the moment, "helping the people we love."

Her words shattered him, simple though they were. He had never seen such contentment on her lovely face. She seemed to him so unwaveringly good, her heart so big that it may as well have taken up all the space in her small form. He saw it in the way she spoke about Christianna, in the way she cared for her family. Her capacity for love was so glaringly obvious that it baffled Aidon that people were not in constant awe of her.

Persephone stared at him with her dark, bewitching eyes, still beaming despite having gained nothing from Christianna's engagement. Aidon adored her.

No, you love her.

Overwhelmed with emotion, he leaned toward her, stopping just as their lips were about to touch.

"May I?" he asked.

She laughed. "I almost thought you'd forget to ask."

It was shockingly easy for Persephone to dismiss the knowledge that she had Lord Follett's letter tucked away when Aidon was pressing tender kisses all over, so easy to let go of what Cassius had said when she agreed to let Aidon undress her, the sun warm on her skin, and so easy to lose herself as he touched and kissed every part of her, his hands working their magic between her legs.

They lay in the flowers together after, Aidon disheveled but still fully dressed, Persephone having pulled her chemise back over her body. She was nestled in his arms, enjoying the feeling of his hand skating up and down her side. She stared at the clouds, her thoughts muddled, her sharp mind dulled by pleasure. She'd been so happy to see him. Waking to the sight of his face had been like a dream.

Her view of the sky was partially blocked as Aidon untangled himself from her and shifted to his side, propping his head on his hand to peer down at her. He ran a hand gently through her hair, and she sighed despite herself. He studied her with an intensity that, surprisingly, did not cause her discomfort. Her insides felt like honey, thick and sweet, but heavy. It was the same feeling that had been frightening her, the same feeling that had led her straight to his study.

A small frown pulled at the side of his mouth for a fleeting moment. She asked, "What are you thinking?"

He looked at her as if he had just realized she was there. "I beg your pardon?"

Persephone reached up to caress his face, roughened by the shadow of his beard. "You were far away. What were you thinking?"

He bent down then, pressing a slow, tender kiss to her lips, the weight of his free hand resting on her hip, apparent through the thin fabric of her chemise. He kept his forehead pressed to hers as they parted, and she was so distracted by his overwhelming nearness that she almost didn't hear him say, "I was thinking about how much I adore—how much I love you, Persephone."

He said her name the way he always did, with a charming melodic lilt, the syllables rolling pleasantly off his tongue. Her mind went blank for a moment, and then, without any warning, she felt tears begin to prick her eyes.

Why are you crying?

She could not parse through the sudden storm of emotions invading her body— happiness, horror, and the overall feeling that this was terrible and that he deserved far more than she could give.

He continued to examine her in that desperate way of his, finally saying, "I don't—I do not want to pressure you into returning the sentiment."

She met his gaze, terrified that she had hurt him. But he did not look hurt. He was smiling down at her, and as he pressed a soft kiss to her forehead, she realized why she was on the cusp of tears.

It was because she loved him, too. The terrible, heavy, honey-like feeling in her chest was *love*. She did not know how it had happened, did not know how even to begin to say it to him. She didn't even know if she was *allowed* to be in love with him after her blatant act of distrust.

She loved Christianna, loved Venus and her father, but this felt entirely different. Deeper. She was no longer teetering on the edge. No, she had gone and fallen without even realizing it. If she had changed at all, if she had softened, it was entirely due to *this*.

It seemed impossible to love somebody and be suspicious of them all at once. She had never read such a thing in any novel. The love between two characters was always pure and whole, unblemished by uncertainty. Her mind went to the Shakespeare plays that littered Honeyfield's library. Duke Orsino and Viola, Orlando and Rosalind—none of their stories matched hers. Hers was a deep, uncertain void.

"Are you sure?" she whispered, wanting to give him the opportunity to change his mind.

"I have never been more sure of anything," he said emphatically.

Another couple crossed her mind. Hades and Persephone. Perhaps this was what it had been like for her namesake, unyielding love with a hint of suspicion. How could the Goddess of Spring not have been suspicious of the King of the Underworld?

What a fool you are, loving the Lord of the Dead, she thought as he pressed his lips against hers in a bruising, delicious kiss. *Just like Persephone, who did not think twice before eating those pomegranate seeds.*

TWENTY-EIGHT

Persephone watched Aidon, a stark figure in black against the pastel wall-coverings of Honeyfield's parlor. She was distracted by the tight fit of his tailcoat across his broad shoulders. It seemed silly, really, for such an imposing man to be so gentle and agreeable.

It was no wonder she loved him.

A wave of terror washed over her at the thought. She had done him wrong in many ways. She'd tried to bring Cassius back into his life. She'd stolen a private letter from his study. She'd betrayed his trust. She'd doubted him.

How could he possibly think to love her? Then again, he did not know what she'd done. When he looked at her, he only saw good. He saw her loveliness despite her sharpness, charm despite her direct way of speaking. He saw the person she wished she was, wanted desperately to be.

"Will you go to Gallowsgate?" she asked. They were sitting on the worn chaise in the center of the room, her question breaking the companionable silence.

Aidon looked at her suggestively over the rim of his teacup. "I thought I might stay here with you."

An ache settled in Persephone's stomach at his implication, but she soldiered on. "You'll be needing your things," she said pointedly.

He considered this, placing the cup in its saucer with a quiet clink. "A lot of what I have planned does not involve very many *things*, my love."

God, he was trying to kill her.

"Perhaps not," she said, swallowing hard and trying *not* to focus on the taut buckskin that stretched across his thighs, "but we should expect Christianna and Mr. Haskett, shouldn't we?"

"I suppose," he said, leaning toward her, the overwhelming size of him making her forget that she was trying to remove him from the house. "Though I would much rather keep to ourselves."

Persephone placed her hands on his broad shoulders. "As would I," she said honestly, "but that is not a privilege we matchmakers have."

He laughed, the sound pulling a smile from her lips. "I'll do as you say, but only if I get to choose tomorrow's activities."

Again, he was trying to kill her.

A few searing kisses later, Persephone successfully managed to shoo her husband out the door. He took a few steps down the path before turning to look at her.

"If I do not return at a reasonable hour, you may assume that Ezra has accosted me," he said. "I've no doubt he'll want to recount his proposal in excruciating detail."

"And I've no doubt you'll let him do so," she said with a smile.

With Honeyfield empty once more, Persephone went upstairs and, for a long while, simply lay in her bed. It was safe to assume that the night would be hers, as the probability of Mr. Haskett's need to discuss his proposal at length was quite high.

She rolled over, reaching underneath her bed to extract Lord

Follett's crumpled letter. The very feel of it in her hands made her pulse quicken.

She should have never taken the letter in the first place, should have never rummaged through his study, but now the object in question was in her hands. Perhaps this was one way to put her mistrust to rest. Cautiously, she unfolded the letter.

> *Mr. Barrington,*
>
> *I must thank you once more for your discretion. I am writing to again remind you to keep the Follett name off the marker. Either use the boy's Christian name alone or, if you must, manufacture a family name if you feel it to be necessary. I trust we will not need to correspond any further regarding this matter. Enclosed is a banknote for £500, as agreed upon.*
>
> *E. Follett*

Persephone felt her stomach sink as she realized the shabbily written letter raised more questions than it did answers. Discretion? Who was the boy, and why did Lord Follett want to distance himself from him?

And what had Aidon done to warrant a payment of five hundred pounds? When she had first arrived at Gallowsgate, Persephone recalled wondering if there was truly so much money in death. She remembered what she had read in Venus's gossip rag about money surreptitiously changing hands between the Lord of the Dead and a client. That had been a Lord K——; this one a Lord F. What were they paying for?

She was more suspicious than ever, and poor Aidon was none the wiser. Persephone felt awful, wishing she could unread the letter, realizing she could have simply snuck it back to

Gallowsgate on her own time. As usual, she had been selfish, prioritizing her curiosity over her marriage.

It was a marriage that gave her hope and held the delicate promise of happiness and lifelong companionship. If only they had met under normal circumstances. No Oxbury, no rumors about the Lord of the Dead, perhaps even a different Persephone who would have approached this whole ordeal from another angle.

But she was not a different Persephone. She was herself, and if there were any consequences to her actions, then she would have to face them head-on. Folding Lord Follett's letter into a small square, she promised herself that she would return it to Aidon's study and think on the subject no more. *That* was how she could fix this particular issue. She could then feel free to love him as he deserved.

Despite her resolve, what she had read kept her up until dawn. She lay in her bed, tossing and turning to escape to the solace of sleep. It was no use—she soon saw the early morning light begin to spill into her bedroom, the first tentative chirps of the birds trickling in soon after. She wondered if her old life had been as bad as she'd made it out to be. She'd spent her days up in trees reading and daydreaming or in the parlor listening to Venus rattle on about ton gossip.

You were unhappy. Lonely.

Anybody else would have found Honeyfield to be peaceful and freeing.

There is no freedom to be found in a cage.

There had been no freedom. She thought about her mother. What Honeyfield had been unable to provide, she had no doubt found in Solomon. He'd understood her implicitly, knew what it meant to be in possession of a deep-seated passion—for mythology, for beekeeping, for *anything.* Persephone recalled the gentle trust they'd had in one another, the soft glances they'd exchanged when they thought the children weren't looking. Honeyfield alone could not have brought Emmeline happiness. She'd needed her family.

Persephone heard the creak of the staircase, the sound startling her into an upright position. She slid off the bed, tucking the letter underneath her pillow before peeking around the doorframe, expecting to see Aidon. Instead, she saw Christianna on the landing, her face flushed.

"Christianna?" Persephone whispered, though the house was empty. "What are you doing here? It is barely morning."

"Yes, I know," Christianna said breathlessly, her voice wavering. "But I—oh, Persephone."

"Christianna, what's the matter?" Persephone asked, a new sort of anxiousness invading her body. "Is your family well?"

"No," Christianna said, her voice barely above a whisper. "It's me."

"You?" Persephone repeated. She gave her a silly, unsure smile. "You look perfectly fine to me."

"Oh, Persephone," Christianna whispered, biting her bottom lip. "I think I'm with child."

Persephone gaped as a chill spread through her. Christianna stood before her, gripping tightly at the dark blue fabric of her muslin skirt.

"Please," she said softly. "Say something."

Persephone wasn't sure *what* to say. She had no idea how this could have possibly happened, unless—

"Did somebody hurt you?" Persephone demanded, breaking the silence. She remembered Cassius and shuddered.

"No. No, nobody has hurt me."

"Then—then the father?"

Christianna's eyes darted nervously around the room before answering, "Do you remember the boy I mentioned? From Little Oxbury?"

Persephone knit her brow.

"I mentioned him to you the day I met Mr. Haskett. I had almost given up hope and settled for him," Christianna said sadly. She gave Persephone a desperate look. "I promise you I have not seen him since I met Ezra. I just—my courses—"

"You do not have to explain yourself to me," Persephone said, taking Christianna's freezing-cold hands in hers and leading her to sit on the edge of the bed. "You would never betray another living soul."

"I should leave," Christianna said abruptly. "This is not your responsibility."

"Wait!" Persephone said, holding tightly to her friend. "Let me help you."

Christianna squeezed Persephone's hands, tears sliding down her rosy cheeks. Persephone pulled her into a hug, patting Christianna's back soothingly.

"Don't cry," Persephone murmured as Christianna tightened her grip. "We can fix this. I promise we can fix this."

Christianna pulled back. "How?"

"I'm . . . not quite sure," Persephone admitted. "But we will think of something."

Christianna let out a long exhale.

"Will you tell Mr. Haskett?" Persephone asked slowly.

"What other choice do I have? I am going to break his heart. And mine. I don't even know how I will muster up the strength to do it."

"Christianna," Persephone said, gripping the edge of the bed until her knuckles were white, "you have time."

"What time do I have? I'm engaged, for heaven's sake."

Panic settled in Persephone's bones as she realized she was desperately looking for a solution that did not exist. *She* needed time.

"Give me a day. Let me think about this. Maybe I—maybe I can tell him. You needn't do this alone."

Christianna froze, turning her sad gray eyes onto Persephone. "I could never allow it. I must do it myself."

"Christianna—"

"I cannot believe you would offer to do this for me," Christianna whispered. "How fearless you are."

The compliment stunned Persephone, who felt very much like a coward.

"Let us be fearless together," Persephone encouraged, forcing herself to feel the bravery that Christianna seemed to see in her. "I promise you that I will be here. No matter what happens."

Aidon hadn't slept, and it was because he was in love. It had been *years* since he'd felt anything other than a constant stream of guilt, shame, and worry.

It used to be that his father's words haunted him often—words that had made up merciless criticisms, words that had expressed disgust and *disappointment*—but now they rarely crossed his mind. He thought about Cassius even less. All he could really think about was Persephone, curled up with her massive encyclopedia of Greek myths, searching for herself in ancient hymns. That he had been allowed into her world, into her bed, was a miracle that had to have been orchestrated by the old gods themselves.

And there was a chance that who he was now was truly better than the person he had been before. Persephone would not have looked at that person, let alone spoken to him. He knew some people missed who he had been. Even Ezra sometimes let slip that he hoped Aidon would allow some parts of his past self into the present. But it seemed he had suffered through everything so he could be the kind of man who could do right by Persephone. The kind of man she could love when she was ready. And he had such hope that she would be, someday soon.

Dawn had barely broken when he mounted his horse to return to Honeyfield. Ezra had, predictably, burst into Gallowsgate after dinner, keeping Aidon up well into the night with excited conversation. He was so desperate to return to Persephone that he had only granted himself a few hours of rest. The trip, thankfully, was short, and he soon found himself knocking on the front door.

Persephone did not answer, likely still asleep.

Aidon pushed the door open. It creaked softly, and he stepped into the entryway. The house was quiet except for the hushed whispers that floated down the staircase. He made his way up the stairs, wondering if Venus and Solomon had returned earlier than planned. He only recognized the second voice as Christianna's once he reached the landing, where he could hear their whispers quite clearly.

Embarrassed at having almost interrupted them, Aidon turned on his heel and began to make his way down the stairs and to the parlor. A heated, nervous sentence reached his ears.

"What am I to do with a baby, Persephone?" Christianna asked.

"Are you sure you are simply not late?" That was Persephone's firm, steady voice.

"I'm quite sure," Christianna responded, her voice breaking. "It has been too long, and I was so distracted, I—"

Aidon's brow knit in a deep frown. They were most certainly discussing a pregnancy—Christianna's—but she had yet to marry. She couldn't be with child.

Well, she could be. But only if—

It couldn't be.

Having heard quite enough, he silently descended the stairs. He let himself out, positioning himself by the busy skeps to wait for Christianna's departure. The early morning sun brought out the glitter of the dew that covered the carpet of wildflowers around him, but he suddenly found he was in no mood to admire them.

A child. Whose child? Ezra's? It couldn't be. Ezra would not jeopardize a young woman's life like that, whether he was in love with her or not. Someone else's, then. How could anyone betray Ezra's loyalty like that? Loyalty that was unwavering and strong, loyalty that Aidon had experienced firsthand.

Christianna left soon after, walking briskly down the path without taking a second look at the hives. Aidon returned to the house, making his way to the bedroom immediately. Persephone sat on the edge of her bed, and the sight of her in the morning light filled him with an ache that, for the first time, he tried to suppress. The dark smudges beneath her eyes betrayed her exhaustion, her worry apparent in the frown that threatened to pull at her lips.

"You've returned," she said, standing up.

"Is Christianna with child?" he demanded.

Persephone paled, her hands grabbing fistfuls of her dress. She cleared her throat. "No, of course not. Why would you—"

"Persephone," he said, an edge of warning in his voice.

She released her skirt, the muslin wrinkled. He could almost see her will to fight melt off her. "She is."

"I see," Aidon said. Persephone looked small and helpless, but he could not hold himself back. "How long have you known? Who is the father?"

"I have known for almost as long as you have," she said, clenching her jaw. "And I don't know who the father is."

"Does her family know?"

"No."

"And Ezra doesn't know."

Persephone shook her head, biting at her lip. "Perhaps—this can be fixed. People needn't know right away."

"Don't they?" he snapped. "Do you know what would happen if people discovered this, Persephone? There is a world outside of Oxbury—a world Ezra belongs to—where something like this could upend his entire life."

Aidon regretted the words as soon as they left his mouth. Persephone bristled, folding her arms across her chest as if shielding herself from him.

"I know there is a world outside of Oxbury," she said. "And there is not much good in knowing that when none of the women here will ever experience it."

"Persephone—"

She interrupted him, voice dripping in fury. "You've no idea what it is to be a woman. What do you think we should do? Let Christianna be cast aside by her family? From society? I would never let such a thing happen to a person I love. I do not care about what *matters* to the world outside of Oxbury. I only care about fixing this."

He remained silent. Damn her sharp tongue, her ability to lay everything out before him without a moment's hesitation. He knew she spoke the truth but refused to admit to it.

He himself had done unspeakable things to prove himself to people he thought he loved.

"Would you have told me if I hadn't overheard?"

Persephone sighed, the sound exhausted and melancholic. "I don't know."

"Of course not," he said, his voice emotionless.

"You've no right to be angry about this," she said. "Wondering what I would have done is pointless. You are the only one of us who has been keeping secrets." Her voice wavered as she reached the end of her statement.

"What secrets?" he asked darkly.

Her face colored, and she loosened her grip on herself for a moment. "Cassius came here—"

"Cassius? Why?"

"It doesn't matter," she said with an impatient wave of her hand. "But he told me—"

"Told you something damning about your dear husband, did he? And you readily believed it, I'm sure."

Persephone took a step back, his words striking a blow. She turned toward her bed, producing a small square of paper out from under her pillow.

"Is this not proof that you have secrets?" she asked, unfolding the paper and presenting it to him.

The letter from Lord Follett.

Aidon felt his blood go cold. He should have tossed that letter into the fire as soon as he'd received it. But it had been in his study, safe from prying eyes, safe from—

"When did you go to my study?" Her silence was heavy with guilt. "Did you go because—*what* did Cassius tell you?"

"It does not matter."

"Doesn't it?" he demanded, furious. "It matters that you took Cassius's word, whatever it was. My God, Persephone, do you trust me at all?"

"I do," she said brokenly, the sound pulling momentarily at his hardened heartstrings. "I am simply saying that people make mistakes."

"*Mistakes?*" he repeated, his anger flaring. "Were you making a *mistake* when you decided to break my trust? My work does not hurt a single soul and—I refuse to explain it any further.

Christianna's condition will hurt Ezra, Persephone. And she will hurt herself if she is discovered."

"Does she have to be?" Persephone asked nervously. "Could we not protect the both of them somehow?"

"If you have a plan, then I would love to hear it," he said.

"I don't," Persephone said, her voice small. "I don't, but I think we should give this time, and if that shocks you, then, well, this is what happens when you marry an odd, unwanted outcast from Oxbury. This," she said, gesturing to herself, "is what you are rewarded with."

He stared at her. Even through his fury, he could not believe that Persephone thought she had been odd or unwanted.

"Please don't tell Mr. Haskett," she said, turning her desperate gaze to his. "Even if we—I—don't think of anything, we must give Christianna a chance to do it herself."

He could not comprehend her clinging stubbornly to a plan that did not exist. Just as she was protecting Christianna, he felt the need to protect Ezra.

"I cannot promise that I won't," he said finally.

With that, he turned on his heel, leaving Persephone in her room as he departed Honeyfield and returned to Gallowsgate.

TWENTY-NINE

I should have never confronted him about that letter, Persephone thought miserably. She sat in the parlor at Honeyfield, holding a cold cup of tea and waiting for Venus and her father to return. She had not heard from Aidon for two days now, and the hours had been agonizingly long since he'd left.

She had only come up with one solution to offer to Christianna, and it involved a tincture that she had heard about from a few of the women in the village who had found themselves in similar situations. She had no idea whether Christianna intended to look into it, or if she planned on speaking to Ezra, but Persephone felt it right to allow her friend the space to decide either way.

She, meanwhile, would have to break the silence between herself and Aidon to ensure that he kept what he'd heard secret. She was angry at him for not understanding, for losing his temper, even for refusing to explain Lord Follett's letter to her.

Why wouldn't he explain it?

Hearing the door creak open, Persephone left her untouched tea in the parlor and went to the entryway. Venus was delicately pulling hatpins out of her golden hair while Solomon struggled with a pile of long rolled-up papers. A few clattered noisily to the ground.

"I told you you'd brought too many home," Venus said primly. Catching sight of Persephone, she broke into a massive grin. "You're still here!" Carelessly stepping over the papers and ignoring their harried father, she rushed toward Persephone and enveloped her in a cozy, warm hug.

"How was the seaside?" Persephone asked, feeling as though her voice was stuck in her throat. Venus's warm hug almost brought her to tears. She hadn't realized just how in need of comfort she'd been.

"Exciting, but only if you've an unholy love of bees," Venus sniffed, untangling herself from Persephone and casting a side-long glance at Solomon. "Papa enjoyed it, of course."

"As did Venus," Solomon said defensively, propping the rolls up messily in the corner by the staircase. He took his straw hat off his graying head and gave Persephone an assessing look. "We expected that you would have returned to Gallowsgate."

"I—Aidon is still in London," Persephone lied feebly. She felt silly and helpless, and suddenly all she wanted was to be alone.

"I am very glad for it," Venus said, all cheer. "It's been ever so lonely here without you, Persephone."

Persephone did tear up at this, sniffing pitifully as her sister peered at her, her blue eyes alight with curiosity. *Persephone* was lonely. She had been lonely her entire adult life, stationed at Honeyfield. At Gallowsgate, she had felt herself crack open like an egg and had slowly felt her lifelong melancholy fade.

Now she was right back where she'd started.

"Are you quite all right?" Venus asked.

"Yes, quite all right. I am simply feeling a little unwell," Persephone said, forcing steadiness into her voice.

Venus did not respond. She gave Persephone a long look, a frown pulling at her rosy cheeks.

Persephone quickly excused herself and spent the remainder of the day keeping her distance from her family. She holed herself up in her room, rereading her mother's tattered novels and ignoring calls for dinner or tea. Anxiety pooled in her stomach every time she thought of Aidon. It was her responsibility to keep Christianna safe, and here she was, hiding. One potential solution was not guaranteed to do away with a problem. She should be spending every minute thinking of all the ways she could prevent Christianna's life from crumbling to pieces.

Selfish.

She could not remember a time she had ever felt so awful. None of this should have happened. She should have remained as she was, Honeyfield's resident sharp-tongued haunt. But one thing had led to another, and fate—or, rather, her father—had intervened. The more Persephone thought about it, the sadder she became. When night fell, she ventured out of her room to seek her father out. Solomon was sitting alone in the parlor, candlelight flickering on his aged, drawn face as he read a book. Persephone pulled her wrap around her shoulders tightly, clearing her throat to get his attention.

"There you are," he said, as if he had been searching for her. He closed the book with a gentle thud.

"Papa," Persephone said, her voice thick, "do you think that Aidon and I are a good match?"

Solomon shifted to make room for Persephone on the soft, worn chaise. He gave her an odd look.

"I would not have consented to the engagement if I hadn't thought him a decent man," he finally said.

A tiny flame of anger began to lick at Persephone's insides. "After you announced the engagement, you yourself asked me what other options I had. As if I should have been grateful for the situation because you could not envision my ever being proposed to, and—"

Unable to finish her sentence, she began to cry, the stress and anxiety she had carried her whole life suddenly becoming too much for her. Solomon looked startled, and he reached toward her awkwardly.

"I did not mean ill," he said, his voice scratchy and tired. "I only meant to protect you."

"From what?" Persephone demanded, tears rolling down her cheeks.

"Ruin," Solomon said, reaching over to wipe her tears away with a rough hand. "And I have always worried what might become of you and Venus when I am gone."

"And so you saw fit to remind me of what a disappointment I have been to you," Persephone said stubbornly, sniffing sharply in a poor attempt to stop her tears.

"Disappointment?" Solomon echoed, tilting his head toward her. "Have I ever called you a disappointment?"

"You did not have to!" Persephone snapped. "I've always known. You *know* what people have said about me, Papa. If you did not agree with them, you would have said something long ago."

Solomon was quiet. Persephone's gaze did not waver, and she continued to pierce him with a hard look. The room was filled only with the crackle of the fireplace and the howling wind that beat mercilessly against the house.

She was so *angry*. She had always thought about what it might be like to be a different Persephone, but perhaps she ought to have dwelled on what it might have been like to be the same but accepted and understood nonetheless.

Solomon finally spoke, and Persephone was surprised to hear his voice crack. "My dear Persephone," he said, as if he were considering

his words for the very first time. "Words have always been my great-
est weakness. Even your mother thought so, bless her soul."

"That's it?" Persephone interrupted. "It is simply a flaw of
yours that I must accept?"

"Yes and no," Solomon said, speaking in that same contemplative tone. "I cannot change what I have said, but I can take
it upon myself to try again, if you'll allow it."

Persephone sighed, a part of her invested in keeping a firm
hold on the sadness that was equal parts painful and comfortable. "Very well."

"Few things in this life have sincerely pained me," Solomon said quietly. "Your mother's passing, for one. And now
this. I cannot bear to think that I have hurt you, Persephone.
I have never felt anything other than blessed to call you my
own. You have all that was good about your mother. You
have her intelligence, her wit—even your fierce protective-
ness reminds me of the way she loved you and your sister.
I have spent most of my life marveling at you." He paused.
"You must promise to tell me when I have hurt you. Do not
hold it inside."

The words were awkward and stilted, but Persephone found
that she did not care. Her father had never said such plainly
affectionate words. Both Venus and herself knew how much
Solomon loved them, but they had also grown up seeing that
love expressed through silent action. These words were a sooth-
ing balm to the little girl inside of her who still struggled after
all these years.

"Has Mr. Barrington done you wrong?" Solomon asked
gently. "Is that why you are here?"

"No," Persephone said quickly. "No, Papa. I simply—I was
thinking of how my engagement came to be. How you were
involved."

Solomon leaned over, pressing a dry kiss to her forehead. The smell of beeswax wafted off him, comforting her.

"Let us be thankful that it *was* a good match, then," he said, patting her head affectionately. "I should hate to think what terror you would have brought upon me otherwise."

Persephone sighed and smiled sadly. She would have brought no terror upon him at all, but she decided that she had pulled enough understanding from his tired, lean body for one night.

The following morning, Persephone was curled up in her bed. She had been reading the same three lines of Shakespeare for the past hour, unable to process the words on the page. A quiet knock echoed through the room, and Venus poked her head in.

"May I come in?" she asked. She replaced her head with a plate, her voice slightly muffled by the door. "I have biscuits."

Persephone laughed despite herself. "Oh, fine."

Venus came in, sitting on the foot of the bed and biting into a tiny iced biscuit, her curious gaze concentrated on Persephone.

"I thought I would wait for you to tell me what has been bothering you, but I've grown a bit impatient," she said guiltily. "I know Mr. Barrington is at Gallowsgate."

Persephone felt a chill creep through her. "What would you have me say?"

"I hoped you would tell me what happened between the two of you," Venus said calmly, offering a biscuit to Persephone. She took it but made no move to eat.

Venus studied her with round blue eyes. The very sweetness of her gaze broke Persephone's composure, and she began to sniff. The walls she had painstakingly rebuilt around herself over the past few days crumbled into dust as she divulged an abridged version of events to her sister. Venus listened patiently, nodding occasionally but remaining mostly silent. She did not even blink when Persephone mentioned Christianna's condition.

"I know that Mr. Haskett has to find out eventually," Persephone admitted, wrapping her coverlet around herself. "But Christianna has to decide what she'd like to do and if she'd like for me to intervene. Why can't Aidon see that?"

Venus shrugged, and despite her nonresponse, Persephone felt herself swell with love for her sister, who had been nothing but a calm and comforting presence throughout the course of the conversation. Venus enjoyed theatrics, but she'd seemed to consciously put them aside as Persephone had poured her heart out.

More remained to be said, but Persephone hesitated. She could not tell Venus about the letter or the gravestone. *That* would surely trigger a whirlwind of dramatics, especially given Venus's penchant for gossip. No, she would have to keep that to herself for the time being.

"You must speak to him, for Christianna's sake," Venus said. "Why haven't you gone?"

Persephone sighed, tucking her knees underneath her chin. "I just—I cannot face him now. I know I have to, but—"

"Perhaps he's changed his mind," Venus suggested. "We'd have heard of a broken engagement if he hadn't."

"Perhaps, but—if he'd truly changed his mind, then he would have come to speak with me."

Venus shrugged again. "Maybe he feels that he cannot face *you*. Have you considered that the two of you may be more alike than you think?"

A short knock came at the door before Persephone could

protest Venus's question. Solomon stepped in, a letter in his hands.

"For you, Persephone," he said, exchanging the letter for a biscuit as Venus swatted his hand away from the plate.

Persephone broke the wax seal, feeling her family's eyes on her.

Aidon.

She stiffened, and Venus seemed to register exactly what Persephone needed immediately. Standing up, Venus dusted the biscuit crumbs off her fluffy pink skirts and onto the floor. "Shall we have some tea, Papa?"

"Yes, yes," Solomon said, allowing himself to be led out of the room. He had been very careful around Persephone since they had spoken, and although she did not usually like any sort of fuss, she was grateful for it.

Once alone, she gathered every ounce of her courage to look down at the letter. Aidon's handwriting was a semi-neat scrawl, stretching across the page in bold strokes.

My dearest Persephone, the letter began. A speck of Persephone's anxiety dissipated. He could have very well started his letter with a curt *madam,* if he'd wished.

> *I pray this letter finds you in good health.*

Persephone bit back a small smile. Of course Aidon had taken the time for pleasantries and politeness. Insufferable.

> *I have spent every night since we parted thinking*
> *on our last exchange, and I regret much of what I said.*
> *Although my feelings have not been dramatically altered*

—she shook her head at this, biting down on her lip—

*I should not have taken such a tone with you. You
spoke of my secrets, which I refused to divulge. This, too,
I regret.*

  In truth, the Lord of the Dead does exist.

Persephone paused, heart thumping in her chest. Here? He
was going to lay it out in a letter, of all things?

*Lord Follett was writing to thank me for my
services, though they were not of the typical funerary
fashion. Many years ago, before I was born, my
grandfather decided to bolster his business by offering
the clandestine service of burying and concealing the
illegitimate children of the rich—stillborn children,
or those who passed from natural causes shortly after
birth—all of them too young to have had their existence
known by anyone outside the immediate family, their
bodies hidden indoors in some mockery of a vigil until
they could be dealt with. It was done for nothing more
than money. When my father took over the business, he
began to use the cemetery at Gallowsgate, thinking it an
affordable and convenient option. Later, he purchased
a hidden plot of land in London for the same purpose. I
myself have continued to use the same plot, only recently
making use of Gallowsgate for the first time.*

Persephone put the letter down, unable to read any further.
Her thoughts were muddled. Of all things for a person to do
to make *money*. But then, of course people would pay for it. In
a world run by gossip and scandal, people would do absolutely
anything to keep their secrets hidden.

She knew one thing for certain: whoever Aidon was helping

most likely did not deserve it. Illegitimate or not, children deserved to be buried with their families.

Aidon must have been haunted by this for the past ten years, and the weight of that fact made her throat tighten in sympathy. She had thought, rather naively, that there was a chance the gossip had simply stuck after his father's passing and had nothing to do with Aidon himself.

Foolish.

> If it helps to lessen your shock, I did not know of any
> of this as a child or young man. Granted, I was too busy
> chasing pleasure and frivolity to notice, but I was also never
> told about it by my father. I only discovered the duties I
> had inherited months into my role as head of the business,
> when a woman came to me desperate for help. She told me
> she had heard that she could seek aid from my family, and
> when I pried further, she told all. I only had to check my
> father's study in London—much like you checked mine.

Guilt pricked her skin. She should have left well enough alone. She had meddled in an effort to push back at the terrifying feelings that had threatened to overwhelm her. She sighed, feeling an acute sense of disappointment in herself.

> Still, I was unable to refuse her. Refusing has never
> quite been my forte, which I am sure explains much
> about me. I took on my father's old secret job of arranging
> funerals under the dead of night to hide the sins of the
> aristocracy. Even if my feelings on the subject were—and
> continue to be—mixed, it seemed a necessity, considering
> what would become of the very same children without
> my family's intervention. Lord Follett's mistress had given

*birth recently in the countryside, but the child lived only
for a few days. He pulled me aside while you and I were
in London to discuss the matter and the cost of a discreet
burial. Many in his position opt for an improper burial
in a potter's field, but he sought to please his mistress,
who hoped he would have the heart to bury the child in
his family's tomb. Many of the men who have engaged
in my services justify themselves in similar ways, or want
desperately to find a way to assuage the guilt of not
wanting their illegitimate children buried where they will
one day lie. When women come to find me, they typically
do so out of a desire to show respect and care to the
children they might have loved, had things not gone awry.*

*These are my secrets, as you called them, written out
in ink. The Lord of the Dead is no figment of London's
imagination, but rather your husband. I hope this satisfies
your curiosity. Whether it will eradicate your suspicions
remains to be seen.*

A few lines under the last paragraph had been crossed out,
though Persephone could barely make out the fragment of a
sentence that began with a devastating *I ache for you.* After, he
simply ended the letter with an abrupt—

*Ever truly yours,
Aidon Barrington*

Persephone crumpled the letter in her hand. Shockingly,
disgust had been the last thing on her mind while she'd parsed
through his words. In fact, an eerie sort of calm began to settle
on her. After a prolonged silence, she began to laugh. She was
Persephone, married to the Lord of the Dead, who took obscene

amounts of money from the rich to hide their *illegitimate chil-dren*, and nothing in her life had ever been so bizarre. Finally, she was living up to her namesake. Persephone, Queen of the Underworld, formerly of Honeyfield.

She would return, and they would discuss this further. Re-gardless of Aidon's attempt to bare his soul to her, he clearly stated that his feelings remained the same. Still, in another life, Christianna may have very well ended up tangled with the Lord of the Dead. If his letter told Persephone anything, it was that Aidon would have had empathy for her—which meant that somewhere inside him was the empathy for the situation Chris-tianna was in now.

Either way, Persephone would be damned if she let any-thing happen to Christianna. If she had to choose between her marriage and protecting her friend, then so be it.

Thirty

The rushed walk to Gallowsgate left Persephone's short hair windswept and wild. She had realized a very important fact on the way here. If she was selfish, then Aidon was a hypocrite. How was it that she was not allowed to protect Christianna while he was allowed to protect aristocrats who, arguably, did not deserve it? At least *she* was protecting someone she loved.

But she was too exhausted to be truly furious.

Baker let her into the house, looking uncharacteristically pleased.

"You have impeccable timing, madam," he said, shutting the door behind them. "We have managed to locate the key to the locked room. I have been carrying it on my person for safe-keeping while awaiting your arrival."

Persephone felt her breath catch in her throat. That room had belonged to Aidon's father. Another Lord of the Dead, keeping secrets behind a locked door.

"Have you gone inside?" Persephone asked as Baker reached into a pocket to produce a slightly rusted key.

He held it out to her with a shake of his head. "No, madam. I made sure to test the key, but as you were interested to know what was left behind, I thought you might prefer if I waited to enter."

Persephone took the key from him, the weight of it heavy in her hands. "Thank you, Baker. Where is my husband?"

"I believe Mr. Barrington is in his study," Baker replied, his expression returning to one of complete neutrality.

"Would you show me where the locked room is?" she asked. She did not know what she expected to find, simply that she was tired of secrets. Gallowsgate would never shake off the shadows of the past until every door had been opened and every room cleared out.

Baker took her upstairs to a closed door, where she slotted the key into its hole. Pushing the door open, she was met with the smell of must. Baker went to the window to push the curtains back, allowing light into the room.

"It will require extensive cleaning," he said, stating the obvious.

A thick layer of dust seemed to cover everything in sight. An overstuffed chair sat by the window next to a writing table. The wall on the left was covered in shelves stacked with books, and on the right was a fireplace filled with soot. Persephone went to examine the portrait that hung above it.

"The late Mr. Barrington," Baker informed her. "He intended to have this portrait moved to the stairwell, but the task was never completed."

Persephone peered into the painted eyes of the man that had, in many ways, broken Aidon's heart. They were an unfamiliar pale, icy blue, lighter than Cassius's and completely different from Aidon's. His mouth was pressed in a firm line, one gloved hand grasping the golden top of a cane. His wife and sons were nowhere to be seen.

"Did he intend to have it replaced with a portrait of his

family?" she asked, studying the strokes of white paint that made up the man's hair.

Baker was silent for a moment. "No, madam, I do not believe so."

Persephone sighed. She went to examine the bookshelf, despite knowing she would find nothing of interest on it. It was mostly occupied by books on English history and analyses of battles long past. She mindlessly pulled an untitled volume off the shelf, cracking the spine open. To her surprise, it was filled with lists in spidery handwriting.

5 January 1742 — Lord Buxton — £100

30 July 1742 — Mr. Wrottesley — £150

10 September 1743 — Lady Jordan, on behalf of her daughter — £125

The entries were from around seventy years ago, each listing a name and a specific amount of money. She turned to the front of the book to see the words *Property of Thomas Barrington* written in the same careless scrawl.

Aidon's grandfather, perhaps? She wondered if Charles Barrington had known of his father's doings before his death, or if he'd been purposefully shut out the way Aidon had been. And this book—was it the first ledger kept by a Lord of the Dead?

"Shall I gather the maids to begin dusting?" Baker asked.

Persephone returned the book to its shelf. She had wasted enough time here, looking for things that no longer mattered. What mattered was Aidon, and they needed to talk. "In a few days, maybe. My husband might want to look through his father's things."

He left with a nod. Persephone, too, made her way to the door, taking one last look at the room. Then, from the corner of her eye, she spotted a book that had been placed at the very top of a shelf, well out of reach.

Strange, given that the other books were so neatly arranged.

Vowing to take only a minute, Persephone walked back into the room, dragging the armchair next to the shelf and standing on it. She pulled the book toward her, blowing off the layer of dust that covered it. The cover was scuffed, the spine almost falling apart.

"*Mythology of the Greeks and Romans,*" she whispered, reading the words embossed on the cover. Her heart almost beating out of her chest, she stepped off the armchair and sat down, barely aware of the cloud of dust that rose around her. Slowly, she opened the book.

Her mother's handwriting was neatly printed across the title page.

Psyche, Artemis, Persephone, Athena.

Names. It was a list of names, written by a woman who had dreamed of naming her daughters after goddesses. Persephone ran her hands lovingly over the faded ink before flipping through the pages. The margins were littered with notes, some of them making connections to other books, others simply stating thoughts—*How I adore this!* was written on a page describing how Psyche was finally granted her immortality. *Poor thing,* next to a passage that recounted Medusa's fate. *Read to my children one day* had been scribbled beside a section titled, "Orpheus and Eurydice."

She remembered the night Emmeline had read that story to her, the tears that had welled up in her eyes when Orpheus turned to look at Eurydice.

"He shouldn't have," Persephone had pointed out.

"He did it because he loved her. You will understand—"

"When I'm older?" Persephone had guessed sullenly.

"Yes, when you're older."

As she continued to turn the pages, she came across a neatly folded piece of paper that had been nestled into the spine.

Dearest Violet,

I find this book an excellent resource for names, and I will be sure to use it when I am finally blessed with child. I have marked a page for you.

Emmeline

Along with the note was a dried, flattened sprig of lavender, delicate and at risk of turning to dust at the slightest touch. Emmeline must have given this book to Violet Barrington years before Persephone was born. Persephone carefully pulled out the sprig of lavender, placing it gently in her lap. As her eyes focused on the words before her, she realized she was looking at a very familiar story.

It was her myth.

I think, her mother had written in the margins for Violet to find, *if I am to have a girl, I shall name her Persephone.* She had written the words near the image of the goddess in question, perched in unusual calm in Hades's onyx chariot. *Hades is a bit on the nose, says Solomon, but what is your opinion of Aidoneus? One of my books claims it was another name for the aforementioned King. It would be delightful (Solomon disagrees, of course, because he is a bore) if we brought a Persephone and Aidoneus into this world, just like in the stories of old.*

Persephone felt her eyes well up with tears, gripped with a longing for her mother.

Aidon. *Aidoneus.* Of course.

Perhaps they had been destined to find one another. Just like in the stories of old.

She had spent so long trying to connect with her mother through this exact book. But now she saw a thread to the past—her past—in Aidon. It was as if her mother had laid the foundation for all that had occurred, for every step Persephone had taken.

Wiping at her eyes roughly with the cuff of her sleeve, she tucked the book underneath her arm and made her way to the study. She knocked but did not wait to be called in.

The room felt very different now that Aidon was in it, less terrifying and cavernous. He was sitting at his desk, his face the very picture of surprise. Persephone found she could not meet his brilliant green eyes for long, so she looked away before speaking.

"You should have told me about your—your deal with the rich, or however you'd like to refer to it, long before it came to this," she began, putting on a brave face. Finally, she looked at him. "But that is a discussion for another time. I want to talk about Christianna. You simply cannot tell Mr. Haskett about her."

Aidon stared at her blankly, shielded by the bulk of his mahogany desk. "Am I not obligated to tell him, Persephone? What of reputation? Honesty?"

"What do you care for reputation?" Persephone said softly, grounded by the press of her mother's book against her rib cage. "You've always had the power to be rid of the gossip surrounding you, and yet you persisted. Even if it did irreparable harm to you."

"I am not speaking of *my* reputation," he said irritably, "but of Ezra's."

Persephone was at a loss. She understood, but did not at the same time. They were about to talk in circles, to repeat what they had said to one another at Honeyfield.

"Christianna will do the right thing," she said confidently. "I know she will. Why won't you give her the opportunity to do so?"

"She's had plenty of time," Aidon retorted. "You know she has, Persephone. Ezra would have come to me if he'd been told."

And Christianna would have told me, she thought.

"We don't know what she means to do, or how," Persephone insisted. She paused. "I know I have disappointed you by asking for your understanding and for time. And by taking that letter." She took a deep breath, grateful for his silence. "I'm sorry I did. I think I might have gone through your study to— to ruin things. Because I have felt unworthy of your affections."

He frowned, the icy front gone. "Unworthy? Why would you even think—?"

"I don't know." Persephone sighed. "I have felt this way my entire life. I don't know if it's the isolation of Oxbury, or that I have never been able to charm people, or that Venus's superiority was hammered into my mind at every turn, I . . . I don't know. But it is what I feel. And I don't think I can ever be rid of it. Not permanently."

And, just like that, it was all out. As much as she resented the pain that had invaded her body, she relished the fact that it could be shed. She had released some of it to her father, and now to Aidon. She would no longer be a reservoir of melancholy. She could still be Persephone, still be herself, without it.

"Venus?" he echoed, standing up and stepping out from behind the desk. Persephone remained rooted by the door. "Why should any of that matter to you?"

"It doesn't," she said. "Most days, it doesn't. It's—it's like a wound. Healed, but if you bump it the wrong way, it still hurts. I cannot explain it."

He looked at her helplessly, and she felt anxiety flutter uncomfortably in her chest.

"I am sorry," she continued, desperate to expel the nervousness from her body, wanting to spill it into the room before it suffocated her, "for allowing Cassius to make me doubt you." She paused and then contemplated aloud, "I don't yet know how I feel about what you do. Perhaps—I think—you have been trying to earn forgiveness for disappointing the person you most desired approval from."

He remained silent, the helplessness on his face melting into a deep sort of sadness. Like her, it was part of who he had become. But if she did not have to hold it any longer, then neither did he.

"I do care. About you," she said. He raised his eyebrows at the admission. She walked toward him briskly and handed him the book. "It seems that you and I were meant to find one another. Even—even if you'd been thinking of your father's will when you agreed to marry me."

The words surprised her, even as they came out of her mouth. It seemed that as much as she'd tried to reason with herself, Cassius's words had lingered in her mind.

"My father's will?" he repeated, holding the closed book. "What are you talking about?"

"You needed to cut Cassius off," she said hesitantly. "Didn't you?"

"No," he said quickly. "I—yes, but—that wasn't *why*—I would never—I swore I wouldn't—"

"Then why would you agree to marry a complete stranger?" she prompted. "Not many people would care about the reputation of a woman who had been, and would continue to be, hidden away in the countryside all her life."

"No," he admitted. "But you've never been a stranger to me, Persephone. You and I—we've never been strangers."

"Of course we were," she said. "Everybody starts out as strangers."

He shook his head. "No, I just—I *knew*—it had nothing to do with the will, and everything to do with my wanting you. The truth is that I never had the nerve to fully cut Cassius off. His household expenses are still paid for and—even when I began to consider marriage, I swore I would not marry simply to protect the family accounts from my brother. I just—I knew it had to be you, Persephone. Everything else was simply a series of convenient coincidences. Believe me."

She knew she was at risk of dissolving into tears. How could she not believe him? No matter what he'd done, no matter what he currently did, Aidon was still the kind, considerate, sensitive man she had known him to be. She'd told herself that he would never have used her simply as a means to an end, and for once, she'd been right about something. Right about him. "I do believe you, Aidoneus."

His eyes snapped to hers, confusion marring his features. "What did you call me?"

"Aidoneus," she said again. "Is that not your name?"

"It is," he said, blinking rapidly in bewilderment. "But how did you—I haven't gone by that name since—"

"Open the book," she said. "There's a sprig of lavender marking the page."

He did so gingerly, eyes scanning the page as he took in her mother's writing.

"This is what you came looking for that first day, isn't it?" he asked softly. She nodded. "Where did you find it?"

"A room belonging to your father. It had been locked until recently."

A flicker of recognition, then, "On the second floor."

Persephone nodded.

"I don't think any of us ever stepped foot in that room. He kept it locked all the time, whether he was inside or not."

"And if my mother's book was there . . ." Persephone began.

"Then he must have taken it from *my* mother and locked it away," Aidon said, a now familiar bitterness tingeing his voice. He let out a slow exhale. "Was there . . . was there anything else?"

"Plenty of other books," Persephone said. "Some of which you might want to look at yourself. I told Baker to hold off on the tidying until you had the chance."

He put *Mythology of the Greeks and Romans* down gently on the desk, taking Persephone's hands in his. She felt her body respond to the contact that she had missed for so many days and nights.

"I had no idea," he murmured, looking at her. He let out a soft laugh. "I thought my mother had a proclivity for odd names, nothing more."

"You said our meeting was fate, once," she reminded him.

"Fate has never been kind to me," he said, running his thumb across her knuckles. "I did not think that would ever change."

Persephone laughed, the weight of his tone causing her to deflect reflexively with humor. "Unless you think of me as some terrible specter sent to haunt you, then perhaps things have indeed changed."

"Do not tease," he said quietly. "I could never—have never—thought of you that way. It is as I said. I love you."

Persephone felt the words melt over her like warm honey, so different from the way she had felt when he'd initially confessed his feelings to her. She wondered what had changed.

Perhaps *she* had changed in the short time they had been apart.

"Even after all this?" she whispered.

"Yes," he said. "Yes, I—may I?"

Persephone smiled and shook her head. "You must learn to stop asking."

"Another flaw," he murmured, bending to close the distance between them. Persephone felt her insides transform into a flurry of bubbles, each of them popping in excitement and anticipation. The kiss was tender, full of longing and desperation, and when they broke apart, she looked up into his eyes.

"If I asked you to promise not to speak to Mr. Haskett about Christianna, would you?"

"I can't do that, Persephone," he said. "You know I can't."

THIRTY-ONE

Reputation, for what it was worth, had only begun to matter to Aidon ten years ago. The disgraceful reputation he'd built in his youth had disappointed his father and made everyone see him as an incompetent fool. And he hadn't cared, really, until the day his father died.

Perhaps—I think—you have been trying to earn forgiveness for disappointing the person you most desired approval from.

Was that it, then? Was that why he had taken on the mantle of the Lord of the Dead? It seemed ridiculous, but Persephone's words echoed in his mind as he rode to the inn at Little Oxbury to find Ezra. That he'd waited to go to Ezra at all was a testament to how convincingly she had made her case—and how much he'd struggled against defying her wishes. He despised himself for still feeling like he had to do this, knowing it would shatter the delicate thread that now stretched between them.

What are you trying to prove?

That he was responsible? A hard, shrewd man like his father, who would never have stood for this? It was less a matter of *what* he was trying to prove but rather *whom* he was trying to prove it to.

The sign outside the inn squeaked noisily in the evening breeze, the sound echoing through the empty square. The sun was just beginning to set, bathing the village in a fiery orange light. Aidon tied his horse to a post by the side of the inn, his insides flip-flopping uncomfortably. Even as he approached the door, he was still uncertain of the path he was going to take once he came face-to-face with Ezra.

By the entrance sat a drunkard on a crude wooden bench, his worn hat drawn over his face. Just as Aidon reached the door, he heard a slurred, "Brother!"

The happy declaration startled Aidon, who looked for the source before finally settling his gaze on the benched figure.

It was Cassius.

He felt a surprising jolt of pity at seeing his brother so run-down, his clothing disheveled, his face ruddy with drink. The pity, naturally, mixed with confusion.

"My God, Cassius, what are you doing here?" Aidon asked softly, abandoning the door and moving to stand before his brother. He reached a hand out. "Can you stand? How long have you been here?"

"Of *course* I can stand," Cassius said happily, clearly tipsy. "And I've been here for an age! Terribly rude of you not to drop by."

Aidon looked at his brother silently, wondering if this was the sight he had looked to other people in the past. The thought sent shame barreling through him.

"Oh, get up, you stupid oaf," he grumbled, pulling a protesting Cassius off the bench. He began to lead him to his horse, hating himself for wanting to take him back to Gallowsgate. He couldn't just *leave* him here. Even if his brother had a room at the inn, he was clearly in no shape to care for himself.

As they rounded the corner to the side of the building,

Cassius piped up with a chipper, "I saw your sweet little Persephone the other day."

Cassius came here—

God, he felt like a fool. He'd been so wrapped up in everything that had passed, he'd forgotten about Cassius's involvement in it all. And, worst of all, he'd been distracted by pity. He released Cassius, and his brother braced himself against the wall in an effort to remain upright. His eyes were unfocused, a stupid smile on his face.

"Very good of you to remind me," Aidon said, eerily calm. "What business did you have with her?"

"Oh, I was bored!" Cassius wailed, sliding down the wall and onto the ground. "She wouldn't entertain me! How's that for hospitality?"

Aidon crouched down, looking Cassius in the eye and speaking very slowly. "Cassius. What exactly did you say to her?"

Cassius grinned toothily. "Don't be jealous, Aidon. We only talked about you."

"What about me?" Aidon demanded impatiently, dangerously close to losing his temper.

"Well, you're the Lord of the Dead, aren't you?" Cassius announced loudly. Aidon winced, grateful that Little Oxbury was sparsely populated even on the best of days.

He stood up, fully intent on leaving his brother to his own devices. "That is nothing more than gossip," he said sharply, beginning to walk away.

"Oh, come off it," Cassius laughed. "I *know* what you've been doing, you silly bastard."

Aidon froze, his blood turning to ice. Impossible. He had covered his tracks well—even clever Persephone would have been none the wiser if she hadn't found that damned letter. And despite the gossip, there had never been any solid proof that—

He's drunk.

As if reading his thoughts, Cassius crowed, "Father did it, too! He told me! I've always known."

At this, Aidon turned on his heel, marched back to where Cassius sat, and pulled him up violently. "What are you talking about?"

"Calm *down*," Cassius said, giving Aidon a pathetic push, his words slurred. "Why do you think I turned the business down?"

Aidon released him, eyes wide. "You—you didn't want the responsibility. I . . . I heard you refuse."

"You think that was the first time?" Cassius taunted. "Father had been begging me for *weeks* by then."

Despite himself, Aidon felt tears prick his eyes. This couldn't be true. Taking on the business, being the Lord of the Dead, performing his duties with controlled efficiency for what he'd believed was the greater good, all of it had sucked the very soul out of him. Cassius could have—

"You—you didn't warn me," Aidon said brokenly. "Why didn't you say anything?"

Cassius let out a noise of pure exasperation. "God, you really are stupid. Would you have taken the bloody thing on if you'd *known?*"

"No," Aidon said immediately. "No."

"And then what would have happened? Who would it have gone to?"

"I—"

Cassius interrupted before Aidon could respond. "Exactly. We wouldn't have had a penny between us, Aidon. No cousin of ours would have spent money on *this*." He gestured to himself.

"But—"

"Of course, I didn't think you'd carry on doing the nasty bits," Cassius said, his tone almost contemplative. "But you've always secretly wanted to prove yourself to Father, haven't you? He isn't even *here*."

Damn him.

Aidon had thought himself largely indifferent to Cassius since they'd grown apart. But they'd still been *brothers*, for God's sake. His only family. Now he saw that he had not felt indifference at all. Love had still been there, now shattered into painful shards tearing up his insides.

Heartbreak—a kind he had never felt before.

"Don't cry, you sod," Cassius sighed. "I did it for our own good."

"*Yours*," Aidon snapped. "You did it for your own good. God forbid we—you—work for money, is that it?"

"Yes, fine, I'm the reason you took on the business," Cassius said, sounding bored. "But nobody told you that you had to be the Lord of the Dead. You can't blame me for that."

Aidon stared at him in stunned silence. Cassius was right. For the first time, he was right.

"Still, you might have told me," Aidon insisted, tears threatening again. "Prepared me for what you *knew* I would have to deal with."

Cassius shrugged.

"No, of course you didn't," Aidon said, shattered. "You don't care. God, you never have. Even before—before all of this—you never cared about anyone but yourself."

"And look at me now!" Cassius chirped, spreading his arms out. "I wouldn't have given this up for anything."

"Not even for me?" Aidon asked desperately, despite already knowing the answer.

Cassius stared at him, gaze unfocused. The silence stretched between them, dark and empty. The last crumbling bridge between them gone.

The sound of his horse whinnying plaintively behind him brought Aidon back to reality. Cassius remained silent still, staring at him with an unreadable expression.

"Why tell Persephone?" he questioned softly. "What in the hell could you have thought to gain from that?"

Cassius raised a sardonic eyebrow at him. "I wanted to get back at you, you bastard. For actually finding a way to meet the terms of Father's will."

"Cassius—"

"I thought seducing her would do the trick, even if she isn't much to look at," Cassius continued lazily. "But I didn't bank on the silly girl actually *caring* about you."

Something murderous spiked through Aidon at Cassius's words. "Say that again."

"You heard me," Cassius said.

Aidon kneeled before his brother, his voice cold. "If you *ever* come near my wife again, I will ensure that the next gift she receives from me will be your *head* on a platter. Am I understood?"

Cassius snorted. "A lucky lady, indeed."

"You are a marvel," Aidon said. "So self-important that you imagined yourself to be the driving force behind my marrying Persephone. For God's sake, Cassius, look at yourself."

"Are you quite done?" Cassius asked.

"I am." Aidon stood. "Thank you for not even *attempting* a lie."

He mounted his horse, feeling Cassius's silent gaze on him.

"I meant what I said, Cassius," Aidon said. "If I ever see you around Honeyfield or Gallowsgate again, I will not be held responsible for my actions." He began to lead his horse away from the inn, away from his brother, his intention to speak to Ezra completely forgotten.

"You wouldn't hurt me," Cassius grumbled.

"Are you so sure?" Aidon asked. "You did not expect me

to carry on Father's work, and yet here I am. Perhaps you don't know me as well as you thought."

Aidon felt his brother's eyes boring into his back as he nudged his horse forward.

Cassius, blessedly, remained silent, rendered speechless for the first time in his life.

THIRTY-TWO

Persephone was at a loss.

She had been fraught with anxiety when Aidon left for Little Oxbury. Now, he had not spoken a word to her since he had returned, choosing instead to remain tucked away in his study. Something had clearly happened in Little Oxbury. Certainly not what he'd intended, or she'd have heard news of a broken engagement by now.

She'd known what Aidon had gone to do, and she had found herself at odds with how to feel about it. Worry had still managed to worm its way into her heart despite her fury and frustration with him. Perhaps this was what it was to care deeply for someone. She loved many a person, as many as she could in Oxbury, but none had ever filled her with fury, worry, and longing all at once.

She had yet to hear from Christianna, the continued silence fueling her dread. Still, she had to trust her friend would do *something*. Most likely, the delay was due to Christianna having to gather up the courage to approach her fiancé. She would not ignore the very real predicament she found herself in, nor would she purposefully hurt another person, especially one she loved—Persephone was certain of it.

The following day, when Persephone passed Aidon in the hallway, she had to violently stamp down her desire to reach out and touch him. They nodded at each other politely, just as they had done when they were first married. Everything between them—the promising, delicate beginnings of intimacy—had disappeared, leaving silences riddled with secrets and broken trust in its place.

Another day passed with no change, Persephone keeping to herself while trying to wade through her feelings. When she finally received a letter from Errwood, an invitation to a celebratory supper for the following evening, she was both relieved and surprised. She hadn't heard from Christianna herself and had no idea what she had or hadn't done. But Christianna would not have let it go this far if she hadn't taken some sort of action. Persephone felt so sure of it that she was finally able to breathe. Any temptation she had felt to burst into Aidon's study to demand to know what had happened in Little Oxbury was replaced with the decision to hold her silence until they went to Errwood.

There was no doubt that Aidon knew of the impending celebration. It was impossible for him not to have heard about it from Mr. Haskett, who had sent a letter mere hours after the invitation had arrived at Gallowsgate. He knew, then, and was doing nothing about it. Though it was possible he still had plans to—plans she was not privy to. She found comfort in the knowledge that Aidon would never cause a public scene, but that didn't mean he couldn't do any number of things before the supper began. He could track Mr. Haskett down, could even respond to the invitation with a damning letter of his own. Every scenario that came to mind demanded that Persephone remain on high alert. If her husband insisted on intervening still, then so would she.

"Persephone, are you in there?"

Persephone shut the doors of her wardrobe, only to see Venus standing in the entrance of the bedchamber. "Venus? What are you doing here?"

Her sister grinned at her, a package held in her arms. "I have something for you. I might have shown up earlier, but I've been wandering the halls for ages."

"Did nobody offer to show you to my room?"

"They did, but I refused," Venus said, utterly unashamed. "I thought I'd take a look around. This place is massive! And look at your room! It's so lovely."

Persephone bit back a chuckle. "If you wanted a tour, you could have just asked for one."

"The point is, I'm here," Venus said, walking in, a cheeky twinkle in her eye. "Were you looking for something to wear to the supper this evening?"

"I was," Persephone said.

"Then I've arrived just in time," Venus said, shoving the package into Persephone's hands. "Open it!"

Persephone did as she was told, a strained smile on her face, expecting a creation both unique and terrifying. When the paper fell away, however, her mouth dropped open in surprise. "Did you *make* this?"

"Partially," Venus said, unable to hide her glee. "That's your green silk. You know, the one you left at Honeyfield because of how you hate it."

"I never *hated* it," Persephone said, despite knowing she

had. The dress had been made years ago and had been collecting dust at Honeyfield ever since. It was not so much the deep color of it but rather its plainness that had made Persephone hide it away. Though she tended to dress simply, something about the unadorned silk had just looked wrong. It caught the light in all the worst ways, with nothing to show for itself.

That was not the dress she was holding in her hands, however. She was holding an expression of her sister's love, each bead and stitch painstakingly placed. Warmth spread through Persephone's chest, calming her unease. For a moment, things felt normal again, Venus showing Persephone one of her creations with a proud grin on her face, the way she had so many times at Honeyfield.

"Yes, you did," Venus said. "I wanted to practice my beadwork, and I knew you wouldn't mind if I tried my hand at this dress in particular. Do you love it?"

"I do," Persephone said, holding the dress away to examine the intricate details. "When did you get so good at this?"

"What else am I to do with my time?" Venus asked. "Learn to keep *bees*?"

"Perish the thought."

"It's not all that good," Venus said, joining Persephone in her study of the dress. "Some of it is a bit lopsided. See?"

Persephone looked to where her sister was pointing, recognizing that it was, in fact, a bit lopsided. "It's barely noticeable. Really, Venus, it's perfect. I love it."

Venus wrapped her arms around Persephone's waist in an awkward side hug. "I'm so glad. The pattern on the hem isn't entirely finished, but nobody will notice. I thought it would be just the thing to wear to tonight's supper."

Persephone lowered the dress. "What about you? You'd usually be readying yourself by now."

"Dressing you was more important," Venus said, untangling herself from Persephone. "And now that I've done that, I can focus on making myself look presentable. Will you show me out? I don't have all day to get lost again."

With a laugh, Persephone walked her sister to the door, making sure to give her a tight hug before they parted. Eager to try on the dress, Persephone went upstairs again, her gait slowing as she passed Aidon's bedchamber. The usually closed door was slightly ajar, an irregularity that caused her pulse to jump. Had it been that way when she'd passed by with Venus?

She looked around the doorframe to see Aidon staring out the window at the cemetery. He struck a depressing figure in the light of the late afternoon, and Persephone decided to leave him to his brooding. As she moved away, her hip bumped the door, the hinges creaking in protest. Aidon turned, and she cursed inwardly. With no other choice, she revealed herself, standing awkwardly in the doorway.

"Hello," she eventually said, the word echoing throughout the room as if to emphasize how silly it was.

"Hello," he responded. He took a step toward her, and so she began to speak quickly.

"I was on my way to my room," she blurted out. "I did not mean to disturb you."

"You did not," he said stiffly, and she vaguely thought she had never seen such rigidity from him. Not toward her. "Was your sister here? I thought I heard her voice."

"Yes," she said. "She was dropping off a dress."

"For tonight's supper, I presume," he said, his voice emotionless.

Persephone felt the blood drain from her face. She thought about lying to avoid the subject of the engagement, but that would be pointless. He already knew.

"Yes," she said plainly. "She did lovely work. It'll be well suited to the occasion."

"I'm glad," he said, not sounding very glad at all. The flatness of his tone frustrated her, and she made the split-second decision to broach the topic of his isolation.

"Is something the matter?" she demanded, taking a step into the room. She kept her eyes averted from the bed, desperate not to be inundated with memories of the night they had spent together there. He raised his dark eyebrows, his eyes widening in surprise at her forwardness.

"What do you mean?" he stammered.

Persephone saw color begin to creep across his face. He was embarrassed.

"You went to the village to speak with Mr. Haskett," she said. "Did something happen there? Since returning, all you've done is sit in your study."

"No," he said slowly.

"Are we to continue to lie to each other?" she demanded with a sigh. "Is that what you want?"

Aidon stared at Persephone in complete bafflement. She stood before him, hands on her hips, small and delicate and full of determination and fire. He had wanted to tell her but had not known how to approach the topic. She had rightfully kept her distance from him, and he had decided to respect that, choosing instead to marinate in his own misery in the privacy of his quarters.

"Well?" Persephone prompted again.

"I—what would you have me say?" he asked, sinking down onto a hard chair by the fireplace and looking up at her. She took a few steps to stand before him.

"I would have you tell me what has been plaguing you so," she said, her voice now gentle. "Or will you return to keeping secrets from me?"

He hung his head, looking at the floor. "You should not want to carry this burden, Persephone. Not after what I set out to do, what—what I almost did."

"You did not speak to him, then," she said. "What happened?"

She expressed herself matter-of-factly, as always. He admired her for it, wished he could just *say* what was on his mind the way she did. She studied him with her wide, dark eyes, a crease appearing between her eyebrows.

"I saw Cassius," he said eventually, his voice a near whisper. "In the village."

Persephone's face fell, the fiery expression melting away. "He's still here?"

"I don't know where he is now," Aidon admitted, feeling guilty despite himself. "I left him there."

"Good," Persephone sniffed. She paused. "That can't have been all."

He looked up at her then, his gaze meeting hers, her face a promise to help him hold this.

"Cassius knew," he said finally, his voice breaking at the admission. "He knew."

Persephone kneeled before him, lightly placing her hand over his and tilting her head to look into his eyes. "Knew?"

"About the Lord of the Dead. He knew what our father was doing. That's why he refused—he knew, and he did not warn me."

"Oh," she said softly.

Her hand still rested gently over his, and he placed his other hand over hers, grasping at it like a buoy. "One of us needed to take over the business, he said. For the money. But he never thought I would take on the mantle of Lord of the Dead—*why do I do it?*"

Persephone stood up, easing her body between his legs, holding his heavy head close to her stomach. The intoxicating smell of lavender reached him instantly. "I don't know," she murmured, running her hands comfortingly through his dark hair.

He let out a long exhale. "Don't you?" he asked into the fabric of her dress.

He was referring to what she had told him earlier, about his desire to earn forgiveness from his father, the man he had so often disappointed. The man he most desired approval from. Her body shifted with a sigh.

"It was only a thought," she said. "I should know better than to—I did not think before I said it."

He pulled away, looking up at her helplessly. "Do you think I—have I become what I am because of him?"

Persephone looked down at him, her hands cupping his tired face. She looked every bit the goddess she was named after, benevolence and redemption a promise in her brilliant, dark eyes.

"I cannot answer that for you," she said, shaking her head.

"But you said—"

"Not everything I say is the truth," she said. "Whatever the reason, I do think you need to stop."

Stop? How could he stop? People needed him. He had been doing this for years. He was doing what his father and grandfather before him had set out to do. This was what his father had intended for *him* to do. And Charles had done it for good reason. Children would be cast aside if discreet burials were not an option. Maintaining the delicate hierarchy of society depended on such secrets being hidden away. Take away what his family had offered for generations, and a whole host of issues would arise. *That* was why his father needed the work to be continued. He was sure of it.

A flicker of affection crossed her face, and he realized he would be disappointing her yet again.

"I can't," he said brokenly.

"Aidon—" she began, but he interrupted her.

"And Cassius—Cassius told me what he tried to do to you. I wasn't able to protect you from him," he said, needing everything out in the open.

"I am fully capable of protecting myself," Persephone said, her tone both gentle and firm.

"I know, but—"

"And you know to protect me from him now."

"Yes, of course," he said.

"Then there is nothing for me to be concerned about," she said. "For now, however, I would have you protect yourself."

"Protect myself how?"

"By doing what I said. You are more than the responsibilities you've inherited, Aidon."

"It's my job," he said, voice barely above a whisper. "I can't."

THIRTY-THREE

Persephone sighed as she looked into her mirror, smoothing her hands over the bodice of her beaded dress. The empire-waisted ensemble was made of the dark, forest-green silk she was already familiar with, but altogether improved by her sister's thoughtful additions. Venus had decorated the skirt and bodice with tiny pomegranates, brought to life by small ruby-colored glass beads. A gold ribbon was tied neatly under Persephone's breasts, the ends of it hanging low by the backs of her knees. On her vanity sat the pair of earrings that Aidon had given her. Threading them through her ears, she sighed once more.

He had refused to stop playing the role of the Lord of the Dead. She had not allowed the conversation to go on longer than it had because, as usual, she'd found that they were talking themselves in circles. A part of her wanted to erase it from her mind, to just stop caring. Indifference had been one of her strong suits in the past, but now—now it seemed a struggle to summon it at all.

She hated to see him hurt himself, and yet she could do nothing to stop him.

After one last look in the mirror, Persephone headed to the waiting carriage that would take them to Errwood. Aidon stood outside of it, politely offering his hand and helping her to step inside without a word. She felt a childish pang of sadness at not being complimented on her appearance. It had been a foolish hope, perhaps, given the strain between them.

The carriage began the bumpy journey to Errwood, the silence beginning to eat away at Persephone. Aidon, pressed and starched to perfection, seemed content to look out the window at the passing emptiness of Oxbury, his handsome face illuminated by the light of dusk. He looked *wonderful*, and she impulsively said so.

"I beg your pardon?" he asked.

"You look wonderful," she repeated, wanting to kick herself.

"Thank you," he said awkwardly. "You look lovely."

The wheels of the carriage rolled over a particularly large bump in the road, jostling Persephone violently as she replied with a dry, "Kind of you to say so."

Something akin to understanding flickered across his features, but he seemed to decide to keep whatever thoughts he'd just had to himself. Persephone huffed and turned to look out the window. The tension in the carriage was unbearable. She hadn't realized it took this long to get to Errwood, especially given the shortcuts she and Christianna had forged through the overgrowth between their two homes.

"I think," she said, her voice sounding uncomfortably loud in the quiet that had once again settled, "it would do us well not to let on that we have had—are having—disagreements. If you could pretend to stand me, at least for the evening, that would be best."

There, she'd said it. She hoped for a begrudging agreement, almost expected one.

Instead, all she got was an incredulous, "Pretend to stand you?"
And, truly, she did not know what to say to that.

The tension in the carriage was unbearable.

Persephone had emerged from Gallowsgate a vision, the setting sun catching the crimson beads that dotted her dress. He was used to seeing her in muslin day dresses, the hems of which were usually stained with grass by midday at the very latest. Those, he found her irresistibly charming in. The dark green of this gown brought out the sparkle in her brown eyes and the peach in her smooth skin. In this gown, she was not irresistibly charming but simply *irresistible*.

As the awkward silence had settled in the carriage, Aidon had begun to grapple with whether or not mentioning her appearance would be appropriate. They had been so close to finding one another again, only for him to ruin it with his un-yielding stubbornness.

And stubborn he had remained. He would not allow him-self even to *consider* abandoning his post as Lord of the Dead. Something inside him was holding on with a viselike grip, and he could not muster the courage to break away from it.

He had been surprised, and more than a little pleased, at her compliment. Even as he had returned it in earnest, Perse-phone's face had not been that of a lady flattered. And so the silence had descended upon them once more, broken only by her primly asking him to pretend to enjoy her company.

"Pretend to stand you?" he asked incredulously. He'd spent half this carriage ride pretending he did not want to tear her pretty dress off her body.

Persephone placed her hands neatly in her lap, running her

fingertips over the clusters of beads that decorated her skirts. The small, delicate movements caught his eye, inflaming him further.

"I should hate for anybody to know our business, that is all," she finally responded, still fiddling with her gown.

"I do not have to *pretend* to stand you, Persephone," he said, his voice rougher than it should have been. He knew he ought to rein himself in, that they would be arriving at Errwood at any moment, but the sight of Persephone in her lovely glittering gown had undone him. The square neckline was cut dangerously low, her chest heaving deliciously with every breath. She was giving him a look of complete confusion, her head tilted, her earrings catching the light. "I told you I love you, for God's sake."

He was being harsh, he knew, but he was finding it very difficult to control himself. Frustration over their disagreements intermingled viciously with the raging desire running hot through his veins.

It was not a kind combination.

"Even now?"

The quiet thoughtfulness of her voice composed him for a moment.

"Do you think it something I can simply stop doing?"

Persephone huffed at this, folding her arms across her chest. The movement was restricted by the tight puff sleeves that capped her pale shoulders.

"You needn't take that tone with me," she said, her voice steady and assured. "I was simply asking."

She was right, and he was being a bastard. But something in him wanted to fight, and her refusal to take the bait was bringing his blood to a low simmer.

"I've an idea," she continued. "Let us bring everything out into the open. That way, we will be able to concentrate on Christianna and Mr. Haskett. What do you think?"

What was she playing at?

At his silence, she said, "I do not think you should continue your work as the Lord of the Dead."

Of course that is where she would start.

"And I told *you* that is out of the question," he replied.

Persephone leaned forward, her breasts almost spilling out of her dress, her knees grazing his. "I think you're scared."

Scared!

A triumphant glint in her eye told him she thought she'd put all the pieces of the sordid puzzle together. He mirrored her, leaning forward so that they were eye-to-eye. Traces of pink began to color her cheeks.

Good.

"There is very little I am afraid of," he said, voice low.

He was lying, of course. There were plenty of things he was afraid of, though being Lord of the Dead was not one of them.

"That can't be true," she said, straightforward as ever. "You are afraid of disappointing your father, and you hate to admit it."

"Persephone," he warned.

She did not back down. Not that he had expected her to. If anything, she was stoking the fire inside of him just like he'd hoped.

"What shall you do, then, if you refuse to admit to it?" she demanded.

Finally, an opportunity to derail this insufferable conversation.

"This," he said, taking her roughly by the waist and pulling her toward him. She stumbled over the minuscule distance between them, straddling him to regain her balance. She blinked at him, eyes wide with surprise.

"What are you doing?" she whispered.

"You asked me what I would do," he replied, feeling her slender hands tighten around his shoulders.

"We've yet to reach a compromise," she said slowly.

"You want to find common ground, don't you?" he murmured.

"Of course—"

Cutting her off, he pressed a kiss at the junction between her neck and shoulder, her skin warm and lightly scented with the familiar aroma of lavender.

"You did not ask," she gasped.

"Didn't I?" he asked, running his hands up her back and reveling in the feeling of her body responding to his touch. "I asked if you'd like to find common ground."

She raised an eyebrow at this. "You're insufferable."

"That's right," he coaxed, trailing kisses down her neck. "Bring everything out into the open."

She sighed, running her fingers through his hair. God, he'd missed this. It felt like an age had passed since he'd touched her last, since he'd been inside her. His lips found hers, their kisses laced with an aggression he had never felt with her before. It was delicious and urgent, and he found he did not care that he was postponing the many heavy, insufferable conversations that lay ahead of them.

"I love you," he said desperately in between kisses. "I love you."

She did not respond, and he had not expected her to. Reaching up, he pulled roughly at her dress, revealing her delectable breasts.

"Don't ruin my dress," she said, scolding him breathlessly, a strangled moan leaving her throat as he took a pink nipple in his mouth.

"Wouldn't dream of it," he said, lavishing attention on her breasts as she ground herself against the growing tightness in his trousers.

Suddenly, the carriage came to a sharp, halting stop. Persephone scrambled out of his lap and haphazardly restored her dress to its previous position. Just as she finished adjusting her sleeves, the door opened to reveal Errwood. Aidon exited the carriage first, taking Persephone's hand as she stepped down.

"Do not think you have succeeded in distracting me," she whispered calmly as they approached the house.

"No? Then I shall have to try harder."

She shot him a look as they were ushered into the entryway, dropping his hand unceremoniously and disappearing up the stairs.

THIRTY-FOUR

Persephone knocked at Christianna's door and waited to be let in. She pressed her cold hands against her cheeks, hoping to drain some of the redness from her skin.

She was so *frustrated*. She should not have wanted him, but she did. She'd wanted him to take her—as thoroughly and roughly as he pleased. But there was still so much that desire could not solve. Perhaps they were simply too different from one another.

Have you considered that the two of you may be more alike than you think?

Persephone frowned as her sister's words popped into her head. She and Aidon were both stubborn. That much, at least, she knew.

The door swung open to reveal Christianna dressed in white, the fabric draped loosely below an empire waist and tied with a pale blue ribbon that brought out the stormy gray of her eyes.

"Oh, Persephone, you look lovely!" she gasped, pulling her inside the room and shutting the door.

"You're a *vision*," Persephone said in wonder.

Christianna blushed prettily, tucking a stray lock of dark hair behind her ear. "Do you really think so?" Her voice dropped to a whisper. "I can't tell you how grateful I am to not be showing yet."

"Showing?" Persephone echoed. A chill spread throughout her body. "Christianna, you did tell Mr. Haskett, didn't you?"

Christianna's hand flew to her chest. "It's been such a whirlwind. Just sit, won't you?"

Persephone sat on the edge of Christianna's large bed while her friend returned to the vanity to fuss over her hair. Christianna's bedchamber was large and white and airy. Her mother had made sure to keep Errwood fashionable, which meant it was very different from the poky hallways of Honeyfield.

Honeyfield, in all its wildness, was Persephone. Errwood was Christianna, elegant and bright.

"I thought about the tincture you mentioned," Christianna admitted softly, breaking the comfortable silence, "and it was nice to have the choice, but I decided to tell Ezra instead."

"But—" Persephone's mouth dropped open, her eyes meeting Christianna's in the mirror. "But this supper . . . he didn't—?"

"I knew," Christianna said softly. "I knew the minute we met that there was something wonderful and different about him."

"And he doesn't mind?" Persephone asked in disbelief.

"It's our secret now," Christianna said, eyes sparkling in the warm light pouring from the fireplace. "Can you believe it?"

"I can't," Persephone admitted. A wave of relief spread through her, and she smiled. "I am so happy for you, Christianna."

"I should thank you," Christianna said. "You gave me as long as I needed. A different person might have tried to intervene for propriety's sake."

"I knew you would do whatever you thought was right for you," Persephone said, feeling deeply exhilarated at having been right.

"I left it far longer than I should have," Christianna said, lowering her voice. "My mother unknowingly forced my hand the minute she began inviting people to supper. I sought Ezra out soon after and told him everything."

"That was very brave of you."

Christianna laughed. "I'm glad you think so because I felt like a terrible coward. Now, tell me, is this the beginning of a blemish on my face, or am I imagining things?" Without waiting for Persephone to respond, she reached for her white powder and began pressing it into her face with a puff. "I do hope Ezra does not notice. I want to look perfect tonight."

Persephone shook her head, still reeling from the news. "He won't. Trust me when I tell you that men are far too distracted by other things to take note of any particulars."

Christianna returned her powder puff to its place. "Spoken like a true expert."

Persephone felt her cheeks warm in response. Ignoring Christianna's teasing, she asked, "Do you think you're in love?"

Christianna whirled around, her hands returning to their efforts to tame her hair into a fancy chignon despite the cloth curlers that still hung by her jaw. Beaming, she said, "Oh, Persephone, I do. I think I shall continue to fall more in love every day."

The announcement and its sincerity caused an uncomfortable feeling to bloom in Persephone's stomach.

It was envy.

She envied that Christianna had been so open to falling in love that she and her soon-to-be husband shared secrets with a freedom she hadn't known. Persephone, meanwhile, remained difficult and stubborn. She believed she loved Aidon but did not have the courage to say so, and she was too stubborn to admit to it while the tension between them persisted.

Even Aidon was a part of Christianna's ranks, his free and

truthful declarations of love driving a stake through her heart with every repetition.

Standing up, Persephone walked toward the window overlooking the gardens. She saw a small group of guests milling about, drinking and chattering. A long table had been set among the flowers and candles, ready to be laden with supper.

"It's lovely," Persephone said pleasantly, remembering how she'd gone to great lengths to make sure nobody in Oxbury knew of her own wedding. Perhaps she ought to have been a little more open.

A little more confident.

"Isn't it?" Christianna agreed, joining Persephone at the window. "Mama planned every detail." After a pause, she asked, "Where is Mr. Barrington?"

Persephone did a quick survey of the garden, searching for the imposing figure of her husband. He was nowhere to be seen. A jolt of electricity ran down her spine as she realized where he might have gone.

"Have things been quite all right between the two of you?" Christianna asked. "I do not mean to pry, but Venus mentioned—well, you know Venus."

Ever the gossip, Venus must have let on that there was something amiss between Persephone and Aidon.

"We are quite well," Persephone said quickly, despite desperately wanting to divulge all to her friend. "I think I shall go find him, actually. I'll see you downstairs soon, won't I?"

"Yes, quite soon," Christianna said.

Persephone fled to the hallway, a twinge of anxiety spiking through her as she left her friend to sit alone once more.

Aidon found himself staring at a cherrywood door somewhere in the spacious, airy maze that was Errwood.

Life had truly descended into chaos, and Aidon was not sure what to turn his focus on first. His tension with Persephone? The open, bleeding wound that had been left by a heartless Cassius? The fact that Ezra was engaged to a woman Aidon had introduced him to—a woman who was also carrying the illegitimate child of another man?

He supposed it made the most sense to focus on Ezra, given that he was standing right outside his door. But, frankly, he did not know how to proceed. Time had not brought any semblance of clarity with it. If anything, it had only brought more confusion.

Before Aidon could finish parsing through his thoughts, the door swung open with a dramatic creak. Ezra stood on the other side, an undone cravat hanging limply around his neck. His freckled face was glowing with excitement.

"I thought I heard someone brooding outside my door," he said cheerfully.

"My apologies," Aidon said sheepishly. "I didn't know if you wanted to be left alone."

"Have I ever?" Ezra asked, ushering him in. He spread his arms out. "Well? How do I look?"

Happy. He looked happy.

Instead of saying so, Aidon said, "Your cravat is undone."

"Yes, thank you," Ezra deadpanned. He walked toward the mirror and began to fiddle with the length of fabric around his neck.

Aidon couldn't help but think how Ezra's happiness would be shattered if he were told the truth about Christianna. How he would be shattered if he were to discover it later, if he put the pieces of the puzzle together months after the wedding.

Aidon felt frustration descend upon him. He hated that his mind kept leading him in senseless circles, and it irritated him to no end that it was only doing so because he was so hesitant to destroy Persephone's hard-won trust. But if Christianna had told the truth, there would be no celebratory supper. It was clear to Aidon that Persephone's friend still held on to her secret, and every moment Ezra did not know was a moment he wasted on being hopeful about the future.

"I can't do this," Ezra finally declared, hands dropping from his neck.

Aidon shook his head fondly, joining Ezra by the mirror to help him tie the cravat into a tidy knot. He could practically feel the joyous warmth radiating off his friend.

You would be ruining this. It is not for you to tell.

But if Ezra were to find out later, his mind insisted, his happiness would be ruined all the same. It would be better for the news to come from a trusted friend.

"Ezra," Aidon began stiltedly as he worked on the cravat. "About Christianna—"

"I was teasing you about finding eligible young women in Oxbury when we first came here," Ezra interrupted pleasantly. "I am certainly eating my words now, aren't I?"

"Yes, but she's—"

The disarmingly joyful look on Ezra's face stopped Aidon's words in their tracks. Ezra had always been good-natured and chipper, even on his worst days, but Aidon suddenly registered this as something different. It was less Ezra's everyday cheer, and more a warm, deep-seated joy.

The kind of joy Aidon felt when he was around Persephone.

He couldn't do this. He couldn't be the one to break Ezra's heart. He could only be the one who helped pick up the pieces when Christianna finally decided to come clean.

Aidon caught Ezra studying his face with a curious expression, a half smile pulling at his mouth.

"She's with child?" Ezra said calmly. Aidon dropped the ends of the cravat in surprise.

"No, no," he replied quickly, shaking his head and lifting his hands to the starched fabric once more. "I was simply going to say that the two of you are a fine match."

Ezra folded his arms against his chest. "Come off it. She told me."

She'd *told* him? Ezra had been prone to dramatics his entire life, and he chose *now* to remain serene and sensible?

"But—you—" Aidon stammered in disbelief. "You did not break the engagement."

"I didn't want to," Ezra said. "I love her."

"Why did you not say anything?"

"To who?" Ezra asked.

"To me!" Aidon shot back, feeling foolish as soon as the words left his mouth.

Ezra gave Aidon a pointed look, gesturing between the two of them.

"To avoid this exact scenario," he sighed.

The innocent, well-meaning words caused a mixture of embarrassment and sadness to flare in Aidon's chest.

"You did not think I would have stood with you?" he asked.

Ezra held Aidon's gaze for what felt like a long moment before sighing again. "Ah," he said, clearly making an effort to choose his words carefully, "I think you might have, years ago. You and I both know you've become a bit stiff, Aidon. A little more like your father than you'd care to admit."

Aidon frowned, Ezra's words striking hard and true. His friend knew the weight of what he'd just said. Had Aidon truly abandoned more than he should have while trying to make up for a lifetime of disappointing his father? As Ezra looked at him, his face apologetic and gentle, he began to wonder.

"I understand," Ezra continued softly. "We grew up together, you and I. You needn't explain yourself."

"Yes," Aidon admitted after a long silence. "I should hate for you to think that you have to keep anything from me."

"I am sure Christianna's decision was not made lightly," Ezra said, shrugging. "Either way, it has no bearing on her character."

Persephone had felt very much the same and had been willing to let her friend chart her own course. Aidon sighed. He'd been a fool, albeit a different sort of fool this time around. Still, he had to know.

"How is it so easy for you to accept?"

"What is the alternative?" Ezra asked, his tone uncharacteristically contemplative.

The question sent a jolt of clarity through Aidon's mind. What *was* the alternative? If Ezra had broken his engagement, he'd have sentenced himself to a lifetime without the woman he loved.

And if Aidon simply chose to, he could live a life with no guilt or shame. A life built solely on trust and love.

"Besides, I think I'd be a lovely father," Ezra chirped.

The seriousness of the moment was broken. Ezra had always been particularly skilled at bringing cheer to dark, somber silences.

"You?" Aidon scoffed. "Your influence will leave the child a little terror."

"Perhaps," Ezra smiled. "But he'll be *my* little terror. Our children can wreak havoc the way we did when we were lads."

The sincerity and hopefulness in Ezra's tone brought an indescribable wave of melancholy over Aidon. He sighed despite himself.

"Struck a nerve, have I?" Ezra said, though the words were not mean-spirited. He narrowed his eyes questioningly. "Have you reconciled with Persephone? Christianna told me there was some tension between the two of you."

Aidon wandered over to the large four-poster bed, sitting down heavily and wrinkling the fine silken coverlet atop it. "It's been difficult."

"Do you care to discuss it? I'm afraid I don't know the particulars."

Aidon thought about all the things Ezra did not know. He knew about the gossip but did not know that the Lord of the Dead was real. He wondered if his forgiveness and empathy would extend toward Aidon if he knew the truth.

"I love her," he said instead, his voice a near whisper.

Ezra whirled around to regard him with wide blue eyes, a glimmer of excitement evident to Aidon even from across the room. "That's wonderful!"

"Is it?" Aidon asked. It had felt wonderful at first but had morphed into feeling terribly painful.

"Have you told her?" Ezra asked, moving toward Aidon. "Has she returned the sentiment?"

"Yes," Aidon said. His friend brightened before Aidon continued with a bitter, "And no, she has not."

"Ah." Ezra sat down alongside him with a soft thud. He looked around the room for a moment as if he'd misplaced something. "She loves you," he said finally, eyes resting on Aidon.

"You can't possibly know that," Aidon said, despite feeling rather desperate for comfort.

"I think our conversation today has revealed I know far more than you think," Ezra said cheekily, standing up again and heading toward the mirror. "Mark my words. Whatever is brewing between you can and will be solved. Love *is* meant to conquer all, you know."

Ezra said this sincerely and calmly, finally managing to tie his cravat into a passable knot.

"There!" he said triumphantly, turning to look at a dazed Aidon. "I'm full of surprises today, aren't I?"

THIRTY-FIVE

Persephone rushed around Errwood like a panicked, harried chicken. If Aidon was not mingling among the guests, then he was undoubtedly with Ezra. And that would simply not do, especially since Christianna had taken care of matters herself. There was no scenario in which Aidon's involvement would improve things.

Persephone did eventually find Aidon. Or rather, he found her. Just as she was passing yet another door constructed from fashionable cherry lumber, Aidon stepped out, causing Persephone to run directly into him.

"Sorry!" she said breathlessly, noticing Ezra peering curiously over Aidon's shoulder. She attempted to smooth herself into some semblance of presentability, running a palm over her wild hair. "Mr. Haskett! Hello."

"Please, call me Ezra," he said pleasantly. "Shall I see the two of you downstairs, then?"

"Yes," Aidon said before Persephone could reply. He gave Ezra a curt nod, shutting the door behind him.

They faced one another in the hall, Persephone lifting her

chin in challenge. Aidon looked at her with a sort of melancholy, and she felt herself deflate. Ezra had seemed rather cheerful for someone who had likely been judged quite harshly by his friend for his decision.

Unless—

Persephone grabbed Aidon by the hand, pulling him toward an empty room at the end of the hall. He followed silently and willingly. The room was a small study, very different from Aidon's, with bright white furniture and walls adorned with a variety of stylish portraits and landscapes, no books on burial rites or funerary practices to be found.

"I wanted to apologize for going through your study," she said. "I . . . I don't think I did a good enough job when we spoke of it last."

He raised his eyebrows, a small smile pulling at his lips. "Is that what you brought me here to say?"

The unexpected humor in his voice disarmed Persephone for a moment, and she felt the longing she should have left in the carriage rise up in her abdomen again.

This is no time for distraction.

Crossing her arms against her chest, she lifted her chin once more and tried to look firmly into his devastatingly beautiful eyes. "No, it is not. Still, it's important for you to know. To betray your trust like that was—it was awful of me, and you did not deserve it. I can promise it will never happen again." She paused to take a breath. "Did you—"

"I didn't get involved," Aidon interjected.

Persephone felt herself relax as the tension released from her stiff shoulders. "You . . . didn't discourage him from marrying her?"

He shook his head. "I did not. And I must apologize to you as well."

"Whatever for?"

"Hiding from you," he said.

"Oh," she said softly. Then, because she had no idea how else to respond, she said, "It's—it's quite all right. I understand."

"I also want you to know that what I said in the carriage, what I've been saying *repeatedly*, is true. I love you. My life was—it was empty before you. Loving you is quite literally the least difficult thing I have ever done."

The admission stunned her, and she felt tears begin to prick her eyes. He believed loving *her* was the least difficult thing he'd ever done. All her life, she'd thought that the people who loved her were performing some godlike feat.

"What you did," he continued, "or what you didn't do, rather, was born of a deep-rooted belief in the goodness of people. I envy that."

Persephone sank down heavily on a nearby chaise, upholstered in white textured fabric. He joined her, his body tilted in her direction.

"You were also doing what you believed to be right," she said, unable to make eye contact even as she felt his gaze boring into her. "And I could do to consider other people's feelings when I resolve to do something." She took a deep breath, feeling as though all of the oxygen had been sucked out of her lungs. Feeling as though all of her anger had been taken along with it. "Thank you for not intervening with Mr. Hask—Ezra."

"He already knew," Aidon said. "Christianna told him."

"I know," Persephone said. "I came to find you because—I thought you might try to change his mind about the engagement."

"Ezra is far too stubborn to have his mind changed." He shook his head. "And it did not even occur to me to challenge his decision. It would have been terrible of me to attempt to destroy his happiness."

She smiled, wide and genuine. "I am glad he reacted the way he did."

Now, if only Aidon could favor his own happiness over duty and responsibility and *propriety*.

"That's Ezra for you," he said. "He has never been anything but agreeable."

They drifted into a moment's silence, examining each other guardedly.

There was still far more to be said, of course, but neither of them seemed willing to take the first step.

Persephone sighed, standing up. "We should go downstairs."

He nodded and offered her his arm. She took it gingerly and, as they navigated the endless halls toward the staircase, began to reflect on how truly troublesome it was to love someone the way she loved Aidon. She almost wanted to believe it was far more trouble than it was worth, but the dishonesty of the sentiment prevented her from doing so.

Despite everything, she would still choose this. Choose him.

"How does anybody find their way around this place?" Aidon muttered, pulling Persephone out of her thoughts.

"You need years of experience," Persephone said.

"I can imagine. All the rooms look the same."

"You would think so," Persephone said, tugging him into a private parlor she had visited many times, "but each one of them has its own unique features. This one, for example, has a rather pretty balcony."

He followed her out onto said balcony, the balmy breeze bringing with it the laughter and chatter of the guests in the gardens below. Persephone peered out over the edge, seeing nothing but dark swaths of land in the distance.

"It doesn't have much of a view, I suppose," she said apologetically. "Not that you would expect one, being in Oxbury."

"On the contrary," he said, his voice low and hot at the back of her neck. "I think the view is rather exquisite."

Persephone scoffed softly, turning right into him, her heart beginning to dance in a staccato beat. "Tell me, has that line ever worked on a single soul?"

"That depends," he said, laughter in his voice. "Is it working on you?"

"No," she said, biting back a giggle. "And it wouldn't matter even if it was, as we are expected downstairs."

"One kiss," he said. "And then we'll go downstairs."

How they had returned to this, Persephone did not know. Desire reared its head, tempting her to remain out on the balcony, insisting that downstairs could wait.

"That's not why I brought you here," she said lightly, wiggling away from him.

"No?" he murmured, capturing her by the wrist, turning her around, and pressing her into the wall. "Why *did* you bring me here, if not to continue what we started earlier?"

The mere mention of what had occurred in the carriage had her blood heating to an immediate boil.

"Just *one* kiss," she told him. "And then we'll go downstairs."

He let out a ragged sigh of relief before slanting his mouth against hers, his body pushing her mercilessly into the wall. Persephone wrapped her arms around his neck, balancing herself on the very tips of her toes for better access. Aidon kissed every bit of skin available to him, from her jaw down to the hollow of her neck and the tops of her breasts.

"It's this damn dress," he said. "I could have taken you in the carriage. I could take you here, against this wall."

Persephone shivered, recognizing the former rake in him out in full force, ready to devour her. She reveled in it, reveled in *him*.

"But you won't," she whispered. "Unless I ask."

He pulled back, his clouded eyes focusing on hers. "Yes."

That single word of affirmation, in all its simplicity, brought a new wave of pleasure crashing through her. She was safe with him. He would always wait for her to consent, and she would always be safe with him.

"I think . . ." she said breathily. "I think—"

"I think you're about to disappoint me," he growled.

Chuckling, she said, "I am. We are expected downstairs, and you know it."

"And if we weren't?" he asked.

Persephone tilted her head up toward his, an indulgent smile on her face. "Then I would hold you to your word."

"At least I have that."

"And besides," she said, untangling herself from him, hoping desperately that the fresh air would calm her, "this supper will not go on forever."

"Is that a proposition?"

Persephone glanced over her shoulder at him as she reentered the room. "You tell me. You are the former rake, after all."

Aidon watched Persephone flit around the gardens of Errwood, looking every bit a flower nymph, the candlelight catching the glass beads of her dress. He could tell Christianna's family was baffled by her as they constantly exchanged glances over her head at the way in which she expressed herself. Despite that, there was fondness behind their eyes, and he could tell she was well loved by them all the same.

How anyone could feel differently, he had no idea.

He, meanwhile, despite still aching with need for her, felt as if a weight had been lifted off his shoulders. The list of disagreements between Persephone and himself now boiled down to one—that relating to the Lord of the Dead. He had tried very hard to concentrate on Ezra and Christianna during the supper, but his mind had kept slipping back to the comparison Ezra had struck between Aidon and his father.

The last person he wanted to be.

And yet here he was, stubbornly hanging on to the ghost of the late Charles Barrington. As if it would change anything or help him to forgive himself.

He couldn't help but wonder why he was so desperate for the approval of a man who, by all accounts, had been a nightmare. Perhaps he was trying to blame himself for his father's shortcomings, lifting the responsibility from his Charles's shoulders and placing it on his own.

If I had been less of a fool, then he would have treated us better.

It was not true in the slightest.

But even understanding all this, he did not know if he could abandon his post. All he'd known for the past ten years had been funeral furnishing and his role as the Lord of the Dead. Who was he without every single facet of the work?

He was almost afraid to find out.

Persephone came to stand by him, cheeks flushed from animated conversations with Christianna's relatives and extended family.

"I'm afraid it's grown late, and we must all retire for the evening," Ezra said, his loud, cheerful voice silencing the dull chatter of the crowd. Everyone murmured in agreement. "But before you all leave, Christianna and I would like to extend our thanks to everyone who has joined us today." His eyes met Aidon's, and he grinned. "And we would especially like to extend our thanks to Mr. and Mrs. Barrington, who went to great lengths to bring us together."

What would the alternative have been?

Aidon returned the smile while the crowd tittered politely. Persephone stood very still, and he felt her small hand find its way to his. She gave it a gentle, reassuring squeeze.

In the candlelight, he saw her expression was one of unbridled joy.

He could not stop being the Lord of the Dead, or at least he did not think he could. But he would do anything to bring that kind of joy to Persephone's face. Ezra and Christianna had overcome an issue that had, to him, seemed insurmountable. They had both simply decided that their relationship would work, that they would love and stand by one another no matter what. Aidon wanted very badly to make the same simple decision. He was still fraught with uncertainty, but seeing Ezra's unfettered elation up close had jostled something inside him. Persephone squeezed his hand again. He would do *anything*, he thought.

And he would not stop until he'd succeeded. That, at least, he could do.

THIRTY-SIX

Persephone had read the myth of Orpheus and Eurydice many times since her mother had first introduced her to it. If her namesake had managed to convince Hades to show some pity on poor Orpheus, then she could convince her tenderhearted husband to free himself from the ghostly shackles of his father. She had yet to speak plainly with him on the subject, and with Christianna off to London, she felt there was no better time. Persephone's heart felt light—light enough to carry. Christianna was safe and happy, for which Persephone was intensely grateful.

On a mild afternoon a few days after the engagement party, Persephone made her way to Aidon's study. The door was already open a crack. She slid into the room silently, not bothering to knock. Aidon had his head buried in a pile of papers, his quill moving quickly across a page. The light that filtered in through the window behind his desk enveloped him in an almost angelic glow.

Ironic, she thought, *considering the circumstances.*

Still, she took a moment to admire him. He was dressed in his shirtsleeves and waistcoat, the muscular broadness of his shoulders still apparent despite the looseness of his white shirt. His overall appearance was slightly disheveled, the dark stubble on his jaw telling her that he had decided to prioritize work over his morning shave. The wave of desire that washed over her did not surprise her. After all, she liked a tousled and mussed Aidon almost as much as she enjoyed him when he was starched and stiff.

She liked all of him, and that was why she chose one more time to broach the difficult topic that hung over them. She hoped very much that he would listen. If he didn't, she was officially out of ideas. And it was very rare for her to be out of ideas.

"I have been thinking," Persephone announced, startling Aidon out of his reverie, "about the Lord of the Dead."

He placed his quill in its inkpot and gave her a silly, lopsided grin.

"He's been thinking about you as well," he said.

Despite her better judgment, Persephone smiled. No amount of teasing would change the nature of this conversation, although the temptation to drop it and indulge in mindless flirtation was far stronger than she would have liked.

"I'm being quite serious," she said, glad her voice was even and firm. She took a deep breath before continuing. "The gossip ruined you. Left you a lonely outcast. And . . . well, you cannot earn your father's approval now."

"It's my job," he said, the response almost automatic, with a now familiar tinge of frustration evident in his voice.

Persephone felt exasperation begin to bubble under her skin. She'd felt an eerie emptiness in her chest when she'd been told of Aidon's secret, but the long days that had followed had given her ample time to process all she had discovered. Now, standing here before him, she strongly believed that she understood what he was doing and *why*. He had changed *everything* about himself for his father. Instead of allowing adulthood to mature him naturally, Aidon had completely gutted himself.

It seemed extraordinarily unfair. Persephone thought of all the times she had been called difficult, wondered at how she had not followed in Aidon's footsteps. Perhaps what differed between them was her inexplicable, stubborn refusal to lose sight of herself, no matter how challenging it was for her to simply *be*. She'd tried, once or twice, to be softer and more agreeable, but the exhaustion had settled in soon enough, forcing her to drop the facade. Receiving an apology from her father had been a balm to her injured soul, and she recognized that that was something Aidon could never experience.

However much Persephone disliked what was inside her, the alternatives had always seemed much worse. But Aidon had been under much more pressure. It seemed, at the end of it all, that living in Oxbury had given her respite from what would have been a far greater number of prying eyes and wagging tongues.

Which was something she had never considered.

Still, for everything to be well and truly peaceful, the Lord of the Dead had to disappear. She just did not know if she had the power to make that happen.

Aidon, despite his resistance, knew this conversation was a necessary one. It was his opportunity to bring Persephone to his side, to make her understand. But as she stood before him with her chin lifted in the air, it occurred to him that he was due for an uphill battle.

"It's my job," he said helplessly.

So much for making a case.

A part of him did want to agree with her. Another part of him, however, seemed insistent on holding on with a tight grip.

"You've made yourself responsible for your father's happiness, and he is not even here," Persephone continued. "Perhaps it is time to mind your own happiness."

"How are you so sure that I'm not doing just that?" he asked, the harshness of his tone forcing her back a step.

Instead of responding, she looked at him in that searching, penetrating way of hers. It was as if she knew that his outburst did not warrant a reply, that it was nothing but a hasty, foolish attempt to cover his old wounds.

"It can end as quietly as it began," she said simply.

"It was my father's work."

What is the matter with you?

Persephone sighed, coming to stand in front of his desk. She reached over the stacks of papers and took his hands gently in her delicate ones. He looked down at where they touched, the freckles of her right hand darkened from the hours she spent in the sunshine.

"You will not admit to it, but you are punishing yourself for disappointing your father. But you should not want his approval, Aidon. He was never there, he treated your mother poorly, and he left you here, alone. Would you have this be your child's work, if we were to have one?"

He paused, finally feeling properly foolish. In the past, he had thought about one day passing all of this down, doing it correctly, keeping it as close and protected as his father had. But he hadn't considered the emotional repercussions his own child would have to suffer as a result.

The ones he had suffered for the past ten years.

"This—this part of it does not need to be handed down," he eventually said.

She pulled her hands away from his. He ached at the loss.

"But the gossip *hurts* you—"

"I thought you did not care for gossip," he interjected.

"No, but I care about *you*," she said flatly. She straightened, smoothing her hands down her skirt. "Think about that."

With those words, she left, closing the door behind her and leaving him at his desk.

Stubbornly, Aidon continued to work, allowing the hours to slip away from him. When nighttime fell, he returned to his room and took to pacing. Naturally, he wanted to go to Persephone as he had been doing every night since their visit to Errwood. The only thing standing in his way was his obstinacy, which was truly something to behold at this very moment.

He would have never taken on the Lord of the Dead's work had it not been for the pressure he had felt from his departed father. His mother would have disapproved, but that had never mattered to him. He had never had to squeeze love out of her. Despite her perpetual melancholy, she had given all she'd had to her children until she could not give any more. Aidon sighed, finally sitting heavily in a chair by the roaring fireplace. He had no idea why it was so difficult to untangle the knot in his chest, why he was so hesitant to do it even as Persephone offered her aid.

Was he truly so afraid of what he would discover? Afraid of who he was without the pressure from his father?

Staring into the flames, he thought of his mother. What would she think, seeing him this way, still unable to free himself from the man that had terrorized them both? Emmeline Honeyfield had made a suggestion long ago to name him Aidoneus, one that his mother had taken. Perhaps she'd known, somewhere deep inside her, that he'd one day need Persephone to bring spring into the Underworld he would build for himself.

In trying to gain his father's approval, he had forgotten about that of his mother.

What would she want for you?

He had loved her—still loved her—and yet had wasted years honoring his father over her. Trying to earn affection that would have never come, even if his father had been alive to see all that Aidon had sacrificed. Like a fool, he had taken the adoration she'd given him for granted. In a way, there was something of his father in him. Why else would he have ignored her memory so thoroughly?

No more.

He kept to himself for the remainder of the night, only seeking Persephone out the following morning. He found her sitting underneath a gnarled tree by the edge of the cemetery. The seeds they had pushed into the earth had begun to sprout, coating the irregular ground with a sparse carpet of green. Aidon stood at a distance for a moment, watching her serenely turn the pages of her novel.

When he approached, she lifted her head, glancing at him with her dazzling brown eyes.

Radiant Persephone.

He did not know how to begin, so he, too, remained silent. They stared at one another, and he was reminded of the day they'd met. He would have continued living on as he had been if she had not crawled through the window at Gallowsgate in search of her book.

A book that had just so happened to show, once and for all, that he and Persephone had been fated to find one another.

Overcome with a sudden wave of emotion, he blurted out, "I'll stop." Saying the words aloud removed an immense tightness from his chest, and he finally felt himself regain the ability to breathe for the first time in ten years.

"You will?"

"I do not have to be the man my father wanted me to be in every conceivable way," he admitted slowly. "You and Ezra . . . it is so easy for the both of you to decide on your own terms what is right. I have not been very good at that as of late."

Persephone sighed, closing her book and placing it gently on her lap. "You *can* be like that. I know there's goodness in you. It's why I was not horrified or angry at what you had done for Lord Follett. I felt that there had to be more to it."

"How do you not feel ashamed?" he asked, coming down to his knees before her. "Of me?"

Persephone stared at him, her expression hard. "Let's go," she said, standing abruptly and offering him her hand.

He took it without hesitation. "Where?"

"To your father's room. Let's go."

Aidon allowed himself to be dragged into the house, unsure of what Persephone intended. When they arrived at the door to a room he had been expressly forbidden from ever entering, he hesitated. He had avoided walking through this door even after Persephone had reminded him of it.

You are not bound to his rules any longer.

"What are we doing here?" he asked as Persephone marched up to a shelf stacked with books.

She whirled around to look at him, her striking face determined. "I think your grandfather kept records of his business as Lord of the Dead."

"And my father stored them here?"

She nodded, pulling a leather-bound volume off the shelf. "Look."

Taking the book from her hands, he flipped it open to see a list of dates, names, and monetary values. It would have seemed innocuous enough had Thomas Barrington not written that a Lady Jordan had come to him on behalf of her daughter. The business's other ledgers were thorough. This one was sparse and vague, all by design.

"Why would my father keep these?" he asked, voice low.

"I've no idea," Persephone said. "But I think you ought to be rid of them."

"Yes," he said softly at first. Then, again, with more conviction: "Yes. What else is there?"

Together, he and Persephone pulled his father's drawing room apart. They found another ledger tucked away in the drawer of a small writing desk, this one written in Charles Barrington's hand, letters shoved in the back pages. Aidon pulled one out, eyes scanning the aged ink.

"A letter addressed to my father," he said, handing it to Persephone. "One of many, it seems."

He watched as she perched on the edge of a small table, reading the letter in silence. Once she was finished, she put it aside, holding her hand out for another. Aidon knew that each one was likely written in the flat, emotionless hand of an aristocrat.

"It's as if they felt nothing," she said eventually.

"They typically do not," Aidon said.

"I feel for the women. It's almost—I can see their stories in between the lines of these letters. They did not deserve such treatment. And I can't—I can't help but think of Christianna, really."

She shivered, and he found himself unable to form a response, overcome with an uncertain sort of nervousness. He had to let Persephone in, choose her above all else. Even above his family's secrets.

"I feel for the children, too," she said sadly. She paused, forcing her next words out with an uneasiness that made him think she was trying to pick them carefully. "What you were doing was not *entirely* for them."

"No," he admitted guiltily.

"Is there something you can do that is?"

Aidon's mind drew an immediate blank. He could not

imagine twisting this part of his work into something less shameful, less dark. "I have no idea."

"In any case," Persephone said briskly, "none of this is of any use to you."

Before he could agree, she took his father's ledger from his arms, picked up the others, and added the letters to the top of the pile. Aidon followed her out of the room, watching her stick her head into one open door after the next until she located a barely smoldering fire. Without a word, she tossed everything onto the dying flames, whirling around to face Aidon with a triumphant smile. "There. I've freed you of it. Although I would have preferred if they had burst dramatically into flame."

Aidon gaped at her, wishing he had her nerve, or even half her resolve.

She wandered to the window, looking out at the cemetery, newly graced with the first delicate green signs of life. "There must be something you can do. Not for your father, or even for yourself. And certainly not for the silly men who write you those letters with hundreds of pounds tucked between the pages."

He joined her by the window and looked out at the tombstones.

"For the people that matter," she said simply.

"So, the Lord of the Dead does not die?"

"Perhaps he does not have to," she said, turning to face him. "Perhaps what he needs is to take on a different form altogether."

THIRTY-SEVEN

Aidon watched the shadows of London travel across Persephone's face as their carriage took them to his town house, exhaustion apparent on her face after three days of travel. Despite it all, she still glowed with the determination she had carried with her from Gallowsgate.

Fear of disappointing his father had held him back, but as his mind cleared during their travels, he realized that he had also been terrified at the prospect of changing once again. Of having to start over *again*. Now, as they moved through the smoky darkness of town, he understood that his dread had been unwarranted. After all, the Lord of the Dead had never really been a fundamental part of him. There was no longer anything to lose.

He had written ahead to Chase, who had responded with a short, *It's about time.*

Persephone leaned against the wall of the carriage and closed her eyes with a sigh. Despite everything, despite every weakness and flaw he had revealed to her, she remained. Before, he had thought that he had suffered through ten years of isolation and loneliness for her, but he was now of the opinion that there was nothing he could have done in this mortal life to have deserved the inimitable, steadfast Persephone.

They slept together that first night in London, entangled with one another, Persephone an anchor despite her size. The next morning, he woke up feeling as if her determination had rubbed off on him. He bounded out of bed and went about his morning routine until he was properly starched and shaven. Persephone still slept, having spread her slender limbs across the width of the bed as soon as he'd risen. Sitting on the edge of the bed, Aidon reached over to gently ruffle her untamed hair. She shifted, cracking a single eye open.

"It's time to go," he said eagerly.

Another eye opened, and she slowly blinked at him in silence for a few moments before responding. "I have somewhere else to be."

"Where?"

She pushed herself up, the sleeve of her nightgown slipping to reveal a smooth, pale shoulder. "I thought I would go to a hothouse. I've never been."

Aidon thought about arguing but quickly decided against it. He needed to find the courage to end this himself, and he could not keep siphoning from Persephone's bravery, no matter how deep and boundless the supply seemed.

And besides, it would give him a chance to work on an idea that had wormed its way into his head the day they had cleaned out his father's private room—the day she had suggested that the Lord of the Dead take on a different form.

Whatever form he took would have to be one worthy of Persephone. That much was certain.

At his office, Aidon stood in the middle of the room, wondering if it had always carried the air of despair that was now settling over him like an uncomfortable, itchy blanket.

Chase leaned against the doorway, his arms folded across his chest.

"You've changed," he said casually.

Discomfort spread in Aidon's chest at the comment. He turned to see Chase looking at him. "In what way?"

Chase shrugged, walking toward Aidon. "I daresay you seem happier. Lighter, even."

The discomfort dissolved in an instant. He hadn't stopped to think about all the ways being around Persephone had changed him, but he supposed it had been bound to happen. He no longer felt the way he had when he'd been in London, shackled to his father's disapproving ghost.

"I have to go through every bit of it," Aidon said, nodding at the packed shelves and drawers. "Until nothing of him remains."

"Would you like my help?"

"No." Aidon looked at Chase from the corner of his eye. "You must think me a fool for letting it come to this. We might have been done with it years ago."

Chase shrugged again, his arms dropping to his sides. "All I can say is I'm grateful that I will no longer have to work throughout the night."

Aidon laughed despite the task that loomed before him. "No, no more nights. And, Chase—"

"Sir?"

"When I'm done, we should discuss your position here. You've been doing far more than assisting me. You always have. You ought to play more of a role in running this place when I'm in Oxbury—if that is something you're interested in."

"Thank you, sir," Chase said, sounding almost surprised. "But—you're to remain in Oxbury?"

Aidon glanced at his right-hand man, who was all but gaping at him. "Is that so shocking?"

"No," Chase said quickly, composing himself. "Not at all. I just—you *have* changed."

"I suppose," Aidon agreed pleasantly.

"Well." Chase turned to survey the room with a long exhale. "I will leave you to this."

"Yes. Thank you, Chase."

"Of course, sir."

Walking over to his desk, Aidon pulled open a drawer, sat down, and began to empty it of its contents. When he was done, he walked a stack of his father's old papers to the fireplace and tossed them into the flames. He continued to do this, quickly losing count of how much he'd burned as the hours slipped by. Very little had been changed about the office after his father had died, with even traces of his grandfather left behind. All Aidon had done was add to what had already been there, which left him with an inordinate number of things to sort through.

He practically gutted the shelves, keeping only what was relevant. As he reached for the last book, he finally felt the tightness in his chest release. He pulled the book off the shelf by its spine, meaning to inspect the cover to see if it was worth keeping. The volume cracked open, and a small journal dropped out onto the floor with a soft thud. What he held in his hand had been a false tome, the insides hollowed out.

God, his father had been unnecessarily dramatic.

Aidon bent to retrieve what had fallen, and he realized it was a journal written in his father's hand. Suddenly the book felt hot enough to burn.

He marched toward the fire to give it this final offering but found himself hesitating.

What if he had been wrong about his father? What if there had been more to him?

Aidon knew he was being ridiculous. But, despite that, he began to turn the pages, searching for any mention of him, Cassius, or their mother.

And he found them.

Words of frustration about their mother's alleged lack of character, about her weeping, overly soft ways.

Paragraphs upon paragraphs about how deeply stupid Cassius was.

All I stand to gain by telling Cassius about the Lord of the Dead, he had written in his untidy scrawl, *is that he will likely turn down the business.*

Of course. Of course he had only been open with Cassius because he had had some ulterior motive. For a moment, Aidon felt a stab of pity for his older brother.

Cassius will undoubtedly tell Aidon. I am unlucky in that I have two foolish, incapable sons—they will be scared off by the work, and the business will be free to go to their cousin, who, I believe, is shrewd enough to continue to generate a healthy profit from it.

Aidon snorted. That was where his father's plan had failed. Cassius had decidedly *not* told Aidon, clever enough to manipulate the situation to ensure that money would continue to flow freely into his pocket—into both of their pockets.

Two foolish, incapable sons from a foolish, incapable father who had never thought that there was more to life than being a shrewd businessman. Two foolish, incapable sons from a man who did not know what it was to love.

Aidon tossed the book into the fire, listening to the pleasant crackle as the pages curled and blackened. He, at the very least, *did* know how to love.

All that was left now was the plot of land tucked away a few paces from the office. He could not leave just yet, however.

Calling Chase in, they began to write, putting into words what Aidon intended the Lord of the Dead to be.

Waking up to the sight of her husband had made Persephone painfully aware of one thing—today, she would tell Aidon she loved him.

It should not have been such a terrifying prospect, especially since he had already made it abundantly clear he felt the same. She fretted needlessly about how the words would sound coming out of her mouth. Stilted and awkward, she imagined, which just wouldn't do.

In an effort to better prepare herself, she decided to use the day to figure out what to say. Something about the eager way he'd looked at her and the soft way he'd woken her up had told her that it was time—or rather, past time. He needed to know she loved him. She needed him to know she loved him *because* of everything he was and not despite it.

Persephone called upon Christianna, who was staying at Ezra's family town house while the banns were posted. Her friend appeared happy and rosy-cheeked, much like she had been before fear had settled into their lives. Ezra, equally happy and rosy-cheeked, was there as well.

"Well, fancy seeing you here!" he chirped. "Aidon didn't tell me you were coming to town."

"Oh." Persephone cast a glance at Christianna, wishing she would put her bonnet on faster so that they might leave. She'd asked her on a walk, and Christianna had cheerfully and quickly obliged. "It was not planned."

"Still, terribly rude of him not to drop by," he said, sounding as if he didn't think it rude at all. "Shall I stop by his office, then?"

He posed this question to Christianna, who glanced briefly

at Persephone, absorbed the expression on her face, and then turned to Ezra with a serene, "Why don't we have them for dinner tomorrow night instead?"

"A wonderful idea," Ezra said, looking down at Christianna with an affectionate glow. He gave Persephone a mischievous grin. "You will tell Aidon that I think he's terribly rude, won't you?"

Persephone laughed as Christianna led her out the door. "If you insist."

"It's silly, but I almost miss Oxbury," Christianna said as she and Persephone walked to the hothouse. She looked up at the gloomy sky and sighed. "The weather here is awful."

Persephone stared at the town that stretched before them, grimy and grand all at once, misty from the sullen murkiness of the sky.

"I don't think it's silly," she said after a moment's silence. "For all my complaining about Oxbury, I miss it whenever I'm here."

"We'd have been trapped either way, I think," Christianna said, fiddling with the pink ribbon of her bonnet. "It's just a different sort of trapped here."

Persephone eyed Christianna as her hand ghosted across her growing belly. "Do you feel trapped still?"

"No!" Christianna said in a burst of earnestness. "Not anymore. *You* freed me, Persephone."

"Nonsense," Persephone said, despite the warmth spreading through her. "You played as big a part in it as I did."

They walked in companionable silence for a long time, and right as the hothouse came into view, Christianna let out a frustrated sigh.

"I should hate for us to only speak of men when we see one another," she said thoughtfully, "but I was hoping you would tell me how things have been between yourself and Mr. Barrington."

"I should also hate for us to only speak of men," Persephone agreed, "but I was hoping you'd ask."

"Well?" Christianna urged, barely concealing the curiosity and excitement from her voice.

They came to a halt in front of the hothouse, and Persephone sighed.

"It's been better," she said slowly. "And I—"

Christianna was looking at her with such eager eyes that Persephone could no longer bear to hold her gaze. She turned to look at the tall glass windows of the building.

"Oh, Persephone," Christianna breathed, perceptive as ever. "You love him, don't you?"

Persephone looked back at her. "Is it so terribly obvious?"

"Perhaps not," Christianna said rather smugly. "But I do know you so well. Have you told him?"

"No," Persephone said sullenly, leading Christianna into the hothouse with a sudden quickness. "I don't know how."

"Oh, well, you just say it!" Christianna said happily.

An extravaganza of plants and flowers greeted them, and Persephone felt her insides settle. This was where she was comfortable, among the fertile plants of spring and summer. She walked toward the flowering bits of greenery and began to study them in silence.

"He loves you, doesn't he?" Christianna asked through some foliage.

"Yes," Persephone replied, feeling horribly and uncharacteristically shy about her response. "Heavens knows why."

"Persephone," Christianna said firmly, marching up beside her and taking her by the shoulders. "Have you ever considered that there are a great many of us who love you? I myself would not be able to do without you. And the lot of us envy your good heart, your sharp tongue, and possibly everything that you do not appreciate about yourself."

Christianna had always spoken freely with her, but rarely with such fervor.

"Fine," she replied, "he loves me because I am wonderfully intelligent and captivating. Is that what you want to hear?"

"It is," Christianna said, seemingly satisfied. "And why do you love him?"

"Oh, Christianna," Persephone said. "He is so kind and— and gentle. Sometimes to the point of foolishness. I don't think he knows how to say no to a single living creature."

"And he's handsome," Christianna said cheekily. "I'm quite sure that helped you along some."

"Frustratingly handsome," Persephone agreed. "I'm afraid anything I say will sound awkward and false."

"It won't," Christianna said, stopping to sniff delicately at a flower.

"How do you know?"

"I just do."

When Persephone parted ways with Christianna, her arms heavy with flowers, she took herself to a small plot of land. She found her path blocked by a low gate. Undeterred, she simply slid her package of flowers through the bars and clambered over it.

It was a cemetery, parts of it dotted with crumbling tombstones, others with worn plaques or nothing at all. It depended, she reasoned, on what Aidon's clients had paid for.

Bending over the tombstones, she gently covered them with flowers, holding the parcel against her body as she worked. Reaching into her pockets, she also scattered seeds around haphazardly, hoping they would take.

"Persephone?"

Persephone straightened, a few petals floating to the ground to rest at her feet.

Aidon.

"How did you find this place?" he asked.

She glanced at him and shrugged. "I wrote ahead to Chase, and he sent a note to the town house."

"Of course he did," Aidon said dryly. "How did you get over the gate?"

"I climbed over it," Persephone said. "It isn't that high."

"I suppose not," he agreed. "I have one final question— what are you doing?"

Persephone looked around, unsure of how to explain herself. "I thought—well, I thought this could be turned into a garden instead of a cemetery. It still honors the people who are here, and hides all that's been done at the same time."

Silently, Aidon approached her and pulled her into his arms. Persephone looked up at him, trying to read his expression.

"I love you," he said, the words heavy with emotion.

Smiling, Persephone placed her hands on his lapels, pulling him forward for a kiss. His lips were warm and yielding against hers. It was a kiss with no hidden meaning, no uncertainty.

It was a kiss between two people who loved one another despite their flaws and wounds. Despite everything.

Persephone broke away, untangling herself from Aidon's arms. She needed to be brave, needed to tell him. She opened her mouth but was interrupted.

"I have something to show you," he said eagerly, his clear green eyes alight with excitement. He pulled out a piece of paper covered in his fine handwriting, offering it to her. She took it gingerly, her mind awash in memories of the last time she had received a letter from him.

It was a restructuring plan. The funeral furnishing business would remain very much the same, but with one major change. The Lord of the Dead would no longer be operating in the shadows. Clients who lost their children were still entitled to a funeral. Not one that cost hundreds of illicit pounds, but one that would be offered free of charge to the grieving families. The offer to keep certain details private regarding parentage remained for those who desired it, but Aidon's time in the dark had come to an end. All of London would know of the services provided by Barrington Funeral Furnishing.

"You said the Lord of the Dead could take on a different form," he said, excitement evident in his voice. "And so he will. We can continue to provide the same services, but without the expense. I thought we might continue our offer of privacy, if only to ensure certain clients still choose this over a potter's field, but there will be no more secrets as far as I am concerned. If there is to be any more gossip, it will not be about me."

At this, Persephone burst into tears.

Aidon appeared startled by this, taking the paper from her and pulling her into his arms. "Not quite the reaction I was hoping for," he said fondly, tilting her chin up so their eyes could meet. "What's the matter?"

"Oh, it's silly," Persephone said, sniffing angrily. "It's just that—that I love you."

His face broke into a wonderful, crooked grin. "Because of this?" he asked.

"No," she said quickly, wiping at her tears. "I loved you before this. I love you for *everything*. Even when you were insisting on being the Lord of the Dead. Even before that. I don't know how long it's been."

He chuckled, the sound warming her. "Why are you crying, then?"

"I don't know!" she burst out, frustrated. "I didn't want to tell you like this."

"Oh, Persephone." He pulled her close, and she breathed

in the familiar, comforting smell of cloves. She felt safe in his arms, small and protected from the world. "It doesn't matter— you could have done it angrily and I'd have still reveled in it."

"I hope that's true," she said, still sniffling. She pulled away from him and looked at the ground, covered in petals and seeds. "The flowers will come in nicely," she said, trying to distract herself from her decidedly embarrassing outburst.

"Only you could bring life to a place that has only harbored death," he said, holding her in his arms. "Look at you, Persephone. You leave a trail of flowers wherever you go."

She smiled softly at him, admiring his irresistible green eyes and the fine, sharp contours of his handsome face.

"How fitting," she said. "After all this time, my name finally suits me."

With that, Persephone Barrington, formerly of Honeyfield, married to the Lord of the Dead, pushed herself up onto her toes for a kiss. As her husband obliged, she sensed, deep in her bones, that all would be well from this moment onward. As long as they remained together, all would be well.

And she was right.

Epilogue

"Persephone!" Venus called, her voice echoing around the great entryway of Gallowsgate. Baker, the butler who had just let her in, did not seem amused at her inability to use a voice suited for the indoors.

"She is in the library, madam," he said stiffly, and Venus wondered if he had ever smiled in his life.

If he had not, then she may have found a wonderful companion for the horribly serious man she had met earlier.

He led her to the library, and Venus found herself walking in on a picture of perfect domesticity. Persephone was lying on a chaise with her nose in a book, and Aidon was by the window, peering out at Gallowsgate—or what was left of it since it was on its way to becoming a facsimile of Honeyfield.

"Venus!" Persephone said, sitting up. "I was not expecting you."

"I won't be here long," Venus said, nodding at Aidon before he could speak. "I simply *had* to come complain to someone."

"You came all this way to complain?" Aidon asked.

"Yes!" Venus breathed. She waited for the library door to be shut before sitting on the chaise next to Persephone. Ignoring her brother-in-law's irritatingly wry expression, she began to recount her story. "I was at Hartwell, and I met the most absurd person."

"Hartwell?" Aidon echoed, coming to stand behind the chaise. "Isn't Hartwell a ruin?"

"*Yes*," Venus said impatiently. "Do keep up."

Aidon sighed.

"Who did you meet?" Persephone asked. Her voice had softened considerably over the years, the consequence of being perfectly loved and understood. Venus had been hoping to become an aunt for some time now, but Persephone had grown tired of discussing it, so Venus took her continued silence to mean that it simply hadn't happened yet. Her sister appeared to be in good spirits today, however, which helped spur Venus on.

"A stupid man who means to buy the land!" Venus announced.

She heard Aidon chuckle behind her, and she wanted to hit him.

"Who would willingly come to Oxbury?" Persephone asked suspiciously.

"Precisely!" Venus all but shouted, folding her arms across her chest. "And Hartwell is—well, it may as well be part of Honeyfield."

"It is rather close," Aidon agreed, though Venus did not recall asking his opinion.

Venus continued to share the encounter, carefully leaving out certain unladylike bits, like the fact that they'd been very much alone or the way his hand had wrapped around her wrist. And she certainly wasn't going to get into what she'd done *after* leaving Hartwell. There would be too many questions if she were to recount her quick visit to the inn—where she'd been caught draped over the front desk rummaging through the post by the same man she was currently complaining about. An abridged version of events would do. Persephone remained largely on her side, much to Venus's delight. She agreed that the man Venus had met seemed insufferable—arrogant, cold, everything that Venus hated in a person.

"He was just impossible," Venus huffed. "So sure of himself, in the worst way. Nothing but an arrogant, overly stuffed, h—"

She had almost said *handsome*. It was a pain to be at odds with someone so—so—

Delectable?

It was a good word, but he didn't deserve it.

"Well?" Persephone prompted, seemingly bewildered that Venus had stopped speaking.

"Heartless," Venus said quickly.

She was rather glad that she had not said handsome.

No, that wouldn't have done at all.

Acknowledgments

I've always said that books saved me. And while they've been my protectors for as long as I've been able to read, I never imagined myself actually writing one. But here I am, and it's all thanks to romance novels. As any reader will tell you, romance is the genre of pure joy. The more I read, the more I wanted to poke around that joyful place myself. In writing *The Temple of Persephone*, I was able to do just that.

This book would not exist without the support of Kate Pawson Studer, who was my first not-related-to-me-by-blood reader and editor. For almost two years, Kate helped me polish this novel until it shone. The path to publication is rocky for the best of us, but with Kate by my side, it was impossible to lose hope. I can never thank her enough for her kindness and super sharp editing skills.

I also owe more than I can say to my agent, Marlene Stringer, who is a fierce advocate for her authors. Her guidance and publishing know-how are unmatched, and I am so lucky to have such a seasoned expert by my side.

Working with Blackstone Publishing has been nothing short

of a dream. A big thank-you to Marilyn Kretzer for standing by me every step of the way. To my amazing editor, Corinna Barsan, I am a far better writer for having had my work edited by you! I also owe my thanks to senior designer Alenka Linaschke for making such a beautiful cover. Finally, my deepest gratitude to Josie Woodbridge, Caitlin Vander Meulen, Ananda Finwall, and the rest of the team at Blackstone. Thank you all so much for your hard work and dedication to this project!

Thank you to my family—Mama, Baba, Sarah, Reema, and Noor—for always making me laugh. I love you all so, so much. And even though he can't read this himself, thank you to my dog Connor for all the cuddles and licks. To my friends Honora, Radha, Danielle, Esther, and Mia, thank you for always being there for me. I cannot imagine my life without each and every one of you.

Finally, to my readers, thank you for taking a chance on my debut! Your support means the world to me.

CREDITS

Marilyn Kretzer **Acquisitions Editor**
Josie Woodbridge **Editorial Director**
Megan Bixler **Editorial Operations**
Corinna Barsan **Developmental Editor**
Ananda Finwall **Managing Editor**
Courtney Vatis **Manuscript Editor**
Caitlin Vander Meulen **Print Editor**
Cole Barnes **Print Editor**
Kathryn English **Art Director**
Alenka Linaschke **Designer**
Katrina Tan **Composition**
Sarah Bonamino **Senior Publicist**
Tatiana Radujkovic **Publicist**
Isabella Bedoya **Senior Marketing Manager**
Francie Crawford **Associate Marketing Manager**
Bryan Barney **Executive Audio Producer**
Jesse Bickford **Senior Audio Producer**